Border Watch

Helene Young

hachette
AUSTRALIA

This novel is a work of fiction. All characters, events and the Border Watch fleet depicted in this work are fictitious. Any resemblance to real persons, living or dead, is purely coincidental.

hachette
AUSTRALIA

Published in Australia and New Zealand in 2010
by Hachette Australia
(an imprint of Hachette Australia Pty Limited)
Level 17, 207 Kent Street, Sydney NSW 2000
www.hachette.com.au

Copyright © Hélène Young 2010

This book is copyright. Apart from any fair dealing for the purposes of private study, research, criticism or review permitted under the *Copyright Act 1968*, no part may be stored or reproduced by any process without prior written permission. Enquiries should be made to the publisher.

National Library of Australia
Cataloguing-in-Publication data

Young, Helene.
    Border Watch / Helene Young.

    978 0 7336 2490 2 (pbk.)

A823.4

Cover design: Natalie Winter
Cover photographs (headshot and Great Barrier Reef): Getty Images
Cover photograph (aeroplane): © Danijel Jovanovic
Author photograph: © Barry Daly Photography
Text design by Bookhouse, Sydney
Typeset in 14/15 pt Spectrum MT Std
Printed and bound in Australia by Griffin Press, Adelaide,
an Accredited ISO AS/NZS 14001:2004 Environmental Management System printer

The paper this book is printed on is certified by the © 1996 Forest Stewardship Council A.C. (FSC). Griffin Press holds FSC chain of custody SGS-COC-005088. FSC promotes environmentally responsible, socially beneficial and economically viable management of the world's forests.

For Graham

Where there's laughter
there is love

1

The gun coughed once in the still, humid night. Without even the breath of a cry, the young man dropped where he stood, his blood a darkening stain seeping into stark white sand that shimmered in the silver moonlight.

With an indifferent shrug, the big man next to him tucked his gun into the waistband of his cargo pants.

Too easy.

Too easy to kill, too easy to take another man's life. Shouldn't be, but it was. Always had been for him.

He grabbed the fallen man around the ankles, the leather gloves he wore at odds with the warmth of the night. Sweat soon seeped into his eyes, burning pinpricks that irritated him as he dragged the body along the waterline, his bare feet leaving footprints to fill with the incoming waves.

Dark water swirled in deepening eddies round the deserted headland, tiny whirlpools sucking away the traces of the tide. That, he knew, was going to make it easier to hide his tracks.

It was another fifteen minutes before he was happy with the position of the body. He wiped the trickles of perspiration from his forehead as he began the long walk back towards the streetlights. With catlike night vision he scanned the dunes and the foreshore. Old melaleucas, with gnarled and ropy feet, reached high towards the night sky and the glistening jewel of a moon. Stringy leaves hung still and limp. The trees' tremendous girths could hide a small gathering, but he sensed a quiet, almost resigned calm in them. No movement anywhere. Another tidy kill and another step closer to disappearing.

Twenty minutes later, he whistled a tuneless dirge as he dumped the gloves in a rubbish bin by the public barbeques. The bins would be emptied before the body surfaced again.

The playground equipment stood like dark guardians of the deserted sandpit. He couldn't resist the childish urge to sit on the swing. It was a simple joy, something he'd never known as a boy. Something he indulged in as an adult, but only when no one was looking. It made him smile with unfamiliar delight, a hidden, forbidden pleasure.

In the gloom of the night, the swing flew higher and higher with each rhythmic push of his legs until he was almost horizontal, the metal brackets squeaking with each pass.

At the very peak, the chain grabbed, the swing jerked. The gun dropped out of his pants, spinning away into the dirt, and he swore, using his feet as brakes.

'Shit,' he cursed. Careless. He fingered the scratches on the snub-nosed weapon. Bloody barrel would be damaged as well now. The ammunition clip slid in and out easily enough; but he had to get rid of it anyway, he supposed, it had a history.

His four-wheel drive was parked in the shadows and he fumbled getting the key in the ignition. After the rush of adrenalin that always went with a kill, the lethargy of the long night slowed him down. A lot more still to do before he could hit the sack, he reminded himself, forcing the fog of tiredness from his brain.

BORDER WATCH

With his seatbelt fastened he drove along the esplanade at a sedate pace. No point in drawing any attention to himself or the vehicle. Bad enough he had to risk leaving the body unburied.

Still, now was not the time for a mutiny and the troops were getting restless. Death was an excellent motivator – someone else's death anyway.

2

The humidity wrapped warm wet tentacles around Morgan's lungs, squeezing the air from them as she opened her front gate. The hiss of automatic sprinklers and the haunting call of a lone curlew were the only other sounds so early in the morning.

She paused for a moment, looking eastward to the early glimmer of sunrise low on the horizon. Dawn on a beautiful day in Trinity Beach, the start of another hot, languid summer.

'Sam,' she whispered over her neighbours' fence, her voice pitched low. 'Sam!' The scurrying of claws on tiles brought a quick grin to her face. Sam would be sliding as he rounded the corner, scrabbling for purchase on the floor before he crashed into the gate.

The fence shook under the impact and a rapturous dog leapt at her as she eased the battered gate open.

'Morning to you too, big fella. Make enough noise or what?' She scratched the floppy ears, her hands sinking into the red fur, the dog's nose nudging her waist.

Having neighbours who were happy for their dog to be walked for them had been a bonus for Morgan when she moved in. She got all the benefits of having a pet with little

BORDER WATCH

or no responsibility. Just why Reg and Elaine had such a large dog she didn't know, but they'd even installed a swing gate in their shared back fence so Sam could come and go between the two houses. Part guard dog, part companion, part therapist, the big dog had heart enough for all of them.

'Come on.' She gave him a final pat and straightened her shoulders as she jogged down the hill. Sam barely broke into a trot to keep pace with her. A defensive curlew, its mottled brown feathers ruffled in outrage, flew at them with wings spread wide as they turned right for the beach. Like a beautiful Egyptian hieroglyph the bird's eyes were outlined in a sharp black border, elongating its already elegant head. Its hissing, spitting defiance made Morgan smile in admiration. The parent bird would have stashed its chick away from danger before it launched itself at the intruder. It stood its ground. Sam dismissed it with a sharp snort.

The sea breeze was still a couple of hundred metres offshore, a faint ripple scarring the surface. Sweat already dampened Morgan's shirt, gluing it to her back. She waved at the caretaker out hosing the night's rubbish away from the local snack bar, cleaning up before the breakfast crowd arrived.

'Morning, Gus.'

'Morning, love. That dog's hardly moving,' he teased her. 'You need to ride a bike.'

'Love you too.' She wrinkled her nose at him and kept running.

'Wish you did,' he called after her, his grin revealing several missing teeth.

'Ha.' Morgan tossed her head in mock disdain, her dark ponytail swinging clear of her shoulders as she pushed the pace up just enough to make the dog break into a jog, trot, jog, trot.

5

The barbeque cleaner was finishing his work down at the beachfront as Sam took a detour to check out the empty rubbish bins.

'Nothing for you there, buddy,' he warned the dog. 'Morning, Morgan.'

'Hi, Larry. Beautiful day.'

She shepherded the scrounging dog in front of her, skirting around the playground and onto the beach, drinking in the soft pinks and purples swathed across the eastern horizon. Rain drifted down from several isolated maritime storms blurring the rising sun in a shifting film.

Her footprints laid an even path across the smooth expanse of beach, swept clean by the night's high tide. White sand, right up to the line of pigface and dune grass, was unblemished. The moon, bright against the dark western sky was just disappearing behind Saddle Mountain. Its perfect roundness signalled the highest of the month's tides, its presence in the sky at dawn a sign that summer was close. A scattering of stars glinted against a backdrop of deepest blue.

As she ran onto the wet sand the cool of the water dropped the air temperature a degree and a light breeze wafted over her, raising a rash of goose bumps despite the heat.

Morgan extended her stride, revelling in the morning and its promise. Back to work after a month's holiday, back to the joy of being airborne, back to the buzz of piloting an aircraft, each machine as individual as the people who flew it. Her passion for flying was lodged deep in her soul. It gave her a view of the world that made all of life's troubles seem insignificant.

In the air, she was Captain Morgan Pentland, a senior pilot in the Border Watch fleet of Dash 8 aircraft. High in the vast blue, it didn't matter where she came from or who her parents were. Nobody cared whether she came from old money, new money or no money. Up there they were a tight-knit crew, the guardians who kept Australia's vast coastline under constant surveillance. Her mouth curved in a satisfied smile. Got to love them when you live that closely with them.

She slowed to a standstill, picking up a smooth piece of driftwood for the bounding dog.

'Go, Sam, go.' She flung the piece of wood out to sea. The dog hit the tiny swell running, leaving white foam in his wake as he swam to retrieve the bobbing wood.

Morgan's thoughts were still drifting. Flying had saved her, had defined her, had given her a purpose. Maybe this was as good as life got? Relationships seemed to be a touch more problematic . . .

Sam distracted her, dropping the stick at her feet. 'Well done, good boy. No, don't shake now. No . . .' She squealed as the water sprayed from Sam's thick fur, covering her in cool drops.

'Okay, big buddy, you can have a run this time.' The stick landed fifty metres along the beach, bouncing as it sprayed fine white sand into the air. Morgan squinted, shading her eyes against the prickling glare of the sun still low on the morning horizon.

'What's that? What the hell . . . ?' Fear spurred her on as she ran along the water's edge after the dog, her heart thudding against her ribcage.

'Sam, stop,' she yelled. 'Stop!' The usually obedient dog ignored her and nosed over to a large pile of clothes, undulating in the tiny swell. 'Stop now, Sam.'

She got to him before he could do more than nuzzle the outstretched leg, its bare toes bloated and pale. Grabbing the dog's collar she pulled him away from the body and bent to pat him, aware she was reassuring herself as much as the muscled dog. 'It's okay, it's okay. We'll be okay.'

7

Her stomach heaved, threatening to deposit her morning orange juice onto the sand, and she turned her back on the corpse, swallowing deeply. Common sense told her she needed to move it up the beach to stop it drifting back out to sea, but the superstitious dread of death curled her fingers, crippled her hands.

She swallowed again, trying to control the nausea that had taken her breath. 'Relax, it can't hurt you,' she muttered. 'Stop being so bloody stupid and just do it.'

'Sit,' she commanded Sam. 'Stay.' He stared up with eyes that managed to look forlorn and she pulled a face as she turned back to the body. The blue shirt was torn across the back and she could see dark tattoos on the bloodless flesh. For an instant a design in the middle caught her eye. A familiar image hovered on the edge of her memory, but she blinked it away.

'Why me?' she sighed as she got a grip on the sleeve and pulled. A small swell pushed in under the body. The whole corpse rolled with the momentum and this time she screamed.

Nothing could have prepared her for the shattered face leached clean by the ocean, for the sightless eye sockets already home to tiny sea creatures, for the horror of death. Nothing, she was sure, would ever completely erase that image.

The hot splatter of vomit drenched her shoes as she swung away. Morgan wiped a shaky hand over her mouth.

'It's just a body,' she tried to comfort herself. 'No one you know, no one you care about. Don't look. Just pull it up a bit further, then get the police.' She stood with her back to it, sucking in air, then jumped as Sam's warm tongue licked the back of her knee.

'Don't, Sam. Don't.' She shuddered, her eyes scanning the dunes. 'Where's Thommo? He's always loitering down here.' A local vagrant who camped among the tall eucalypts that lined the beach, Thommo was usually out fishing for breakfast by now. Logic told her the corpse behind her was too big to be the stringy, half-fed tramp, but where was he?

She frowned as she took a deep breath, thankful the clutching roll of her stomach seemed to be subsiding. She looked back down the beach towards the barbeques.

Too early for anyone else and if she left him to get Larry, he might wash back into the ocean.

'Damn it,' she said, turning back to the body. Keeping her eyes focused on a portion of blue sleeve, she forced her fingers to grip it. Her muscles strained, shoulders tightening in protest, as she heaved the body until it was out of the water, then rolled it over to lie face down again. The small wound in the back of his head seemed disproportionate to the horrific injury the bullet had caused.

Unexpected hot tears stung her eyes. Someone's father, someone's husband, someone's son, shot and dumped into the ocean. She squatted on the sand, confused by the overwhelming connection she felt with a man she'd never met, her sadness for a life that had become detritus washed up on a beach.

An irrational urge made her want to pick up the pale lifeless hand and tell him it would be okay. Clearly, it wouldn't ever be okay again, but she felt compelled to give comfort. 'I'm sorry,' she whispered. 'I'll get someone to look after you.'

Morgan's fingers dug into the damp sand as she pushed to her feet. 'Come on, Sam.' The urgency finally hit her and she started to run.

She skidded through the door of the snack bar. 'Gus? Gus!'

'Here, love.' His voice echoed out of the storeroom.

'Can I use your phone?'

'Only if you're ringing lover boy to tell him you're eloping with me.'

'No, the cops.'

'What?' His balding head appeared in the doorway.

'Body on the beach.' She jerked her head to the north.

'Yeah?' His eyes widened. 'You're kidding?'

'No, 'fraid not.'

'Ugly?' He came through to the shop, his gaze locked on Morgan's face.

'Very.' Morgan couldn't stop the quaver in her voice as the breath hitched in her throat.

'Here.' Gus dialled and held the receiver out to her.

'Hi, my name's Morgan Pentland, I'm out at Trinity Beach and I've just found a body . . . Sure . . . I'll wait. It's the northern end. Phone number? Hang on. Gus, what's your number?'

She repeated the details to the police call centre and handed the phone back to Gus.

'They'll be about fifteen minutes. I can't just leave him there for someone else to stumble over.' She shook her head, biting down on her lip to stop it quivering.

'Do you want to mind the shop and I'll go?' Gus offered.

'No,' she said, her voice still unsteady. 'No, I'll be fine. I'll wait on the rock wall near the road. That way I can stop people from going any further down the beach. Can you send the police along when they arrive?'

Gus peered at her, concern crinkling the corners of his eyes. 'Seen a body before?'

'No.' Morgan shook her head, automatically denying her past. 'You?'

'Yeah, did a stint in Vietnam. Saw lots of bodies, lots of body parts. It never quite leaves you.' He went to the sink and returned with a glass of water. 'You need to talk, I'm here.'

'Thanks, Gus.' It was only when she tried to raise the glass to her lips that Morgan realised her hands were shaking. She stiffened her spine, willing her hands to follow suit. If she could cope with any emergency they could throw at her in an aircraft, then she could deal with one lonely body on a beach.

A whisper of memory slid behind her eyes. Her mother's face, bloodied and bruised, eyes staring unseeing, her hair a dishevelled halo. Morgan's stomach contracted, pushing hard against her lungs until she banished the image from her mind.

She sat on the rock wall, her back to the road. The metre drop to the sand gave her a good vantage point to keep an eye out for the police and anyone going for a morning walk. Sam sat at attention below her on the beach, unwavering eyes trained on his prize.

Wrapping her arms around her now cooling body, she glanced over at the mound of clothes further along the beach.

Where had he come from?

She guessed his size was more to do with being in the water, his clothes straining to contain the bloated body. Black hair, swarthy skin and young. A tourist? A visiting sailor who'd been dumped off a boat after a brutal argument? Or something more sinister?

Morgan brushed loose strands of hair back from her face. A siren wafted in on the breeze and she shook her head wryly. No point, boys, he's not going anywhere.

By the time she'd given her story to the police, a small crowd of locals had gathered on the road above the rock wall. The Scenes of Crime forensic vehicle had to thread its way through them.

Morgan scrambled up to the road and waved at the two police officers in the SOCO car as one of them called out to her.

'Hey, Morgan, you find the stiff?'

'Yep, though he's not looking very stiff at the moment.' She hoped humour might ward off the aftermath of the horror.

'Carl home today?'

'Apparently, though I'll believe it when he walks in the door. You know what SERT's like.'

'Yeah, right. You never know where the Special Emergency Response Team really are.' The policeman winked at her, cynicism in his words.

'Thanks, Uncle Harry. I'll remember that.' Morgan grinned at the grizzled, grey-haired man.

'Don't uncle me. I'm not that old.' He wagged a fatherly finger at her. 'You okay?'

'Fine.' She nodded, managing to stretch her lips into a tight smile.

'Make sure Carl gets you a counsellor if you need one. Might get the odd nightmare or two out of this.' The concern in his eyes made her blink at the sudden burn of tears.

'Thanks. I'll keep an eye on myself.'

'You do that. Better go.' The car drove off, leaving Morgan to run the gauntlet of the curious crowd. Sam trotted to heel as if enjoying his fame in some way. Did dogs do that?

Reg met her at his gate as she returned Sam home. 'Bit of action this morning? Heard the siren going through.'

'Some poor bloke, with what looks like a bullet hole in his head, had washed up on the shore. Sam found him.'

'Really?' Reg looked horrified. Morgan leant over to give his shoulder a quick pat.

'Give him an extra bone.'

'Right.' He focused sharp eyes on his young neighbour. 'You okay?'

'I'm fine. Got to go to work now.'

'It's not easy, Morgan. First time's the hardest. When do you leave?'

'Soon. But I'm back the day after tomorrow, all being well.'

'Drop round then.'

BORDER WATCH

He waved as he shuffled back to his house. A paramedic, he'd been forced into early retirement by a back injury. He and Elaine had adopted Morgan the day she moved in.

She opened her front door, feeling the wave of air-conditioning chill the sweat on her bare arms. Leaning against the kitchen bench, she tried to put the morning into perspective.

According to the clock on her kitchen wall, exactly one hour ago she'd left the house with a spring in her step. Now she felt like a deflated balloon, her stomach churning and tears hovering.

'Just a body.' She said the words out loud, hoping they would bring some perspective to the morning.

It didn't work.

'Okay, just a corpse then. No one you know, no one you love, no one you care about. Just a stranger.'

She looked around her tidy cottage, a beach house that mirrored the woman she'd become. Its whitewashed walls were cool and austere, several bright pieces of artwork the only decoration.

Simple furniture, bright cushions, soft billowy curtains. A house with few trimmings, an honest home and it was all hers. It steadied her.

She straightened up. Yep, her legs weren't so wobbly. Her stomach was a little less queasy. She glanced at the clock again, a bright yellow sunflower, a rare relic from her childhood. Time to get moving or she'd be late for work.

As she drove out of Trinity Beach, she saw the local media cars leaving as well. Her stranger was now a news item. An image of his ravaged face flickered at the edges of her mind and she stamped on it.

'No you don't,' she said through clenched teeth. 'Not today. This is *my* day.'

3

The hectic bustle of the crowded office distracted Morgan when she arrived at the Border Watch hangar.

'Hey, Lauren, how was the end of your holiday?'

The young blond woman swung around from the computer she was peering at. With a wide smile she stood up to hug Morgan. 'Shopping in Melbourne was outstanding, you should have come with me.'

'Only so many clothes a girl can wear,' Morgan replied as she dumped her bag next to her colleague, hooking a chair with her foot.

'Nah, can never have too many clothes,' Lauren retorted with a throaty laugh, making way for Morgan.

'Both of you on holidays for a month? How did commerce in Cairns survive?' The young man who joined them pushed thick glasses up his nose, changing the magnification of his blue eyes alarmingly.

'Lauren is the legendary shopper, thank you, Gavin. I just succumb to greed when she's there to give advice.' Morgan slid into the chair. 'What's happening?'

Gavin sat on the bench and smiled. 'Missed you, skip. And,'

BORDER WATCH

he jerked his head in Lauren's direction, 'your sidekick. Have you spoken to the boss yet?'

'No. Why?' Morgan glanced up at him in surprise.

'Echo Charlie's probably unserviceable.' He nodded towards the Dash 8 aircraft parked near the fence with its registration, BEC, in large letters along the fuselage.

'Hasn't it only just come out of heavy maintenance?'

'Yeah and the test flight was fine. Found a hydraulic leak in the number-one side this morning when they dragged her out of the hangar.'

'Have you seen it yet, Lauren?'

The woman shook her head in answer. 'No, just finished signing on.'

'No worries.' Morgan tapped her codes into the computer. 'Give me a second. We can go together.'

Lauren flicked her long ponytail behind her and rested back on her hands with a sly grin at Gavin. 'So,' she drawled, 'anything interesting happen while we were away? New romances, divorces, affairs?'

Gavin shook his head. 'You can wait for the gossip until we know whether we're going anywhere.'

Morgan heard the note of panic in his voice and glanced up at Lauren. At twenty-four, the young woman was very aware of her own good looks and the overpowering effect they had on men. Morgan hid her smile as Lauren moved closer to Gavin and continued teasing him.

'You do have some goss. Spill it, Gavin,' she breathed in his ear, long red-tipped fingers trailing down his arm.

He tensed, clearly flustered by the close contact.

Morgan took pity on him and turned from the computer.

'Righto, that's done. Let's go, Lauren. Keep you posted, Gav. Did we have much on task today?'

15

He managed to move fast enough to put a desk between himself and Lauren, but still looked nervous. 'A full day today and tomorrow. The rest of the week depends on what we find. I reckon there's something big going down up the Cape. I'll keep setting the gear up. Let me know.'

Even the backs of his ears were pink as he left the room in a hurry.

'You really shouldn't wind him up so much,' Morgan chided Lauren as they headed for the hangar floor.

'I know, but it's so much fun. He's my best friend. He can't hold out on me. Gossip is gossip and we're meant to share.'

Morgan grinned at her. 'Not every man has a best friend nicknamed Bacall because she's drop-dead gorgeous.'

'The gods gave me these gifts. It's my duty to share them. So . . . Oh my god.' She emphasised each of the last three words. 'Look who it is. The Latin lover himself, over talking to the chief engineer.'

Morgan turned a stony gaze in the direction Lauren pointed, her mouth tightening in disapproval. Rafe Daniels. 'And look which aircraft he's loitering around.' She resisted the urge to curse.

The first and only time they'd flown together, he'd been auditing the flight for the Customs department, and that trip had proved to be a battle of wills from the moment he'd boarded the aircraft.

'Maybe you two can kiss and make up,' suggested Lauren, her grin showing white, even teeth. 'I always reckoned he thought you were hot last trip.'

'Hot?' Morgan snorted. 'On fire more like it. Just because he's up the top of the food chain in some secretive branch of Customs, he doesn't have the right to jeopardise the flight.'

'So try charming him next time, instead of sitting him on his arse.'

BORDER WATCH

'Ah yes. The wisdom of youth.' Morgan's nod was sage. 'How would you suggest I do that, Lauren?'

'Easy.' The younger woman reached across and flipped open Morgan's top buttons. 'Use some of your god-given beauty to pacify him. And before he gets wound up,' she added, messing with Morgan's collar.

'Lauren.' Morgan grabbed her hand to prevent any more damage just as the grey-haired chief engineer got to them.

'Hey, ladies, she's broken, I'm sorry.' He nodded at the aircraft. 'And we're waiting on a part. Trying to see if we can borrow one from the other operator on the airfield, but if that doesn't work, it'll have to come from Sydney. Won't make it until tonight.'

'Okay, Chief,' Morgan nodded, her buttons forgotten.

'Operations are champing at the bit. There's some unusual activity up in the Gulf, but we can't send you out like this.'

Lauren interrupted. 'Who's the mission commander?'

The chief jerked his head at the tall figure standing by the disabled Dash. 'Rafe. He's not auditing this one, he's running it for real. Been here for a couple of hours already. If it is tomorrow, I think he wants an early start.'

'That'd be right,' Morgan grumbled, feeling the muscles in her neck tighten up in rebellion. 'Calling the shots before we've even left the ground.'

The chief grinned at her. 'Morgan Pentland, I do believe the big guy makes you nervous.'

He left Lauren laughing and Morgan fuming, but before she could think of a suitable retort Rafe was heading towards them. She crossed her arms and relaxed her face into a polite smile. He was a colleague not the enemy, really he was.

'Rafe.'

'Ladies.' He nodded at the two of them.

17

'Hey, Rafe, heard you were mission commander with us today. That'll be cool,' Lauren drawled in her smoky voice, nudging Morgan with her foot. 'We're both fresh back from holidays today, so we're ready for action.'

'Really?' The quiver in the deep voice had Morgan wincing. The look in his eyes said clearly he'd gone where Lauren had intended with her innuendo.

'Looks like we're hanging round for a bit till they fix the aircraft. Got time for a coffee?' Lauren twisted her silky pony-tail over her shoulder.

'Thanks, Lauren, but I've got some phone calls to make. See how the day goes.'

'Okay, no worries.' Lauren pouted her red lips just enough to look sexy, her long lashes fluttering just enough to draw attention to her vivid blue eyes.

Rafe looked unmoved. His dark gaze ran over Morgan, stopped on her cleavage for a moment, then met her eyes with unambiguous laughter. 'New style of uniform, Morgan?' He didn't wait for her reply. 'Catch you later.'

Both women watched in grudging fascination as the tall lean figure strode away, command in every stride, authority in the set of his shoulders.

'Nice arse,' Lauren whispered to a bemused Morgan.

'Hmm. What's wrong with my uniform?'

Lauren grinned. 'Check out your cleavage.'

Morgan looked down. 'Lauren,' she hissed, horrified. 'My bra's on show. For god's sake.' With furious fingers, she fastened her green uniform over the black lacy bra.

'So now he knows,' Lauren shrugged with an unrepentant toss of her head. 'All that buttoned-up-repressed Saint Morgan thing's an act. Underneath your ever-so-proper uniform you dress like a sex goddess.'

BORDER WATCH

'And that's so important for the captain of a surveillance aircraft.' Morgan's sarcasm was lost on Lauren.

'Where's your sense of humour this morning?'

'Disappeared about the time I stumbled over a man's body washed up on the beach.' Morgan regretted her words as soon as she'd said them.

'What?' Lauren turned with a perplexed smile. 'A body, as in a dead one?'

'Yeah, very dead.' Morgan avoided her friend's curious stare. 'To my untrained eye it looked like he'd been shot.'

'Wow.' Lauren grabbed her arm and steered them towards the staff lounge. 'You need to debrief me, and now.'

Morgan's shoulders sagged in resignation. Lauren would not let this go until she had all the details, so more fool her for having mentioned it.

Two hours later the part for the aircraft still hadn't arrived and operations finally sent them home.

Morgan parked the car in the drive behind Carl's old four-wheel-drive ute. At least he'd made it home. Special Emergency Response Team, SERT to its members, was the branch of the Queensland police that got all the dirty jobs. The riots in outlying communities, drug busts and undercover operations kept them busy.

Not for the first time, Morgan wondered if there was a future in this relationship with Carl. It was a relationship of habit more than anything else – still together because they didn't see each other enough to break up. Thanks to their respective careers they weren't often in the same town. And his job messed with his head, big time.

He could be demanding, domineering, driven even, and never more so than when he first returned from an assignment. The

19

sex was great, though, or it used to be; there hadn't been much in that department recently. In fact, she frowned in concentration, she had to go back a while to find the last occasion.

The emotional side?

She'd convinced herself she didn't need any emotional support.

Almost.

Morgan slipped off her flying boots at the door, and padded through the house in her socks. Carl must be sleeping, she figured, or the music would have been pumping. She dropped her bags on the lounge room floor and started to peel off her flying suit. Her fingers locked to the buttons, the plastic biting into her skin.

Whose shoes were they?

She peered at a strappy pair of high heels then followed the trail of clothing that led straight to her bedroom door. Her senses went into overdrive. A hint of unfamiliar perfume hung in the air and she could hear the hum of the air-conditioner behind the closed door.

And something else.

She stopped.

Something much more primitive – the sighs and cries of someone in the throes of very noisy sex.

Anger, frustration and hurt, heightened by the day she'd endured already, blinded her. She wrenched the bedroom door open. The entwined limbs, tousled hair and rumpled bed were like a hard slap to her face. For the second time today, she felt her stomach heave.

She only just made it to the bathroom, dry retching into the toilet as the door slammed behind her.

Could this day get any worse? Bending over the sink, she rinsed her mouth with water. When she looked up, she was surprised by the composed face staring back at her in the mirror, haunted grey eyes the only sign of anything wrong. Her dark hair hung in tidy order, a sharp contrast to the turmoil in her head.

With a huge effort she straightened her shoulders, and breathed, forcing oxygen back into her bloodstream as she heard heavy footsteps in the corridor.

'Just get it over with, girl, it's been coming for too long,' she whispered to the woman in the reflection with smooth golden skin and anger in her wide-set eyes. 'Just do it now.'

Carl confronted her as she unlocked the door. How, she wondered, taking in the angry set of his jaw, had she been so blinded by his blond good looks?

'What the hell are you doing home? I thought you were away for a few days,' he snarled at her.

She laughed in disbelief at his attack, his arrogance further fuelling her anger. 'Sex good, was it? Hope she has a nice big house for all your gear because you're out of here.'

'Morgan, you're being ridiculous. It's nothing. She just turned up here. I didn't invite her.' Carl's hands slid up the wall, his arms trapping her as he changed tack. 'I missed you.' He dipped his head to kiss her and she recoiled, the scent of sex strong on his skin.

'Don't touch me,' she snapped, gathering her anger around her for strength. 'Missed me so much you couldn't wait?' She twisted away from him and glanced down at her watch. 'I'm going out for an hour. I want you out of here when I get back.'

'For fuck's sake, Morgan, don't be such a precious little drama queen.' The big hand that shot out to grab her was hard and callused. He shoved her up against the wall, knocking the breath from her body.

Morgan froze, feeling the tingle of fear strengthening her resolve. 'Drama queen? I'm supposed to be happy I've found you crawling around in my bed with another woman?' She shook her head. 'You've made a fool of me. That's not happening again. Just get out. Now!'

'Morgan, I'm sorry. I know this looks bad.' Carl ran one tanned hand down his sweaty, tattooed chest, his tone wheedling though the grip on her arm still hurt. 'Look, she doesn't mean anything.'

'Oh, she does to me, you cheating arsehole.' Morgan pushed off the wall, glaring up at him. 'She does to me.' She tried to push past him but, with a flick of his wrists, Carl pinned her up against the wall again, towering over her.

'Listen to me, babe. Just listen to me. I'm not going anywhere. Okay?' He shook her, snapping her head back against the timber. The sharp jolt of pain bolstered her courage, crystalised her anger to purpose.

'Oh yes you are.' She ground out each word separately.

'And who's going to make that happen?' he jeered, his grip on her arms still solid.

'One hour. You've got one hour.' She spat the words at him. 'Or I call Harry. And you know he'll throw the book at you.'

As the pressure in his hands slackened at her threat, she ripped her arms from his grasp and fled out the front door, slamming it behind her.

Glancing in the rear-vision mirror she saw him standing in the middle of the street as she left burnt rubber behind and careened down the hill. Serve him bloody well right if she pressed charges for assault. Damn well deserved it.

But she wouldn't.

The hopelessness of that thought triggered a quick flood of tears. She fought them back. She didn't give up, never had. It was not her way. And yet . . .

She drove aimlessly, unseeing, uncaring. The patterns of her family had woven tight bands around her. How many

BORDER WATCH

times would she have to fight them off before she was free of them?

Images she kept buried deep intruded despite her control.

Her mother bleeding on the ground, each breath a ragged gasp. Her father standing over her, alcohol on his breath and blood on his bare hands. Her brother screaming at her to run, run, *run*.

Then, on legs long even for a twelve-year-old, she was sprinting next door to the neighbours for help, the jab of sharp stones on the roadway going unheeded.

When her vision blurred, Morgan pulled into a lay-by and rested her head on the steering wheel. Why couldn't she break free? She was not her mother. She was not her father. She was most certainly not her brother. Violence and addiction were not her way and yet . . .

'And yet, I only find jerks who use me,' she whispered with a deep sigh. 'Why do I let them? Why do I think I can change them? Why do I do it?'

Morgan sat for another few minutes. When she blew her nose, she caught sight of herself in her side mirror. If Carl was still at home, the fright she looked now should be enough to send him running.

The drive home took half the time.

The ute was gone. Good start.

The house was silent and calm. She locked the front door behind her. They hadn't even made her bed.

She couldn't look at it without seeing their naked bodies. Tears threatened to spill over and she brushed at them, angered by her own weakness. 'Damn them, damn them, damn them.'

Dragging her bags into the spare room she dumped them on the linen bedspread, the old wooden bed groaning under the sudden load. She slumped down next to them.

23

If the aircraft hadn't broken down, she might never have known. It didn't console her at all.

Did she love him? She turned the question over in her mind. No more than the other couple of men she'd attempted to have relationships with before. And what the hell was love anyway? Could sex somehow translate into a love that could withstand the anger, the jealousy, the lies that went with being a couple?

Morgan's hand smoothed the soft bedspread next to her, trying unsuccessfully to soothe away the pain and the hurt.

How did a thirty-two-year-old competent professional woman make such obvious mistakes in her love life?

Patterns, she thought, resignation in her sigh. Patterns she'd never really broken. Patterns she'd inherited from her parents that foster care had done nothing to erase. Patterns that ruled her life.

'I can beat them,' she whispered fiercely, as she wandered back out to the kitchen. 'I must beat them.'

4

Lauren took one look at her face and thrust her own coffee cup into Morgan's hand.

'You shouldn't be here.' The younger woman kept her voice expressionless. 'Carl?'

Morgan's mouth twisted up at the corner. 'Yep. I had the pleasure of interrupting him in my bed with someone else.'

'Bloody hell, Morgan. Why didn't you call me, text me? I would have driven through a cyclone to be there.' Lauren poured herself another cup of coffee, avoiding Morgan's eyes for fear of what she might see, and knowing her question was futile. Morgan never asked for help, she only gave it. 'But you did throw him out this time, right?' She didn't understand how an attractive woman like Morgan, so successful in her career and so well liked by her colleagues, could get mixed up with a gorilla like Carl.

'Yep. He's packed his bags and gone.'

'And you're changing the locks too?'

Morgan sighed. 'Yes, Reg is seeing to it for me since we'll be gone for the next week it seems. Where's Gavin?'

Lauren knew the conversation was over and gave in grace-fully. 'Out in the aircraft already. He and Rafe have been poring over some new gizmo they've got for fine-tuning the infrared photos.'

'Great, so we've still got the Latin lover on board. Rafe's just what I need today.' Morgan shook her head ruefully, then sipped her coffee.

'Thanks, I'm happy to be here too.' The deep rumble had both women spinning around, Morgan choking on her drink.

'Hey, Rafe.' Lauren beamed at him, running interference for Morgan. 'I thought you were out in the aircraft.'

'Obviously.' He smiled at Lauren before turning quizzical dark eyes on Morgan. 'Latin lover?'

Morgan flushed under the frank inspection. 'I didn't invent your nickname. Sorry.'

'Come on, Rafe. They've been calling you that for the last year.' Lauren rested her hand on his arm. 'It's a compliment. It's because no one's actually got you into bed yet.' No need to tell him there was a bet out there regarding who was most likely to achieve that either, she decided.

Rafe's eyebrows just about disappeared into his dark hair. 'Got me into bed? No one's tried very hard.' He glanced over at Morgan, who was looking mortified. 'You got a problem working with me?'

'No.' Morgan's chin came up. 'No.' She amended the assertive tone of her voice. 'We work with the mission commander we're allocated.'

'I know Lauren does, but how about you? This is going to be a long, stressful assignment. We might not be home much in the next month.'

'Then I'm the man for the job, if you'll excuse the expression.' Morgan's grey eyes were bleak. 'I'll get planning and let you know when we're ready to depart for Weipa.' She spun on her heel.

BORDER WATCH

'I don't tolerate prima donnas,' Rafe said to her departing back, but her stride never faltered. Lauren hid a quick grin at her captain's subtle defiance.

Lauren dropped her voice. 'She found a body washed up on the beach yesterday with a bullet hole in its head. Then she caught her boyfriend screwing someone else in her bed. Go easy on her.'

'She shouldn't be at work,' Rafe replied flatly, his dark eyebrows drawn down in a quick frown.

'What?' Lauren said, with a shake of her head, not prepared to admit she'd had the same thought. 'You reckon it would be better to sit at home and stew over the day from hell she's just had? Didn't they teach you any psychology in the big bad world of the SAS?' Lauren kept her voice light, but her large blue eyes pinned Rafe.

'She needs her friends and that's Gavin and me. Play your cards right and you might get adopted too. There are worse things could happen to you.' Lauren left him staring after her, glad she'd got the last word in. A wayward bubble of temper surfaced.

Rafe could be so bloody high-handed when he felt like it. Just because someone looked like a cover model it didn't make them a nice person. Carl was the living proof of that.

'Gavin? Still here?' she called up the airstair door of the aircraft. A muffled reply made her grin. He would, as usual, have his head buried in something electronic. It was going to take some woman to distract him from his computers.

Lauren smiled. She had a bit more living to do yet, but one day she might just be that woman.

'Morgan's submitting the flight plan. We're headed to the west of Weipa out over the Gulf of Carpentaria. You ready to go?'

'Yeah, yeah. Of course. Rafe's got some great software to enhance the infrareds. Talk about random.'

'And he's already rubbed Morgan up the wrong way this morning.'

'No way?'

'Heard her calling him the Latin lover. I think he's ticked off with her.'

'She okay this morning?'

'Yes, but no. She'll cope, but she found Carl screwing around in her bed yesterday afternoon.'

'Shit.' Gavin's mouth gaped. 'We always thought he was a jerk.'

'Yep, well, that's life. I'll go load the catering. Rafe looks like he's champing at the bit.'

'Ready when you guys are.' Gavin bent towards his computers again, but Lauren sensed the concern in her colleague. No need to tell him to give Morgan a break; she was his hero.

An hour and a half later the heat and dust in Weipa's air was burning her throat. The flies descended in clouds. The exhaust from the aircraft's auxiliary power unit blew straight over the refuelling panel. Lauren clamped the ear protection tighter against her head, squinting up at the fuel bugs on the gauges. The noise from the auxiliary power unit prevented any conversation with Sarah, the refueller, so the two women stood side by side watching the needles move steadily upwards.

'Up here for the week are you?' Sarah asked hopefully, once they'd retreated to the air-conditioned cab of the fuel truck to do the paperwork.

'At least, according to Rafe. It might be a month. Our briefing was pretty sketchy, which always makes us a bit suspicious. Have the boys seen anything unusual in the Gulf?' Lauren referred to the fishing fleet that operated out of Weipa.

BORDER WATCH

'More illegal fisherman than usual out and about. The lads on the *Lady Musgrave* chased a couple the other day. So much for the two-hundred-mile exclusion zone. They need more Customs boats and aircraft to patrol it. Bloody bureaucrats in Canberra. What do they know? Most of them think Queensland stops at Noosa.' Sarah sounded bitter.

Lauren nodded, understanding better than most the enormity of the task. Securing a vast coastline that had so little habitation and too many overpopulated neighbours was a costly impossibility. The fishermen were the ears and eyes best placed to see something significant, but the law wouldn't support them if, by deliberate action, they injured or damaged an illegal fishing operation.

'Rafe's being very tight-lipped about details. Everything's on a daily, need-to-know basis.' Lauren rolled her eyes. 'You'd think he was still in the SAS.'

'Any luck yet?' Sarah knew all about the bet. Lauren didn't consider discretion a necessity.

'No, but there might be some action if we're spending a month together.' Her grin was wicked. 'Better go now. Four hours flying for us before we stop for the night. Busy day for you?'

'State Police Airwing's due in this afternoon.'

'Really?' Lauren pursed her lips. 'What brings them here?'

'Flying in SERT boys.' Sarah shrugged. 'I'm not complaining. Between them and you, I'll have done my week's fuel quota in a day. Makes for six days of retirement money.'

'Or drinking money. See you at the pub tonight.'

'Righto.'

Lauren chewed her bottom lip as she walked back around the aircraft. No point in worrying Morgan. Carl might not be with this SERT unit anyway.

29

5

'And the landing place? You'll be there, Woomera?'

'I'll be at the site to meet you.'

'Good. *Allahu akbar.*' The line went dead.

Woomera smiled a tight little grimace as he keyed down to memory and erased the caller's details.

His codename meant 'spear thrower' in the local Aboriginal dialect. He'd chosen it with care. It was the name of a rocket-testing facility where the Australian and British governments had cooperated in a joint rocket program in the aftermath of the Second World War. The range still existed, though it was now used for space research.

The same name had been given to the infamous Australian immigration detention centre where brutality reigned. Did his controller get the irony? he wondered.

He closed his mobile phone with a snap and opened the back with surprising delicacy for fingers so large. Flipping the SIM card out he replaced it with another. In such a remote location he wasn't going to risk being tracked by his phone. Rebirthing the phone had been expensive, but it was worth the money. Now he just had to keep changing the service providers and stay one step in front of ASIO, the domestic arm of Australian

BORDER WATCH

intelligence. Nothing tied the phone or the calls received to him. Some poor bastard whose IMEI number they'd used would no doubt find armour-clad heavies kicking his front door down in a couple of weeks. That thought made him grin.

All the pieces seemed to be falling into place. The prawn trawler would be in position for a pick-up by the end of the week. The troops had worked out that apathy or mutiny could be life-threatening and the bomb maker had just left Roti on his way to Australia.

An Indonesian island south-west of Timor, Roti was home to subsistence fishermen whose livelihoods were being threatened not just by environmental degradation, but also by political boundaries imposed from thousands of miles away. Woomera knew first-hand how government decisions taken in isolation could wreak havoc quite contrary to their intent.

Though only eighty by twenty-three kilometres, Roti punched above its weight. More fishermen from this tiny island than from any other region in the Indonesian archipelago, were caught illegally fishing in Australia's Exclusive Economic Zone. The seas they fished were the same seas their fathers' grandfathers had fished. An arbitrary line on a map drawn by politicians in another country had no meaning.

Many of the illegal fishermen came from the village of Pepala, tucked in the north-eastern bay of Roti, with its deep-water access and protective coral reefs. That made it the perfect place to hide illegal activity of a more devastating nature. The fishermen needed money, new boats and little other encouragement. What better place to hide a tree than in a forest, as the saying went? Woomera grinned to himself. And it would do Abu Nadal no harm at all to endure the hardships of a fishing prau for a couple of days. Would bring the arrogant prick down a peg or two. He spat the quick taste of bile from his throat, hawking into the red dust.

He'd worked with plenty of Muslims over the years and the vast majority believed in their religion, practised their faith and lived good lives. There were the few for whom religion represented power or revenge or an opening into the untold wealth of corruption. Then there were those who considered it their fanatical duty to impose their religion on the world. Unstable, unpredictable and often unmanageable, they sure as hell gave him something to whinge about. But, shit oh dear, they paid well. And Nadal topped the last list by a couple of hundred thousand dollars. It helped that Woomera spoke his language and knew enough about his religion to avoid giving offence. But he wouldn't trust Nadal any more than he had to. Working as an agent in Indonesia and the Middle East for the Australian Secret Intelligence Service, the overseas arm of Australian intelligence, had taught him many hard lessons. And opened many doors.

He slipped the phone into the pocket of his cargo pants and wiped the sweat from his forehead. Nineteen days until 9 November. It would all be over then, leaving Australia to weep and wail and wonder what next. Anniversaries were such powerful symbols.

6

When they met for dinner, there was no sign of Rafe.

'Hey, Ben, miss me?' Lauren leant over the bar to peck the barman on the cheek.

'I haven't slept a wink since you left. I'm a shadow of my former self.' Ben patted her shoulder with avuncular affection.

'Still putting on a brave face?' They grinned at each other.

'Can you two stop your little mutual admiration session and get a thirsty man a drink?' Gavin complained, slapping a twenty-dollar bill on the counter in mock annoyance.

'Got your boyfriend in tow still,' Ben laughed. 'And the lovely Morgan.' He stopped pulling Gavin's beer for a moment. 'Good to see you, lass.'

'And you. It's like coming home.' Morgan smiled at him. 'Mary's looking well.'

'She's on a diet. Again.' Ben rolled his eyes. 'Has me walking every morning after breakfast as well.' He patted his considerable stomach. 'This has to go.'

Lauren turned her head and regarded his girth with a critical eye. 'I can see it getting in the way during a night of hot passion, Ben. No wonder Mary's got it on her hit list.'

Gavin almost choked on his first mouthful of beer, while the publican beamed at her. 'You must have been a right little horror to your mother.'

'Well, she should have given me a baby sister or two, instead of six brothers.'

'Lauren just needs a good man to make her settle down,' Morgan chipped in dryly.

'It'll take one hell of a man to keep up with our Lauren.' The barman placed a glass of lime and soda in front of Morgan. 'The cops are in town. Isn't your man in the SERT team?'

Morgan's smile didn't reach her eyes and her back stiffened. 'I'm a single woman so I hope my ex isn't in town.'

'Ah.' Ben nodded, and wiped the bar down again. 'They're here on some top-level investigation. Something brewing up the Cape.'

'Really? Looks like we'll be here on and off for the next month or two as well.'

'Mary mentioned you were booked in all week.'

'Days off in Cairns and back up here beginning of next week.' Morgan sipped her drink. 'Not sure what we're hunting. Our illustrious commander has lockjaw when it comes to defining the task.'

'Just as well or the whole pub would know what we were doing. Remember signing a confidentiality clause, Captain Pentland?' The caustic voice was right at her shoulder and Morgan felt her cheeks flush. 'Or did that slip your mind after one too many drinks?'

Damn that man, Morgan fumed to herself, keeping her face bland. Why did he have to turn up right at that moment? Ben knew their job. It was just chitchat, harmless.

She kept her eyes on Ben, who'd reached for a glass and started pouring. She could almost feel Lauren holding her breath. Gavin shuffled his feet, looking uneasy.

BORDER WATCH

'Ben, remember Rafe?' She gestured vaguely over her shoulder. 'He's our mission commander. Doesn't seem to enjoy working with us mere civilians. We're an undisciplined lot compared to his military pals. I'm sure he'd like one of your cold beers though. Put it on my tab.' She had to stop her teeth from grinding together.

Lauren dropped her foot from the rung of the bar stool with intent and Morgan hid a smile as she touched the younger woman's shoulder to forestall one of her friend's tirades.

'Let's get some dinner, Lauren. Rafe seems to be a little busy for us.' She finally let her gaze slide over the tall rangy figure as he moved up beside her. 'Catch you in the morning, mate.' Her eyes locked with his and she was surprised to see a glimmer of amusement in their darkness. Had she just misinterpreted an attempt at humour?

'I'll be joining you. Table for four, thanks.' He smiled at the barman. Morgan was unsettled by the sudden jolt in her stomach. When he bothered to smile, it lit up the harsh angles of his face and warmed the forbidding brown eyes. His mouth, usually a firm line, relaxed and his lips were unexpectedly sensual. She dragged her eyes away and raised her eyebrows at Lauren, who shrugged in resignation.

'We're honoured, Rafe.' No mistaking Morgan's sarcasm. 'Where would you like us, Ben?'

'Take your pick. By the window if you like?'

'Thanks.' She took the menus from the barman and walked to the nearest table, keeping her face impassive. Rafe was not going to needle her outside work hours, nor in public.

'We can go get takeaway and leave him to it,' Lauren whispered.

Morgan was not about to let Lauren get caught up in the animosity between herself and Rafe. 'What happened to your bet? Can't waste a moment.' She pulled a chair out and patted the seat next to her. 'Sit here and bat those baby blues at him all night. Maybe he'll get scared and leave.'

'Gavin has to sit next to him then.'

Gavin shrugged. 'He's fine. I think he's just nervous around you two. Lots of guys are, you know.'

'You're not,' retorted Lauren.

'I'm not most guys,' Gavin whipped back.

'Enough, here he comes.' Morgan peered at the menu. 'Red meat for me, I think. A nice juicy steak with a huge pile of chips. Lauren?'

'Don't know yet.' She kept her eyes on her menu as Rafe slid into the seat opposite.

'How about you, Gav?'

'Steak with mushroom sauce. No one does it like the chef here. Share a bottle of wine, Morgan, since you've only had a soda water?' His question was pointed, and she smiled her thanks.

'Only if the others are going to have a glass as well.'

'Hmm, I will,' replied Lauren, distracted by the dessert menu. 'Red's good.'

'Rafe?' Morgan kept her voice polite. 'Wine?'

He looked up before he answered, a tiny smile lifting the corner of his mouth. 'A glass of red will be fine. You choose.'

Morgan narrowed her eyes. It felt like a peace offering, but she wasn't that easily pacified.

The waitress took their order and after she left there was momentary silence.

'So . . .' Gavin cleared his throat. 'Looks like we've got good weather for the week anyway.'

'It does. I guess we can expect that, this time of year.' Rafe's response was courteous, careful even, thought Morgan.

'Forecasting south-easters for most of the week,' Gavin continued.

Lauren broke in with a sarcastic laugh. 'Nice day, bit of wind about, shame about the weather,' she chanted. 'Gav? What are you doing? Are you insane? The weather, for heaven's sake?'

'Someone's got to get the conversation rolling,' he protested, flushing at her dig.

Lauren rolled her eyes, tucking her hair back behind her ears. 'But the weather? Can't you do better than that?'

'You try then,' Gavin replied sharply, pulling his beer across the table. Morgan intervened, knowing Lauren could tease Gavin for hours if the mood took her.

'Mary says the fishing's been great so far this year. They're booked out for the next few weeks with fishing tours. Ever done one of those, Rafe?' Her smile was interested, but she made sure there was no warmth in her eyes as she met his gaze.

'No.' He shook his head. 'I haven't been out on the water up here. I'm not much of a fishing fan.'

Gavin lifted his glass in salute, Lauren's taunts forgotten. 'You haven't lived until you've caught your first barra.'

Morgan knew that Gavin's passion for fishing could keep him talking for the whole evening. She raised her soda to her lips and found Rafe's dark eyes on her again. She met his gaze, trying to fathom the expression hiding in the blackness before he looked away.

The waitress returned with the bottle and Morgan gestured to Rafe's glass. 'The gentleman can taste it.'

He half nodded at her, acknowledging her ironic use of 'gentleman'. 'Thank you.'

'It's red, it's got alcohol, it's Australian. Who needs to taste it?' Lauren held out her own glass. 'Me too.'

'You just don't want to miss out on any, do you?' teased Gavin, as he finished off his beer. 'She can drink like a fish when she puts her mind to it. Never ever get into a drinking contest with her. She'll win.'

'Really?' Rafe looked surprised and Morgan couldn't help herself.

'Try it some time. I'd have my week's pay packet on Lauren. No worries at all.'

'You encourage her?' Rafe clearly disapproved and Lauren laughed, cutting in before Morgan could defend herself.

'No, she doesn't encourage me, but after hours she's not the boss any more than you are, so bottoms up, lover.' She raised her glass and caught Morgan's eye. 'Oh, all right. I'll behave. Otherwise she'll get shitty and make my life hell.' Her sigh was theatrical. 'It's so hard having a sober, sensible captain.'

Morgan trod on the younger woman's toe.

'So, where's home for you, Rafe?' She tried to steer the conversation on to another safe topic.

'Wherever the job takes me.'

'And in between operations? Nowhere you call home?'

'I've got a place in Brisbane, but I'm not there much.' Rafe's shrug was noncommittal, dismissive.

'Wife, kids?' Lauren's curiosity got the better of her.

'No.'

'Never ever?' Lauren was back on task.

'Never ever. Came close once.' Rafe looked puzzled at the direction of the conversation.

'So you don't have a total aversion to them then? Wives, that is.'

Lauren really did the ditzy blonde to perfection when she tried, thought Morgan, sipping her wine, the conversation washing over her. That she just happened to be an exceptional pilot and a very tough lady was something Lauren kept largely to herself. She'd explained to Morgan several years ago when she joined Border Watch that men didn't appreciate women who knew more than them, so who was she to try to change their genetic defects?

BORDER WATCH

Lost in her own thoughts Morgan finished her steak with a debate about the sanctity of marriage raging around her.

Rafe's voice jolted her. 'And what about you, Morgan?'

She lifted startled eyes to him.

'What about what?' She'd obviously been silent too long.

'Marriage. Is it overrated?' He nodded at Lauren. 'Lauren claims it is. Gavin reckons not, that it's still relevant. I'm with him. I think our society risks falling apart without it. So?'

She cleared her throat, swirling the wine around her glass, looking for diplomacy. 'Then it's a tie. I'm with Lauren. Marriage and commitment don't mean a damned thing to most people.' She met his steady gaze with a tiny apologetic shrug. 'Sorry.'

'No need to apologise.' He shook his head. 'Just seems a bit strange that the two men here believe a lifetime commitment is possible and the women don't. Isn't it supposed to be the other way round?' He kept his eyes on her face and she wondered where he was going with this.

'Life teaches us different things, I guess.' Her shrug was more obvious this time. 'White weddings and Prince Charming belong in glossy magazines and fairytales. We can't wait around for some alpha male to come along and sweep us off our feet. He'll most likely have feet of clay and we'll be disappointed.'

'I'm not saying you can't have relationships that last,' interjected Lauren. 'But monogamy doesn't seem so relevant anymore. If both sides know where they stand, then no harm done. Just poor form if one partner thinks the relationship's monogamous and the other one doesn't.'

'Very ugly.' Morgan nodded and glanced at the silent Gavin whose miserable expression betrayed him. Would he ever have the courage to voice his feelings to Lauren? She sighed and looked at her watch. Probably not.

'Time for bed for me, guys. I'll go fix up the account. Cough up.'

39

'I'm with you.' Lauren pushed her chair back, digging into her purse. 'Gav?'

'Yeah.' He dropped thirty dollars into her outstretched palm.

'Looks like we're all in for an early night.' Rafe pulled a credit card from his wallet. 'I've got to pay on card. I'll catch you guys in the morning.'

He waited by the register for the waitress to process his card. Absently he watched the other three leave. Morgan, flanked by her team, was a petite, raven-haired woman with enough curves to be alluring. Was she what she appeared to be?

Rafe's gut instinct said yes, but someone was leaking details about the surveillance operation and the evidence all pointed to Morgan. He needed to find the truth. He'd given up judging people on face value years ago. He knew terrorism spawned strange bedfellows. His faint smile held no humour. Plato's question, over two thousand years old, had new meaning in today's world. 'Who guards the guards?'

He knew the answer to that one. He did.

Without fear, without favour.

And without love, a little voice whispered in his head before he could prevent it.

He dashed off a signature on the docket and waited for his receipt. Focus, he cautioned himself. Focus on the issues.

With Lauren and Gavin, Morgan had a formidable team. The three of them were almost to the door when a group of men came through it. Rafe watched Morgan freeze. Gavin and Lauren moved closer, a protective reflex. The man in the centre with short blond hair had a smile that set off alarms on Rafe's radar. His photo was in the file Rafe had been sifting through before dinner.

BORDER WATCH

Morgan's boyfriend — make that ex. Carl Wiseman. The elite police officer looked different from his official mug shot. The photo didn't convey the power or size or presence of the man. In the flesh dangerous charm oozed from him.

Rafe nodded to the barman and threaded his way through the tables, his pace measured, not wanting to draw attention to himself. The rest of Wiseman's companions had trickled in and headed for the bar. They were the SERT team Customs had asked to be stationed here. They didn't know him, nor did they need to yet.

Wiseman was big. Six-foot-five with muscles toned from hard living as well as gym sessions and, right now, he looked to be doing his best to intimidate Morgan. From his stance, he was clearly one of life's bullies, Rafe decided.

He stopped behind Morgan. 'All done, guys. Let's go.'

Morgan looked up at him with anger still blazing from her eyes, long dark lashes framing their intensity. 'Thanks for that, we just got held up.' She went to push past Carl, but he put out a restraining hand.

'We've not finished yet, Morgan.' With his deep voice Rafe could see how the whole package might be attractive to a woman on a superficial level.

'Don't think we've met. Rafe.' He held out his hand knowing it would be ignored.

'Yeah, right.' The blond man barely looked at him, dismissing him as another pilot no doubt, thought Rafe smugly. Just the way he liked it. Wiseman kept talking, focused on Morgan. 'I'll get you a drink, babe.'

'No. Let go of my arm, Carl.'

Rafe didn't bother to hide his smile at the tone of Morgan's reply. Let's see how she handles this one, he thought.

'We haven't finished talking.' Carl hadn't let her arm go and Rafe could see the veins standing out in his hand. It must be

41

hurting Morgan, but she kept her spine straight and her eyes trained on his face. No one could fake a look of such venom. Things must have got really ugly between them.

'Yes we have.' She bit out each word. 'Let go of me now.' She tried to pull her arm free, but Carl held on, glaring at her.

Time for a bit of muscle, Rafe decided. Lob a hand grenade, so to speak. 'Morgan said she's ready to go now, mate. You're blocking the doorway.' Rafe moved in a little closer, his voice raised just a notch.

For the first time Carl seemed to register the size of the other man. 'Really? And who the hell are you?'

'A friend of Morgan's.' Rafe tipped his head sideways at her. 'And we're all on our way out now.'

Carl kept his hand on Morgan's arm, but the pressure had eased just enough for Morgan to break free. Rafe saw Carl drop his chin. He tensed for the punch. With a small roll, he moved his own body into position. Just give me a chance, you fucking ape, he thought, the sharp surge of anger taking him by surprise. You'll be on your arse and out that door before you know what hit you.

Carl must have sensed the other man's tension and rocked back on his heels, his eyes darting between Morgan and Rafe.

'You screwing this guy already? Shit, Morgan, doesn't take you long, does it?'

'You hypocritical bastard,' she hissed at him, icy with disdain.

'She's not bad in the sack,' Carl smirked, his eyes on her face, mocking her.

Lauren caught him across the cheek with a flying hand before the words were out of Carl's mouth and he spun towards her, his fist raised in retaliation. Rafe didn't hesitate. He blocked the big man, putting all his strength into the grip, aware that he was now involved whether he liked it or not.

But Morgan wasn't finished. She grabbed Lauren before she could take another swing and thrust herself forwards between the men.

'No,' she said, her face inches from Carl's. 'It's over. Get out of my way. Now.' Whether the tone of her voice, the rigid set of her body, or the fact they were in a public place finally pierced his anger, Carl capitulated.

He lowered his shoulders, though his eyes stayed watchful as he glared at Rafe over Morgan's dark head. Rafe didn't release his grip on the bigger man's fist, not convinced it was over yet.

'Really?' Carl moistened his lips, the glimmer of a smile tugging at his mouth.

'Yeah, really,' Rafe said, before Morgan could respond. He kept his voice measured, an undercurrent of anger swirling. Carl's tense wrist suddenly went limp and Rafe released it. 'Wise choice, mate.'

He turned to the others. 'Ladies, you first.' He formed a protective barrier behind them, leaving Carl glaring at their backs. Gavin closed the door in his face.

'Friend of yours?' Rafe asked the question into the silence.

'My ex-boyfriend. There are a few things I don't do well. Choosing men tops the list.'

Morgan's harsh voice tugged at Rafe. Despite all that front, all that composure, all that potential duplicity, she was still a vulnerable woman.

'At least I can see now why you might not think marriage is such a good idea. But we're not all arseholes, are we, Gavin? Nice right hook, Lauren. Night all, see you in the morning.'

'Shit, Morgan. Did you see that? He would have taken Carl out easily. I didn't realise how big he was until he measured up behind you.' Lauren looked impressed.

'But he didn't take him out. He just politely stood his ground. I should have thanked him.' Morgan, more shaken than she wanted to admit, locked her knees as they wobbled. 'I wonder if Carl's up here all week.' She bowed her head. 'Wouldn't that be fun.'

Gavin spoke up. 'He can't touch you, and believe me, Rafe won't be letting him. You didn't see his face through all that. I did. Bloody hell, I hope he never gets me in his firing line.'

'Well, I hope he lines up on me,' purred Lauren.

'Oh for god's sake, Lauren. You aren't seriously trying to get him into bed?'

'Why not? He's cute and there's two hundred bucks, at least, riding on it.'

'Shit, Lauren.' Gavin stomped off to his room shaking his head.

Lauren turned to Morgan. 'You okay?'

'Yep, thanks. Lauren?' Morgan looked down at her hands. 'Thanks for sticking up for me, but don't. I don't want to see you caught up in my disaster. You've never seen his anger . . .'

'And I'm not standing by while you're bullied.' Lauren rolled Morgan's arm over. 'Nice bruises in the morning. He's a jerk and I'm glad you got rid of him. I know it's not our place to have an opinion, but neither Gavin nor I could stand him. Sorry.' She gave Morgan a quick hug and left her standing outside her door.

Morgan entered her room and sat on her bed, forcing down the anger that still roiled and bubbled inside her. She folded her hands in her lap, trying ineffectually to stop them trembling.

BORDER WATCH

Carl might be the icing on the ugly cake of her private life, but her distress went deeper than that.

The last few months had been hard, confronting, bewildering. It had all started with Patrick.

After twenty years of absence, her brother had finally bothered to track her down. She still didn't know how she felt about that.

Angry? Definitely.

He'd left her in foster care even after their father hung himself in a fit of belated remorse for killing their mother. He hadn't bothered to look her up for twenty years. And the only reason he'd bothered now seemed to be money.

Guilt? Sure.

She should have tried to find him, but the horror of that night, the fear of really knowing the truth, had held her back. Locking it away and refusing to acknowledge she'd played any part in it had allowed her to function.

Scared? Yep.

The patterns she fought so hard to break might reassert themselves anyway, regardless of how hard she battled to prevent that happening.

When the dark-haired stranger had knocked on her door and she saw her own eyes staring out of his face, she'd felt the ground tilt under her feet. She hadn't looked for him, hadn't needed him, hadn't dared to hope, so why now? What would it change?

His second visit didn't make things any better. It left her unsure about her own choices, about her own life, about her own capacity to love. No doubt some of the anger from that had spilled over into her relationship with Carl, tainting it even further.

And now here was Carl in her face in a small town like Weipa. As if she needed reminding of how lousy she was at

45

relationships. She pushed to her feet, wandered into the bath-room and met her eyes in the mirror. 'I can beat them. I must beat them.' She spoke the words for courage, her mantra, and felt the quick surge of belief. 'I will beat them.'

7

'The water's glassy in the Gulf this morning,' Gavin's voice said through the headsets. 'Should be a good day for you two passengers with the window seats.'

Morgan laughed at his jibe. 'Just get your nose glued to that screen again and put some meaning in our day.' The Gulf of Carpentaria was a wide, shallow body of opalescent water bounded by Cape York in the east and south, Arnhem Land to the west and Papua New Guinea to the north.

On its western side the mighty Roper River flowed across the Roper Bar, a natural rock barrier that separated the warm artesian fresh water from the salt water of the Gulf. South of it the McArthur River emptied the floodwaters of the savannah land, coursing around Kangaroo Island, flushing prawns into the Gulf and muddying the clear waters. In the east the Leichhardt, the Gregory and the Nicholson, the wild rivers of Cape York, spewed their lifeblood of nutrient-rich waters in pulsating surges. The tannin-stained flow created a sharp edge with the warmer currents of the Gulf. Good rain meant fish and prawns in abundance.

Between the enormous influx of water and the prevailing winds a short, sharp choppy swell could build up quickly in the right conditions, making for an uncomfortable crossing by boat.

Lauren, her foot up on the front panel next to her flight instruments, peered out the window.

'Coral spawning looks impressive.'

'Must have happened last night. Reefs are deep here. Twenty, thirty metres down. Couple of days after a full moon, slack tide and water temperature just perfect for reproduction.' Morgan squinted down at the water. 'Don't ever let it get stuck on the side of your boat though.'

'Yeah, right. It sticks like glue and stinks worse than rotting fish,' Gavin added.

'You too,' Morgan laughed back at him.

'Yep, took me a couple of hours to scrub the tinny clean.'

'See,' Lauren interrupted. 'I've always told you, you're swimming in fish pee in the —'

'We've got a contact reported at about one hundred and fifty miles, bearing two-nine-zero from Weipa.' Rafe's authoritative voice cut through the chatter. 'It's been reported by a couple of the fishing fleet and it moves too fast to be just an old prau. Probably Type 3, shark boat.' The illegal fishing vessels were categorised by length. The largest ones, with enclosed cabins, were Type 3. Shark was their usual catch.

Lauren had leant forwards to load information into the flight management system before Rafe finished speaking. Morgan altered the course of the aircraft to an approximate guess as she and Lauren confirmed the navigation details. They were forty-five nautical miles from Weipa and tracking north already, so they only had about twenty-five minutes to run to the target. She went over the details in her head.

'What height do you want us at? High level?'

'Twenty-five thousand.' Rafe's reply was curt.

BORDER WATCH

He's distracted this morning, thought Morgan. She turned in her seat and looked down the cabin to the consoles at the rear of the aircraft. Gavin was hunched over his radar, refining the settings for the target. Rafe had the Satellite phone tucked under his chin while he scanned the computer in front of him, a frown etched on his face.

She turned back to the aircraft controls and re-engaged the lateral navigation function on the autopilot. Rafe had looked uncomfortable this morning when she'd thanked him for his support last night. She knew her cheeks had flamed red, embarrassed that she'd entangled him in her little soap opera. But she'd persisted, knowing she needed to acknowledge that he'd involved himself in something he could have walked past. She smiled to herself. Lauren couldn't be any more impressed with their gallant mission commander if he'd single-handedly saved the world.

'What are you smiling at?' Lauren was watching her.

'Nothing important.'

'Really?' Lauren reached forwards and flicked the switch, isolating their headsets from the rest of the aircraft. 'Looks like a sinful smile to me.'

'And you'd know.'

'Absolutely. I think you're warming to our illustrious leader. And you looked very fetching this morning, Captain Pentland. I'm sure he noticed.'

'How do the other captains cope with you interfering with their lives?' Morgan tried to sound stern.

'Ha, I don't, but you love me helping you out.'

'You're so right. I just love having you tell me I'm the most beautiful captain in the company. Short on competition, I suspect.' Morgan laughed outright.

'Even if there was another female captain, you'd still top them.'

49

'The sublime confidence of youth.' Morgan's retort was wry.

'Ladies?'

'Yes, Rafe.' She switched the intercom over again.

'How long to top of climb?'

Morgan studied the flight management system. 'FMS says another five to six minutes.'

'Okay. Endurance once we get to the search area?'

Lauren answered this time. 'About six hours, high level. Four and a half if we go low and that'll be from the point of expected contact.'

'Okay, give me a latest divert time then.'

Lauren and Morgan both looked at the clocks in front of them. 'Twenty-five to target, six hours after that. It's six-thirty now, give or take a couple of minutes. So thirteen hundred for a high-level search,' Lauren looked at Morgan for confirmation.

'Yep, thirteen hundred, or less if you need us low level.' Morgan wrote it down on the notepad on her control column.

Minutes later, Gavin had the target vessel on radar and confirmed its speed was in excess of twenty-five knots. That made it almost twice as fast as an Indonesian prau. Its general direction of travel would take it to the north of Weipa, almost on the reciprocal track to their flight path. They'd exhaust all of their endurance to shadow it to the coast at its current speed.

'Hold that course. We'll get some stills and video footage as we go over the top.' Rafe had command now and the aircraft would go where he ordered it.

'Gavin, get the details on the FLIR and I'll pass the info onto the BPC.' Border Protection Command was the central government agency tasked with collating all the intelligence information on Australia's borders. The FLIR was the Forward

Looking Infrared Radar that could pick up a heat source from twenty-five thousand feet and accurately pinpoint how many people were on board.

Gavin grunted as he hunched over his equipment. He was the true genius on the flight, in Morgan's opinion. The pilots flew the aircraft, the mission commander ordered the searches, but the observer worked his equipment like a symphony orchestra conductor. Gavin was the best they had in Border Watch.

'Six bodies on board and they're not moving around much. Two very large inboard diesel engines, probably a couple of hundred horse a side, but it's not much of a boat size-wise. Maybe a bit bigger than six tonnes? I'd say just on ten metres in length.'

Rafe was already on the line to the BPC and nodded at Gavin.

'Okay.' He disconnected. 'They want us to observe high level. Break off only if we're getting close to international airspace. A "no visible contact" run. Gav, we'll need to stream video footage back to the BPC. Let them know when we have to break off. Morgan?'

'That's fine with me. Way they're tracking we'll be following them back to Weipa. Is this illegal fishermen or a SIEV, people smugglers?' She used the abbreviation for suspected illegal entry vessel.

'Looks like a typical shark boat and only has six on board,' Gavin answered before Rafe could. 'Fishermen taking their new boat for a spin? Checking out the lie of the land for a future smuggling run maybe? SIEVs normally carry more people than this one is.'

When Rafe didn't answer Morgan filled the silence. 'Okay, we'll fly a five-minute right-hand pattern moving with him. Need that to change, just sing out. Let me know when to start turning.'

Smoothly she brought the aircraft engines back to holding power. No point in going round and round in circles at twenty-five thousand feet any faster than necessary. Save the fuel and increase their endurance. She mulled over Gavin's reading of the boat. Fishermen weren't often spotted this far east. It could be an exploratory run, the start of a new wave of boat people.

She turned to Lauren. 'Been a spate of illegal-immigrant incursions in the last few months. Don't know how they keep most of them out of the media.' Lauren shrugged as Morgan continued. 'The press have no idea how many boats are apprehended and the passengers bundled onto charter flights and sent home the same day. They, and all the human rights activists, would have a field day if they ever found out.'

'Yeah,' Lauren replied. 'And what about the damage they could cause if they wanted to? Remember the boatload that tied up on one of the oil rigs in Western Australia?'

'The Front Puffin rig, west of Darwin.' Morgan nodded. 'Spent the day on the rig before the navy could get out to them. The rigs are sitting ducks.'

'Politicians are never going to admit they can't really control these borders.' Lauren flicked her long nails in dismissal. 'They can't stop them fishing, they can't stop the people smugglers and, god knows, they probably have no idea what the terrorists are doing.'

Morgan didn't hide her cynicism. 'Something would have to blow up in their faces before they accept the threat's real. Australia has been very, very lucky so far, considering it's involvement in Iraq and Afghanistan.'

'And that is not for us to speculate on.' Rafe's voice cut through their conversation. 'We're not paid to have an opinion.'

'I know, I know,' Morgan said sharply. 'Thanks for reminding us, Rafe.' The tension crackled in her voice and she didn't try to disguise it. With an impatient click, she isolated the

BORDER WATCH

women's intercoms from the rest of the aircraft. He might be right, but she did have an opinion and no government could stop that.

She had limited sympathy for illegal fishermen. Most of them knew where the boundaries were and flouted them. Maybe it wasn't fair that those reefs had been absorbed into Australia's Exclusive Economic Zone almost thirty years ago without consulting them. Then again, most of them were too young to be able to claim the reefs as traditional hunting grounds.

But the people smugglers?

The jury was still out on how she felt about illegal asylum seekers. Part of her saw only desperate people in need of help. A more cynical side saw queue jumpers with money denying other legitimate immigrants a place in a country they all saw as lucky. She'd met a couple of illegal immigrants, taxi drivers in Cairns, who'd been through detention centres. Nice enough guys who, without exception, were sad, broken people.

'You know, I was in Broome when they escorted a big boat-load into harbour.' Morgan knew she sounded edgy. 'They were these terrified-looking people with nothing but the clothes they were standing up in and a small tatty bag each. We were unserviceable waiting for the engineers. A BA 146 roared in late afternoon, loaded the lot and flew them back to Indonesia. I had this insane urge to try and stop it.'

'Yeah, I know what you mean.' Lauren paused for a moment. 'I still think a country like ours has room enough for a few more.'

'I guess after September 11, it's hard to sort the real refugees from possible terrorists.'

Lauren snorted this time. 'The ones that look like they don't need a feed are probably the terrorists. Australia's borders are just so vast. Anyone could slip in through the Torres Strait

53

and work their way down the Cape, bringing supplies and explosives with them.'

'So best we do our job and stop them.'

'Yeah, well at least we're out of the action up here. An observe-and-report mission is like an armchair in front of a widescreen TV.'

'Hope you're right, Lauren. Remember that cargo aircraft hit by a SAM departing Baghdad back in 2003?'

'Yeah, I remember looking that up on the web. Hard to believe they managed to land the freighter safely.'

'May it never happen to us,' Morgan replied. She settled back in her seat, glancing at the expanse of ocean rolling below them. 'Wouldn't want to be forced down over this lot.'

Lauren nodded, adjusting the tilt on their weather radar. 'Don't know what would be worse. The sharks out here or the crocs back on shore.' She flashed a wicked grin. 'Though I'm sure they'd find the guys more to their taste. Do you reckon we'd survive the impact?'

Morgan shrugged, still looking out the window. 'Depends, I guess. If we went in with a full load of fuel on board, it'd probably fireball and we'd burn to the waterline.' She glanced across at Lauren. 'Empty? After our showing in the simulator, girlfriend, we'd give it our best shot anyway. Wouldn't like to hear a playback of the voice recorder, though. I'd be swearing the whole way down to the ground.'

'You reckon I wouldn't be? My vocabulary is much bigger than yours.'

'And you're proud of that?' Morgan rolled her eyes.

Lauren smiled broadly. 'You bet. It's taken me a long time to memorise enough of them so I can now make up my own combinations.'

Gavin interrupted them with a request for a heading change and they focused back on the task.

BORDER WATCH

★ ★ ★

For the next five hours they followed the vessel sedately back to the Australian coastline. Several times, Australian fishing boats came within close range. Each time, the shark boat slowed to a snail's pace, crew came on deck ostensibly fishing with hand lines. Each time, it accelerated as soon as the trawlers were over the horizon.

The track they were holding started to veer further north-east up the Cape from Weipa towards Skardon River, an isolated stretch of coast with little or no habitation. The mangrove islands on the west of Cape York formed impenetrable barriers, sometimes miles across. Without exception the river mouths were wide tributaries with shallow bars, providing safe anchorage and myriad hiding places.

Rafe chewed on his lower lip, weighing up his options, knowing he couldn't consult his crew.

'Do you think they're camping up here?' Gavin asked. 'They seem to be heading on a set course.' He swivelled his chair towards Rafe. It was not unheard of for illegal fisherman to run their boats ashore for some land-bound R and R and to collect fresh water. The authorities didn't like it, but they chose to ignore it.

People smugglers in SIEVs were another matter. Once they landed on Australian soil they had new avenues to claim asylum. The whole Border Watch operation was designed to prevent that happening.

Rafe frowned with a noncommittal shrug. He knew he couldn't risk telling the crew the real situation. The operation had reached its final stages and he already knew exactly where the vessel would land. All he had to do was the daily head count and wait for the order from Border Protection Command to move in.

'BPC should be able to pinpoint that from our photographs. By my reckoning, we've got another hour of flying time and we're still thirty miles to the coast. They'll need to slow down once they're in the shallows so we may miss their landing spot.' And that was exactly what he wanted to happen.

Morgan had left Lauren in charge of the aircraft and had come down to make them all a drink. She stopped beside the two men with the mugs in her hand.

'We could always cut and run now. Be back in Weipa in ten, twelve minutes, refuelled, airborne and back on task in less than forty minutes total. No patrol boats in our neck of the woods?'

Rafe considered her words, kicking himself for not having blocked off that course of action earlier. Too easy to underestimate Morgan's ability to think outside the square. He shook his head.

'Too risky, some of these boats have crude radar and might pick us up if we come down to land. I don't want to tip them off. And no, the patrol boat is busy further north.'

Morgan raised her eyebrows. 'Sounds more serious than a bit of illegal long-line fishing to me, but you're the boss.'

Rafe watched her walk through to the cabin, the sway of her hips in her green flight suit distracting him for a moment. Damn her for being so quick. He caught Gavin watching him, his eyes far too knowing, curiosity lifting his mouth in a half-smile.

Disconcerted, Rafe turned away. These people were his team for the next couple of weeks, even while he investigated them. He'd worked with several teams since being seconded to the Customs Patrol Division. None of them were a match for the intuitive cohesion he saw here. They were living proof that good teams were greater than the sum of the individual parts. Their loyalty to each other, which made them so easy

BORDER WATCH

to work with, also muddied the source of the leak. At least one of them was not what they seemed. So he wouldn't be taking any chances.

'Just keep logging them and we'll predict an area of probable landfall once we have to leave them. BPC can do the rest.'

'We're close enough to shore. If the navy isn't in a position to help can't you just call in a Customs vessel? There are normally a couple of them operating out of Weipa.' Gavin frowned at his screen again, sounding unconvinced.

'For now, we're on an observe-and-report mission. That's all I can tell you, sorry.' The apology in his voice didn't need to be forced. He'd be glad when this operation was finished. Lies and half-truths were necessary in his job, but neither sat comfortably with him.

Morgan had floored him with her apology this morning. Her cheeks had flushed a delicate shade of pink under her light tan, her grey eyes held only honesty. He hadn't been able to stop his eyes flicking over the bruises on her arm. Defensive, she'd crossed them, her eyes darkening. The sharp pain he saw pass across her face made him wish Carl had pushed him just a fraction further. He deserved to run up against someone harder than a woman.

A glimmer of last night's flash of anger surprised him and he turned it over, examining it before discarding it. None of his damn business what went on in Morgan's private life.

Unsettled, he turned back to the computer screens and keyed the intercom to the flight deck. 'Can you give me ten minutes warning when we need to head off?'

'No worries,' Morgan answered him.

They followed the boat to within twenty miles of the mouth of Skardon River before they broke off the search and commenced descent into Weipa.

57

'Coming fishing this afternoon?' Gavin tapped his pen on his desk, the rhythm erratic.

'Thanks, but I've got reports to write. Give it a miss this time.' Rafe didn't see much pleasure in sitting on a hot jetty in the fierce sun with stale bait prawns for company.

'You don't know what you're missing. Weipa's the only place I know in Queensland where you can fish off a mainland jetty, a cold beer in your hand, and watch the sun set over the water.' Gavin spun his pen in the air. 'Who cares if we catch barramundi? It's just an excuse for being there.'

'Maybe next time.' Rafe knew it was easier, no matter how good the team, to keep a little distance while they were on the job. And the complexity of this particular job made it mandatory.

He ignored the twinge of regret. No one paid him to be sentimental and soft. Never had, never would. And there was no point in comparing them with his team in the SAS. It was not possible to reclaim what he'd lost in smoke and heat and flames and a living hell. There was no going back.

That thought steeled him.

'Gets pretty rough for the last few thousand feet into here. I'd strap in if I were you.' Gavin had already tidied his equipment away and collected Rafe's empty mug. The look on his face said he understood where Rafe was coming from and the big man looked away.

He fastened his seatbelt and watched out the window. Wide, flat sandbars emerged from the clear water. Saltwater crocs, large enough to be visible even at altitude, sunned their prehistoric bodies like tourists on a tropical resort beach. The dark green of the mangroves hid their own secrets.

For the inhabitants of this primeval northern corner of Australia, the untamed wildness of the country was commonplace. For anyone else it would be confronting. Everything,

BORDER WATCH

from the virus-carrying mosquitoes to the oversized reef fish and the giant mining trucks that plied the roads in Weipa, was larger than life.

And so were the characters that lived here.

The ocean gave way to the red bauxite-rich land surrounding Weipa. A frontier town, it had been built on the back of mining and fishing. Both those industries attracted tough people who worked hard, partied hard and lived life with the throttle jammed wide open.

New housing estates were springing up to the south-west of the main town. A worldwide commodities boom had seen the price of bauxite go through the roof. Fat pay cheques burnt a hole in the miners' pockets and there wasn't much to spend it on in Weipa, except alcohol, boys' toys and adventure. Pig shooting, deep-sea fishing and four-wheel driving over terrain so rough that NASA had tested lunar vehicles on it were respectable weekend picnic outings. Mum and the kids, if they hadn't cleared out for the bright city lights, went along for the ride.

The fishing industry wasn't quite so robust. Illegal fishing still cut a swathe through the trawler men's livelihoods. And there was nothing he could do about that right now, Rafe thought, shifting in his seat, uncomfortable with his department's lack of resources. A crappy government policy, it had little to do with solving the problem and much to do with re-election promises. There would be time later to work on that.

This time, he reminded himself, he was hunting much bigger prey than some shark-fin-poaching, impoverished Indonesian fishermen. There was a hell of a lot more at stake than the survival of an industry. No chance of him losing sight of that.

8

'I'll see you guys at dinner. Do you want me to ask the chef to cook up our catch?' Morgan pushed dark strands of hair back off her sweaty forehead.

'Nah, you go run off your excess energy. Gav and I'll sort it out.' Lauren waved her away, her face hidden by a large shabby straw hat. 'Leave your rod, I'll take it back with me.'

'Okay, see you at seven in the bar.'

'And don't go bumping into that great gorilla you dumped either,' murmured Lauren, as the older woman walked away.

'Should one of us go with her?' Gavin turned the winder on his fishing reel a couple of times, frowning as he concentrated.

'Have you seen her run? She'd leave us both in her dust, and red dirt's not on my menu today.'

'Let's hope he's off doing something more constructive than beating up women then.'

'Maybe she'll run into Rafe. I saw him head out wearing a pair of flash new running shoes.'

'I thought *you* were trying to get him into bed.' Gavin didn't try to hide the annoyance in his voice.

Lauren looked at him and laughed. 'You know I love it when you sound jealous.'

'Piss off, Lauren. I just hate seeing you get hurt.'

'I'd have to have something invested emotionally before I got hurt by my lovers.'

'One day you're going to realise there's more to a relationship than sex.'

'I know that, and when I'm ready for such a serious, long-term commitment I'll know exactly where to look.' She picked up her fishing rod along with Morgan's and blew him a kiss as she sauntered off.

'Why me?' Gavin muttered, hauling on his line impatiently. 'Two billion women in the world and I have to fall for a blonde with attitude.' The line jerked hard in his hand and he spent the next ten minutes working a good-sized barramundi onto the jetty.

He regarded it sourly. 'At least she can't say I didn't catch her a good dinner.' He'd almost finished packing up when he saw Carl heading down the jetty towards him.

'Hi, Gavin isn't it?' Carl was all smiles and Gavin kept his face neutral.

'Carl. How's it going?'

'Bloody hot up here, isn't it? Morgan about?' Even Gavin could see why women might fall at Carl's feet when he was being charming, but his bullshit detector had ramped up to high alert.

'Sorry, just missed her.'

'Where are you going for dinner? I thought I should buy her a drink to say sorry.'

'Don't know.' He shook his head, pretending to mull it over. 'We didn't discuss it. You're not going to be up here for long, are you?' He didn't stop the note of censure creeping into his voice and Carl reacted with predictable scorn.

'Listen, you computer jerk, it's none of your fucking business how long I'm up here. Tell Morgan I'm looking for her.'

He marched off, heavy footsteps shaking the old timber jetty. Gavin's grin was broad.

'I'll do no such fucking thing, mate,' he mumbled under his breath. Damn, but it felt good to antagonise a man twice his size. Lauren must be rubbing off on him.

Morgan made it to the airport in a little over twenty minutes and stopped in surprise. The airstair door hung open with the auxiliary power unit running to provide electricity to the aircraft.

'What the hell?' She raced to the fence and keyed in the password, only waiting for the gates to move far enough for her to slip through.

'No one touches my aircraft,' she said aloud as she ran towards it.

She could see through the front windscreens that the flight deck was empty. That meant they were messing around down the business end. She stopped at the bottom of the airstairs, her breathing still ragged from the run.

Common sense reasserted itself and she ran the scenario through her head. No car in the carpark, so they'd come on foot like herself. It couldn't be Lauren or Gav, so that left Rafe.

Why would he bother coming out to the aircraft and not do her the courtesy of mentioning it? Her anger shot from simmer to boil. He better have a bloody good reason for not letting her know first. She crept up the stairs, confident the noise of the APU would obliterate any sounds she made.

Two steps from the top she felt the cool wash of the air-conditioning and heard Rafe's deep voice. The words weren't quite distinct and she strained to hear.

'I'd rather we ran the way we are. If we can pinpoint the exact numbers . . .'

Damn, thought Morgan, she was only getting half of it. With care she edged further up the stairs.

'Terrorists . . . do anything if they're cornered . . . if they are . . . JI . . .'

Morgan froze. JI? Jemaah Islamiya? The fanatical Muslim extremist group, with its centre in Indonesia, had master-minded the Bali bombings at Kuta Beach in 2002 and again in 2005. Was that who they were hunting? Not fishermen at all, but terrorists who targeted westerners?

She craned to hear more and almost screamed when a heavy hand descended on her shoulder. Attack, she decided, was the only appropriate response here.

'What the hell do you think you're doing?' she demanded, shaking herself free. Putting her hands on her hips, she glared up at him.

'And the same back at you, lady.' Rafe was angry. Morgan could see it in the flare of his nostrils and the grim line of his mouth.

'Securing my aircraft. I often check on it last thing. I don't expect to find mission commanders with APUs running and the aircraft powered up. Are you endorsed for that, mate?' She snapped out the words, sorry that being on the second step from the top gave him a height advantage of over a metre.

'Yes, I am.' He ground out each word.

'Really? You're a hot-shot pilot as well?' Morgan put all the sarcasm she could muster into her taunt.

'Yes, really.' His expression mellowed to smug for an instant. She fired straight back at him, annoyed at his arrogance as his hands slid to his hips.

'The aircraft is my responsibility. What if something went wrong and the APU caught fire?' Morgan knew she'd backed down, but being this close to him, when he wore only a brief pair of running shorts and a body-hugging singlet, unnerved her. He was just too male, all male. She couldn't miss the toned muscles that bulged as he crossed his arms again. Distracted, her anger slipped a notch despite herself.

'Then I'd follow the QRH and shut the bloody thing down. Come inside. It's too hot to argue out here.' He turned back into the aircraft, leaving her with no option but to stomp up the stairs behind him.

So he knew about the Quick Reference Handbook pilots used in emergencies, she fumed. That still didn't make it okay for him to be messing around in her aircraft.

He stopped by the observer's station and faced her. 'I'm sorry. I should have let you know first. It was rude, unprofessional.' With one stroke, he'd stolen the high moral ground from under her. That annoyed her almost as much as his original transgression.

Feeling cheated, she faced him over the console. 'Apology accepted,' she said, not meaning it, and showing it.

'How much did you hear?'

She hesitated a moment, considering whether to bend the truth a little. Didn't seem worth it, she decided. 'JI.'

'Ah.' He regarded her for a moment. Defiant, she kept her gaze level. Silence remained her best weapon.

'You know about JI?'

'Just what I've read in the press.'

'Hmm.' The sound rumbled in his throat. He looked down, running a lean hand through his midnight dark hair, leaving it sticking up in sweaty clumps. Morgan found it oddly endearing, as though behind the tough facade lurked a dishevelled schoolboy.

'You know it's not policy to tell you guys more than strictly necessary.' He met her gaze.

'I know.' She kept her tone haughty. 'But if this involves terrorists then it's a little different.'

BORDER WATCH

'And your team is a little different. You're too quick to analyse everything.'

'Quick?' She snorted derisively with an impatient shake of her head. 'We didn't pick our targets as terrorists. We figured if they weren't fishermen or people smugglers, they were drug runners probably hauling in ice or something similar.'

'Then you're right. JI finance their overseas operations with all sorts of money-earning schemes. Methamphetamine is just one of them.' He patted Gavin's chair. 'Sit. I'll give you a thumbnail sketch, but don't try to convince me the other two need to know as well.'

She slumped into the chair and shrugged at him. 'We'll see.'

His jaw clenched and he ran his hand up his throat, tipping his head back. 'I'm breaking all the protocols here.' He pinned her with his dark eyes, but she refused to back down.

'So?'

He eyeballed her for several more seconds, the tension, the anger, crackling between them.

'We've had reports of a prawn trawler with links to Cairns. We believe they're picking up drugs from the Indonesian praus, stockpiling it up the Cape, then ferrying the shipment south in among their catch of prawns. We think this run is part of a particularly big consignment. It'll be the last this year with the wet season almost on us.' Rafe was referring to the monsoon trough that made its yearly journey south from the equator, bringing with it driving flood rains, fierce storms and the ever-present risk of violent cyclones. Conditions in the Gulf of Carpentaria would be too dangerous for the praus.

'So you need to pick them up in possession of the drugs otherwise they'll claim they're simple fishermen.' Morgan nodded her understanding, gratified by the unguarded surprise on his face. 'If they're fishermen, then the courts will only

65

impound their boats, try them and send them home with a
fine. Next season they'll be back doing the same thing.'

'Exactly why I didn't want to tell you. You're too quick for
your own good.'

'So?'

'We observe and report. Ground crews will do the rest in a
couple of weeks' time.'

'Just as Gavin said.' Her quick grin was triumphant. 'You think
Gav won't put the picture together in a couple of days?'

'So let him try. If you hadn't overheard me, I wouldn't be
telling you this now.' He leant against the rear bulkhead, arms
crossed, a quick flare of anger in his eyes.

Morgan's temper heated up again. 'Despite what you think,
I understand that what we do for a living is classified. I also
understand that I could endanger my crew by being indiscreet.
You clearly don't know me if you think I'd ever do that.' She
made sure her scornful smile reached her eyes. She had no
intention of trying to placate him.

He kept his gaze on her face, but didn't respond. If he was
trying to unnerve her, he'd have to work a lot harder, she
decided rebelliously. The silence stretched out, the background
rumble of the APU the only other sound. Impassive, she didn't
waver under his relentless stare. She was not going to be the
one to break the standoff.

A muscle in his jaw twitched and she wondered what it
would take to snap his control. A tiny bubble of mischief
sent the unruly thought through her mind. With deliberate
slowness, Morgan let her gaze drop from his face, across his
shoulders, down over his resolutely crossed arms and back up
to his eyes again. With muscles rippling every time he moved,
there was much of the warrior in his demeanour.

He appeared unmoved, the hard glint in his eye a challenge,
the arrogant tilt of his head a rebuke. A slither of traitorous

BORDER WATCH

desire snaked through her stomach. Misplaced, inappropriate and unwelcome, it rattled her. She broke first.

'So that's it? And I can't tell my crew?' Her chin lifted. Her cheeks heated with the rush of blood. Damn it, why did she think she could play games with this man? He was in a different league.

He pushed off the wall and came to stand in front of her, the subtle smell of clean male sweat playing havoc with her jumpy nerves.

'Let's see how long it takes them to work it out.' He met her eyes with a quick grin, at odds with the hard glint in his eyes. 'Two hundred bucks says Lauren gets it first.'

Morgan laughed at his oblique reference. 'You know.' She shook her head in amused disbelief. 'You know all about the bet. Lovely.'

'Lauren is not profiting from my body.' His smile reached his eyes this time. The air of menace, of antagonism, that had simmered only moments before vanished with one quick flash of humour.

'She'll be so disappointed.' Morgan laughed again and got to her feet, giving in to the strong urge to put some distance between them. She assumed the conversation was over. Rafe clearly wasn't going to be telling her any more. 'Are you finished here?'

'Almost. Can I get a lift back with you?'

'Sure.' She tucked her hair behind her. 'I think I could carry you a couple of paces before my legs give out.'

'Oh.' He snorted. 'You ran out too.'

'Race you back?'

His grin held only challenge. 'Winner buys dinner.'

'Fine by me. Hope you like fish. Gav is a very special fish-erman.' Morgan crossed her fingers that Gavin had, as usual, caught enough fish to feed an army.

67

'I'll shut the comms down. You want to turn the APU off?'

At least he had the grace to look embarrassed, thought Morgan, as she headed to the front of the aircraft. And apologise. Suppose I should cut him some slack, she grumbled to herself. Secure phone lines were guaranteed from the aircraft, plus he had access to everything he needed. Still, most mission commanders used their mobile phones. As she understood it, those phones were routed through scramblers, diverters and god knows what else to make them secure. Why run all the way out here?

She reached up and deselected the generator before she hit the overspeed test switch, silencing the APU. Battery loads looked good, she noted, so he'd done the right thing when he'd got to the aircraft.

And a pilot as well? Seemed a little hard to believe, but ex-SAS could mean a lot of things. As well as way too disturbing for her peace of mind, she decided, as she cast one long last look around the flight deck.

Those itty-bitty little shorts left nothing to her imagination. And that imagination was going into misplaced overdrive. She really did have to get it under control. He was a colleague after all.

Distracted by her thoughts, she didn't hear him come to the flight-deck doorway and slammed into his rock-solid chest as she turned to go.

'Sorry.' She struggled to regain her balance, the physical contact with him sending her heart rate skittering.

'Easy, easy. You'll do damage.' His hands steadied her and she fought against the urge to break free. As if sensing her rebellion, he released her, though his fingertips lingered just a moment, which did nothing at all to steady her jumping pulse.

BORDER WATCH

He held the door open, giving her room to stand. 'After you.'

'Thanks.' She kept her distance, refusing to meet his frank gaze as she walked down the stairs. He did not need to see any telltale signs in her eyes. That would be embarrassing for both of them.

Looking back at the aircraft, she gave it a final once-over to check all was secure again on the deserted airfield and used the moment to steady her breathing.

'How long did it take you to get here?' He'd bent down to retie a shoelace and squinted up at her in the waning sunlight.

Deliberately she added a few minutes. 'Half an hour.'

'Along the road?'

'Yep, might get lost taking a detour.'

'Okay, let's go.'

She started running, her pace steady and slow, warming her muscles before she applied the pressure.

Running was many things for Morgan.

It had started as an escape from the violence that defined her childhood, a refuge from the pain of death and loss. It grew into a tool she'd used to survive during the endless search for safety in the years after her parents died, when each foster home brought new challenges.

Most importantly, it became the key that eventually opened the doors of opportunity.

Her last foster family had recognised her talent and found a way into her shuttered heart. When she won a Queensland cross-country championship, she'd been headhunted by the Australian Institute of Sport. A serious injury cut short a promising track career, but by then she'd come to like herself enough to imagine a life where she made the choices, a life where she could dare to dream, a life where she could live on her terms.

69

She pushed her thoughts aside and concentrated on the length of her stride, the angle of her foot hitting the ground. With a sideways glance she assessed the big man next to her. Rafe was so much taller, his long legs outpaced her easily and he moved well.

It would be a sprint to the finish, but she was confident.

'You run often?' he asked.

She hid a quick smile. 'Every day if I can. And you?'

'The same. Too much sitting around in my job.' His breathing hadn't sped up much she noted. Maybe she should keep him talking.

'What else do you do to stay fit?' She couldn't stop her gaze dropping to those impressive biceps.

He looked down at her and she was sure his lips twitched in a knowing smile. 'Too long in the SAS. Push-ups, sit-ups, martial arts, yoga.'

'Yoga?'

'Yeah,' he said with a grin. 'Surprised?'

'Can't see you meditating.'

She pushed the pace up a little. Was that what was behind that secretive little smile of his?

'A Zen moment every now and then.' He looked down at her with a self-deprecating laugh. 'You should try it yourself. Might bring you some peace.'

'Peace?' She controlled the quick blast of indignant anger by increasing her speed. Damn, but he was fit.

'Sorry, poor choice of words. Try inner calm. Works for me when I have issues in my life I'd rather I didn't. Puts things in perspective.' He shrugged, an off-hand dismissal of his own words.

She didn't miss a step, intrigued at the philosophical turn the conversation had taken. It wasn't what she'd expected, but she felt he deserved an answer.

'Carl is not going to disappear because I meditate. Wish it were that easy.' She tucked a stray strand of hair back behind her ear and cast a wry grin his way. Her own temper had always been too quick to rise. She'd learnt to meditate to control it. Why was she surprised that a warrior like Rafe might use the same techniques?

'Wiseman treated you like a victim. I don't see you as one at all.'

She heard approval in his voice, surprised that it mattered. The tingle of warmth she felt in the pit of her stomach was unfamiliar. 'Thank you.' Her chin inched up and she knew the battle light would be glowing in her eyes. 'It's just a matter of standing my ground until he gets bored. Which he will,' she added, with a toss of her head.

In an almost companionable silence, they ran along the roadside, red dust lifting in tiny spurts from their shoes.

Stringy red kangaroos and scrawny dingos with their distinctive tan and white fur skittered away from the unfamiliar noise. Animals that were used to the drone of heavy machinery and the roar of diesel four-wheel drives careening down the road were nervous of the rhythmic thud of running feet.

Perhaps, mused Morgan, it was a memory locked in their cells of thousands of years' hunting by the local indigenous tribes, a memory passed down from mother to joey, from bitch to pup, that kept their species alive.

A flock of white cockatoos flew screeching from the decimated top branches of a young ghost gum, wheeling in flight across the road only to settle again in the same tree. The hardy eucalyptus scrub, scrappy remnants of once vast tracks of forests cleared by the giant mining company gouging for bauxite, provided no shade or relief.

Not the sort of environment in which to venture off the beaten track, Morgan knew, as her running shoes sank unevenly into the super-fine red dust. Several dirt-stained four-wheel drives passed them with laconic waves from the occupants, the windows wound up tightly locking the cool of the air-con inside. People mostly worked too hard up here to need exercise at the end of a long day. Rafe and Morgan were being dismissed as lunatic out-of-towners. Tourists.

From the corner of her eye, Morgan saw Rafe check his stride length then stretch out. Unconsciously he'd fallen into step with her and that was going to cause him pain if he kept shortening it. They were entering the outskirts of the town now and Morgan gestured ahead.

'First one to the pub door buys dinner?'

'Yep.'

She didn't wait for his one-word answer, just took off. She got a five-metre lead on him before he realised what she was doing.

Best part of a kilometre to go, she reckoned, arms and legs pumping to keep ahead of him. She hadn't intended to sprint the whole way there, but she would if she had to.

He moved up to sit on her shoulder. 'Fit little thing, aren't you?'

She tossed a grin over her shoulder. 'Not too bad yourself. Ready?'

'After you.' He waved towards the pub.

She accelerated again. God knows, she'd be paying for this in the morning, but she hadn't had so much fun on a run in years.

He pulled level with her, but couldn't quite get ahead of her even with his longer stride. They hit the front post at full speed and Morgan swung around it laughing.

'A dead heat, I'd say.' She bent over, gasping for air.

'Go you halves on dinner then.'

BORDER WATCH

'You two idiots right there?' A local fisherman on his way to the pub looked them over with disbelief. 'It's gotta be thirty degrees still and that'd be in the shade.' Shaking his head, he pushed open the door to the bar, releasing a quick blast of cool air onto their hot bodies.

Morgan caught Rafe's eye and couldn't stop the laughter bubbling out of her. In the way of lunacy it was infectious and they both stood there, sides heaving, laughing with a touch of hysteria.

'He's right,' Rafe managed to get out. 'We're bloody nuts. I need a swim or I'll never cool down. Where'd you learn to run like that?'

'AIS. Sorry, that wasn't fair, was it?' She was laughing still, her head thrown back and her chest heaving.

'I think you set me up. You must have been walking if it took you thirty minutes to get to the airport.'

'So I stretched the truth a bit.' She stretched her arms behind her, hauling her hair off her neck. 'I'm off for a shower. See you for dinner at seven.'

Rafe let her go with a nod. The different faces of Captain Pentland. Women with abusive boyfriends had abusive fathers, low self-esteem and a propensity to repeat that cycle. Morgan must have fought hard to build her confidence. She obviously hadn't quite broken that cycle yet though. Maybe she wouldn't and maybe, he reminded himself, it wasn't his problem anyway.

Had she deliberately followed him today? The blast of anger when he found her sitting on the aircraft steps had rendered him almost speechless. Towering over her, he'd had to use all his control to rein that anger in. The temptation to shake the truth out of her had lasted several seconds longer than it should have. His purpose and training had eventually exerted themselves and he'd taken the other route.

73

The misinformation he'd fed her contained enough valuable details to keep it plausible. They'd find out pretty fast if the leaks were coming from her.

A complex woman, she had plenty of reason to tell lies. And if fitness was a prerequisite for terrorist activity then she had all the attributes.

9

Three days later they'd flown daily sorties out over the Gulf at twenty-five thousand feet. No more shark boats. They'd chatted with HMAS *Atherton* out on patrol, shared a laugh with the Customs vessels as they checked the fishing fleet and recorded the prawn trawlers pulling in their catches.

Did that mean the shipment had already landed on Cape York? Morgan wondered. Did that fit with Rafe's explanation of a large quantity of drugs? Something didn't quite gel, but she couldn't discuss it with her crew and, even with the new-found spirit of cooperation between her and Rafe, she didn't think she should ask him. She would, she reasoned, find out eventually.

Morgan gazed down at the cerulean blue of the Gulf of Carpentaria, the last of the coral spawn dissipating. The coral reefs were deeper here, invisible to satellites and aerial photography. A government mapping program had discovered them accidentally. Too deep for recreational divers and in areas too remote for most tourists, scientists speculated they would provide refuge for coral species threatened by warming sea temperatures. On the surface the waters of the Gulf stretched unbroken ahead of her all the way to the western edge of Cape York.

The best view in the world out your office window, she thought with a smug smile. It was almost the end of day five and the team was indeed a team.

Morgan glanced across at her colleague. She'd miss flying with her, but Lauren was due to be upgraded to a captain in the next couple of months. She'd do a fantastic job, provided she kept her hands to herself. Morgan hid a quick grin. Not that she seemed to be making any headway with Rafe, which didn't mean she'd tried everything in her repertoire yet. But so far their mission commander remained resolutely self-contained and unmoved by Lauren's charms. And, thought Morgan, I have to admit I kind of admire him for that. And for his remote, but somehow sexy authority.

Some people were born giving orders. Now that she was used to his delivery she appreciated his honesty. It was a whole lot easier working with him this time. Might even be able to describe it as fun. She smiled at the thought. Who would have believed she'd come to like the forbidding soldier?

'There's that grin again. It tells me you're having seriously sexy thoughts. Spill.' Lauren tapped her on the arm, peering over her lowered sunglasses.

'I've no idea what you're talking about, Lauren.' In vain, Morgan tried to rearrange her face.

'Yeah, right. You can share with me, I won't tell anyone. Really.'

'No point batting those big blue eyes at me, I'm immune, remember?'

'So, spill. It's me, your bestest-ever friend and ally,' Lauren persevered, digging Morgan in her ribs where it tickled.

'I was just thinking what a great captain you're going to

BORDER WATCH

make, if you can just keep your hands off the boys.' Morgan couldn't resist needling her.

'What?' Lauren was outraged. A frown marred her beautiful face before she laughed at herself. 'Okay, okay. If my command depends on it, I guess I can leave them alone. Does that mean the men are out of bounds as well?'

'You're incorrigible.'

'And irresistible.' She leant over to Morgan, pushing the microphone from her headset clear of her mouth. 'D-day tonight. All or nothing with Rafe. See if he can really turn me out of his bed.'

Morgan looked sideways at her young friend. 'Don't want to sound like your mother, but are you sure that's a good idea? He doesn't seem the nasty type but . . .'

'There is nothing, not one little thing, I'd call nasty about Rafe. Great face, body to die for, wit, charm and power.' She deepened her voice on the last word. 'No other aphrodisiac is as potent as power. Gets me going every time.'

'You do realise he must be fifteen years older than you? At least?' Morgan refused to examine why the idea of Lauren in Rafe's bed was disturbing her so much.

'Fine wine, just gettin' better in the bottle as every year goes by.' Lauren winked at her and, for a moment, Morgan thought she detected an ulterior motive behind her first officer's words.

'Just don't get too technical with the details tomorrow morning. It might upset my breakfast.'

'Time's up, ladies. Back to Weipa and a cold beer all round.' Rafe's voice came through their headphones making both women jump with guilt.

'Sure thing.' Morgan hit the heading select on the autopilot and turned the aircraft towards Weipa, gentle hands adjusting the power levers as she nosed the aircraft over into a descent. 'Any wins today?'

'No.' Rafe sounded disappointed. 'Not happy that we're heading back to Cairns either.'

'Sorry about that, but we don't write the flight and duty regulations.' Morgan referred to the regulated hours restricting a pilot's flying time. Fatigue on the job was closely monitored. The team needed two days off and a grudging Rafe was headed to Cairns with them. Another crew and aircraft would take their place.

'I know, but it sucks.'

'Any idea what our target really is this time?' Gavin looked up from his screen.

'I'd have to kill you, remember, Gav,' Rafe replied affably.

'I forgot, sorry.' Gavin was unrepentant.

'Can't blame us for trying,' Lauren cut in.

'No, and I'd like you less if you stopped.'

'See, I knew he liked us. Just take that next step, Rafe baby. You could find yourself in love with us,' Lauren purred into her microphone.

Morgan laughed as Rafe shook his head, refusal in the stubborn set of his jaw.

'Too old for love,' he growled back at her.

Rafe took his headset off, ending the conversation, and strapped himself into his seat, making sure any hint of his thoughts remained hidden.

Looking out the window unseeing, he didn't appreciate the rich, red landscape beneath the aircraft's flight path.

Flirty Miss Lauren was beautiful and far too young. He'd made the mistake of loving once and that was one too many times. A man could live without the soft comfort of love if his work challenged him.

He was sure of it.

10

Lauren pushed her glass away, leaving a wet trail of condensation on the table, and stood up.

'Sorry, guys, I'm off for an early night tonight. Catch you in the morning.' She blew them a kiss as she went and Morgan did her level best not to grin into her wineglass.

'She okay?' Gavin frowned with concern.

'Seemed fine today. Probably just tired, it's been a busy week really,' Morgan answered, evading his eyes. He grunted and turned to Rafe.

'So what have you got planned for your time off in Cairns, Rafe?'

'Wish I could say I had days off, but there are things to do with this,' he nodded off in the direction of their search area to the north, 'that still need finalising. How about you guys?'

'Depends. Golf, fishing, take the boat out to the Reef. Depends on who else is around. Most of my mates are in aviation as well. If we get lucky, Morgan asks us round for dinner and man, for that, I'd walk ten miles in bare feet over hot rocks.'

'Really?' Rafe turned intrigued eyes on Morgan. 'You cook as well?'

79

Embarrassed, she waved Gavin's compliment away with an airy hand. 'Been known to dish up a decent meal once in a while.'

Gavin snorted. 'If she ever gave up flying she could be a five-star chef.'

'Yeah?' Rafe was laughing at her, but she knew Gavin was right. If she had to choose another career, then haute cuisine would be her calling.

'How about it, Morgan? We can't leave him loose in Cairns for three nights. I'll catch the mud crabs, you do that chilli sauce thing and I'll pressure Lauren into buying a couple of bottles of good wine.'

'It's fine, Gavin. Thanks for the invite, but I really do have to work.' But there was something in his voice, a slight hesitation, which told Morgan he'd like to join them, despite his words.

'Gav's right. It's our town and you're a visitor to North Queensland. Have to eat somewhere, might as well be at my house. Work it out tomorrow which one of you gives him a lift, Gav. Day after tomorrow. Okay?'

'If you're sure it's not too much trouble?' Rafe's dark eyes watching her were making her jittery.

'Cooking for these two is always trouble. What's one more? Of course, the chef never washes up.' She tilted her head at Gavin, who groaned.

'And while she can definitely cook, she needs to use every pan in the house to do it. Took me half an hour last time. I reckoned she'd saved the dishes from the whole week for me.'

Morgan patted his shoulder. 'There'll be three of you this time. Be a walk in the park. Done, then.' She got to her feet then stopped with a frown. 'And Gav, do you think you could have a look at my laptop for me? It's doing something weird

BORDER WATCH

when I send emails. And running a whole lot slower than usual. I hope it's not about to crash.'

'Sure.' Gavin nodded. 'I'll bring my tools and check it out at dinner.'

'Okay, thanks. Well, I'm off to bed too. See you guys in the morning.'

She could feel Rafe watching her as she made her way out of the restaurant. Sometime in the last week, they'd reached a compromise. The antagonism that had bubbled up between them at their first meeting, then burst into flames during the confrontation in the aircraft at Weipa, had mellowed into respect for the other's professionalism. And a little misplaced desire on her part, but nothing she couldn't ignore, she reminded herself.

And he was a pleasant dinner companion. Who would have thought it?

She grinned. Plus any man who could put up with Lauren's taunting without missing a beat had to be all right. Wonder where Lauren is now? she thought, as she passed the younger woman's door.

Rafe turned back to Gavin and waited for him to speak first.

'That okay with you?' Gavin asked.

'If I'm not intruding.' Rafe kept his expression neutral at the turn of the conversation. This could be an opportunity to fill in some more blanks in Miss Morgan's file.

'No, mate. We don't want to leave her alone too long. Not going to be easy for her to walk back into her house after finding that dickhead at it with someone else in her bed.'

'Ah.' Rafe waited.

'And we know the cops want to talk to her some more about the body she found. They've phoned a couple of times

81

since we've been up here. Some photos they want her to look at. Shit . . .' He sipped his beer with a shake of his head. 'She doesn't deserve this. She had some family trouble a couple of months back. And she really needed a break.'

'Family trouble?'

'Yeah, her brother, the guy who abandoned her when she was twelve, is back looking for money for his drug habit.'

'Abandoned her?' Rafe kept his voice light though the hairs on his neck went straight up. The brother?

'When her dad murdered her mother during a drunken argument, her brother let the authorities put her in foster care. He was about seventeen, eighteen years old, maybe. Then her dad hung himself in jail, fit of remorse or something.' Gavin half shrugged. With one too many beers to the wind he clearly had no idea how much he was revealing. 'The brother still didn't come and get her. Shit, they were orphans then. You'd think . . .'

It shouldn't be possible to wrap a tragedy up in so few bland sentences, Rafe thought, absorbing the horror of Gavin's words. What a battle Morgan must have fought to gain the composure and strength she wore round her like armour plating. Reading the hard facts in a government file hadn't given it quite this perspective.

'I had no idea.'

'Didn't you run her file? Every other bloody mission commander does.'

'I figured she'd tell me anything she wanted me to know.'

Gavin looked pained. 'I guess there's no point in asking you to forget it either, is there?' He peered into his glass. 'I should never drink more than three beers.'

'Lauren told me about the body and finding the boyfriend in the sack with another woman.'

BORDER WATCH

'Yeah.' Gavin's sigh came from the very bottom of his lungs. 'Morgan spends so much time looking out for us, I guess we figure we owe her.'

Rafe held his silence, watching the agitation on Gavin's face.

'She still finds time to go out with the soup kitchen for homeless kids on her days off.' Gavin gulped down another mouthful of beer. 'Any Christmas she's not working, she cooks up a storm for the Salvos.' His grin was lopsided. 'But don't ever try to say what she's doing is great, she'll bite your head off.'

Rafe nodded, examining his beer. 'She doesn't take compliments easily?'

'Huh,' Gavin snorted. 'Only if they're for her team, then it's okay.'

'So how did her brother track her down?' There'd been no reference in the report to any contact with her sibling. Was that something important they'd missed?

'They did a profile on her and Lauren in a women's magazine a year or so ago. Her brother was sitting in a rehab clinic flicking through old mags and saw it. Easy from there, even for a druggie.'

'She said she went to the AIS?' Rafe felt a twinge of guilt for pumping the inebriated Gavin, but dismissed it.

'She won a scholarship. Someone talent-spotted her at a school meet.' Gavin settled back in his chair.

'Yeah, she burnt me off coming back from the airport the other afternoon,' Rafe remarked.

'Photo finish, she told us.'

Ah, thought Rafe, so she does discuss me with her crew.

'Technically she won, but she was very gallant in victory. I think she took pity on me.'

'She's like that. She got tripped in a trial for the Olympic squad, not that she tells it that way. Tore her right knee ligament so badly they had to operate. She took that in her stride and signed up for a uni degree in aviation.'

'A high achiever,' Rafe observed, thinking that all the facts Gavin was supplying tallied with the official version. Apart from the brother.

'I reckon it was her way of erasing her past. Lauren reckons she's just a natural-born leader who can't help herself.'

Rafe nodded, understanding so much better the haughty composure that kept Morgan's spine straight and her grey eyes level. 'You're probably both right. Escaping the past is easier if you're born with the right instincts.'

'And you'd understand that.' Gavin's face went red before he'd even finished talking. 'Sorry, that was out of line.'

Rafe smiled without rancour. 'No, I know that in a small company like this, people gossip.'

'Still, sorry.' Gavin regarded his empty beer glass. 'Must have been hard to leave the SAS.'

'Especially after the rest of my team was killed.' Rafe finished the other man's train of thought. 'Yeah, it was, but I needed to get out for my sanity or every mission after that would have been personal. There's no room for personal when you're killing people.'

Gavin's gaze sharpened as he met Rafe's. 'You've actually killed people?' He sounded incredulous and Rafe bit back his bark of harsh laughter. People were so naive.

'I sure as hell wasn't playing tiddlywinks for fifteen years. It came with the territory. Kill or be killed, as they say. Morgan seen a dead body before?'

'Dunno, don't think so. That's why Lauren and I reckon she needs company for the next couple of days.'

84

'She'll see that body for years to come, at totally inappropriate times. Little snatches, fragments of the picture. She'll need you. Lucky girl to have good friends.' Abruptly he got to his feet. 'See you in the morning.'

He pushed through the glass doors, feeling an unfamiliar tightening in his chest. It had been a long time since he'd felt the need for companionship. Sure there'd been girls and sex. That came with the territory as an elite soldier. Had to let off steam somehow, and healthy uncomplicated sex was perfect for celebrating surviving another vicious encounter in an inhospitable far-flung corner of the world.

Rafe rubbed his hand over his jaw, feeling the scrape of day-old growth under his fingers. Morgan Pentland had got under his skin. Must be getting soft, mate, he chided himself. She's still a suspect and too many questions are still unanswered.

His hand froze halfway to his door handle and he frowned. He was sure he'd left a light on when he'd gone out for dinner. What the hell was going on?

Quietly he opened the door, his senses on full alert.

The smell of perfume was foreign in his room, but it was a very familiar scent. Instead of reaching for the light switch, he closed the door and let his eyes adjust to the dark.

His bed was definitely in use and the pale hair spread over the pillow betrayed the identity of the intruder.

'Nice try, Lauren.'

'Damn.' The bedside lamp clicked on. 'How did you know it was me?' Her eyes were deep blue in the soft light, her blond hair a golden skein across the pillow.

'You wear the same perfume every day. Even a guy like me can work that out.' He shook his head in disbelief. 'How'd you get in here?'

She grinned with pure mischief. 'Mary can be bought if you know the right price.'

'Really?' He eyed the neatly folded clothes on the chair with relief. At least she still seemed to be wearing underwear. 'Put your clothes on and head off to bed.'

Lauren's mouth curved in a sexy smile, her lips inviting and moist. 'Are you gay or something?'

'Just particular about who shares my bed.'

'Really?' Lauren sat up, the bedspread dropping to her waist, revealing her pale pink lacy bra, clinging to what Rafe acknowledged to himself were particularly impressive breasts.

'Yes, really. I've got a kid sister around your age and she'd never forgive me if I brought someone the same age home. So out. Put your wares away and do us both a favour.'

'I'm not talking marriage here,' she sulked at him, sliding her legs over the side of the bed.

'Neither am I, so scat. I prefer my relationships long term.' He folded his arms across his chest.

She wrinkled her nose at him in disbelief. 'Yeah, right.'

'No, really.' He reached out and gingerly picked up the pile of clothes before dropping them in her lap, losing the battle to keep his eyes on her face as she turned away.

The rest of her was pretty spectacular too, he admitted as she pulled her jeans over her hips. A man with fewer scruples would be tempted.

'I think you're being unreasonable. We could be good together.' She smiled from under thick lashes, turning around as she buttoned her shirt.

'And I think you're just bored. A serious attempt to seduce me would have involved being naked in my bed. You were just amusing yourself.'

Lauren stopped with her shirt half buttoned. 'Is that a challenge? Lord knows, I could do with one.'

'No, Lauren, it's some brotherly advice. Don't try this trick on anyone else or you might get more than you offer.'

BORDER WATCH

She snorted, the grin splitting her face. 'You think I don't know that? Honourable guys like you are suckers for a pair of big blue eyes.' She stopped at the door. 'If it had been Morgan in your bed, would you have been so chivalrous?'

'Out, Lauren.' He was still amused by her, but she'd just hit a nerve he didn't want to examine.

'Well, would you?'

'Morgan would not pull a stunt like this. It's not her style.' His eyebrows drew together.

'I think you're sweet on our boss and I think you'd be good for her.'

'Lauren . . .' He kept his voice mild, but his body had tensed.

'And the way you just changed your body angle tells me I'm right. Night, Latin lover.' She blew him a kiss from her fingertips and the door closed behind her.

'Bloody hell,' Rafe exhaled into the empty room. 'Didn't see that one coming. Gavin really needs to make a stand. Or is there something else going on?' He crossed to the table and checked his files and laptop. Nothing seemed to have been disturbed, but he booted up the computer and checked its history. He'd look a right fool if the operation was compromised by his negligence.

No attempt to enter his password showed up. A quick scan down the files showed nothing had been touched since he left the room. Morgan's file hadn't been opened and neither had Operation Spearthrower.

He switched on the TV, then straightened his bed. Even with his iron control, those sheets smelling of pure woman were going to be a bit disconcerting tonight.

'Silly little brat,' he muttered. 'Would it have been different if it had been Morgan?' he mimicked Lauren's words. 'Lucky for both of us it wasn't.' Having a suspect break into his room would prove very embarrassing. He slouched down into the cane armchair and refused to contemplate that scenario.

Half an hour later, he was fast asleep in the chair with the remote control resting on his stomach, late-night TV lulling him with white noise.

11

Clouds of mosquitoes swarmed towards any exposed flesh, the whine of their wings disturbing his light sleep. Woomera pushed his swag down around his hips and eased himself out from underneath the heavy canvas. The filmy mosquito net wafted with his movement. Tied above him to the lower branches of a melaleuca, pale in the weak moonlight, it kept the army of tiny insects at bay.

The soft bark on the tree trunks glowed luminescent. It didn't take a large leap of imagination to understand why the local Aborigines thought the trees were their forebears' spirits keeping watch over their people. Paperbark guardians.

The silvery white sheen of the tree trunks curved to his right, showing the way to the sweep of old riverbank. When the monsoon trough dropped its load of precious water, the bed of soft sand he lay on would become a raging, roaring torrent of life. It would sweep through the ancient riverbed, spilling out over these banks, swirling across miles and miles of parched forests.

For now it was a convenient place for him to sleep, but sleep was evading him. He checked the gun nestled in the swag beside him and cocked his head to listen.

Nothing. Only the buzz of the mosquitoes and the flap of dark wings high overhead. Silhouetted against the waning moon he could see the flight of black flying foxes heading for a night's feasting on the berries and fruits in the forest behind him. From the screeching and babbling he'd heard earlier the colony must hold thousands of the furry airborne mammals.

Their daytime roost lay near to his main camp – further upstream away from the risk of flash flooding. He'd chosen to spend the night closer to the landing point in case Nadal's prau made it in tonight. Calculated risks were his business, but this was a high-risk operation even for him.

He'd need to be back in town before the offensive was launched, but he didn't trust the leaders of this cell not to go off half-cocked. His nerves were stretched tight, chaffing against the edges of his mind. Must be getting too long in the tooth for this, mate, he remonstrated with himself. Time to take the money and run. It's been a good life. Time for some new horizons. Fourteen days and you get to stop pretending.

Playing both ends against the middle was a young man's game and he hadn't been young for a few years now. Maybe it was time to find a woman and settle down, have a family. A twinge of unwelcome regret wormed its way through his defences. After the life he'd had that would be as likely a scenario as winning the lottery. Both would bring more changes than a man needed. No point in even contemplating it, mate, he reminded himself. You've got nothing to offer a family.

The faint slap of oars on water reached him. He strained to hear, his eyes scanning the channel where the water lapped in a dark shimmer. No local would be up this far without a decent outboard going full bore. The crocodiles were too damn big.

A light flashed several times, the sequence correct. He pushed the netting aside, feeling the immediate rush of insects around his face. The beam of light he directed back at the vessel steadied the rhythm of paddling and the sound headed towards him. Silently, he crossed over the dry riverbed and made his way to the landing stage on the next branch of river. He could smell the prau as well as see it now. That peculiar odour of rotting fish, cooking fires and the great unwashed bit the back of his throat. Bloody glad I didn't have to sail down on that little heap of shit, he thought with a wolfish smile. Wonder how Nadal's feeling?

The vessel grounded on the mud banking still short of dry land by a couple of metres. Sharp angry words were hissed into the night air. Woomera stifled the urge to laugh. Nadal's Indonesian now ran to a few swear words, but berating the fishermen wasn't going to encourage them to solve this problem. Arab bastard would just have to get his feet dirty if he couldn't walk the plank.

Woomera's call was pitched low, just enough to carry. He used the same language, directing the fishermen to the wood he shoved out across the mangrove. With a bit of care it would work. Wet boots weren't a good look in this neck of the woods. Parasites made short work of the soles of feet. Some of them stayed for life.

The scrawny fisherman who made the crossing first carried a heavy pack. Probably weighed more than the little guy himself, thought Woomera. Trust Nadal to bring the kitchen sink with him as well as the hardware.

Nadal made the crossing without incident, but Woomera didn't miss the sweat on the man's palms as they grasped hands.

'Welcome to Australia, mate.' He didn't keep the amusement from his voice.

'The arse-end of the world, you people say, I believe.' The cultured tones were incongruous in such a primitive, steamy setting. There should have been a white-coated waiter with a long cool drink balanced on a tray, Woomera thought, with a quick smile. Instead there were miles of mud, a million mosquitoes, no ice and the nearest bar was fifty kilometres away in a straight line through endless stands of mangroves with crocs lurking in wait. And what would a good Muslim be doing in a bar anyway?

'Don't know that we Aussies appreciate anyone but us calling it that, but yeah, it's pretty fucking black up here.' He deliberately coarsened his language and tone. The olive-skinned man opposite him never quite knew how to take him and Woomera planned on keeping it that way. 'The troops are a couple of hundred metres away. Stick close behind me.'

He turned back to the fisherman and spoke a few quiet words. The dark head nodded in reply and within a minute the faint splash of oars faded into the night.

'This way.' He made no move to pick up the backpack and he turned away before Nadal had hefted it onto his shoulders. He was not the man's fucking pack animal. Killing was his specialty and Nadal was in his territory now.

12

Rafe slid into the passenger seat of the VW Beetle, folding his long legs to fit them under the small dash. 'An original Beetle? This must be worth a mint.'

Gavin smiled, pride oozing from him. 'The mechanic who fixes her offers me a thousand bucks more every time I bring her in. Can get minimum fifty thousand for it on the Japanese market, but she's not for sale. I bought her from my aunty so she's only ever had two owners.'

'Two loving owners,' Rafe observed, running a lean hand over the tiny dash.

'Obsessive, you mean. Hi, Rafe, lovely to see you too.' Lauren was jammed in the back seat, her slim legs tucked up to fit into the cramped space.

'Hi, Lauren.' He ducked his head to grin at her in the reflection of the side mirror.

She poked her tongue out at him. 'I always get the front seat, but apparently you're more important.'

'Is she always this cheerful on leave?' Rafe asked Gavin, wincing at the solid knee that jammed into the back of his seat.

'I made her shell out for a couple of good bottles of wine. Lauren only believes in spending money on clothes.'

Rafe rattled the backpack on his lap. 'I brought a couple of good ones too. We can save the brat's bottles for her to take home.'

'Brat?' The outraged squeal was deafening and she tugged at his seatbelt.

'Only a brat would be trying to force my kidneys out through my stomach.'

'Know the old saying "Hell hath no fury like a woman scorned"?' She thrust her head between the seats, the scent of familiar perfume wafting from her silky hair.

'Not scorned so much as politely refused, Lauren,' Rafe retorted.

Gavin swung stricken eyes on her. 'Tell me you didn't put the hard word on him?'

She sat back, examining her polished nails.

'Did she?' He'd stopped watching the road and Rafe nodded ahead at the slowing line of cars.

'Traffic's stopping.'

Gavin returned his focus to the road, his face bright red, and Rafe felt sorry for him. 'She was playing silly games, so no, she didn't.' He laughed. 'Maybe you could teach her to play chess.' He caught Lauren's eye in the mirror again and squinted at her threateningly. Gavin was a good man. It was painful to watch her toying with him. He didn't doubt that the young woman felt more for Gavin than she'd admit to anyone.

He decided to change the topic. 'So you had a good day off today?'

'Caught the muddies that are in the esky in the front, that was about it. Lauren went and checked on Morgan.'

'Yeah, I got to spend the captain's money.'

Gavin groaned. 'How many clothes can you two wear?'

BORDER WATCH

'Way better than clothes shopping. We went bed shopping.'
'What for?'

'Because somebody else had been screwing in it,' Rafe interjected, before Lauren could reply.

She beamed at him. 'Got it in one, I knew you were smarter than you looked. God, if I'd found my boyfriend screwing around in my bed, I'd probably have burnt it. You know,' she leant forwards again, her sulk forgotten, 'that lovely old bloke next door, Reg and whatever his wife's name is, cleaned the house and washed all her bedding for her as well as changing the locks. He's a retired ambo and was telling me all about Vietnam. I think he's worried Morgan will get some sort of delayed reaction to the body on the beach and dickhead Carl.'

Rafe nodded. 'Yep, he's right. Maybe it's still not really hit home yet. Maybe she's still holding it inside. You know her better than I do. Has it affected her behaviour?'

'She's quieter than usual. Normally she gives Lauren a run for her money. Been a bit distracted this week.'

'Doesn't show up in her work.' Lauren, as always, defended Morgan against any criticism. 'The cops were round yesterday as well. She'd hardly got home before they were knocking her door down.'

'And?' Gavin changed down a gear as they approached the turning to Trinity Beach.

'No trace of the dead guy on the missing-persons list and no one's been reported off any boats. They were interested in who else was on the beach. Asked if she'd seen anything that might suggest he'd been shot on the beach, then dragged down to the water, rather than drifted in on the current. Harry came out with some other copper.'

'Harry's sweet on Morgan,' Gavin added. 'I know he would have hauled Carl's arse off to the watch house in an instant if she'd let him.'

'Who's Harry?' Rafe figured he might as well ask. Neither one seemed too concerned about keeping secrets.

'SOCO. Head of the Scenes of Crime team. He's old enough to be her father and knows it, but you can see it in his face when he talks to her. And he's not the only one,' Lauren added. 'Carl was just more persistent and wore her down.'

'Persistent?'

Gavin looked sideways at him. 'You're good, you're really good. You ask innocuous one-word questions and we spill our guts.' He looked embarrassed.

'Techniques I've honed for the last thirty-nine years.'

'Are you that old?' Lauren asked, her innocent blue eyes wide.

He caught her eyes again in the mirror and smiled, not deigning to answer her. 'So how was Carl persistent?'

'Just kept turning up at her house. Being the sweet, silent type. I think he'd run her name through the computers and found out all about her. Someone else in SERT told me he has a pattern of picking up successful, good-looking chicks and demeaning them before he ditches them. Glad she got in first.'

'I don't think she's too upset about kicking him out, but she is still pissed that he was screwing around in her house. Here we are, Chateau Pentland.' Lauren gestured grandly out the window.

The house was a typical 1960s wooden beach house, with a small veranda. Its entry had been widened to accommodate French doors that stood open and inviting. Soft, pale curtains stirred in the faint breeze.

It was on the western side of the street and developers had bought up the land opposite, building wedding-cake tiers of apartments. What would once have been a sweeping view of

BORDER WATCH

the Coral Sea was now blocked by banks of air-conditioners and the car park.

Rafe scanned to the north. Hell of a view there still. The lengthening shadows as the sun slipped behind Saddle Mountain sharpened the contrast between sea and land.

Two islands. For a fanciful moment the large one looked like a sleeping man on his back, the small one a discarded hat set beside him. They seemed to float in the shimmering water. A couple of trawlers bobbed on their moorings in the lee of the larger island.

Further out, where the sky met the sea in an almost seamless harmony of blue, several white-sailed yachts drifted before the breeze. An indolent summer evening in paradise.

Rafe unfolded himself from the car and enjoyed the cool wash of sea air over his sticky shirt. The smell of roasting garlic made his nostrils twitch.

'That smells great.'

Lauren pushed past him. 'So don't just stand here admiring the view, there's eating to be done, and bring that wine with you. I'm not driving home.'

With a last glance at the view, he followed the other two up the wooden stairs. As his foot hit the top step, uncharacteristic nerves twanged and he hesitated. Why had he come this evening? He'd rationalised it as work. Morgan was still under surveillance. Just a shame he hadn't told his boss about this little side trip. If she was the link to the terrorist cell, he was playing with fire. Being turned to ash if this all went up in flames didn't appeal to him. And yet, here he was.

Morgan appeared from the back of the house and his thoughts stalled. Her loose dress floated round her, accentuating rather than hiding her curves. Tendrils of dark hair, escaping from a silver clasp, drifted around her face.

Gavin whistled. 'Very nice.'

'See, I told you it looked great.' Lauren kissed her lightly on the cheek. 'She reckoned it was too young and tizzy for her. What would she know? It's perfect.'

'You also thought the red hotpants looked sensational,' Morgan retorted, leaning over to peck Gavin's cheek before extending her hand to Rafe. 'Welcome to my place. Hope you like seafood.'

He felt the warmth in her hand and a faint tremor that tugged at him. His breath hitched in his throat as he met her smoky eyes. This feminine, gentler version of Morgan was so much more compelling, so much more unsettling, so much more everything than the tough professional he worked with.

'Thanks for inviting me. Nice house.' He swivelled his gaze away and looked around, taking in the bright artworks. Skilfully arranged, they gave a feeling of peace, of home, of serenity.

'She did the decorating herself, too,' Lauren chimed in, flashing a grin at Morgan, who started to protest. 'Well, you won't tell anyone anything, so someone has to shine a spotlight on you.'

'Thanks, Lauren. What would I do without you, I wonder?' Morgan led the way back to the kitchen where several pans simmered on the wide rangetop.

She reached up into a cupboard for glasses and for an instant Rafe had a perfect view of her body silhouetted by the down lights. His body reacted with an unwanted rush of blood and he quickly shifted his gaze, trying unsuccessfully to stem the unwarranted blast of anger. Raving bloody idiot, he rebuked himself. Playing this sort of game will end your career and god knows what else. Concentrate.

Morgan held the glasses out to Lauren. 'You pour. Whichever. I've got some sparkling white if anyone wants a change.'

'How about a sparkling red?' Rafe held up a bottle, focusing on Lauren. 'Might be okay with the chilli crabs.'

'We celebrating something?' Lauren frowned as she reached across and took the wine from him, reading the labels. 'A De Bortoli — and,' she squealed, turning the second bottle to face the other two, 'he's brought a Penfolds as well. How good is that?'

'Open it and find out.' Gavin rolled his eyes at her. 'How'd it go with the cops yesterday, Morgan?'

Her grey eyes flashed a quick glance at Rafe before she answered. Did that look indicate she was lying? he wondered.

'Not sure, really. Harry was great, but the other guy was an out-of-towner with a chip on both shoulders for some balance. I'm almost convinced I shot the guy myself and threw him into the water. I reckon if he'd been able, he would've inter-rogated Sam as well.'

'Why are they so interested in him? Was he a drug runner or something?' Lauren handed out the glasses of wine. 'Cheers, everyone.' She touched glasses with Morgan, who still frowned.

'Don't know. I'd mentioned a tattoo on the guy's back that looked familiar when I first stumbled across him.' She hesitated for a moment. 'They showed me a dozen photos of similar tattoos — circles with a strange-looking cross in the middle. Wanted to know if I'd seen any of them before.' She shook her head uncertainly. 'I couldn't place them, but I'm sure I have seen something similar, I just can't remember where. Harry wasn't giving anything away, but they can't find Thommo, the old guy camping out up the end of the beach.'

'Thommo? Do they think he's seen something?' Lauren asked. 'Didn't you say he's off with the pixies?'

'Well, I wouldn't call him a reliable witness,' Morgan replied. 'He's always got some new story to tell me. I'd hate the cops to take him in for questioning. He'd probably end up in a psych ward and that would kill him.'

'So where is he?'

Morgan sipped her wine. 'Hmm, good, thank you.' She raised her glass to Rafe before answering. 'I haven't seen him since I got back and Reg reckons he's not been around for at least a week.' She pushed a bowl of crisped chickpeas across the counter top. 'It's not him, but they are wondering if there's a connection. My guy's apparently of Middle Eastern descent.'

'So why would they be connected?' Lauren propped herself up on one of the stainless-steel stools.

'They didn't say, but they did ask some strange questions.' Morgan turned back to the fridge and pulled out a plate of tapas. 'I told them I was out again day after tomorrow. All the other guy said was, "Leave a contact number."'

'Maybe Thommo was injured during some sort of struggle and that's how the guy ended up in the water?'

'Maybe. I still think there's a connection here I'm missing. Something literally staring me in the face,' Morgan said. 'I just need to piece it all together myself.'

Lauren swung around to Rafe. 'You're into all this cloak-and-dagger espionage stuff, what's your take on it?'

Rafe shrugged. 'Middle Eastern appearance could mean anything or nothing. Didn't a boatload of Indonesians lob up on one of the beaches near here a few years ago?' He wasn't going to be drawn into this debate if he could possibly avoid it. He'd made adroit deflection one of his specialties.

'Yep and that's when they increased the number of surveillance aircraft operating around the coast. They'd sailed all the way down Cape York and beached it at Holloways. First anybody knew about it was when one of them phoned a taxi.'

BORDER WATCH

Gavin couldn't help laughing. 'Must have been some bloody red faces over that one.'

'Yeah, almost as good as the ones who tried to catch a commercial flight out of Weipa or the boys they found floating in that commercial esky north of Horn Island. Anyway,' Lauren slid off her stool, 'enough shop talk, come and see Morgan's new bed.' She tugged at Rafe's hand. 'See whether you approve?'

'Lauren,' Morgan turned from the stove, a threatening wooden spoon in her hand. 'Stay out of it.'

'What? *What?*' Lauren shook her hair. 'What's the point in having such a beautiful bed if no one sees it? Gavin, you come too.'

Rafe was amused by the sudden flush in Morgan's cheeks and the spark of anger that darted from her eyes.

'Lauren, it's my bedroom.' Her tone was exasperated.

'I know, so hopefully you've put those lacy knickers away or you'll be giving these boys bad thoughts.' She headed off up the corridor with Gavin in tow. 'Rafe,' she called back at him, imperious command in her voice.

'Need some help in the kitchen?'

Lauren flounced off, leaving him with an irritated Morgan.

'Thanks, it's all under control.'

She flushed again under his steady gaze and he searched for something to say. Being tongue-tied was not normally one of his problems. 'Lived here long?'

'Five years now. I got a bargain. My little slice of paradise.'

'You've worked for Border Watch for that long?'

She smiled at him and he sensed the tension starting to drain from her. 'I have. I came here for the job and here is where I'm planning to stay.' She gestured around the large airy room. 'Probably not very grand to you, but it's my place and that makes it special.' The pride of ownership was in her

101

voice and Rafe recognised the determination that had got her this far.

'Makes my one-room apartment in the middle of Brisbane look like a shoebox.' He glanced around again, realising there were no photos, no pictures of family and friends, no images of Morgan with a boyfriend, no past. Had she swept it out of her life or was there another reason?

'Must be lovely when it rains on the tin roof.' He smiled at the surprised look she shot at him. 'One of those evocative sounds from growing up in Queensland. Wooden houses and iron roofs that creak in the heat or the cold and positively roar in a thunderstorm. My little sister used to be terrified of storms. Hid under the beds, in cupboards, anywhere Mum'd let her. Me? I've always loved the soothing sound of night-time rain on corrugated iron.'

Morgan returned his smile. 'Storms electrify me. I love the energy, the fury, the life that pours out of them. Your sister must have had a fright during a storm.'

It was his turn to be surprised by her insight. 'Yeah, she did. We had a guy break into the house in the middle of one. He didn't take anything, never got a chance. We chased him out with a piece of four-by-two.' He chuckled at the memory.

'We?'

He cleared his throat, embarrassed he'd started this conversation. 'More me, I guess.'

'How old were you?'

'Fourteen, I think?' He downed a quick swallow of wine, wishing Morgan's calm gaze would shift somewhere else. 'Grace was only a toddler. When he went past her room she saw him and started screaming. First thing I knew was this big guy rushing at me.' He put his glass down and reached for a delicate wafer topped with a prawn. 'My dad had always said attack was the best defence, so I jumped on him and hung on. He took off and as we went out the front door I grabbed a piece of wood that we used to throw for the dog and started into him.'

He looked up and was surprised by the sheen of tears in Morgan's grey eyes. 'I didn't hurt him, I was only a lanky kid,' he apologised, wondering whether the talk of family or violence had upset her.

'I bet Grace still thinks you're her hero. She must have hated you joining the SAS.' Morgan pushed plates and napkins across the bench top towards him. 'Does she worry about you?'

Rafe smiled at the thought of his very competent sister ever not worrying about him. 'She's a sergeant in the police now and I have to put up with her endless interfering.'

'And you wouldn't have it any other way.'

'What about your family?' He raised his glass to his lips as he asked the question, trying to be offhand. 'They live here?'

'No family, it's just me.'

Lauren and Gavin reappeared as she spoke, preventing any more questions.

'Jeez, Morgan, is it big enough?' Gavin reached past Rafe for a prawn wafer. 'You'd spend half the night finding your way round it.'

'He doesn't believe me that it's only a queen size,' Lauren complained. 'Nothing wrong with a bed with plenty of room to move.'

'Room to move? Have a sleepover for a cast of thousands.'

'What a great idea.' Lauren's face lit up. 'We could try it out now.'

'Thankfully for me and my bed, the entrée is ready.' Morgan pulled trays of delicate scallops wrapped in prosciutto, and creamy pastry cups topped with smoked salmon from the oven. 'Lets eat out the back where it's cooler.'

She pushed the screen door open with her hip. The deck overlooked a sparkling pool surrounded by a tropical garden. Rafe held the screen open for the other two, admiring the simple colour that filled the garden, spotlights highlighting a couple of giant trees. Its serenity rolled over him, like a long cool drink in the heat of a hot day. He caught Morgan watching him. 'Meditation heaven.'

'My Zen room.' Her eyes were luminous in the soft glow of the candles and the dimmed spotlights.

For an instant, Rafe had the illusion it was just the two of them, standing in their own private world, where anything was possible. He saw the connection in her face and saw the instant she pulled the shutters down and turned away, saw her dark hair float in the light breeze, saw a delicate blush bloom on her slanted cheekbones.

He dismissed the inappropriate thoughts that skittered across his mind. His job was to find the truth, not get involved with the very woman he was investigating.

Deliberately he sat opposite Lauren, Gavin on his right. It shouldn't take much to keep the focus on the pretty blonde. She'd been born hogging the limelight. And she didn't let him down. Her bitingly funny story of the shopping trip for Morgan's bed took all of the entrée to tell. Rafe felt sorry for the salesman, who'd no doubt been duped out of his commission, befuddled by two good-looking women trying out row after row of mattresses.

Still laughing, Gavin finally cleared the plates. 'Poor bastard didn't stand a chance against two of you. I'll get your laptop, Morgan. Better fix it before I have any more wine.'

'Sure. It's on the desk in my bedroom.' She went to stand up, but he waved her away.

'I'll get it.'

BORDER WATCH

Gavin carried the laptop out and fiddled while the others talked, his fingers flashing over the keys.

'Hey, Morgan, you've got one hell of a spyware program on here. Who's been working on this for you?'

'Spyware?' Morgan stopped halfway through a sentence. 'What do you mean?'

'There's something here that's sending out a copy of all your mail, tracking any sites you've visited, probably transmitting all your keystrokes as well.'

'But how can that be? You set it up with the world's most determined firewall, you said so yourself. And I always keep my virus protection updated. How could that happen?'

'Dunno. I'll be able to remove it but hang on . . .' He frowned again. 'It might be hardware, not software. Give me a tick.'

'How would hardware get into my computer? That's crazy, Gavin.' Morgan slid her chair back and came around to stand behind his chair.

If she were acting, she deserved an Oscar for her performance, thought Rafe, as he watched her face for miscues. He saw only anger and worry dipping her eyebrows and tightening her jaw.

Gavin turned the computer over and with a few deft moves had the back open, his tiny screwdriver hovering over the components as he identified them. 'Processor, video card, memory. What's this?' He flicked a tiny processor board out onto the table and squinted at it, pushing his glasses up his nose. 'Don't recognise this little sucker.'

'May I?' Rafe used Gavin's small pliers to pick it up and held it up to the light. 'I don't recognise it either. No serial numbers,' he added, looking it over.

'Well . . .' Gavin turned the computer on again. 'It's running without it and I'd bet fifty the spyware will have disappeared.'

105

'So how did it get there?' Morgan asked again, leaning forwards to inspect the offending device. 'You're the only one who ever fixes it for me.'

'And I certainly wouldn't be bugging your computer. You should probably report it to the police, though I don't know what they'd do about it.'

'Who would bother to bug me?'

'Didn't you have to get a new battery early this year, when Gavin was on leave?' Lauren spoke for the first time and Rafe glanced over at her.

'That's right. I did. I left it at a repair shop in town to see if they could repack the cell. Ended up I needed a new battery anyway. I've still got the receipt. But why would they bug me?'

'You should definitely tell your boss. Maybe it's got something to do with your work.' Rafe kept his tone neutral. 'I could take the chip with me and get the Customs gurus to look at it.'

'My work.' Morgan looked stunned. 'I file all our flight plans from this.' She gestured at the computer. 'Get the weather, briefing, maps, everything through it. Oh my god.' There was no way she could be faking the sudden pallor or the faint tremor to her hands as she spread them across her stomach. At least Rafe now had an explanation for how the leaks were happening. Now all he needed was the why and who.

'Well it's not your fault that somebody hacked your laptop, is it?' Lauren replied. 'Let Rafe take it and see what it is. The boss would only have to do that anyway. Will there be paperwork and more interviews?' Her concern for Morgan was transparent and Rafe could only shrug.

'Don't know. Not really my department.' A lie, he knew, but necessary right now. 'I'll let you know what I find, but you should change passwords and check your bank accounts to be on the safe side.'

BORDER WATCH

'I'll fix those up for you, Morgan.' Gavin pointed back at the kitchen. 'You don't want to ruin six good muddies just because some nasty has had your private life under a microscope for the last eight months. You cook, I'll fix and Rafe can investigate.'

Morgan's hand clutched her stomach as she silently obeyed. Lauren followed her into the kitchen, putting a reassuring arm around her friend.

'Eight months?' Rafe queried, turning back to Gavin.

'Yeah, the program had data files dating back eight months. My money would be on whoever replaced the battery.'

'Yeah, right,' Rafe said. Morgan's computer had been the donor, now he needed to find the recipient machine. Maybe the repair shop was responsible. He'd need to investigate that angle before he could discount it. And maybe this was all an elaborate act to confuse him. Either way, he'd be working late tonight.

Close to midnight, back at his accommodation, Rafe switched on his laptop, mulling over the evening. The Customs tech he'd given the chip to would have an answer for him by morning. That left him to sort out the human dimension.

Morgan Pentland. An intriguing woman and he was no closer to a definitive answer. The chip would explain why none of the details he'd told her in the aircraft in Weipa had surfaced, yet the details of their movements had.

Did that mean Lauren or Gavin were the real leaks? Nothing in their background suggested even a remote connection with terrorists, undesirables or anything illegal. Nothing in their behaviour tonight seemed contrived.

What was he missing?

Tomorrow he'd follow up on Morgan's repair work.

107

He logged on to check his emails, drumming his fingers on the desk as they downloaded. The questions the federal police officer had asked Morgan were consistent with the surveillance operation Customs and the feds were running in tandem.

Rafe ran an impatient hand through his hair. He couldn't help feeling the feds' informant wasn't being entirely upfront. Were they being spun a load of crap? Only half interested, he focused back on the computer screen, scanning down the list of emails. A couple of red alerts jerked him back. One was a request for a meeting with a federal police officer. Special taskforce. Probably the one asking Morgan questions. Rafe slid into his seat, frowning now. He could read between the lines of his boss's email. Don't tell them anything we haven't already shared. He could do that. With pleasure. Rafe knew their own Customs operation was clean, but the other agencies? After tonight?

The email also raised suspicions about the fed's informant. The information supplied by the man codenamed Woomera had been consistently high grade, but now they were concerned he might be playing a double game. For Rafe, that raised some ugly questions. ASIO, with its domestic focus and ASIS, charged with gathering intelligence offshore, played a mean game of poker. Were they involved as well?

He sat back in his chair. He needed more information.

He entered the police officer's number into his iPhone. Too late now, ring him in the morning. Blinking the fatigue from his eyes, he opened the other flagged email and froze.

Why hadn't they rung him with this one?

His eyes narrowed as he scrolled down. A credible bomb threat on Australian soil did not happen very often, especially not one raised by the Indonesian authorities. He chewed the inside of his lip as he assessed the information and its ramifications for his operation.

The date was 9 November: the anniversary of the execution of the Bali bombers. He glanced at his iCal. Twelve days. He did a double-take. No, midnight was long gone so that made it eleven days to go. Dates like this were bread-and-butter stuff for fanatics. The demise of Amrozi and his pals would have great significance to extremists. To them the death of two hundred and two people including eighty-eight Australians, in a single night of hate, was a victory for their beliefs. Nothing like an anniversary to drum up new martyrs willing to take up the challenge of being suicide bombers.

He examined the four attached photos carefully. None matched the cell he'd been working, but he was watching the money-making arm of JI, not the bomb squad. The first photo was labelled Abu Nadal. A symbolic name, he wondered, chosen by the latest Abu to engender fear?

Rafe sat back in the chair, dredging up what he knew about the original Nadal. A Palestinian extremist, last name either Nadal or Nadil, depending on the interpretation, had been killed in about 2002. The product of a wealthy Palestinian father and a servant mother he was responsible for a reign of terror for over twenty-five years against the Israelis and anyone he perceived as sympathetic to their cause. His preferred weapons were bombs delivered by uneducated young men trapped in impoverished lives. Indonesian fishermen fitted that description perfectly.

And this new Nadal — son, nephew or copycat — had risen through the ranks of al-Qaeda leaving a trail of bomb victims behind him. If he'd made it to Australia then carnage on a scale not seen before would follow. That was a certainty.

Rafe opened another file and read down it, matching names and locations of confirmed members of the group he had under surveillance. Did that mean his cell was involved in more than drug running to pay the bills?

His muscled shoulders hunched forwards as he dragged tired hands through his dark hair. 'God, I hope I'm not right.' The words held menace and resignation in equal parts in the silent room. The move he'd been waiting for, expecting, might have much more tragic ramifications than extra drug addicts on the streets of Sydney.

He sent a response to his office, requesting a video hook-up in the morning with all the stakeholders. Time to bed down the final details and make sure his covering teams were in place. If it were more than drug imports this might just be about to blow up in their faces, literally.

Flat on his back several hours later, sleep still wouldn't come. Something kept niggling at the back of his mind.

The pattern of the vessels they'd been tracking didn't ring true. The explanation was unthinkable, but his mind edged around it anyway. The cell could have kept something secret from his informant so it could be his group that had prompted the warning from the Indonesian authorities. The feds' informant may also have given them misinformation or outright lies.

Either way, terrorists could well be plotting to blast away the innocence of Australia.

13

Woomera peered at his PDA in the half-light.

Shit.

The transponder he was tracking had stopped transmitting a couple of hours ago. Now it was back online and doing some weird shit. The chime of an incoming email made him start. With another expletive he shut the phone down as soon as he saw the address. Australian Customs. That could only mean one thing.

They'd found it.

Fuck, fuck, fuck. He needed to move fast. Nadal could not be caught on Australian soil. He'd have to get him out of the camp just in case they decided to send in the SERT guys early. He glanced at his watch as he removed the SIM card from his phone. Now he'd need to manufacture some pretext to go jaunting up the Cape again. And organise a ride down to Cairns for Nadal.

How the hell had they found it?

He inserted a new SIM then snapped the old one between his fingers. It was of no use now.

When had they figured it out? he wondered. If they'd managed to find the tracker then it might just lead them to

111

him. If that happened then the feds would start to question his reliability. He couldn't allow that. Damn it. He cursed again, curbing the urge to hit something. He'd need to give them some more information without compromising the operation. The tight rope just got a little more wobbly.

Half an hour later he'd made the arrangements. Another boat would collect Nadal and move him further up the Cape until he could get the prawn trawler into position.

Now he needed to manufacture his own excuses and feed his handler some lies and half-truths.

He ran his tongue around his teeth to ease the sudden dryness in his mouth. Initiating contact could be problematic. First he'd have to get his story straight. Then he'd need to give them enough information to keep them looking at the wrong person, but without making them panic. If they panicked, they'd pull everyone in for questioning.

If that happened they may well discover that when he claimed two and two made four, it in fact added up to a hell of a lot more. He'd invested too much time, too much frustration, too much anger in this little escapade for it to be brought undone by a woman.

14

Rafe closed the lid on his laptop with a snap and coiled the power lead in his hand.

At 6 am the tech had woken him up to confirm the hardware from Morgan's computer had the ability to send out anything she accessed on her computer as well as providing a tracking signal. After the tech explained that the email he'd sent with its own spyware had been received and the connection immediately terminated, Rafe had woken his boss.

That was something you didn't make a habit of doing, but this time? Too many things were adding up for Rafe and the sum didn't equal drug running. He was convinced the Indonesians' warning was accurate. Which meant that the group up the Cape were terrorists intent on harm, not making money. Nadal meant bombs. He just needed to convince the other agencies.

Half an hour later he'd been in a video hook-up with men and women he'd never met before, detailing his theory. They all looked like they'd been dragged from their beds. That gave him some small satisfaction after his own sleepless night.

Their lack of response frustrated the hell out of him. Video conferencing might be necessary in a country as large as Australia, where the threats tended to be in remote, inhospitable regions far from the cities where decisions were made, but a video couldn't give you the subtle nuances that revealed a person's real opinion.

Right from the start Rafe got the impression they weren't prepared to listen to a Customs agent telling them their informant was lying. Especially a Customs agent who'd started life in the army with the SAS. Woomera was the fed's golden-haired child of informants. Woomera could do no wrong. Woomera could be trusted and they wouldn't even believe that he may have made a mistake. Woomera was their asset.

It became clear in the first five minutes they still considered Morgan a risk. Rafe didn't bother mentioning that her brother had moved back into the picture – that would only give them more ammunition for their witch-hunt. He'd already decided that she had no knowledge of the device in her computer. He trusted his instincts. And the only time he hadn't trusted those instincts had ended in a fireball and the loss of twelve good men.

Despite his eloquent argument, despite his own boss presenting solid backup, the meeting had ended with no decision other than a request that he produce more evidence to prove his case. And that, he decided, he would bloody well do, and then enjoy ramming it down their throats. Just unfortunate that it was only eleven days to 9 November. And, if he was right, that didn't leave much time to prevent a devastating terrorist attack on Australian soil.

In another hour he had a meeting with the federal police officer who'd interviewed Morgan. Maybe he could convince him to provide some more resources. If not, too bad. He'd be back up the Cape by mid-morning and he'd find the missing piece if he had to stay on it twenty-four seven. Too much at risk to take no for answer. Too little time.

15

They'd been back in Weipa a day and already Morgan felt the heat bearing down on her. The humidity seemed to be intensifying by the minute and a quick glance at the weather charts confirmed the monsoon trough sitting over Cape York. Cyclone season had arrived early.

For the next four months air and sea travel would become the only way in and out of the far north. Roads and railway lines would be submerged under metres of muddy flood-waters as the monsoon rains fell. Bridges and causeways would be buried under a deluge of debris swept along by the rising torrents. Infrastructure would be literally washed away, leaving the north isolated.

And the people wouldn't complain or panic or even notice particularly. Stoic, enduring, laconic. They accepted that the Australian landscape bowed only to raging flood rains, scorching droughts and intense fires. That juxtaposition of lethal elements produced a harsh beauty seen only by a lucky few and they took it in their stride. Morgan smiled her appreciation to herself.

She finished her pre-flight walk around the outside of the aircraft and gratefully climbed the stairs into the cool interior.

The surveillance equipment was humming. Both Gavin and Rafe were bent over their screens with frowns on their faces. She left them to their worries and joined Lauren on the flight deck.

'All good to go outside.' She fumbled with her oxygen mask, checking the flow as she spoke, and Lauren grunted back.

'Yeah, fine here too. I've entered the coordinates for the search. Just need you to confirm them before I activate the plan.' She plonked a pile of paperwork up on the dash. 'Looks to me like we're crawling around the scrub today.'

'Rafe mentioned we'd be low level.' Morgan nodded. 'Weather systems finally turned tropical as well. There's a low pressure building up to the north-east that looks like it might develop early.'

'Late October, early November? Cyclone? Bit bloody early for that, isn't it?' Lauren looked surprised. 'Don't they usually start in January?'

Morgan shrugged. 'Depends. We've had them through here at Christmas and that one had spent almost three weeks wandering around intensifying. I'm not saying it's going to happen tomorrow, it's still a couple of hundred miles away and it's only a low. Just has potential, that's all.'

'Okay, but I'm not sitting around in the middle of a cyclone.' Lauren tossed her head. 'Being stuck in Weipa with no power and no cold beer would be a tragic thing.'

'What's wrong with Weipa's power?' Gavin stuck his head into the flight deck and both women groaned at him.

'Nothing yet, but if a cyclone comes through?' Lauren shrugged.

'But there's not one on its way, is there?' Gavin's alarmed face made Morgan laugh.

'No, Gavin, there is no cyclone, Weipa still has power and the pub still has cold beer. We were speaking hypothetically. Okay?'

BORDER WATCH

'Whatever.' He looked miffed that she was laughing at him. 'We're ready to go when you two are. Rafe's strapped in and champing at the bit.' He looked over his shoulder. 'I'd say he's pretty keyed up about this, so let's get it right.'

'Really?' Lauren used her best bored voice. 'And have you ever seen us not get it right, Little Mr Computer?'

He flushed. 'That's not what I meant and you know it. I meant all of us.'

Morgan interjected smoothly, 'And we all will. Strap in and we'll get moving, Gav.' She shook her head at Lauren. 'Just give it a rest for a day, would you?'

Lauren fired off a high-wattage grin. 'But it's fun tying him in knots. He never quite knows when I'm joking. Just the way I like it. My man on a dangle.'

'Don't drop him, you just might break him.'

'That I won't be doing.'

Ten minutes later the fully fuelled aircraft roared into the air, the heat taking its toll on the climb performance. The cloud base made a solid line of grey above them with embedded thunderstorms to the north-west painting a warning magenta on the weather radar.

'Level off at three thousand, thanks.' Rafe's voice was businesslike over the intercom. 'Set holding speed and give me a yell when we're ten miles away from the start of the first run.'

'Will do.' Morgan engaged the autopilot and eased the power levers back. The turbulence wasn't as bad as she'd expected, but it was still early. As the heat of the day built, the mechanical turbulence would keep increasing with it. She snuck a look at her first officer. Lauren was never her sparkling best when the air turned rough. Her good humour deserted her and she even stopped teasing.

For reasons that Morgan had long since stopped wondering about, she belonged to the flip side of the coin. She loved

117

turbulence. Each bump and roll was like a giant massage chair easing her muscles and loosening her spine.

Morgan keyed the intercom. 'Start of the run in ten miles.'

'Thanks. Aircraft feels nicely set up.'

'Any time for you, Rafe,' Lauren replied with a wink at Morgan, who just raised a disapproving eyebrow at her.

'Can you concentrate on work instead of your ovaries,' Gavin complained.

Lauren stifled a quick giggle. 'Yes, sir. All hands on.'

Morgan touched her shoulder. It may have been a light brush but it held a warning. Lauren grinned, unrepentant.

For three hours, they threaded backwards and forwards over the forest and coastline of Cape York, their track taking them ever closer to Skardon River. The river deltas were wide and shallow. Massive saltwater crocodiles sunbaked on the exposed sand left behind by the falling tide. The water was a brilliant azure even with the cloudy sky above. Morgan knew if she could dip her feet in, it would be warm, heated by the fierce sun over the shallow Gulf of Carpentaria.

Just after lunch they made contact with a boat moving too fast to be part of the fishing fleet. Not a prau, but a nondescript converted fishing vessel. Its current track suggested it had left Skardon River and was now headed up the Cape.

'Hey, Rafe,' Gavin called. 'By my count on the FLIR this thing's got about fifteen bodies on board and a couple of big donks hanging off the back that would give it a top speed of twenty-five maybe thirty knots in smooth water. It's got to be a SIEV.'

'Really?' Rafe peered over Gavin's shoulder. 'Can we have a closer look at this one, Morgan?'

At their current altitude, the aircraft was visible to the boat and they circled menacingly overhead. Rafe streamed live

BORDER WATCH

digital video-feed back to the BPC, as he talked to the analysts in Canberra.

'Don't know what you're thinking, Rafe,' Gavin said. 'But there's a few too many people on that for fishing. They all shot inside when we flew over them. They hiding something?'

Rafe grunted noncommittally as he ended his phone call. He didn't answer Gavin's query. 'Okay, ladies, one last orbit then we'll pick up the search pattern again. We've got about an hour's endurance left, right?'

He sounded pleased and Morgan looked over her shoulder. He had his back to her and, for a tiny moment, she admired his broad shoulders and slim hips. He cut a very impressive figure in his flight suit. She caught Gavin's interested gaze and turned back to the front, pink with embarrassment at her momentary lapse.

'We're about thirty miles north of Weipa still burning seventeen hundred pounds an hour. Yeah, that's another hour of this before it's time to head back.' Morgan looked across at Lauren for confirmation.

The younger woman frowned, distracted, and nodded before turning back to her window. 'It's stopped dead in the water. Is that significant?'

'Really?' Rafe moved to stand behind Gavin. 'Gav, can you zoom in on the man on the back deck there?'

'Sure.' Gavin rotated the joystick and the man's face shot into focus.

'Fuck.' Rafe breathed the word. 'Fucking hell, this isn't drugs. I'm right. Damn it.' He crossed to the window, grabbing binoculars. 'Bank a little more, Morgan.'

Morgan disengaged the autopilot and banked the wings over, giving him a view that was almost straight down on the boat. He pressed the high-powered binoculars up against the window. 'Nadal.' Rafe spat the name.

119

The word meant nothing to Morgan and Lauren shook her head as well.

'Nadal?' asked Gavin.

'Shit, turn left, turn left. Now.' Rafe's words had such urgency that Morgan responded automatically, forcing the control column back to the left and pressing them all into their seats with the g-force. Rafe did well to stay on his feet. 'They've got a SAM. Stay low. Go. Go. Go!' His words struck at Morgan as she pushed the power levers up to their maximum range, feeling the aircraft leap forwards.

'They've fired something.' Gavin's voice was calm as he watched his FLIR screen.

'A surface-to-air missile,' Rafe replied. 'Hang on.'

With a deafening roar and a bang the missile hit. The impact tipped the aircraft over to just short of ninety degrees, ripping the controls out of Morgan's hands. At that sort of bank angle, they started to lose height rapidly and Morgan grabbed at the column, hauling back on it as a cacophony of alarms deafened them.

'Roll jam,' she called, fighting with the controls, unable to right the aircraft from its steep turn as it accelerated down.

Lauren reached forwards, panic making her fumble, and grabbed the striped handle. 'Roll control.'

'Confirmed. Do it, do it.' As Morgan answered her, Lauren pulled and rotated the handle, disengaging the clutch between the two controls and abruptly the aircraft turned back to the right as Morgan's column came free.

'My controls.' Both women were breathing hard, the sudden rush of adrenalin pushing them into territory they'd trained for, but never visited before. Morgan fought to stabilise the aircraft, the controls sluggish and unresponsive as it screamed like an injured animal, shuddering in its death throes.

The warning panel had lit up like a Christmas light show. Methodically the women silenced the alarms and acknowledged the system warnings.

Rafe picked himself up from the floor. The only one not strapped in, he'd been hurled across the cabin and blood trickled from a cut on his head, his left arm hung from a damaged shoulder. He limped across to his console where the Sat phone dangled from its cord, feeling the aircraft yawing beneath him as the right-hand engine surged, mortally wounded, but still fighting to provide power to the stricken aircraft.

Gavin watched his screens.

Waiting for the next rocket to be fired, Rafe thought as he tried to dial out. Nothing. The line was dead.

'Gavin, have we got any comms left?' he asked, desperation hardening his voice.

'Just the VHF at the moment. The girls will get a call out.'

Rafe picked up his headsets in time to hear Morgan's emotionless voice crackle through.

'Number two engine failure.'

'Number two's confirmed.' Lauren's voice cracked fractionally.

'Engine shutdown drills on number two,' Morgan ordered her first officer, her voice flat and businesslike.

They completed the drill securing the damaged engine, but still they had multiple warning lights illuminated.

'Status report thanks, guys.' For the first time Morgan acknowledged the crew in the rear of the aircraft.

'My equipment's on UPS and draining, FLIR's still working,' replied Gavin. 'But there doesn't seem to be any more activity from the boat.'

'Right. Rafe, can you see the damage on the wing?'

'Looks like it tore through the right wing. It's almost ripped the engine off. Your props mangled, still attached, not turning. Fuel's streaming out. No sign of fire yet, but there's smoke.'

'It's still in the engine?' Morgan sounded shocked.

'Don't know. Don't think so, but those missiles aren't that big.'

'Shit, shit, shit. Lauren, distance to shore from here?'

'Fifteen miles in a straight line but that boat would be in the way.'

'Not going there again. Terrain up on the radar and let's head in the most direct route we can manage. Lauren, mayday call with anticipated ditching position. Guys, life jackets on. We're already down at two thousand feet and I'm only managing to hold a rate of descent around three to four hundred feet a minute. Six minutes to impact.'

Lauren had already started her mayday call, her voice unsteady. The others waited in tense silence. Only static came back.

'No answer,' Lauren said. She tried again with the same result. 'I'll broadcast again later. Someone might pick us up. We'll be lucky to make the coastline.'

Damn, Rafe swore to himself. He had a vital piece of information and no way of getting that message out.

As Lauren flicked through the checklist for emergency operations, he turned to Gavin. 'Can you send anything out other than the FLIR?'

'Data link probably still works. It might only be the Sat phone itself that's stuffed. Why?'

'Long story but they need to know Abu Nadal is in Australia.'

Gavin's eyes widened. 'Holy shit, the al-Qaeda bomb maker? He's the Nadal on that boat?'

Rafe nodded, surprised at Gavin's knowledge. 'Yeah.'

BORDER WATCH

'They would have received that last stream of footage before they hit us. It should have been a clear close-up of his face. Will they work it out?'

'They should do.' Rafe didn't relax. 'Can we check?'

'Sure.' Gavin's fingers were already tapping the keys. 'Ah, shit. It's not working. See what I can do.' He kept typing and Rafe tuned back in to the conversation from the flight deck.

'We've lost the number-two hydraulics altogether and . . .' Lauren bent forwards to the gauges in front of her. 'And the way the quantities are dropping, we won't have anything left on the number-one side either. Sprung a big leak.'

'Guess a missile'll do that every time,' Gavin quipped, looking up from his equipment. 'But you can pump the undercarriage down, can't you?'

'We will if we've got time, but that'll reduce our glide performance, smart arse.' Lauren's answer was tart.

Rafe looked at Gavin in amazement. 'You two can bicker at a time like this? When there's so much at stake?'

Gavin shrugged. 'No point in worrying about things I can't control. If anyone can get this down safely, Morgan and Lauren will. And I'll do everything in my power to tell the world there's an arsehole like Abu Nadal on Australian soil.'

'Okay, guys. Plan of attack. Tell me what you think,' Morgan intervened. Her voice had tightened with the effort of flying the stricken aircraft. 'It'll take about one minute to manually extend the gear. We'll wait until we're five hundred feet or lower. Get the life raft ready. If we make it to shore, throw it out anyway. It's full of survival gear. With power on the left engine still, it'll be a controlled landing so if we can find a flat area, it's our best chance. We'll transmit our position before we land and activate the emergency locator transmitter. Lock the flight-deck door open and anyone left standing grabs the others.'

123

There was silence as the other three looked for alternatives.

'Gear down? Even though it's probably not going to lock in place?' Rafe had flown enough aircraft to consider it illogical to want to land an aircraft on two and a half legs rather than on its smooth belly, gear retracted.

'Manufacturer's recommendation. Anything is better than nothing. Gives us some protection.' Morgan's reply was terse.

'How far do you reckon it'll drop down on the right-hand side?' Lauren twisted in her seat, straining to see the damaged wing. 'Looks like it's gone straight into it so the chances are it won't extend at all.'

Morgan was still focused on flying the aircraft. 'So what are you thinking?'

'If we can't make it to land and have to ditch, we might be better off clean,' Lauren replied.

'You're right.' Morgan managed a nod. 'Okay. So if we get to five hundred feet and think we can't make dry land, we'll leave it retracted. Otherwise, we'll pump it down.'

'And if we end up in the water, we have one hundred and eighty seconds to evacuate, they reckon,' Lauren added.

'So we'll set a new record evacuating and email Bombardier the info when we land.'

'We've got maps of this area?' Rafe broke in, looking at Gavin, still bent over his screens.

'Dunno.' Gavin looked up. 'You two got WAC charts?' He referred to the topographical maps pilots were required to carry.

'Yeah, but I don't want to be orienteering my way back to Weipa off them,' Lauren answered, digging into her flight bag. 'It'd be like driving across Sydney with a map of the world.'

'Better than nothing.'

'You bring the compass, boy scout?'

BORDER WATCH

'We've got the hand-held GPS and my mobile phone has one as well.' Rafe looked back out the window. 'There're flames out of the right-hand side now. Have you fired the extinguishers?'

'Of course,' Morgan answered crisply. He heard the control in her voice. She had no options left to fight the fire.

'Okay, we'll secure the cabin. Give me a heads-up with a minute to go.'

'Will do.' Morgan was still concentrating on holding the aircraft steady on one engine as the turbulence started to intensify.

'Lauren, emergency landing checklist and then we'll brief the emergency gear extension. Two and a half minutes to go, guys.'

Gavin unhooked his headset. 'No joy, Rafe. Just have to survive this and tell 'em yourself.'

'You tried, mate. You tried. Thanks.' Rafe gave him a brief clap on the shoulder as he continued to stow away the loose gear. The noise of pieces of metal hitting the aircraft side sounded like hailstones and Gavin glanced at the windows, apprehension stamped on his face.

'At least we're not pressurised,' Rafe said, trying to find a positive spin.

Gavin nodded. 'Could have been worse, but shit, a fucking missile?'

It was the first emotion any of them had shown. Rafe felt his own anger, held in check only by the urgency of their situation, simmering below the surface. The two women had calmly, methodically dealt with the damage as though it were routine. To an outside observer it looked controlled.

Rafe swallowed a swift rush of bile. The missile was in all probability still live and still in the engine. That meant it might well explode when the aircraft impacted. That meant fire.

125

Having survived a chopper crash, the only one of his team to make it, the fear in him sent a wave of heat through his body. It wouldn't, couldn't show on his face. He was responsible for their predicament, perhaps indirectly, but he'd make damn sure he did his utmost to extract them from it.

And he'd be after blood when they got back to Weipa. They'd dismissed his suggestion that Nadal could be in this area only this morning. Now, from the direction he was headed, they'd have a hard time finding him again. God help Australia if he made it south from Cape York. Ten days, now closer to nine. Less than a week and a half until the ninth. Would he live to stop whatever carnage had been planned?

'One minute to go,' Lauren yelled down the cabin and both men stopped, exchanging quick glances. 'Strap in.'

'All done?' Gavin asked as he made one last attempt at communication.

Rafe nodded. 'All done.' He squeezed Gavin's shoulder. 'You did your best. Let's hope they got it.'

He sat in his seat and fastened his harness, his fingers slick with sweat. Out the window, he saw the undercarriage struggle to free itself of the tangled wreckage. Watched as a shower of debris, shaken loose as the gear doors opened, sprayed back, making him flinch away involuntarily. The big strut stuck halfway.

'Right's only half down.' He couldn't see the pilots from his seat.

'Thanks, the other two are down and green.' Green meant locked into position, so they'd be landing with the right-hand side significantly lower than the left. He could see the water changing in colour as they neared the coast and wasn't surprised when Morgan spoke up.

'We'll make land, just.'

'Well done, ladies.'

BORDER WATCH

'Here we go, folks, brace, brace, brace.' Lauren's voice remained calm and both men obediently assumed the brace position.

Morgan pushed hard back in her seat, the belt already locked to prevent her falling into the control panel. She knew that the column would be slammed back into her and that her chances of surviving were slim.

Too busy to dwell on it, she acknowledged a certain amount of regret that her life could end here on a sandy shore far from home. An image of the body on the beach flashed at her. She too might just end up debris, washed up on the shore, rejected by the ocean as a foreign body.

'Fifty, twenty, ten . . .' Lauren counted down on the radar altimeter. As she got to ten, Morgan closed the throttles and pulled back on the column to flare the aircraft. The moment of truth, she thought, and barely a word had been spoken.

The left wheel dug into the soft sand, dragging the aircraft around and lifting the opposite side high. Morgan struggled to hold the nose up, preventing a cartwheel. Water sprayed from the wheels as they ran over damp sand. The still-turning prop sucked the spray even higher in a chaotic whirl and the edge of the narrow beach seemed to rush towards them.

Then they ran out of airspeed.

16

With a sickening lurch the right side dropped hard. The nose wheel slammed in, burying itself before it snapped off. A giant spray of sand shot into the air, coating the windows in white. The control column was torn from Morgan's hands as the great elevator on the tail flapped violently with the sudden deceleration of the aircraft.

She felt the yoke slam into her chest, forcing the air from her lungs. Then it bounced forwards again, her hands groping to contain it.

'Impact drills,' she shouted, her voice only coming out as a croak.

Lauren had already reached for the remaining fuel and hydraulic shut-off handle. With her seat locked further back, she'd escaped relatively unscathed. Her oxygen mask had flown forwards under the impact and clipped the back of her head with its sharp metal edges. Blood trickled down her shoulder.

They were both left hanging in their seatbelts as the aircraft finally dug in and buried its right side. The damaged under-carriage collapsed completely under the huge forces, but its sacrifice cushioned the impact.

BORDER WATCH

Thick dust swirled in the flight deck. The only sounds were creaking, straining metal and the hiss of escaping oxygen.

'Shit.' Morgan struggled weakly to move. 'Lauren?' Both their headsets had come off in the impact. Dazed, she peered around at the destroyed flight deck. Nothing was where it should be. It left her disoriented, searching for a focal point she could recognise.

'I'm okay, I'm okay,' Lauren fought the buckle on her harness. 'I'm okay. Bloody belt.' Her fingers fumbled with the catch.

'The guys?' Morgan felt for her own buckle, too sore to bend forwards. Hers came free immediately and she hung onto her seat, fighting gravity, half wedged against the displaced centre console. She twisted in her seat and came face to face with an ashen Rafe. 'You okay?'

He nodded, even his iron composure rattled. 'Yeah, Gavin's beaten up though. Some of the equipment fell on him.'

'No! Gavin!' Lauren shrieked his name, tearing at her seatbelt.

'Lauren, stop.' Morgan's voice cut through her panic. 'Try your lock. There's too much tension on it.' She reached over herself to the lever on the side of the seat, fighting the nausea that crippled her. She didn't know whether it was fear, adrenalin or the pain that twisted her stomach, but she didn't think she'd be able to control it much longer. She needed to get out of the aircraft before she threw up.

'There, try again.'

Lauren pushed free of her seatbelt and Rafe pulled her out into the cabin, steadying her against the awkward deck angle. Morgan sat still for a moment, her head bowed with the pain. Her chest hurt, her shoulders ached and the bile was flooding her mouth. She gritted her teeth. Just do it, girl. You've faced worse, much worse. Too much pain for dying, not enough blood, girl. Just do it.

She shoved herself out of her seat, stumbling over the wreckage and into the destroyed cabin. Lauren was talking to Gavin – words of encouragement, reassurance.

Rafe had managed to crack the lever on the airstair door and had all his weight against it, trying to force it open. Unlikely that will work, Morgan thought. Airframe's buckled. Emergency exit would be better.

She bent to peer out the right-hand side and sucked in a grunt as the pain in her chest stopped her. The smell of aviation fuel, thick in the air, mixed with a briny saltwater taint. It coated the back of her throat. That side was out of the question, she decided. Which left the door Rafe was attacking or the exit under the wing.

'Morgan.' Rafe turned to her with urgency, not anger. 'Lean on it with me. It's almost gone.' A sharp explosion followed by a shower of metal on the skin of the aircraft emphasised the danger.

She pressed forwards, leaning her shoulder into the stairs beside Rafe, feeling every muscle in her chest and back screaming in complaint. Ignore it, it's only physical, she thought. The door groaned and opened up a hand span.

The muscles on Rafe's neck, inches from her face, were corded with effort. A pulse beat strongly in the V above his collarbone and she wanted with sudden desperation to press her lips to it, as though in this world so unexpectedly alien and dangerous he was a beacon of hope, a haven of safety. Instead, something finally gave and with a sharp crack the door dropped away from them, sending Rafe stumbling down the stairs. The drop at the bottom was high with the aircraft half rolled on its side. He disappeared over the edge.

His head popped up again next to his hands as he hung on the bottom edge of the door, forcing it further down. 'Go. Get the others and a first-aid kit. Get out.'

BORDER WATCH

Morgan swung around to Lauren, who'd pulled Gavin clear of the wreckage and propped him up against the side wall. His legs were out in front. Morgan winced. The lower half of his pants was sodden with what could only be blood. Lauren had the first-aid kit open, but the task looked to be beyond her.

Morgan pushed her way through the wreckage. 'Gavin, we need to get you out. Now.'

His eyes flickered open. 'Mate, it fucking hurts.' She squatted down next to him, a muted popping from outside the aircraft going unnoticed.

'You'll be right. We need to get you out of the aircraft.' She prodded at Lauren. 'Now. We need to get out *now*.' The younger woman didn't seem to register the urgency, but before Morgan could get through to her, Rafe pounded back up the stairs.

'Out, now!' he yelled. 'The fire's spreading fast. Go, now. Jump!' He grabbed Morgan and pushed her to the door, ripping Lauren away from Gavin's side, thrusting the first-aid kit into her hands and sending her staggering after Morgan.

'Gavin, hang on.' He lifted the younger man, hearing the scream in the other man's chest before Gavin passed out. 'I'm sorry,' he said. 'I'm so fucking sorry.' He hit the sand running, Gavin held tight in his arms, and lurched in the soft sand.

'Get away from it,' he yelled back at the two women.

'But what about . . . ?' Lauren raised her voice in protest.

'Move. That missile's still attached to the aircraft. It'll blow.' His tone left no room for argument. He was by training, and by instinct, the leader. He was also the least injured.

Morgan grabbed the younger woman and pulled her up the beach. 'No, Lauren. We'll salvage what we can later if it doesn't burn to the ground. Run!'

They hung onto each other as they followed Rafe up the beach, the fire spreading rapidly behind them. The muted popping had become a crackling roar and the heat of burning

131

metal built quickly. With a deafening bang the missile finally exploded. The pressure assaulted their ears, a physical hit that left them all reeling. Debris rained down around them as they cowered under the trees. The heat was intense, the smoke an acrid black pall that clawed the backs of their throats, stole the air from their lungs and seared their streaming eyes. They watched in silence.

Morgan was shocked. From a capable, versatile machine to a mass of twisted metal in little more than five minutes.

The destroyed aircraft continued to burn and settle as Rafe worked to stabilise Gavin. Lauren cradled his head in her lap and Morgan dug through the first-aid kit in silence, relieved that Rafe seemed so competent. It was obvious to all of them that Gavin would probably lose his legs, but none of them voiced it. His eyes were closed, his breathing rapid and shallow. The morphine gradually took effect.

Close to twenty minutes later Rafe ran a weary hand across his forehead. 'That's about as much as I can do. We need a doctor, and soon.' He looked back at the still-smouldering wreckage. 'Hopefully they'll see the smoke and come looking quickly.'

'ELT won't have survived the fire,' Morgan said, her eyes dark with shock and huge in her face. 'We'll be lucky if the satellite even picked it up.'

'You got the coordinates out to Brisbane Centre, didn't you?' Rafe demanded sharply.

'I kept trying,' Lauren answered, 'but no one ever responded to the mayday call. Too low possibly, or the antenna was damaged. I can't guarantee anyone heard me.'

'Shit.' Rafe turned his frustrated eyes skyward. 'Gavin needs help now. Not in twenty-four hours when they work it out.'

'We're only about forty kilometres up the coast from Weipa. I think it's closer to there than Mapoon, the next settlement

BORDER WATCH

up the Cape. If we can find a road we'll meet someone on it.'
Morgan rubbed her chest unconsciously, her ribcage aching,
each breath a knife jab. 'What about your mobile phone?'

Rafe pulled it out of his pocket. The face was smashed.
'Something hit me in the chest and the phone bore the brunt
of it.'

'Shit.' It was Morgan's turn to swear this time. 'How much
water did we get out?' She looked at the other two.

Lauren shook her head. 'Nothing.'

Rafe held up a sports bottle half filled. 'That's it.'

'We didn't get the life raft out either.' Morgan scrubbed her
eyes with weary hands. 'Damn, damn, damn.'

Rafe gripped her shoulder. 'We'll survive this. We haven't
come this far to let them win. You girls stay here with Gavin
and I'll get to a road. The smoke should act as a guide to any
searching aircraft.'

'Yeah, till the tide rises and puts it out,' Lauren replied
bitterly.

'Maybe it won't.' Rafe pushed himself to his feet and Morgan
saw him wince as he straightened. He might be pretending to
be unhurt, but she knew that he had to be injured as well.
A dark red stain ran down his face from a sizeable cut on his
head. Letting him go alone was not a good idea. They were
better off in pairs.

'Lauren, you stay with Gav and I'll go with Rafe. We've each
got backup then.'

'No way, you'll slow me down.' Rafe spun to face at her,
anger in his dark eyes. 'I'll be quicker alone.'

'And if you've got internal injuries and collapse somewhere?
What do we do? Sit here waiting indefinitely? I'm coming. Don't
argue.' She made it to her feet before she finished speaking,
hands on her hips despite the pain that gripped her. She knew
the drill. She understood what it took to cope.

133

For a long moment, they faced off over Gavin and Lauren before Rafe finally shrugged. 'Okay. You keep the water, Lauren, and the first-aid kit. Use the morphine if he needs it and keep the fluids up as much as you can. You'll be all right?'

Lauren nodded, her hands gently stroking Gavin's hair back from his forehead. 'Stop asking dumb questions and go find a doctor.'

Morgan smiled, just a glimmer, at the young woman's tenacity. 'See you, kiddo.' She dropped a light kiss on her cheek and touched Gavin's shoulder, wondering if he'd make it. Would she see her friend alive again? Did Lauren realise how serious his injuries were?

Rafe watched in silence as she retied her bootlaces and she sensed his impatience. 'Ready.' She didn't meet his eyes, knowing she'd see anger there and she didn't want to fight with anyone right now, let alone Rafe.

He nodded and turned to Lauren. 'Take it easy.' She smiled up at him with tears filling her blue eyes.

'Just don't take too long, I don't want to lose this one.' She looked down at Gavin again, now semiconscious in her lap.

Morgan and Rafe battled through mangroves, up to their knees and occasionally their waists, as they worked their way through the creek system. Perhaps the noise they made or the urgency of their pace kept the snakes away, and the crocodiles mustn't have needed a decent feed, thought Rafe, as he sank up to his thighs in brown mud. The pervasive odour of the swamps filled his nostrils. Debris caught in the distinctive upside-down root system of the mangrove trees festered in the heat. Even clear of the mud they couldn't push the pace much above a jog. The twisted roots seemed to delight in tripping the unwary foot.

BORDER WATCH

Sweat trickled down their faces in rivers, soaking their clothes as they ran. With little or no breeze, the heat sapped their energy. The cloud cover raised the humidity and did little to reduce the temperature.

As they left the coast, the vegetation became more sparse and easier to negotiate. It barely helped. Rafe kept checking the sun behind them as it continued its inexorable descent. He looked at his watch again. They were headed south and east by his rough reckoning. This would eventually lead them to Weipa, but just how far they had to go was anyone's guess. Did they have enough daylight left?

Finally they hit a road, a red-dirt graded track with a smattering of animal paw prints and no signs of fresh tyre marks. It did nothing to lift their spirits. By now fatigue had slowed their pace even more. Rafe knew Morgan's feet would be bleeding from burst blisters. Didn't help to keep immersing them in smelly swamp water either, he guessed.

'Gavin's not going to make it, is he?' Morgan finally broke the silence and Rafe glanced away, without answering.

'If by some chance he does, he's going to lose his legs.' Her voice was flat and Rafe guessed that shock was setting in hard. Nothing in her training could prepare her for an actual crash or surviving it. He knew where her thoughts were headed. He'd been there before. That merry-go-round of guilt and anger and pain whirled faster and faster and faster, making it near impossible to get off.

'Maybe, maybe not. Either way, the damage is already done. No point in blaming yourself.'

'If we'd landed with the gear up, we might not have burnt. It could have been a smoother landing.'

'And then the props might have dug in and we'd all be dead or the missile might have exploded before we got clear and we'd have horrific burns. That'd definitely be better.' His tone

135

was sarcastic, deliberately cruel. No time now for Morgan to feel guilty. She'd done everything she'd been trained to do and more. She would need sympathy later, but now she needed strength and focus. Anger at him should provide both.

He saw her chin rise and hid his grim smile as her hands made small fists.

'He's more than a workmate. Gavin's as close to family as I've got.' Her voice stayed level, but there was no hiding the fire in it.

'So do him a favour and don't dwell on it.' Rafe shrugged. 'We've only got a couple of hours of daylight left and we need to get a rescue chopper back to them before sunset. We need to pick up the pace.' He left a small pause. 'If you're up to it.' Again he put an edge in his voice and saw her lengthen her stride. He knew she must be hurting like hell because he was, but she was doing her best not to show it. One tough lady.

'We can try running again.' She looked down at her steel-capped flying boots.

'Game if you are.' Rafe kept his eyes forwards, refusing to give in to the urge to comfort her. They both needed to push through the pain. There was more than just a man's life at stake here. Rafe still had no idea if the footage of Nadal had made it through. Until he knew, he'd push the two of them as hard as he had to. No exceptions.

'Okay.' She shuffled through the first few steps and Rafe winced with her, seeing the sweat immediately bead on her forehead. The side of her face was rigid with the effort, but not even a whimper passed her lips.

'Okay,' she said again, the word defiant. Rafe silently applauded her courage.

Magnificent.

It was a shame he had no time to appreciate the strength, the determination, that pushed her on. A shame to watch her suffer yet another unimaginable tragedy after all she had endured so far.

And a shame you need to stay impartial, mate, he cautioned himself, willing his thoughts back to the task at hand.

They kept up a slow run for almost half an hour before the sound of an engine drifted in on the breeze.

'Chopper.' Rafe stopped in the middle of the road. 'Can you see it?'

Morgan shook her head, scanning the skies. 'Nope.'

'It's low and big. Sounds like the rescue chopper.' Its deep note was getting closer. 'Coming from Weipa?'

Morgan twisted her head to hear, trying to marry the sound with any glimpses of an aircraft. 'There, there!' she screamed suddenly. 'Two o'clock and low. Heading past us.'

Rafe leapt in the air, waving his hands frantically over his head, yelling. Morgan put her fingers in her mouth and whistled, a shrill piercing blast. Neither one really expected to see the chopper turn, but suddenly it banked over, dropping lower as it shot towards them.

'They've seen us,' Morgan hung off Rafe's arm even as he kept waving at it. 'They've seen us!'

The chopper landed down the road from them, blowing the bright red dirt up in giant swirls and buffeting them with the rotor wash. The rear door slid open and a helmeted crew-member ran towards them.

'Rafe? What the fuck happened? We saw smoke up ahead.' The burly man clasped hands with him as he shouted over the noise of the rotors. 'Only you two survive?'

'No, mate, the others are back where we got shot down. Back up the Cape.'

'Fuckin' hell. They bad?'

Rafe nodded. 'One is. You got a doc on board?'

'No. Just me and the pilots. We've been tasked by AMSAR to find you guys. They didn't have great coords on you though.'

Rafe nodded. 'Let's go. I need your comms.' He turned to Morgan to find tears rolling down her cheeks. Shock was definitely allowed to set in now and he pulled her close against him, feeling the unyielding set of her body and wishing he could ease her burden.

'Let's go get them, Captain.' She stumbled and he didn't hesitate. Swinging her up into his arms he carried her to the chopper, bending low as they neared the spinning blades. His own aching body screamed with the extra weight, but at least he could offer her this one small comfort.

Rafe had the helicopter's Sat phone in his hand before the blades had spun up again for take-off. Some of the tension drained from his spine. Gavin had been correct. The final images from the aircraft's video had made it through. Resources all over Australia were being mobilised. They just needed to find Nadal now. In a coastline as vast as this one that would not be easy. His day wasn't over.

Finding their way back to the crash site proved much easier. The smoke pall still hung over the wreck. They landed on the beach upwind of it and Lauren came pelting down the sand towards them. Horror was stamped all over her face, tears streaming from her swollen eyes.

'They took him. They took him, the bastards, they just dragged him.' She choked over the words, screaming at them as she got closer, the noise of the rotors subsiding as the chopper wound down. She ran straight into Rafe's chest, clutching at him. 'They took him.'

'Lauren, Lauren.' He held her away, searching her face. 'Who took him?'

BORDER WATCH

'The bastards that shot us down. They beached down there. Men with guns. I thought they were going to shoot him, but they just dragged him down the beach. He was screaming, screaming. Oh my god.' She bent over, her sobs wracking her whole body. 'Gavin.' His name came out as a wail and Morgan wrapped her arms around her tightly, rocking the grieving woman.

'How long ago?' Rafe demanded as the chopper crew looked on, horrified. Lauren sniffed and gave a shake of her head. 'Lauren,' he repeated, 'how long?'

She raised red eyes to him. 'About an hour after you went. I went for a pee in the bushes and saw them land. I thought they'd miss us, but they searched around the aircraft and then one of them saw Gavin. I didn't do anything. I hid.' She whispered the last word, anguish distorting her face. 'I let them take him.' Fresh tears rolled down her cheeks, but Morgan steadied her before she could break down again.

'Stop, stop now,' she soothed. 'You couldn't do anything against guns. You did the right thing. Which way did they go?'

Lauren pointed north, still crying too hard to speak.

Rafe looked at Morgan. 'The SERT team are on their way in one of their choppers. You two go back to Weipa, get a doctor, get her sedated. Don't talk to anyone outside of the company about this.' His tone was hard, but his eyes didn't give the same message. His big capable hand touched her shoulder gently and she leant her face against it.

'Find him, Rafe.'

'We will.' He let his hand drop and shepherded the two women to the helicopter. 'I'll be in touch.' He pressed a gentle hand to the back of Morgan's neck as she held Lauren close. 'Well done, Captain. Well done. You did everything you could.'

As he turned his back on them and headed up the beach to the crash site, he wondered if Lauren realised they wouldn't be

139

finding Gavin alive. Even if the terrorists didn't shoot him, his injuries were life-threatening without surgery. Lauren wasn't going to have anyone to tease and she would miss that much more than she realised.

And Morgan? His mouth tightened. Morgan was a woman used to losing people she loved. She would most probably bury it away deep and silently blame herself. At least there was something he could do about that, he decided grimly. No matter how far she might push him away, he'd be coming right back to her.

Night was creeping closer, the sun a bright orange orb low on the horizon, turning the waters of the Gulf blood red. Rafe wasn't superstitious, but the colour had an ominous tinge.

17

'Fuck.' Woomera's breath escaped in one long snort. 'Just for fucking once.' He swore again as he shoved the phone back into his pocket. How the hell did they think they would get away with shooting down a surveillance aircraft? What sort of fucking idiots were these people? Now not only did he have to clean up their mess and get Mr Abu bloody Nadal out of the way, but he had to explain to his other masters why he hadn't shared this more vital information with them. What a bloody cluster fuck.

And he now needed to be in two places at once.

His blinding rage built quickly. He turned away, looking for something to distract him before he exploded. A coconut fallen from its tree made an easy target and he hurled it against the trunk, the sweet smelling juice spraying in a glistening arc. Pieces of creamy coconut flesh flecked his arms as he reached for another and sent it rattling after the first. The pile grew and his anger dissipated until, with a heaving chest, he'd exhausted the supply.

He walked away, flicking open his mobile phone. Time to fix the problem now.

Less than ten days to go, then no more dealing with incompetent idiots and deranged terrorists. He'd dealt with enough fools and morons to last him the rest of his life. Maybe he needed to cut and run. Tip off ASIO anonymously and let them sort it out. He would have proved his point. Maybe not with the same spectacular force he'd dreamt and planned for but . . .

He spat onto the red dirt of the bedraggled garden bed.

Maybe not.

Too much effort to just waste it like that. And the moral dilemma still reared its ugly head. How many dead constituted too many dead?

'Yeah, hi,' he said into the phone. 'I'll be a bit late for the briefing. Can you cover for me?' He grunted at the reply before hanging up. Much more of that and his team would be asking awkward questions.

His boots echoed on the floorboards. The house seemed empty, but he checked through all the rooms before he dialled again. His next call took a little longer. Sweat slicked his palms by the time he'd finished talking. He couldn't be entirely sure his controller had believed him.

Impatiently, he tugged his shirt over his head and rummaged in his pack for the regulation dark blue shirt and pants. Buckling the heavy weapons belt low around his hips, he walked back into the kitchen and downed a litre of orange juice, wiping a trickle from his chin. The clock on the wall said six.

Time to go. He locked the front door as he went, silencing the phone and burying it deep in one of the many outside pockets of his fatigues.

18

Morgan crawled back to her room late in the evening. The doctor wanted more scans done, but they would have to wait until she got to Cairns. Weipa's hospital was rudimentary, used to dealing with mining injuries and the usual first-aid traumas. CT scans were done in Cairns and while the Royal Flying Doctors did a fantastic job of transferring the seriously injured, neither Morgan nor Lauren fitted that description. And they weren't leaving until they'd found Gavin. So far there was no word.

Morgan leant over the hand basin, ignoring the sight of her face in the mirror. Haggard with exhaustion, the colour had drained from it leaving her warm-toned skin alabaster. With dark circles under her eyes, the bright spots of cuts stood out dramatic and red.

She pushed her wet hair back off her face, feeling the pain in her shoulders, chest and ribs, despite the heavy dose of pain-killers the doctor had injected.

'Gavin,' she whispered. 'Oh, Gavin, what have they done with you?' The tears that she'd held onto so tightly all day trickled down her cheeks, a flood that dripped off her chin and into the basin. 'Why does this happen to people I love?' Her voice broke and she buried her face in her hands, deep sobs shaking her slender frame.

'Why?' The anguish was so very real, tearing at the scars she'd healed so many times before, breaking all the fragile grafts she'd painstakingly grown, ripping deep into her like a jagged, rusty knife blade.

The day had been a maelstrom of emotion, a storm that had broken over her without warning, without pity, without mercy. A storm that washed away her ironclad control, made her doubt herself, doubt her hard-won abilities.

She turned to her bed and sat forlornly on its edge, reliving the crash, the moment they'd been hit, the screeching, wrenching impact of the aircraft's final landing and the last image of Gavin, semiconscious in Lauren's arms.

Lauren had eventually given in to the doctor and taken a sedative. Describing her as distraught would be an understatement, thought Morgan. Not only had she lost her best friend, in Lauren's eyes she hadn't saved him and she should have.

There was no point in trying to tell her she was being irrational and would herself have been killed if they'd found her. She'd gone beyond reasoning. She had failed a friend, and for Morgan it was all too easy to understand the younger woman's logic.

Hadn't she spent the last twenty years wishing she'd stopped her father? Wishing she'd put herself between her warring parents? Wishing she'd at least tried, instead of hiding in her room, her head under a pillow to block out the screams?

She knew what it felt like to be betrayed and to betray someone you loved. You can run, girl, but you won't change history, she reminded herself. You have to live with your actions and the regrets.

She lay down on the bed, staring at the ceiling, absently counting the speckles of mould scattered across it. The hum

BORDER WATCH

of the air-conditioner cocooned her. She would dream tonight, she knew, of faceless bodies and death. It was a nightmare that had recurred so many times she knew it by heart. No doubt a nice polite counsellor would make much of that. She knew it for what it was — a deep-seated subliminal scream that only she could hear.

She pulled the covers over her head, knowing it was childish and it would never work, but the warmth, the darkness, the solitude might eventually bring sleep, even if it didn't bring peace.

Rafe landed back at Weipa close to midnight. The Queensland SERT boys and their federal counterparts had wasted no time. Within an hour of him phoning in a positive ID on Abu Nadal they moved in and wrapped up the terrorists' camp. Bigger than anyone had estimated, the camp was unprepared for such immediate reprisals. Nadal was missing, but they captured twenty and left two dead without more than a dozen shots being fired. A couple of casualties were acceptable collateral damage, he figured. Two less to tie up the courts with hard-to-prove terrorism charges. The fact that Morgan's ex had been the one doing the shooting made him uneasy. Carl Wiseman was hiding something. His intuition didn't lie.

He headed down the side of the pub to his room. Worry about Wiseman and Nadal tomorrow. Today had been testing enough. He'd even managed to sit in a helicopter again without freaking out completely.

The things we do, mate, he consoled himself, rubbing a weary hand across his face. He probably should get his ribs examined. Gingerly, he poked around his left side where his phone had conveniently taken a hit. Something grated. The pain, a sharp stab, took his breath away. He straightened up. A

145

medic would only strap him up anyway. Nothing they could do that his body wouldn't accomplish for itself, just as it had done many times before. Not like Gavin.

He almost stumbled. Shit. It would fall to him to answer the questions of two very gutsy ladies tomorrow morning. Nothing could ever teach you how to deliver bad news, he thought dispassionately.

Nothing.

The sudden surge of anger made his stride longer, his steps heavier. There had been no sign of Gavin and the only answer from their captives was a jet of tobacco-stained spit directed at Rafe's shoes. Gavin was probably even now being returned to the food chain inside a large saltwater crocodile, Rafe guessed.

Let's hope none of the fishing fleet find him in their nets. Enough people have been traumatised today, he thought, exhausted to his very core.

He stood for twenty minutes under the steaming hot shower, palms flat on the wall, his head bowed, cleansing water pouring over him. He knew he was trying to wash away a multitude of emotions. Recognised every single one of them like old adversaries.

Fear. He'd faced death in an aircraft again and beaten the odds one more time.

Regret. He'd tended to a seriously injured young man only for other forces to take his ebbing life without a damn thing he could do to prevent it. Again.

A tiny dart of satisfaction. They'd smashed a terrorist cell and closed down a gateway of chaos into Australia.

But the overriding emotion was anger. Customs, ASIO, ASIS and the AFP had all underestimated the strength and aggression of their foe and now Nadal was loose in Australia. He personally had put an aircraft and its crew in jeopardy and cost a man his life. Now the whole country was at risk because

BORDER WATCH

of errors he and others had made. That he would have to live with forever.

The hot water started to cool and reluctantly he turned off the tap. He knew he wouldn't sleep yet. Too much adrenalin, too much emotion. He shrugged on a pair of track pants and a light T-shirt. He needed to wind down.

As he walked past the row of doors towards the road, he paused outside Lauren's, wondering how the young woman was holding up. He never doubted there was a deeper side to Lauren than the flirty little madam who teased, shopped and partied hard. To be so secure in her own skin, she had already discovered her strengths and weaknesses. Tomorrow she would learn some new ones.

He turned away, but a soft cry from the room next to Lauren's stopped him.

Morgan?

The cry rose a little higher, a sob that ended in a name.

It was Morgan.

He hesitated, then walked back. Her voice rose again.

Nightmare. He knew those feelings too. Damn it. How much did one woman have to have thrown at her?

He tried the handle and it turned unexpectedly in his hand. The layout of the rooms was identical to his own so he didn't need lights to find the bed.

Morgan's dark shape was screwed into a tight ball, her hands shielding her head from imaginary blows, her bedding a tangle of damp sheets. 'No, no! Not again, please, I won't tell.'

He felt his muscles bunching with inadequacy. He shouldn't be here, but no one should be suffering this much. He flexed his hands, unsure what to do. Would it scare her even more to find him in her room?

'Nooo,' she wailed, rolling over. Was she escaping long-remembered fists, he wondered, or something else?

147

He touched her shoulder, felt her shivering despite the heat of the night, felt the sweat that slicked her skin and felt her recoil from him, the only real touch she couldn't see.

She was deeply asleep and as his eyes became accustomed to the dark, he could see the furrows on her forehead, the rigid muscles of her arms and the fine strands of dark hair stuck to her face. It fractured something locked deep, deep inside and the need to comfort and be comforted proved greater than his own fears.

He gathered her up against him as a father would his child.

With a gentleness at odds with the strength of his hands, he stroked the tangle of her hair, soothing her knotted limbs, brushing away the horror.

He smelt the clean scent of her even through her terrified sweat, felt the soft catch of her hair over work-roughened palms, absorbed the pliant softness of her body as she faded back into sleep. Her breathing ever so slowly eased.

She cuddled closer against him, burrowing into his chest, her arms crossed defensively still. Rafe rested his chin on her head, wondering at the sudden blast of loneliness that tore through him. The warmth of a woman relaxed in his arms had become a forgotten pleasure. What memories he did have had never instilled this sense of deep comfort, of connection with another.

Each warm caress of her breath on his arm tugged at him. For the first time in his life he felt the overwhelming urge to put down roots, take another person into his life, share uncomplicated laughter with no secrets. He wanted to live, just live.

Suddenly, he realised he was crying, a tiny trickle of tears that wet his cheeks. It had been a very long time.

The warm body in his arms moved and a gentle hand slid across his jaw.

'I think you've sprung a leak.' Morgan's voice rasped with the night's fears.

'Hmm.' His answer rumbled in his chest.

'How'd you get in here?' She made no move to leave the sanctuary of his arms, compliant, still wrapped close.

'I heard you yelling out. I know a bit about nightmares so I kinda let myself in. You didn't lock your door.'

'Oh. Sorry.'

He snorted gently. 'No need for apologies.'

She stayed silent before twisting her head to peer up at his face. 'You didn't find Gavin, did you.' It wasn't a question.

He shook his head in the dark, unable to lie to this tenacious woman. 'No. He wasn't at the camp.'

'He'll wash up on a beach and someone will find him and wonder at his life and the journey that brought him to that lonely place. Alone, so alone.' Now she was crying, a flood that dripped off her chin and onto his chest. He tightened his arms around her, willing his last reserves of strength into her weary body as she continued. 'We need to find him so Lauren can say goodbye. She loved him, you know. She told me that one day there'd only be room for Gavin in her life.' Her voice broke. 'I hope she told him that on the beach.'

Rafe pulled her more securely into his arms, cradling her in his lap, holding her against the sobs that shook her. 'I'm so sorry, Morgan. So, so sorry. Gavin was a good man.' She nodded against him, sniffing back her tears. He dug a hanky out of his pocket and handed it to her.

'Yeah, I know.' She blew her nose. 'And the bastards who shot us down?'

'We got them. Two dead.' But not all of them, he added silently. And, he continued his internal conversation, your mate Carl was in the killing quadrant and it looked like a deliberate hit to me. And no sign of Abu Nadal, so now there's a full-

149

scale alert out and no one has a fucking clue where he's gone, but we're winning, really we are.

'Where are they now?'

'Under wraps at their camp. The feds don't want the story to get out. For now, our shooting down is being described as a crash, no mention of missiles.'

She moved and he loosened his hold, expecting her to move out of his embrace, hoping she wouldn't, wanting, needing to feel her still in his arms, but aware of the sound of his heartbeat thudding in his ears.

But she only turned, resting her back against his chest, the thin cotton of their clothes the only thing separating their bodies. What had started as a need for comfort was giving way to something much more disturbing.

He spoke to distract himself. 'Too much else at risk for the truth to come out yet.'

'So Lauren and I have the distinction of being the only crew to lose a Border Watch aircraft. Something special for our résumés.' The bitterness in her voice made him blink.

'Anyone who matters will know what really happened. You can only keep the lid on these sorts of things for so long. The feds just need enough time to wrap up the rest of the cell. The camp was only the tip of the iceberg.'

'JI.'

'Yep, Jemaah Islamiya. We've set them back a couple of years at least.'

'I hope Gavin's life was worth it.'

'No one should have to pay the ultimate price, Morgan, but let these guys loose in Australia and you'd have carnage. They don't respect us, our country or our values. We are just arrogant, decadent westerners oppressing their religion. I'm sorry Gavin's gone, sorry for Lauren and sorry for you, but we can't change that. We can try to make sure it doesn't happen again.'

BORDER WATCH

'You underestimated them, didn't you?'

He nodded in the dark. 'That's right. I made a mistake and it cost a good man his life. Don't for a moment think I've not reviewed all the data in my head a hundred times to see where I went wrong.' He struggled to keep the anger from his voice, knowing not only that it was misplaced, but unnecessary. But it kept his mind from the other more primitive urge that was running riot through his veins.

'You too, huh? I guess we're both beating ourselves up over might-have-beens.'

'And we both know we can't change the outcome. We need to move on. Lauren is going to need your strength today.'

Her hair tickled his chest as she tilted her head back to draw a deep breath. 'I'll tell her about Gavin. It should come from me.'

He felt the tension tighten in her and ran soothing hands down her arms. 'We can do it together. You're still hurting.'

'Feels like I've been hurting forever,' she whispered, the despair in the sudden slump of her shoulders ripping at him. Her grim acceptance of a life that had delivered so many knockout blows blew away the last of his defences. Morgan was a victim who'd recast herself as a winner and yet life kept throwing more challenges at her than was fair. He couldn't leave her to face them alone, not tonight, not tomorrow, not ever again.

Never.

The thought terrified and surprised him in equal measure and his voice was rough with the unfamiliar emotion.

'We'll do it together. Save your strength for you.'

'Strength?' Her voice cracked. 'I'm not strong tonight.' She turned her face to his chest and her lips brushed his bare arm as she spoke. 'Stay with me for tonight. I just need . . .' Her

151

words trailed off. She paused. 'Just hold me. Nothing . . . Just hold me.'

Rafe looked up at the ceiling and, blinking away fresh tears, tightened his arms around her. He knew she wasn't talking about sex, but just the comfort, the reassurance, the feeling of another's arms.

It was the least he could do, even if the proximity of her warm, soft body was wreaking havoc with his self-control. Even if the gentle rise and fall of her chest was heating his blood. Even if the steady beat of her heart was the sound of a tribal drum echoing through his soul. He would stay because she needed him tonight and that was enough.

19

Morgan stirred, feeling damaged muscles and bones that had seized. She ached in every joint, her head was pounding and she seemed to be trapped under a great weight.

Panic engulfed her.

It couldn't be another nightmare, could it?

She tried to sit up, wrestling with the dead weight across her body. The grunt close to her ear froze her. Then reality came pouring down on her like an icy deluge.

Yesterday she'd crashed an aircraft, she'd lost a friend and she'd asked a man to hold her all night. That same man was now regarding her through sleepy midnight-dark eyes.

'Sorry.' She cleared her throat, her voice scratchy from last night's firestorm of despair.

'Don't be. It's time to wake up anyway and my other arm's gone to sleep completely.'

'Oh.' Morgan struggled to sit up, her aching muscles hampering her, embarrassment flushing her cheeks.

One firm hand steadied her and gently urged her to the edge of the bed. Rafe stifled a groan and she looked at him. A frown creased his face as he wiggled the fingers on the hand she'd been lying on.

153

'Sorry.'

'Do me a favour and stop apologising.' He spoke with his eyes still closed, concentrating, she guessed, on returning blood to his numb limb. The amusement, rather than anger, in his voice disarmed her and she rested on the bed, taking in his chiselled features and rumpled hair. The dark shadow of new beard on Rafe's solid jaw made her want to reach out and touch it. She resisted the temptation. That was a path to more self-destruction if ever she'd seen one.

But it didn't stop her hand itching to touch.

Unsettled, she turned away and levered herself to her feet. Yesterday's wrenching sense of loss twisted inside her, intertwined with her confused feeling of attraction for her colleague. Unsteady still, she made her way to the tiny ensuite, wondering why it felt so natural to have Rafe, fully clothed, in her bed.

She washed her face in the hand basin, sluicing water down her neck, every move costing her. The doctor obviously had a better appreciation of pain than she did. She pushed two painkillers from their foil packet and swallowed quickly.

Lauren. She stopped with her glass half raised. Gavin, she had to tell her about Gavin. The glass clunked onto the shelf as it slipped from her shaking hands. Damn it. She grabbed at it to stop it falling further and the sudden action tore at her ribs.

'Rafe?' she asked, pushing open the door.

'Yes?' Rafe was sitting on the only chair in the room, dwarfing it with his bulk. His mouth was grim and Morgan wondered how he was dealing with the pain of his own injuries.

'Did you see a doctor last night?' Her thoughts had wandered off, following that new tangent. 'You can have some of the painkillers she gave me. I've got a whole box full.' She frowned at his shaking head. 'No, you didn't see a doctor or no, you don't do painkillers.'

'Both, they're bad for your health.' A ghost of a smile flittered across his face. 'I'm all right. I've had worse.'

She looked down at her hands, realising she was wringing her fingers and willing herself to stop. 'Is there any hope Gavin might turn up?'

'There's always hope, Morgan, but . . .' He stood up, forcing her to lift her chin to meet his gaze. With a gentle touch he smoothed her hair back from her face and for an instant she saw desire in his eyes. 'We'll tell Lauren the truth and see what today brings. They'll have had searchers up since first light so maybe . . .' He shrugged, shifting his gaze over her shoulder and dropping his hand. 'Have a shower, it'll ease your aches. Take two more painkillers. I'll come and collect you in half an hour?'

She nodded, unable to meet his eyes, feeling the burn of tears prickling. 'Okay.' She looked down at her feet and swallowed, wanting to press herself against his broad chest and find the safety of the night. 'Okay.'

The kiss he feathered across her temple shot a shiver of desire right through her body. He'd gone before she could draw in a deep shuddering breath.

The door closed behind him and she sank onto the bed again, burying her face in her hands. Surviving the crash suddenly seemed like the easy part. Today would only get worse.

20

Rafe closed his replacement phone, tucking his fresh shirt into clean jeans. Damn, damn, damn. So much to do. A trawler had found a body and was bringing it in. He glanced at his watch. Eight o'clock, time to get Morgan. His own body cried out for some more sleep and the oblivion of a good bottle of rum, but he knew from long experience the only way to push through pain and exhaustion was to ignore his body and its whining.

He hadn't slept until the sun came up. Keeping watch, he thought sadly. Scaring away any demons that threatened to disturb Morgan. She'd felt so real, so right, in his arms, as though they'd been there a thousand times before.

In the dark of the night, tired of going over the crash and his sighting of Nadal, he'd given in and tried to analyse his reaction to Morgan, tried to put it in perspective, so that he could then dismiss it as momentary madness, a lust-induced fever. Instead, all he'd done was catalogue the reasons why he wanted her in ways that stunned him and frightened him, elated him, challenged him.

They were both flawed people who had the courage to change themselves, single-minded, honest, blunt even. Both were committed to careers, both cared about the people close to them. Both had trouble articulating their feelings. He saw the world as black and white. She saw the colours of the world in all its infinite possibilities. He wanted some of that for himself. A touch of magenta, of gold and silver, of indigo. The colours of Morgan and her garden.

And, damn it, she fitted perfectly in his arms. The scent of her, clean and sweet, soapy and elemental, was imprinted in him now. He needed her in a way he'd never needed before.

It was going to be a long chase, he knew. She wasn't necessarily going to see it the same way. One more person she loved had died and she would, because she was Morgan, hold herself and him responsible. That made for a big hurdle he'd have to work hard to get over.

The corridor was empty as he left his room and he almost made it to her door.

'Rafe?' Lauren's voice croaked from behind him.

'Lauren.' He turned to face her, drawing his lips into a smile. 'How're you doing this morning? You two should have spent the night in hospital.'

She brushed his words aside. 'I'm fine. Gavin, did you find Gavin?'

'Let's go get Morgan.' He nodded towards the other woman's door. He put a protective arm around Lauren, feeling the slim shoulders shaking. Morgan opened the door as soon as he knocked and gathered her friend into her arms.

Rafe looked away from the women, disconcerted by his own urge to cry. Morgan shook her head at the question in Lauren's vivid blue eyes. 'I'm sorry, baby, they didn't find him,' she whispered. 'I'm so sorry.'

How many times did a man have to watch people grieve for their loved ones? Rafe wondered. How were people supposed to just pick up where they'd left off, when a cornerstone of their life was gone, taken in an instant? He felt isolated from them, knowing that his training gave him coping mechanisms that others didn't have, but this death had bitten deep, touched places he'd buried a long time ago, and it ached.

Morgan ushered Lauren to the chair, the young woman's grief destroying her composure, and raised teary eyes to Rafe. He tried to hide it, but saw her recognise the anger, the loneliness, the grief in his face. Her tiny smile was meant to reassure him, but it simply ripped into him. He wanted to be the one to comfort Morgan, to draw strength from her arms.

How bloody selfish could he be? He closed his emotions down, drawing dark covers over his eyes, and turned away.

He decided impulsively that he would meet the trawler and identify the body, just in case. Just in case? Who are you trying to kid? he scoffed at himself. There were unlikely to be two bodies floating around the mouth of the Skardon River.

He cleared his throat. 'I've got to meet a guy at the docks. I'll be back in an hour or so. You have my new number. Anything, just call me.' He saw Morgan make the connection between Gavin and his reference to the docks. She'd worked out he was meeting a rescue vessel. Her eyes met his over Lauren's head, distress and understanding stamped on her face. He shook his head at her, imploring her silence.

He watched her weigh it up, then acquiesce. 'Okay.' With a decisive nod of her head, she made up her mind. He was relieved.

The trawler had already docked and one of the local police was there.

'Morning, Rafe.'

Rafe nodded as he clambered aboard. 'Morning, Pete. Is it my boy?'

'Yeah, 'fraid so. Wearing his green flying suit still and the boys on the *Lady Jane* knew him from the pub. They're pretty upset.'

'Who's talking to them?'

'My offsider. Trawler men are tough nuts, but a body in your nets would give anyone a friggin' fright.'

Rafe nodded. 'Where is the body?' He couldn't quite say the name and knew he was being a coward.

'In the freezer. Just waiting for the undertaker to drive him up to the hospital. They've got a room they use for autopsies.'

'Can I see him, ID him? I need to let Morgan and Lauren know once and for all.'

The police officer pointed at the stairwell. 'Down there on your right, mind your head as you go. It's not pretty. He'd been in the feeding frenzy when they picked him up.'

Rafe raised his eyebrows, not understanding his words.

The door to the freezer room was taped up with scene-of-crime tape and Rafe picked enough free to open it. Gavin was face down in the middle of the small room, ice piled around him. Normally, there'd be bins of prawns or rows of fish lined up. Today's catch was a tragic reminder that the world was a changed place.

Rafe crouched down and rolled the body over. It was unmistakably Gavin, even though the meaning of the officer's words was now clear. Jammed into a net, Gavin had been attacked by the sea creatures caught with him. Any bare skin was red and angry with bites, prawns were inside his clothes and no doubt the coroner would have a grisly task dissecting him. Rafe had seen death so many times, too many times, but this battered at his defences.

He rocked on his heels, tilting his head back, feeling tears burn his eyes. It had been Gavin, but it wasn't anymore. Just another corpse. He knew anything could be rationalised with time.

With steady hands he rolled Gavin over and got to his feet. 'Hope it was quick, mate. I'll miss you.' His voice echoed in the cold steel and forced a momentary crack in his composure.

Rafe emerged back on deck to find the police officer had been joined by the local undertaker. 'Yep, that's a positive ID. You won't need Morgan or Lauren to see him, will you?'

Peter shook his head. 'No, you're good enough. They okay?'

'They're two very strong ladies, but Lauren is devastated and Morgan still feels responsible. Both of them should have stayed in hospital last night,' Rafe replied.

'Bloody idiots. Survive being shot down, hiking for a couple of hours, seeing your boyfriend kidnapped by terrorists. You'd reckon they'd listen to the doctor.'

Rafe turned sharp eyes on the policeman. 'Shot down? Terrorists?' he barked.

Peter squirmed under his angry glare. 'Well, the SERT boys are telling it that way.'

'Which ones?'

'What does it matter?'

'It matters. Who was it?'

The undertaker looked decidedly uncomfortable and shuffled his feet, moving out of the firing line of Rafe's anger. 'I'll just be over there.' He didn't wait for an answer.

Rafe lowered his voice, but not his anger. 'It matters that more lives might be lost if this gets out before the feds clean up the remaining cell members. You want that on your conscience?'

The police officer shot a sullen look sideways. 'The big bloke that used to date Morgan. Wiseman.'

'Really? And where were you when he let this slip?'

BORDER WATCH

'At the snack bar up the road from the police station this morning. I was getting breakfast and he'd tracked me down to confirm we could accommodate some extras in the house until they organise pick-ups.' The policeman shrugged the indiscretion away. 'He's a funny guy, tells a good yarn.'

Rafe towered over him. 'Maybe you are unaware of the far-reaching implications of this operation.' His mouth was grim as he glared down at the shorter man. 'If word of this gets out, many people in Australia with terrorist links will be spooked. That will precipitate violence the scale of which hasn't been seen on our shores. The federal police need twenty-four hours to pull everyone in. Do you understand what the loose lips of one idiot can do?'

'He was just making conversation.' Peter started to puff up with indignation. No doubt, Rafe thought, deciding that the big man in front of him had no real power.

'And you didn't need to repeat that in front of the local undertaker. I will be filing a report with your superior, mate.' Rafe's voice, though quiet, held menace. 'Don't go getting any ideas that just because I'm only Customs I can't make real trouble for you. I'll see you at this afternoon's debrief. Better get your explanation ready.'

His boots rang loudly on the wooden planks of the dock. He knew his anger was disproportionate to the crime of stupidity, but he didn't want to lose any more people.

One was already too many.

And telling two women who he'd come to care for such sad news would test every one of the skills he'd learnt the hard way.

Morgan opened the door and saw the answer in his face. 'Oh dear god,' she whispered. 'Gavin.'

161

She turned to Lauren, who was propped up on the bed with a cup of tea in her hands.

'Lauren . . .' Morgan's eyes filled with tears, her voice full of anguish, her soul awash with sorrow as she watched her colleague crumple. With all the composure she could muster she reached out, wrapped her arms tight around the trembling woman and rocked her as she sobbed.

She had to be strong for Lauren.

Had to be strong, had to survive.

No one knew better than she how much it hurt to lose someone you loved, how easy it was for that grief to take away your will to live, take away your ability to dream, take away your right to hope.

She knew.

Through the blurring veil of her own tears she couldn't help but watch Rafe. He looked as devastated as they were, she thought. Would he blame himself forever for something that someone else had done?

'Did you see him?' Her voice shook and clearing her throat did nothing to ease it.

Rafe nodded and she saw a flash of horror cross his face. 'I did. He's been taken to the hospital for an autopsy. They found him in fishing nets near Skardon River. It would have been quick.'

Morgan let his lie slide by, knowing there was no way he could have told that from the body, but grateful for his attempt to comfort Lauren. The fleeting expression on his face belied his words.

'Cup of tea?' She nodded at the kettle. 'It's still hot.' Lauren was quiet in her arms and she handed her another tissue from the box on the bedside table, watching Rafe's competent hands preparing the tea.

'So what happens next?'

BORDER WATCH

Rafe kept his back to her as he answered, but she saw the stiffening of his spine. 'The federal police will want to interview you, but only when you're ready. The Australian Transport Safety Bureau's been directed to talk to me initially, but they will investigate the crash site and need to talk to you to understand some more of what happened.'

'This will drag on for weeks, won't it?' Morgan ran her fingers through her hair, the dark strands falling back into place.

This time he met her gaze, the half-smile of sympathy wrenching her heart. He nodded. Weighing his words carefully, Morgan thought, looking for a reassuring answer. This time the truth was in his eyes, even as his gaze shifted to a spot on the ceiling above her.

'To make it worse, they've found a connection between your stranger, washed up on Trinity Beach, and this JI cell. The guy who interviewed you the other day?' He looked back at Morgan.

'The one with Harry who seemed to have a different agenda?' She did her best to keep her face expressionless.

'Yeah, I spoke to him the next day and he confirmed the body had been identified as a fringe member of a JI splinter group. They think he'd been found telling outsiders info he shouldn't have. Maybe a falling out between teammates. Probably dumped off a ship that left Cairns heading north to here.'

'Have they found that ship then?'

'Some of your colleagues are tracking it past Thursday Island at the moment. There's a welcoming committee once they clear the shipping lanes.'

'How big is this thing?' Lauren had managed to stem the flood of tears, though her voice still trembled.

'At least a cell in each capital city on the east coast that I know of, but there may be more the feds know about. My involvement was with the money-making arm of JI. Fundraising through illegal immigrants has become much harder for them with the new immigration laws. Drug running, in this part of the world, is easier and more lucrative.'

'So you didn't know about the terrorism angle then?' Morgan was puzzled. 'It wasn't part of your brief?'

Rafe glanced away, his face impassive. 'I found out there was more to it at a briefing in Cairns the day before we left. The feds admitted they suspected JI was bringing arms, as well as drugs, down through the top end. No one bothered to tell Customs that.' He met Morgan's steady gaze. 'No one mentioned missiles.'

'So there was no way you could have expected them to be carrying them, let alone using them.' Morgan's voice left no room for dissent, but he shook his head in denial anyway.

'It was my call to apply pressure by circling over them. Turn up the heat a little and see what got shaken out.'

'Certainly shook something out,' Lauren interjected, heat licking at her words. 'We don't blame you for what's happened so neither should you. I know it's clichéd but . . .' Her voice broke before she managed to finish her words. 'But Gavin would have approved of your choice, of what we're doing and what we helped achieve.'

She buried her face in her hands. Morgan ran a soothing hand over her friend's back. Lauren struggled for words. 'I blame the bastards who dragged him away, not you. If anyone carries blame it's me, I was the one hiding in the bushes, chicken-shit scared and hopeless.'

'And if you hadn't stayed out of sight, you'd be dead too, and that, Lauren, would be even harder for us to take.' Rafe's voice, gentle with concern, surprised Morgan. The subtle, hidden depths of him unexpectedly touched her.

'They will be charged, found guilty and locked away for life and I know, I know —' he shook his head at Lauren, 'I know that doesn't bring him back, but I will see they pay the full price.'

'You and me both then.' Lauren had cobbled together some shreds of control and blew her nose. As far as she was concerned, thought Morgan, the conversation was finished. 'So do we just sit here and wait?'

Rafe straightened up and placed his half-empty mug back on the shelf. 'You two have appointments with the doc again. You should have stayed the night in hospital anyway.'

Morgan raised a haughty eyebrow at him. 'Since you haven't even seen one, I don't think you're in a position to lecture us.'

'That's why I'm taking you there myself after breakfast.'

Lauren looked up. 'I don't think I could eat anything.'

'No,' replied Morgan. 'You won't feel like it, but you need to. Something light. I'll check with Mary in the kitchen and bring it back here. Rafe?'

'No, thanks.' He opened the door. 'I'll be back for you at nine-thirty. Stuff I need to do. Will you be okay?' He addressed the last directly to Morgan.

'Yeah, we'll be fine.' A glimmer of a smile touched her lips. 'Yesterday seems like a lifetime ago, doesn't it?'

He nodded and left them sitting on the bed.

A very long lifetime.

Without the aircraft, he didn't have access to the secure comms that he was required to use for top-level communications. The news that Abu Nadal had already left the camp would have caused panic among the security organisations and he felt very isolated without direct contact. The vessel that fired the SAM had clearly been carrying more men than they thought. Maybe they'd learnt some tricks to shield themselves from the FLIRs. Space blankets could be very effective reflectors.

A charter flight should land shortly, bringing in his team along with more equipment and members of every other department connected to Australia's security. He'd get some more answers then hopefully.

He was still seething at his conversation on the boat. By now the undertaker would have told his friends, who would be ringing their friends, and no doubt the wonderful world of the internet would spread the news faster than a raging bushfire up a gully. He'd have to explain to ASIO, the federal police and his boss why there was a leak from his side of the operation. If they'd listened to him yesterday and pulled Wiseman off the team, there wouldn't be this added complication. There was no place for that sort of incompetency in an operation this critical.

He headed over to the police accommodation house, his mouth grim. No time like the present to kick some arse, he reasoned. He was still angry enough to pin the idiot up against a wall.

'G'day, mate, you're up early after a late night.' The SERT guy who opened the door was an amiable giant and Rafe kept a pleasant smile on his face in reply.

'Yeah, looking for one of your team: Carl Wiseman. Is he around?'

The other man rolled his eyes and gestured to the rear of the house. 'Probably out pumping weights on the back veranda. It's where he usually is.'

'Cheers, can I just go through?'

'Yeah, sure. How's Morgan doing and her blond friend?' The other man's gaze sharpened when Rafe hesitated.

'As you'd expect after a crash and then losing a close friend.'

'Yeah, I heard they'd brought a body in. What happened?'

'Sorry, mate. It's all still under wraps for now. You should know that.'

BORDER WATCH

There was a hint of surprise on the other man's face. 'Yeah, but we're all on the same side, right?'

'Any leak could jeopardise other operations. We're not the only ones working on this.' Rafe's dark anger transmitted itself clearly and the SERT guy stepped back clearing the way for him.

'Okay, okay.'

Rafe felt the other man watching him as he walked through the cool house, the air-conditioning humming.

Carl was on the back deck doing bench presses with another elite police officer and didn't stop when he saw who the visitor was.

'I'll stand for him, if you like.' Rafe's tone brooked no argument and the other officer, a stringy short man, stepped aside without comment. 'And I'd like some privacy too, thanks.'

Rafe positioned himself behind the weight's cradle, not bothering to see if the other man had left. A big powerful presence could be a useful tool.

Carl continued to pump the bar, sweat dripping off him, the veins in his neck taut with the effort, his muscles straining. Tattoos covered his chest and arms, intricate designs within designs. Contemptuously, he ignored Rafe until he was ready to hang up the weights.

'Here.' One word, a command.

Rafe leant over to take the weight, but instead of lightening the load he pressed down, forcing Carl to fight against him. 'Heard of confidential briefings, Carl?' he asked softly, in complete contrast with the pressure he was exerting.

Carl just grunted, fighting to keep the bar above his neck.

'If one of my men dies because you have loose lips, I will see you charged under the anti-terrorism act. As it is, you'll be kicked out of SERT once my report hits your superior's desk.'

The veins in Carl's arms were corded with effort. 'You can't touch me,' he spat at Rafe.

Rafe leant a little harder on the weights. 'Don't bet on that, mate,' he ground out. 'And what can you tell me about a tracking device in Morgan Pentland's computer?'

He felt the slight hesitation in Carl and let the bar go. The weights shot up, almost catching him on the chin as he stepped back.

'Fuck off, arsehole. You can't touch me, you can't prove anything,' Carl snarled, lowering the weights with considerable effort to rest across his heaving chest.

Rafe smiled bleakly. 'You're off the job as of now and you'll go back to Cairns on the charter aircraft that's due in sometime soon.'

'You can't prove a fucking thing or I wouldn't still be here,' Carl growled back, arrogance in every word.

Rafe didn't bother to answer, just walked back through the house to where the other two men were watching TV. The big bear who'd let him in looked up.

'You didn't hurt him too much, did you?'

'No, but he's out of here this morning.'

The other man's grin was wolfish. 'He's had it coming for a while. Just took a man with bigger balls to show him the way.'

'Don't know about balls, but I won't have my assignments compromised by idiots.'

'Just don't judge the rest of us by his yardstick,' the little man added mildly.

'I don't. I think he needs some help out there.' He gestured to the back veranda before he let himself out.

Rafe cracked his knuckles as he walked back to his car. It felt good to be still able to intimidate a man like Carl. Did that make him as bad as him? he wondered.

Probably.

BORDER WATCH

He hadn't expected Carl to admit to bugging Morgan's computer, but the man's belligerence spoke volumes. If pressuring him made it easier to get information from him then Rafe would happily rationalise his own behaviour.

He understood what he was doing, knew how to identify that behaviour and knew why people, including himself, did rationalise their actions. The truth was sometimes too unpalatable, too unthinkable. Who wanted to admit they were capable of bullying others, capable of terrorising people, capable of killing so easily? Once you started down that slippery slope, finding level ground again could be difficult. He'd seen the depths. He knew where rock bottom lay. He understood that he never wanted to see that blackness again. Ever.

21

Morgan walked in her front door, dropped her bags on the floor, and turned the lights on, chasing away the darkness. She could hear Lauren behind her, dragging her feet up the stairs. Despite her own exhaustion she knew she needed to function, needed to focus on Lauren, needed to keep moving. They'd flown out of Weipa on the last flight of the day. The AFP's priority was to shift the men from the terrorist camp down to Cairns using the Queensland police aircraft.

Bad enough she and Lauren had to wait around so long to leave, but once they arrived in Cairns, it took Morgan a very tough half hour to convince the AFP that neither she, nor Lauren, should be put in hospital under guard. Just as she was getting ready simply to walk away, someone, somewhere in the hierarchy recognised the two women were victims now, not suspects, and intervened.

Lauren's family lived in Sydney and Morgan didn't want to let her go home alone to her empty townhouse. She insisted on keeping Lauren with her. The AFP eventually capitulated. So here they were, out at Trinity Beach, in her peaceful cottage. She didn't think she'd have any easy wins tomorrow with the ATSB or the feds.

BORDER WATCH

Car doors slammed in the street and Morgan sighed. And she hadn't won the battle about the minders. Two of them, at least, were here until they'd got the answers they needed.

'Better grab a shower now, Lauren,' she said, as her friend came in. 'I'll see if our guests want something to eat.'

'Okay, but don't cook me anything.' Lauren's voice was listless. 'Thanks,' she added.

'See how you feel later.'

'I'd rather just go to bed.' Lauren's eyes were red. 'I just want to sleep.'

Morgan knew how she felt. She picked up her bags again, flinching as her muscles protested. 'Whatever you need, Lauren. Whatever you need.' She didn't think either one of them would get much sleep.

Morgan woke to the unfamiliar sounds of strangers in her house and lay still, trying to bring her thoughts into focus. Today would be even harder than yesterday. Swinging her legs out of bed, she paused for a long moment, before she found the strength to stand up. Her body still ached, sudden movements jarring her. The best she could hope for was that they'd conduct the interviews here, in an environment that at least gave her comfort.

She got that concession and the interviews started after breakfast. By ten o'clock, Morgan was hanging onto her patience by a thread. The government departments involved in the operation seemed to have the bureaucratic knack of duplication down to an art form, she decided, as she sat with her arms crossed, describing the terrorist attack yet again. She'd told the story so many times now, she felt tempted to type up a copy and hand it out.

Common sense said it was a necessary part of the investigation process, but the strain on her, and Lauren, of telling

171

and retelling, was immense. Locked away in her grief, Lauren remained monosyllabic.

Just after eleven o'clock, Sam almost got himself arrested as he pushed his way through the garden gate. Unperturbed by the strangers, he went and sat by Lauren as if sensing the deep hurt. He rested his big head on her knee, brown eyes watching her. When one of the minders tried to shoo him away, Morgan didn't hold back with her sarcasm.

Sam stayed.

At midday, Morgan called a halt, donned her favourite apron and started cooking. No one argued. No one tried to stop her. She cooked as though her life depended on it. And perhaps her sanity did, she acknowledged, as she handed out toasted paninis to the crowd of people who now invaded her home. From her last foster mother, the only woman after her mother to encourage her, she'd picked up the coping mechanism of feeding the people around her in times of crisis.

It kept her busy, something practical that needed doing, and something she could do effortlessly, without engaging her emotions. As she loaded a tray of biscuits into the oven, she knew it was futile, that the food tasted like dust to Lauren, even to herself, but she couldn't completely control her compulsion. She knew from bitter experience that, if she stopped, and allowed herself to think, then grief might sweep away her sanity. Again. She'd clawed it back before, but this time it felt different, darker, more despairing, more powerful.

Night fell with summer-time abruptness, from bright heat to black humid darkness. The minders adjourned outside, giving the two women their first moment of peace for the day.

The knock on the door startled them both, but Sam's wagging tail was reassuring.

Morgan held her breath as she opened the door, knowing from the silhouette who stood outside. Rafe looked uncertain, fatigue greying his skin, the cut on his temple stark red in contrast.

'Rafe.'

'May I come in?'

Morgan realised she'd been staring, half blocking the door, and she stepped back. 'Of course.'

Her heartbeat steadied again to a dull thud. In the preceding forty-eight hours the axis of their relationship had tilted so dramatically she didn't know what to expect. Safety like she'd never known, never understood, never dreamt of, stood inches away from her. She felt herself sway towards him and had to pull back. Something in his expression held a warning. The boundaries, the borders were back in place. They were pilot and mission commander again. And she understood that. And understood why. The sanctuary of his arms would always be a memory when the dark pressed down.

'They've left you alone finally?' His voice was gentle with concern.

'Yes.' She led the way to the back deck, acutely aware of how different it felt between them today.

'Lauren.' He brushed his hand over the young woman's shoulder.

'Rafe.' The hand she reached out to him trembled and Morgan saw him squeeze it tight before he released it.

Morgan cleared her throat. 'So how was your day?'

'Marginally better than yours I'd guess.'

'For your sake I hope so. Do we ever get our questions answered?' Censure had crept into her voice.

'That depends.' He looked uncomfortable as he dropped into a chair, stretching out a hand to rub Sam between the ears. 'On whether it's classified or not.'

'Oh for goodness' sake,' Morgan complained. 'We've been shot down, lost a friend and been interrogated for eight hours and no one will tell us anything. I hate to sound ungrateful, but it's starting to piss me off. Aren't we part of the classified scenario?'

'And I hear you tried bribing them with homemade chocolate cake and Anzac biscuits,' Rafe replied. His weary smile dispelled some of her annoyance. 'Beats me how they didn't fold under that onslaught.'

Lauren managed a tiny snigger and Morgan gave him half a smile.

'So if I produce biscuits and cake will you fold?'

'Take more than that, Morgan.' His smile made it to his eyes this time, the creases fanning out to his temples. 'But I was wondering if Carl had made contact or tried to?'

'Carl?' Morgan narrowed her eyes. 'No, and he wouldn't want to. Why?'

'Seems he's gone AWOL. We need to find him, Morgan.'

'Why?'

'We think he may have been bugging you.'

'He planted that device in my computer? The one Gavin found?' Her voice wobbled as she said her friend's name.

'Yes. They lifted a partial print from it. He may be involved in some other shit as well. If he does contact you, we need to know.'

'You or the feds or ASIO?' Bitterness edged her words. 'I had no idea we had so many different departments involved in this operation.'

'Me first.'

'Right.' They were all silent again before Morgan got to her feet. 'Staying for dinner then?'

Rafe shook his head. 'No, thanks. I've got more to do tonight.' Pain showed itself in his involuntary wince as he pushed his chair back and followed Morgan into the kitchen.

BORDER WATCH

'How's she really doing?' he asked, jerking his head towards Lauren.

Morgan sighed. 'It's hard for her. Every conversation leads back to Gavin. It will take time for her to come to terms with losing him let alone work through the belief she abandoned him.' Her voice cracked on the last two words and she busied herself in the fridge, knowing tears were glimmering in her eyes.

'And you?' His voice came from right behind her and she turned, shutting the door and keeping the bottle of milk between them. He touched her hand and she couldn't stop the quiver that shook her.

'I'll be fine.' She kept her eyes focused on her hands so he wouldn't see the naked want in them. His white shirt clung to his chest, the skin a dark sheen under the fabric. She trembled with the strength of her craving.

'Morgan.' The one word caressed her and she recognised his own need in the rigid set of his wide rangy shoulders. The memory of that body curled around hers, the sanctuary of his embrace, the solid defence of his arms washed over her, engulfing her in a rush of emotion. She wrestled it back under control. It was inappropriate.

'Morgan.' He whispered her name this time and in it she heard not just his desire, but also his conflict.

'Don't.' She shook her head and stepped back, breaking the contact. It could never be, would never be. Too much, too late, too impossible. 'Don't.' She met his gaze this time seeing the battle in his midnight dark eyes. 'It's enough to know you care. So don't.'

He nodded his understanding, the fierce demands still in his eyes. Pain flickered across his face before he masked it.

'Did you see a doctor?' she asked, moving the conversation to safer territory.

175

His laugh was his answer and she shook her head as she turned to her oven.

'Not very bright of you. You might have internal injuries from the crash.'

'They are the least of my worries.'

'Abu Nadal?' She risked a quick look at him, gauging his reaction.

'I wondered if you'd ask.' He leant back against the kitchen bench and folded his arms, tension keeping his back straight, his face grave.

'So?' She tried one word and caught the end of his tired smile.

'So . . .' He took a deep breath then thrust his hands into his pockets. 'What do you know about Nadal?' He didn't look away, didn't blink, didn't surrender anything.

She shrugged, her hands busy slicing. 'Not a lot. Gavin perused the most-wanted lists that occasionally come up in the press. He figured we should know in case we spotted one of them. I heard you say the name just before we were hit. Had to be someone important on that boat to risk shooting us down.'

'Yeah.' Rafe nodded this time. 'It was Nadal.' She could see from the expression on his face that he'd made a difficult decision as he continued talking.

Five minutes later Morgan stood slack-jawed, '9 November is only . . .' She put the knife down on the bench, counted up the days, then stopped and looked up at him. 'If your theory's right, you only have seven days to find him and stop it.'

'Yes,' he agreed.

'And who's in charge of finding him now?'

'Oversight's with the AFP. They have more power to arrest than ASIO, but ASIO have the operatives and analysts.'

'So where do you fit in?'

He turned away as he answered, but not before she'd seen an unguarded look of regret touch his face. What the hell was going on? she wondered.

'Tidying up the loose ends from the group up the cape. A few things.'

'Like Carl?' She hesitated not sure if she wanted to hear his answer. The feeling that she'd been used by Carl had been growing in her mind since Gavin had removed the tracker from her computer.

Her mobile phone rang before he could reply. She looked at the number before she answered. Not one she recognised.

'Hi, it's Morgan.'

'Hi, it's me.' She felt the colour drain from her face and held the phone away from her mouth as she turned to Rafe without looking at him. 'Excuse me a mo. Just need to take this call.'

She walked out the front door, her heels striking a staccato rhythm on the wooden floor, leaving Rafe frowning behind her.

'What the hell do you want now?'

'Are you okay?' Concern rasped in the deep voice, then a slight hesitation. 'I heard your plane crashed.'

'I can't talk about it. Where are you?' Morgan didn't want to hear this, didn't want this conversation, didn't want him close.

'It's all right. I'm not coming near you. I just wanted to make sure you were safe. The report said you were in hospital, but no one would tell me anything when I rang.' Morgan thought she heard a quiver in the voice.

'Why would you care?'

'Morgan.' The man's tone was pleading. 'Don't, please. Don't hang up on me. I'm trying here. I know it's been hard on you. I know I should have done more but —'

'But fucking nothing,' Morgan snapped, giving in to an irrational surge of anger. She didn't want to care. 'I owe you nothing so just leave me alone.' She closed her phone, holding it up to her cheek as she breathed in, feeling a rising tsunami of grief overpowering her, swamping her. The debilitating tide left her legs shaking, her hands trembling. Why? Why did her brother want to claim a place in her heart now? Now, when she had no strength left.

The call from Patrick had been the final stroke that severed her tenuous hold on her emotions. The air in her lungs burnt with each harsh sob, tears left wet tracks down her cheeks. She knew she couldn't face anyone, let alone Rafe, like this. Her feet stumbled as she made her way down the stairs and out into the darkness of the street. She lowered herself to the footpath, pressing her back against a pole. 'Why now?' she whispered to the velvet night.

In the kitchen, Rafe frowned. Who the hell was that? he wondered. He hadn't missed the colour draining from her face. Wiseman? The phone tap would pick it up anyway, even if she didn't tell him.

He fiddled with the kitchen knife she'd discarded. His instincts couldn't be wrong. Not this time. For five minutes he stewed over it before finally following her out the door.

Standing in the middle of the street the silence surrounded him. The smell of warm bitumen, the whiff of meat on a barbeque and the pungent odour of tropical decay saturated the air. The pools of light under each lamp-post didn't quite intersect and he peered into the dark patches between looking for her.

She'd disappeared.

Seven o'clock. The hands on his watch glowed as he watched the second hand tick round. Had she gone to meet the caller? What the hell was going on now? Had she run from him?

He knew he hadn't misread the look in her eyes. He'd seen the conflict, felt her tremble when he touched her. The barriers between them had been literally blown apart and yet . . . And yet he still hadn't told her the truth. Even now. When would he ever find the courage to tell her she'd been a suspect, part of the operation? Was that what this was about? Had she found out?

Just as he turned to go back into the house, he heard a muffled, snuffling sound. In the darkness, sitting on the kerb Morgan had merged into the night. He could see the distress in the bowed head and the rigid arms wrapped tightly around her legs, pressing them against her chest.

Without a word he sat next to her, feeling the heat from her body across the tiny gap. Each intake of breath rattled a tiny sob from her. Each intake of breath ripped a little deeper into his heart. Each intake of breath rammed home how inadequate he felt in the face of such powerful grief. Rammed home how little he had to offer her. Rammed home how overwhelming the urge, the need, the desire to touch her had become.

As the storm gradually subsided, he could see her struggle to unlock her arms and straighten her shoulders. He watched her regain her composure, wipe her face on her sleeve and dig a tissue from her pocket.

Still he stayed silent. There were no words he could offer.

When she turned to him in the shadows he couldn't see the expression on her face.

'Thanks.' Her voice croaked and she tried again. 'Thank you.'

He could only nod. When all this was over there could only be truth between them. Until then . . .

She scrambled to her feet and cleared her throat, her voice husky. 'We'd better go in.'

'Yeah. I'm sorry about this, Morgan, but we need to find Carl. Anything you can tell me might be vital.' He tried to read her face in the low light.

'Yep, right.' She stood looking down at him, the anguish in her palpable. Then she gave a decisive nod. 'Let's do it.'

For an hour and a half they sat on her lounge and sifted through her year-long relationship with the policeman. He could see only honesty in her face as her words came out flat, emotionless. The cost must have been huge, but she made no attempt to seek pity or comfort or escape from his questions. None of her answers rang alarm bells, but he kept on tapping the keys on his laptop. He had to. He'd sift through it later.

Lauren came in from the back deck, her laptop under her arm. 'Rafe?'

He looked up, surprised by her interruption and the sharpness in her tone. 'Yeah?'

'Morgan needs to eat and sleep. She can't do any more. Look at her.'

Morgan's hands lay limp in her lap, shoulders hunched, fatigue in the taut pale skin across her cheekbones.

'I'm fine,' Morgan said, waving away the younger woman's objections. 'I'm fine,' she repeated, the denial dropping a note. 'And we need to find him, Lauren.'

'So let them look a little harder. You need to sleep.' Lauren crossed her arms and turned to Rafe. 'She cooked like a madwoman all day and answered every question they threw at her, even when they insinuated it was her fault we got shot down. And she still found time to keep me sane, so now it's my turn to look after her. I've listened to you grilling her for the last hour and a half. Enough. She needs to sleep. Come back in the morning.'

Rafe closed the lid on his laptop, acknowledging she was right. They were getting nowhere. Maybe he could spot something himself from his notes.

BORDER WATCH

He stood up. 'I'll come back tomorrow. If you think of anything, Morgan, phone or at least write it down.'

'Right.' The plum-coloured bruising around her eyes screamed exhaustion, but she hauled herself to her feet and followed him out the door.

'That call before on my mobile?' She paused as he clicked the remote on the car and the alarm cheeped. He heard barely disguised despair in her voice as she continued. 'It was my brother, Patrick. I don't think it's relevant, but you should know he's only been in contact with me for a couple of months. Ricky Pentland. Look him up.'

'Patrick Pentland?'

'Ricky, I think. He stopped using Patrick a long time ago.'

'Right.' He filed it away. 'I'll see you tomorrow.' Resisting the urge to touch her proved harder than he thought possible. He slammed the car door, a loud thump in the quiet street.

As he drove down the hill, she cut a forlorn figure in his rear-vision mirror, arms still wrapped around her body, face turned skywards. So her brother had sparked the emotional meltdown. One less question he'd be coming back tomorrow to try to resolve. So many others sat heavily on him still. When would he be able to talk to her without lies? And when he did, would she believe him, trust him again after he explained it all? In less than seven days' time it would be over one way or the other.

Morgan waited outside until the pounding of her heart subsided. Rafe had sat beside her, offered her the comfort of his presence then let her draw herself back from the edge without judgement. It unnerved her. She'd needed strength and it had been there in his broad shoulders and silent acceptance. God, but she wanted him in ways she'd never before imagined.

Lauren had taken over where she left off with the kitchen knife.

'He said he'd drop in tomorrow.'

'Dinner'll be ready in twenty,' Lauren responded with an extra vicious slap of the blade.

'It's okay, Lauren. It's what he has to do.'

Lauren swung around to glare at Morgan. 'Bullshit. They're treating you like you're responsible. You're not. They are.'

'Lauren . . .' Morgan did her best to keep her voice level. Agreeing with Lauren wouldn't make it easier to bear.

'You did the best you could. I heard what Rafe told you in the kitchen. They're the ones who lost track of Carl and Abu Nadal. Not you, not me, not Gavin. It's their intelligence gathering that failed. They need to fix it.'

'It's okay. Really.'

'It's not okay. You two should be lovers not adversaries. Instead . . .' She burst into tears, pushing the cutting board away from her. 'Oh dear god, when will it end?'

'I know, love.' Morgan rocked her young friend, rubbing soothing circles across her shoulders, understanding the depth of the girl's despair. 'I know.'

Later, as she spat toothpaste into the hand basin, Morgan caught sight of her face and straightened, smiling cynically at her reflection.

How easy it was to be strong for other people and how very hard to ensure her own shaky grip didn't slip. Would there ever be a time when she could lean a little, depend on someone else? Would there be a time when she allowed that to happen, let down her guard and opened up the borders of her heart? Too late, she told the woman in the mirror. Far too late.

22

Thommo greeted her from up the sand dune as she shuffled, still aching, down the beach the next morning at a half-pace jog, Sam barely bothering to run to stay with her.

'Hey, Morgan.' He hailed her from his plastic patio chair perched under a coconut palm. 'You all right?'

She stopped, hands on her hips. 'And back at you, Thommo. Where've you been?' Her sides were heaving from the effort of running. 'We've been looking for you.'

'The cops have, you mean,' he answered sourly, patting the spare chair next to him. 'I didn't see nothin', but they don't believe people like me.' He hawked and spat on the ground beside him. 'Druggie no-hoper, they reckon. Interferin' pigs they are.'

'I looked for you that morning and couldn't see you.'

Thommo eyed her shrewdly and Morgan wondered for the umpteenth time just where this strange man had come from originally. 'I saw you. I saw you throw up.' He cackled with laughter, but she wasn't offended.

'Thanks for your help, mate.' She didn't try to hide the amused sarcasm.

'No worries, mate.' He clapped his hands in childlike amusement, making Morgan smile with him.

'Did they give you counsellin'?' He leant forwards, suddenly serious. 'It's hard the first time. I know. You have nightmares for months. It's okay.' He nodded at her. 'It's normal. Psychiatrists can be good for some people.' He fell silent as tears welled in Morgan's eyes before she could blink them away. 'Hey, love. I didn't mean nothin'. You're okay.'

'It's not the body, Thommo, it's . . .' She brushed at the tears, not sure what had started them. The concern in Thommo's eyes had unsettled her and the irony of being analysed by an unemployed vagrant with no material possessions nor a roof over his head did not escape her.

She sighed. Thommo didn't read papers or have a TV in his little humpy, so the events of the week would have passed him by. 'Just some other stuff that's gone on. No biggie.'

'Yeah, must have been a shit to prang an aircraft.' Thommo's answer was sly as he watched her reaction with laughing eyes, though she judged the humour to be complicit with her, not directed at her.

She held her peace, knowing he loved to needle, always looking for a rise. 'So what other gossip have you heard?'

'That your jerk of a boyfriend finally got caught and you threw 'im out. I'm not sorry. He was never good enough for you.'

'Gee, thanks for telling me,' she retorted, wondering how her private life had become public knowledge. Reg must have gossiped with Gus, who could have told Thommo.

'He wasn't. He'd marked you. I saw 'im. You never did, not when he first started hangin' round.'

'Marked me?' She frowned at him. 'You're wrong.'

'Marked you, watched you, picked you, before you even knew he was there.'

'Mate,' she warned him. 'I met him in the pub. I'd never seen him before then.'

'Maybe not, but he'd seen you 'cause I'd seen 'im.' He cackled at his own brilliance. 'Dumb arse even asked me who you were. I didn't tell 'im. I hate blokes like that, think their fists rule. Fuckin' thug.' He spat again, putting real distaste into it. 'Not good enough for you.'

'Well . . .' Morgan drew the syllable out. 'He's history now. Just another bad dream.'

'You have too many of those, girlie. Not right. You see someone. Gotta go.' He stood up suddenly. 'He fought, you know. Big fight, lots of swearing. I seen 'em, but I'm not tellin' anyone I seen 'em.' He spun away and stomped up the dune towards the thicker scrub and his little humpy. Just before he disappeared through his makeshift door he stopped again. 'I heard 'em, I know,' he yelled down at her, shaking his fist. 'I heard the gun.'

Morgan stared after him, bemused by the conversation. Had Carl been following her before she met him? She replayed their first meeting in the pub, looking for inconsistencies.

She whistled Sam and started walking to the end of the beach, sifting through her memory. It was possible he'd engineered the meeting. He'd bumped into her as she turned from the bar with her hands full of drinks, spilling half of them. He'd offered to buy fresh ones. She'd been taken by his blue eyes and easy smile and invited him to join them. That was it.

She mulled it over all the way home as her jagged breathing stretched her damaged ribs. Lauren had left a note to say she'd gone out and would be back by eleven. Rafe had phoned and would drop by early.

Morgan contemplated the scrap of paper. It was the old Lauren's style to simply disappear and leave her and Rafe alone.

She pinned her hair back and tied an apron around her waist. No point in worrying. What would be would be. She needed to talk to Rafe about Carl anyway. If Thommo was right about this then he'd seen the murder actually happen. And all the other stories he told her about flashing lights and boats in the night might be true too.

Rafe parked outside the house. Guilt prickled his conscience as he picked up the delicate orchid, dwarfing it with his hands.

Too late now to back out, he told himself. Just do it. Maybe it would have been easier to go with a basic interrogation instead of exploiting what lay unacknowledged between them. But they were running out of options with a week until the deadline. They hadn't found Wiseman and they hadn't found Nadal. If Morgan could unlock even part of that puzzle this was worth it. However he had to engineer it.

His breath hitched in his throat when she opened the door. Unsettled, he held out the orchid. 'For you. I thought you needed some pink in your garden.'

Her smile was almost shy as she took the plant. 'Thanks.' She turned to lead the way inside. 'Come in, Lauren's out, but she can't be far off.'

'How is she today? A little less feisty?' Rafe settled himself on a stool, appreciating the smells from the rangetop.

Morgan rested her hands on the bench. 'She's doing okay, I think. Her mum and dad have been overseas on business. They get back to Sydney in a couple of days and they'll fly up to Cairns then. Two of her brothers should be here tomorrow at the latest. That will help.' Her smile was sad. 'There're flashes of the old Lauren. Last night's defence of me.' She shrugged. 'But she's got a long road to travel yet.'

She turned back to the stove. 'Gavin was the first person close to her to die. Grandparents and elderly friends are bad enough, but someone that young? Someone she genuinely loved? Too hard, way too hard.' He knew from the thickening of her voice that she was on the verge of tears.

'So the feds have wrapped up all the sites they'd marked out. I know there are lawyers all over the country trying to free their clients, but the terrorism laws are pretty tight.' He carried on talking about the case, giving her time to regroup. He had too much respect to offer her sympathy when she didn't ask for it, no matter that he would have taken any easy excuse to draw her close against him and touch his lips to hers.

She placed a mug of coffee on the counter and slid the milk and sugar across to him.

'And Carl?' She kept her eyes down.

'Nothing.'

'Right.' Her chest rose and fell with a deep breath. 'I saw Thommo this morning and he had an interesting theory.'

Rafe's phone rang and he peered at the caller ID as he asked, 'Thommo?'

'The guy who lives at the end of the beach. I told you he was missing when I found the body.'

'Of course. You said he's got a humpy down the end of the beach?' He let the call go through to voicemail. This was more important.

Morgan nodded. 'That's him. He was hiding that morning, in case the police made trouble for him. He had a lot on his mind when he spoke to me and it was hard to follow his train of thought.' She took a pot off the stove and continued, 'He claimed that he'd seen Carl hanging around before I met him. Thommo decided he was casing me out. At least that's what I think he was trying to say.' She frowned and Rafe went very still. 'I'm hoping he's just having one of his delusional phases . . .' She shrugged. 'Though for his sake I hope not. He gets really scared and hides for days at a time. Doesn't eat,

187

dehydrates, hears voices in his head, the whole box and dice. It's really sad to watch.'

'You've seen him like this before?' Rafe put his coffee cup down.

'Yeah, a couple of times now. I go fish him out and take him to the doctor, provided I can find him. He's harmless and I can't let him starve, can I?'

'No, you can't. Plenty of others would.' He turned the full force of his dark eyes on her, making her squirm a little in her seat as he waited for her to go on.

'Yeah, well, we all travel our own roads. Not my place to ask how he got so far off the beaten track.'

She paused again, tucking her hair behind her ear and he prompted her.

'So?'

'So there was something else he said at the end as he walked away. "There was a fight, a big fight, I seen them but I'm not telling." His words not mine. Then he yelled back from his humpy, "I heard the gun." The only sense I can make of that is that he saw someone fighting on the beach and he thinks that one of them turned up floating in the water.'

'And who do think that was?'

'He was talking about Carl just before he followed that tangent off into the wilderness and I don't know . . .' She looked at him, confusion in her eyes. 'What if he's right and Carl did fight on the beach? What if he actually shot a man and dumped him in the water? It's so far out of left field it's unbelievable, but . . .'

Rafe regarded her calmly, waiting for her to finish.

'But he may have engineered our first meeting. Bumped into me at the pub and then joined us for a drink. I'd never questioned it before, but it would have been easy to do.'

'And now Wiseman's missing.'

'Lauren and Gavin couldn't stand him.' She looked down at her mug. 'You probably think I'm an idiot for going out with him.' She didn't meet his eyes. A wash of pink stained her cheeks.

'I think men like Wiseman are very good at targeting vulnerable people who are weaker than them. He misjudged you.'

'Thanks, I think.' She turned away again. 'Have you had breakfast? I can scramble some eggs. Another cup of coffee?'

'Thanks, but I've eaten already.' His gaze skimmed down her body, remembering again her warmth cuddled close against him, the soft touch of her skin and the steady beat of her heart. And to cover the wave of desire he tried some humour.

'But you can try bribing me with some Anzac biscuits if the guys didn't eat them all yesterday.'

'There are a couple left,' she laughed. 'Lauren's favourite. I made heaps.'

'So, back to Wiseman again.'

She pushed a glass jar half full of caramel-coloured biscuits across the counter. 'Back to Carl.'

'Any more ideas about where he might go?'

Morgan pursed her lips, a frown creasing her forehead. 'You never realise how little you know someone until you get asked these sorts of questions. I don't know. Do you think Thommo's right about him?'

'It's possible.' His phone rang again. 'Sorry,' he apologised, looking at the number. 'I need to take this one.' He went outside to answer it.

Morgan tidied their cups away, watching Rafe pace across her small front veranda. Everything about him screamed anger and worry. She appreciated the approach he'd taken this morning, but she knew an interrogation when she saw one. Just like last night had been. Her gaze stopped momentarily on the pale pink orchid. He may have come bearing gifts, but he came for answers. No point deluding herself. It certainly wasn't all about her. It was all about Carl.

She pulled the tea towel from its rack and went to load the washing machine, still wrestling with her thoughts. Maybe she should talk to Thommo again about the flashing lights. Maybe she should have mentioned them to the investigators. Maybe . . .

'Morgan, I've got to go. I'm needed back at the office.'

'Okay.' She turned to look at him.

'If you think of anything, no matter how small, call me. We've got just over six days, Morgan. We're running out of time.' His tone was brusque, but she saw worry in his eyes and something else that unnerved her, left her a little breathless.

'Six days.' She nodded, recognising the gravity of the situation. 'If I think of anything, I'll call.'

23

Silently, for such a big man, Woomera made his way through the scrub. His dark clothing and cap, pulled low, made him virtually invisible in the dark. His footsteps were soundless on the compact sand.

There was no light ahead of him, but he knew what he was looking for.

Lucky he had good contacts in the police and found out early enough they'd interviewed the derelict. If they believed Thommo, they'd be asking more awkward questions. Stupid fool of a tramp was only going to get what he deserved. Telling stories. He was a nutter anyway. People like him should be locked up. And they would be, if it wasn't for bleeding hearts bleating about putting the mentally ill back into society. Part of what was wrong with western democracies really. Interfering politicians made excuses for all sorts of excessive behaviour and never took any hard stands.

But he was different. He'd known that early on. High IQ, borderline genius, but he got his kicks from the dark side of life. The double life of an ASIS agent had suited him for a while until he found his god.

Money.

The lure of two pay cheques instead of one proved irresistible. So here he was, cleaning up the loose ends before he changed his identity one last time.

The big shoulders moved in readiness under his dark jacket, pumped-up muscles straining the fabric. The bottle of fire-lighter fluid sat comfortably in his pocket alongside a cigarette lighter.

Without a sound, he lifted the flap of towelling hung as a door and peered into the dark interior, his eyes adjusting to the lack of light. He could barely make out the huddled shape sleeping in the middle of the floor.

Silly bastard would be drunk or tripping at this time of night. He'd never wake up. Just a vagrant burnt to death.

Woomera laid his trail carefully, circling the bark humpy so there could be no escape. The leaves and grasses were tinder dry. The monsoon rains hadn't come this far south yet. An accident waiting to happen.

The first touch of flame from the lighter started the ring burning. It crept around the little shack and began the inexorable climb up the paperbark walls. Tea-tree burnt so well.

He waited twenty metres away. No human sound came from the funeral pyre. No burning figure struggled to free itself from the fiery embrace.

Hiding in the shadows, Woomera felt cheated. He shrugged. Probably best if it was a clean kill anyway; less chance of questions being asked.

As he made his way back along the waterline he tucked his cap into his pocket and undid his top buttons. Just a lonely man out for a walk on the beach.

The glow of the fire was hidden from the road. The only person who might notice was the old lady who lived on the slope above the humpy. Not likely she'd be up this late, let alone looking out the wide front windows of her magnificent house.

He took one last look and spat the taste from his mouth, grinning contentedly. A good night's work, mate, he congratulated himself. Only Morgan left to warn off and that shouldn't be too hard. He'd think of something.

She'd made it more difficult for him to keep an eye on the operation. Still, Morgan didn't deserve to die for being gullible. Plenty of other women had fallen for his charm. He'd been trained to charm, and he was good at it. And Morgan was different. He'd known that from the start. It was the reason he'd had to dominate her sometimes, or at least try to. A small corner of him admired her resilience, envied her strength, and therefore wanted to destroy those very same qualities.

Maybe he'd try messing with her head a bit. See if he could prod her down the road to depression. With her family history, it shouldn't be too hard to do, though she was a tough one. Should have been damaged goods, but she wasn't. Pity really, but that's life, he decided, pushing aside an unfamiliar twinge of regret. That's life and there was no room for introspection.

24

Morgan was relieved to find twenty-four hours made a world of difference to her injuries. She managed to run down the hill, round the corner and along the beachfront before she was forced back to a walk.

Larry had just arrived to clean the barbeques. He hailed her as she got closer.

'Morning, love. I think there's been a fire down Taylors way last night.' He motioned towards the house at the end of the road.

'Bad?'

'Dunno? But I'll check as soon as I'm done here. I've phoned the fire brigade and I'll drop by Smithfield on the way to Yorkeys and tell the cops.'

'Seen Thommo this morning?' she asked.

'No.' Larry shook his head. 'Not yet.'

'Oh no!' Morgan started to run, Sam bounding to catch up. Dread clutched at her stomach and she fought it off, pushing her legs to pump faster in the soft sand.

She faltered as she got closer, the smell of burning cloying.

Thommo's humpy was gone.

Just a pile of ash and charred branches.

Her hand went to her throat, feeling the tightness.

BORDER WATCH

A section of bush had been burnt out to the north of the house on the hill and it looked as though low scrub was still burning on the hillside.

'Thommo!' she called, staying clear of the campsite. 'Thommo, can you hear me?' On the vast expanse of beach her voice barely made a sound and she felt futile anger welling up inside her.

Sam sniffed the air and Morgan stopped to do the same. 'Don't they say burning human remains stink, Sam?' She sniffed again. 'In that case, Thommo got out, because this just smells like a bushfire.'

The ashes were still warm, but there was nothing left intact. She was no fire expert, but it looked like a perfect circle around the site where the humpy had stood.

For the second time on this beach, she heard sirens on the breeze and cocked her head to listen.

Fire engine this time. Heading up the road to the top of the cliff. That was quick.

Thommo would have gone bush again for sure. Had he seen something the night the guy got shot? If so, that would make this payback.

Morgan puzzled over what had happened as she ate breakfast, willing Lauren to wake up so she could talk it over with someone. She resisted the urge to pick up the phone and ring Rafe. What did she have to tell him? He had enough problems trying to track down Nadal and Carl.

Had Thommo accidentally burnt his humpy down or was someone trying to warn him off? Did it have something to do with the body on the beach and the fight Thommo said he saw? Rafe had seemed to take note when she'd mentioned it yesterday, but he hadn't dug any deeper. Maybe she was just being fanciful.

195

She filled the sink with soapy water, suddenly feeling the need to go back to work. The more time off she had, the more her thoughts crowded in on her.

The chief pilot at Border Watch had outlined what she and Lauren would have to do to get back in the air. A simulator session in Sydney and a line flight with a check captain. Then, if they and the checkie were both happy, back into it. No pressure though, and if it was all too much that was fine too.

She was grateful for their support, but she understood now why when children fell off horses and bicycles it was important to put them straight back on.

Lauren finally emerged, looking refreshed, just before ten o'clock. She had her duffle bag over her shoulder.

Morgan was sitting on her lounge contemplating the many unanswered questions jostling for attention in her mind.

'Morning, Morgan. I need to swap some clothes at my place. Anything you need from town?'

'No thanks, Lauren. You're looking good.'

'Yeah, I know.' Lauren plopped into the chair opposite her. 'I've wallowed for long enough. Yesterday's run to the hairdresser's was probably a little premature but I'm getting there.' She rummaged in her bag for keys. 'And I need to pack for the trip to Brisbane. If it's okay with you, I'll sleep at my place tonight. Probably spend a couple of days in Brissie after the . . .' Her words faltered. She tried again. 'After Gavin's funeral.' She cut the last word short and rushed on. 'Mum and Dad are going to fly from Sydney straight to Brisbane. I'll see them then. I think I convinced my brothers to stay home for now. If they do turn up today, they can sleep at my place.'

Well done, thought Morgan, gutsy girl. You've managed to say the word *funeral*. 'That's fine. As long as you need, there's always a spare bed here.'

BORDER WATCH

Lauren rolled her eyes. 'And I'm not going to sleep with ear plugs in to stop the sounds of someone else's fun disturbing my sleep.'

Morgan gave a rare giggle. 'I wouldn't do that to you either. There is no one lining up to park their shoes under my bed.'

'Yeah, right. I saw the look on Rafe's face the other night before he turned into the interrogator from hell, but hey, hey, hey . . .' She held up her hand to forestall Morgan's protest. 'I'll let you have your virginal little fantasies. My lips are sealed.' She stopped with the door half open. 'He's a good man, Morgan. You deserve that.' She was gone with a swirl of blond hair and flashes of long tanned legs.

The French doors closed with a tiny clunk before Morgan could reply.

The silence rolled on for a moment. Morgan felt the blood heating her face, smelt the mangoes ripening in the bowl on her kitchen bench, saw the bright heads of the wild gingers outside her window waft in a tiny breeze, and knew she was alive. Whatever else she took from the last week she knew her senses were awake again in a way they may never have been since she outgrew her ankle socks and Barbie dolls and her family had fractured around her.

Commander Rafe would have a place in her heart whether he wanted to claim it or not. And Patrick, the brother she'd adored for twelve years and mourned for another twenty, would have a place there too. And instead of that thought shackling her, burdening her down with an obligation to reciprocate, it released her. She managed a smile and that gave her renewed determination to find some answers. She jotted down a list of possibilities and grabbed her car keys. Sitting around wasn't going to solve anything. Doing something positive had to be better than worrying at home. Buoyed with new enthusiasm she drove down the hill feeling almost optimistic.

197

Helene Young

★ ★ ★

Tired, frustrated and still without answers as the sun passed
the high point and started its steady descent towards Saddle
Mountain, Morgan pushed open her door. Nothing.

In three hours of searching she'd achieved nothing. She'd
scoured all Thommo's usual haunts and not found even a hint
of his whereabouts. No one had seen him. That only left the
hilltop ruin and she didn't have the energy to check that out
today. It would have to wait until tomorrow. And Carl? She
hadn't tried all that hard to track him down. He could look
after himself, and surely the police would find him more easily
than she could.

The red LED was flashing on her answering machine and
she hit the play button as she walked past. It beeped to begin
its replay, but she didn't hear a voice. She backed up to the
machine and pressed play again, turning up the volume. This
time she could hear heavy breathing that finished with a
menacing chuckle. It sounded like the call she'd missed this
morning on her mobile, which had gone through to voicemail. She'd dismissed that one as a wrong number. Maybe it
wasn't.

'Sicko,' she said, hitting the delete button. 'Who the hell
would bother doing that?'

The second message was similar, but she hesitated before
she erased it. Maybe she should keep it, tell the police? She
couldn't make up her mind, so she saved it, then continued
opening up the house.

She found the body of the sunbird chick on her back deck
as soon as she opened the French doors, letting the accumu-
lated heat flow out of the still house. She gathered it into her
hands. It felt warm and there was no sign of injury. The two
adult birds, and the second chick, were cheeping in the bushes,

198

BORDER WATCH

outrage in the pitch and intensity of their cries. Morgan stroked a finger down its tiny body, sad that it had come so far and hadn't made it.

She wrapped it up in newspaper and hauled her shovel out of the shed. The parents flew around her as if they knew she had their chick. And probably they did, she guessed. The sweet little birds had been nesting in her garden when she'd bought the house and every plant she'd added had flowers to give them food. They were her good-luck charms.

The oppressive heat stuck her shirt to her back as she finished shovelling. The water from the hose came out warm and she grimaced as she washed the dirt off her hands. A swim might revive her. The pool sparkled in the bright sunlight, pale blue and refreshing. She walked around to check the skimmer box for leaves from the overhanging gum trees. The scream left her throat before she could stop it.

A baby possum, obviously dead, lay curled up in the basket. Squeamish, she pulled the whole container out just as Reg spoke from the side gate.

'You all right?'

'Yeah, sorry about that. There's a dead possum in the skimmer.'

'Oh bugger.' Reg and Sam came into the yard, the big dog bounding over to the pool fence, adoration in his brown eyes.

Reg gestured at the dog. 'He was pretty upset earlier today. 'Bout ten, ten-thirty, not long after you went out. I couldn't see anything, but he sat by the gate and growled for an hour or so. Eventually, I let him through and he shot off to the front of the block. Hope he didn't scare the possum into jumping into the pool.'

Morgan shook her head. 'I doubt it. He only chases butcher-birds and magpies.' She looked around the garden. 'I wonder if someone was here. There was a dead sunbird on my deck as well.'

'Maybe. Sam doesn't normally bark during the day.' Reg peered at his young neighbour. 'No one in their right mind would kill animals and leave them for you to find, though.'

'Someone's left heavy breathing on my answering machine and voicemail, so who knows?'

'No kidding? That's disgusting.' Reg sounded outraged. 'Get the cops. You don't have to put up with that.'

Morgan sighed. 'Maybe it was a wrong number.'

'And maybe it's not.' Reg gingerly picked the skimmer basket up, grimacing with distaste.

'Here, I'll fix that, Reg.'

'No worries, love. I'll dig a big hole in the corner near the compost. He'll end up being recycled in ten years' time.'

Morgan knew he was trying to make light of it, but all she felt was the weight of grief pressing down on her again. The morning's optimism seemed misplaced, premature.

'I'll be right.' She held her hand out, wanting to do something, but not wanting to confront the thought her pool had been filtered through a baby possum.

'You might be, but you don't have to be. I'm doing it. Come on, Sam.' Reg shuffled back through the gate, leaving Morgan standing morosely outside the pool fence.

She couldn't face the pool and she knew the stinger net at the beach was closed after irikanji were found in the daily drags. The tiny marine stingers, smaller than her thumbnail, could inflict an immensely painful sting that could kill. It wasn't worth the risk.

She poured a glass of cold water, noticing as she did that her flyscreen on the side window was askew.

Frowning she walked outside to refit it and stopped dead in her tracks. The fleshy stems of the wild ginger growing up against the house had been disturbed. She bent and looked closely at the plants. Several had been squashed flat, their stems broken underneath a foot.

She stood up, goose bumps of alarm spreading up her arms. Someone had stood here and prised her flyscreen off. The plants were green, the moisture still in their leaves, so it couldn't have been all that long ago.

'Sam, my friend, I wish you'd managed to catch the bastard,' she muttered. She left everything as it was and hurried next door to Reg.

She'd hardly got into the explanation before he handed her the phone. 'Ring the cops.'

'What the hell do I say to them? I think someone pulled my flyscreen out? Do you think they'll actually bother to investigate that?'

'When you tell them the intruder left a calling card — a sunbird dead on your deck for no apparent reason and possum with its throat slit — they will.'

'Someone *did* kill the possum and dump it in my pool?' Morgan was horrified.

'Know a bit about injuries, love. Its poor little throat had been opened up with a very sharp blade. I wasn't going to tell you; thought maybe it was a prank. But someone breaking into your place?' He shook his head. 'Sam can stay with you for a while.' The dog thumped his tail, recognising his name. 'There's a nutter out there.'

She dialled Harry's number and got through to his voicemail. She left a message then handed the phone back to Reg. 'Thanks. Guess I'll go and see if anything else has been touched.'

'You want me to come with you?'

'Thanks, Reg, but I'll be right.'

He pointed at the giant red dog. 'Take Sam for company anyway. Let me know if you need me.'

201

'Thanks, I will.'

She stood inside her front door and scanned the lounge room, looking for anything out of place. Everything seemed fine. Walking into the kitchen, her eyes went straight to the knife block, but nothing was missing. Indeed, nothing had been taken that she could see. Her artworks were still there, the sound system, TV, computer. She walked into the bedroom where her suitcase lay on her new bed and looked around.

It was a simple room with little clutter and nothing seemed to be any different. But as she turned to go she noticed that the wardrobe door was slightly ajar. She pulled it open and recoiled with a gasp. Her clothes had been slashed.

She turned to her drawers, jerking them open, but nothing there was damaged. She couldn't tell if anything had been taken; she wouldn't necessarily miss something until she went to wear it.

Her skin crawled. Her private sanctuary had been despoiled.

Her phone rang and she raced back into the kitchen to answer it, glancing at the caller ID.

Private number.

She stopped with her finger poised over the button, waiting for the answering machine to pick it up.

'Hi, Morgan, Harry here. Sorry I missed you. You sounded upset, ring me back.' She shut the machine off and grabbed the receiver.

'Harry? Harry, it's me. Sorry.' She ran a shaky hand through her hair. 'Someone's broken into my house. All the clothes in my wardrobe have been slashed, cut to ribbons. And they left a dead possum in my pool.' She knew her voice was shaking but it wouldn't stop.

'Go next door to your neighbours. I'll be there soon. Go. Now. Morgan?'

'I hear you. I'm okay.'

BORDER WATCH

'Morgan, just hang up and go.'

'Okay, okay.' She raised a hand in resignation and hung up. 'What the hell is happening to me?' she wondered out loud as Sam followed her from room to room. Nothing else seemed to have been touched, but she couldn't shake the image of a stranger ferreting through her things.

As she pushed open Reg's gate, her eyes narrowed. Was her brother sick or desperate enough to come back to Cairns and do something like this? He wanted money, so it made no sense since nothing was missing. She couldn't believe Ricky would be that violent. He'd always been soft, too soft. Maybe it was Carl being malicious? That she could imagine.

'Hey, Reg, sorry to butt in again.'

'No trouble, girlie,' he called from the back of the house. 'Come in, come in.'

Reg's house was as old as Morgan's, but he and Elaine had lived there for thirty years and decorating wasn't a high priority. The crocheted doilies that protected the faded sofa needed a wash, the floorboards were worn to the pattern of many foot-steps. The paint, which had once been a delicate yellow, had faded to off-white with time yet, like Morgan's home, the house was welcoming.

'Harry's coming out.'

'Good, good,' Reg said. 'Coffee? I'm just making one.'

'That'd be lovely.' She followed him into the kitchen. 'Someone did break in.'

'Oh, love, did they steal much?'

'Just my bloody peace of mind. And trashed my clothes in the wardrobe.'

'What do you mean?' He'd stopped spooning coffee into the cups.

'You said the possum's throat was cut?'

He nodded, looking uncomfortable. 'Yeah.'

203

'Probably used the same knife on all my clothes.' She said it matter-of-factly, but her voice caught on the last word and her face crumpled.

She waved him away. 'It's okay, I'm okay.' She took a deep breath and sniffed away the threatening tears. 'It's all right. They weren't even clothes I liked anymore, but . . .'

'But some bastard's been in your house. Sit down, love. I'll bring the coffee over.'

Sam nuzzled his big head hard into her knee. His soft fur was familiar and steadying under her fingers, but Morgan's knees still trembled as she perched on the edge of the sofa.

'Have you seen anyone hanging around at all?' She took the mug Reg held out to her, her face composed again.

Reg shook his head. 'Nope, no one who didn't belong here, anyway.'

'No guy who looked like me?'

Reg's eyes narrowed. 'How like you?'

She shrugged. 'Dark hair, grey eyes, slim build. Scruffy.'

'And that would be . . . ?' Reg let the question hang.

'My brother. Patrick. I haven't seen him in years and he called me a couple of months ago after a free handout.'

'Oh.' Reg's eyes dropped to the red dog sitting between them. 'Sorry, love.'

'No need. It's my problem, I'll fix it. Just wondered if he'd been here before and I didn't know about it.'

'I know I'm a nosy old bastard, but I'm in the garden a lot of the time and unless he came to the back of the house I might have missed him.'

'Maybe I'm just jumping to conclusions anyway. He's supposed to be in Sydney with his family . . .' She trailed off as she sipped the coffee.

'Did you find Thommo?' Reg asked, easing his stiff frame down onto the chair next to her.

BORDER WATCH

'No, he's vanished again.'

'You shouldn't waste your time worrying about him, girlie. He's a no-hoper who's been here forever. He'll outlast you and me both. Elaine feeds him up at the Red Cross centre some days and even she reckons he's a lost cause.'

'Yeah, probably, but he reminds me of an abused dog. Hard to just ignore him. It's not his fault really.'

'Maybe not his fault, but his choice.' Reg patted her shoulder as he stood up. 'Car's outside. Probably Harry.'

Morgan listened distractedly to the voices at the door. How do you explain to people that your brother is a junkie with a family to support and you've turned him away?

'Morgan, how you doing?' Harry sat down next to her on the sofa.

'Fine, Harry. Sorry to bother you with this.'

He shook his head, waving away her apology. 'Do you want to come with us? We can do a check by ourselves, if you want.'

'No.' Morgan kept her voice under control. 'No, I'll come with you. There's not much to show really. A few squashed plants and some ruined clothes.' She got to her feet, grateful her knees had stopped quivering. 'Let's get it done.'

The younger constable nodded at her as she led the way next door. At the rate she was going, Morgan thought, she'd soon have met most of the Smithfield police.

Harry took photos of the damage outside her window as the other man dusted for fingerprints. The conversation between them was short and sharp. Little bursts of sounds and comments that meant little to Morgan. She wandered to the back of her house.

The three remaining sunbirds were busy in the torch gingers. Had they forgotten their other little one so quickly? she wondered. Death just another by-product of life? Maybe

205

humans did do everything too intensely. Lived, loved and lost as though their lives depended on each outcome.

'Whatever happened to smelling the roses?' she said to herself, running her hands through the bright orange flowers massed on her fence. 'Watching clouds grow from wisps into giant thunderheads with silver tops?' Tears filled her eyes, a quick burn of self-pity that she dashed away with angry hands.

She was alive. She was still making choices. She was still winning.

'Hey, Morgan?' It was Harry's voice.

'Coming.' She held her breath as she squared her shoulders and pushed her hair clear of her face. 'Find anything?'

'Plenty of fingerprints, but we'll have to check them out. Plenty of smudges as well. Probably wore gloves, but Ned got some more traces. Fibres, some blood traces on your wardrobe door handle. No promises. We'll be in touch.'

Morgan nodded her reply.

'You got your friend staying with you still?'

'Carl?' Morgan shot a quick frown at the older man.

Harry snorted. 'Nah, I heard the good news on the grapevine about that arsehole. And that they're looking for him still. No, your blond friend.'

Morgan didn't try to hide her tired smile. 'You mean my beautiful blond friend, Lauren.'

'That'd be the one.' Harry gave a quick, appreciative grin.

'She's flying down to Brisbane tomorrow. We'll both be in Brisbane next week for Gavin's funeral. She's gone back to her place for now.'

'Can you stay somewhere else until we sort this out?'

'Reg and Elaine will put me up if I ask, but I think I'd rather just have Sam sleep over.'

'Well, be sure you lock up at night.' Harry patted her shoulder reassuringly. 'And call me. Any time.'

BORDER WATCH

'Sure. Thanks for coming out so fast.'

'Any time, any time.' He led the way out to the police car, but Morgan couldn't help noticing that he glanced up and down the street. His vigilance should have reassured her, but instead it made her uneasy. Who would do something like this to her? Patrick? Carl? Or just some idiot who wanted his five minutes of fame?

She turned to head back into her house and stopped, her gaze drawn to the ocean. Something flashed on the periphery of her vision out near Scout Hat, the little island perched to the east of the coast. It flickered again, a tiny wink of light just off the island. Without binoculars she couldn't make it out. Maybe light glinting off a small boat? Morgan blew the air out of her cheeks with a soft sigh. Probably nothing but paranoia, girl. Time to face your house again.

Standing in the lounge room, she surveyed her little domain. It didn't feel any different. The only reminder of the ugliness in her wardrobe were the smudges of fingerprinting dust. It may as well not have happened.

The yellow sunflower clock told her it was only four o'clock in the afternoon, but she felt exhausted. She knew it was stress, depression. She'd known that particular blackness before. Only one way to deal with it and that was exercise. Maybe a paddle in the kayak? Water would be good.

She could check out the light over by the island. It would beat the hell out of trying to clean up all the grey dust that now decorated her house.

207

25

Woomera pushed his sunglasses down to the tip of his nose so he could read the text message.

'*At the first mark in channel.*'

'About bloody time,' he said softly, the metal chair scraping across the tiled floor as he stood up. Keeping a low profile in a town the size of Cairns got harder each day. The heat of the afternoon was fierce, the sun still high enough in the sky to send refracting light skittering across the waters of Trinity Inlet. He opened the sliding door, but stayed in the air-conditioning, reluctant to go outside until he needed to.

The fishing boat chugged down the channel, its ever-widening wake spreading out among the mangroves and stirring the debris of plastic bottles and driftwood floating on the shore. It was a long journey down from the tip of Cape York. Three days straight steaming, if the winds were favourable. The passenger he was collecting was not amused, it seemed, and that brought a wolfish smile to his face.

Nothing like having the upper hand when dealing with someone from further up the food chain. Not that there were many further up than he was, Woomera knew. He'd made sure of that.

BORDER WATCH

The vessel made its stately way into the marina, both deck-hands ready with the hawsers. He didn't move to help them. No point drawing any attention to himself. Just another punter having a beer and a bet on the horses. He'd pick his man up once the prawns had been offloaded.

Dropping back into his chair, he stretched his neck muscles, freeing the tension there. This was his final week. Silly bastard of a Customs agent did him a favour getting him stood down. No need to take a sickie or explain where he'd been. Easy. By next weekend he'd be sunning himself in a luxury villa far away from Australia, secure with his new identity. He knew ASIO was snapping at his heels. He'd seen their file on him. He'd heard the whispers about the investigation. Being ex-ASIS had some advantages. Lots of contacts who still owed him favours. But time to get out now.

Shame there would be bloodshed on Australian soil, but better like this, in a controlled way. A small attack rather than wholesale slaughter. Then they might take security more seriously.

He'd warned them about the risks of easy entry though Cape York when he was still an active agent and they'd dismissed his concerns. That pissed him off so he'd resigned and joined the Queensland Police.

Dickheads.

He coughed to clear the bitter taste from the back of his throat. Dickheads running the country didn't know jack-shit about the way a fanatical terrorist's mind worked. Prissy little boys with degrees and pedigrees and no real world experience.

'Another drink, mate?'

'Sure, darlin'.' He grinned at the curvy waitress, letting his gaze linger on the full breasts almost spilling from her low-cut T-shirt. 'Put one on the tab for yourself.'

209

'Cheers.' Her accent was European and he debated taking up the offer that was clear in the tilt of her hip and the smile on her lips.

But he didn't.

Too much to do today and no point in being distracted. He jingled the change in his pocket feeling arousal tightening him. Too much at stake for a fuck, but then the knowledge of what he was planning made him horny as hell.

The waitress slid the beer across the table and he handed over a twenty-dollar bill. 'Keep the change for next time.'

'Sure.' Her smile was pure come-on and she brushed his arm as she leant over to wipe the table down, the softness of her rounded breasts strengthening the surge of desire. He sat back in his chair, knowing his tight-fitting jeans weren't going to hide anything.

'Out here on holidays?' he asked, letting the tip of his tongue touch his lip. Her gaze dropped to his lap before she answered and he watched the flush creep up her neck.

'Going home in a couple of weeks. It's been great, but time to do something serious again.' Her breathless voice said so much more than words. She'd drop her phone number by next time she visited his table and he might just use it.

'That's a shame,' he drawled, raising his glass at her. 'A real shame to see you go.'

Her smile was wide as she cast another glance at his lap. The sway of her hips was a beautiful sight as she walked back to serve her other customers. Women were such uncompli- cated creatures, really.

Except for Morgan.

The thought took him by surprise and he brushed it aside to peer again at the steadily growing pile of boxes on the wharf. Morgan had been a challenge and he wasn't entirely sure he'd won that encounter.

BORDER WATCH

'Fuck her,' he muttered. 'Forget it.'

The deckhands were standing with their hands on their hips contemplating the stack of prawns. Must be almost done. Time for him to move. He left the half-drunk beer on the table and headed for the docks.

The swarthy man, aged somewhere in his mid-forties, stayed in the shadows of the wheelhouse. Woomera grimaced. The authority in his stance was unmistakable. Doing business with him was always a delicate balancing act. Not for much longer, though. And that thought almost made Woomera smile.

26

Rafe absently acknowledged the waitress as she placed the coffee in front of him. He didn't notice the pout of her lips or the extra kick of gently curved hips as she swung away from him. Hunched over his computer he had eyes only for the screen in front of him.

The office held too many distractions for him at the moment. At least here he could turn his phone to silent and concentrate on the information he'd gathered in the last few days.

The raucous cacophony of a fire engine wailed up the street outside and he turned his shoulder against the beat of its noise and the endless ringing of a fire alarm. A sudden image of a tranquil garden forced its way into his mind. He felt the punch of desire and rebelled against it, unsettled, annoyed even, by the intrusion.

He moved the laptop closer and squinted at the list of intercepted emails. There was a pattern here that just eluded him, fingered the edges of his mind, but stayed tantalisingly out of reach. He didn't need images of the delectable Captain Pentland blurring his judgement.

But his mind, it seemed, was being particularly singular today.

BORDER WATCH

A pair of long slim legs gliding past the cafe windows on needle-sharp stilettos distracted him. They forced another image of long legs sprinting for the finish line in Weipa into his mind. Damn it, he thought, pushing the computer away. Never get involved with women, mate, he reminded himself. Especially never when you're on a job. Not that you're really involved yet. No sex, no commitment, no kiss even . . . And who are you trying to kid? Just waiting for the right moment and you know it.

The fire truck backed out of the building opposite, flashing reversing lights like warning beacons of alarm. Sourly, Rafe gulped down a mouthful of coffee before reaching for the sugar with a grimace. He really was distracted.

He sat back in his seat, stretching his legs under the table. Might as well give in to temptation for five minutes. Enjoy the coffee anyway. Memories might end up being the only thing that kept him warm.

He'd never made room for a woman in his life, never wanted to make room for a woman in his life, and never allowed the softness to touch him this deeply before.

Was he getting old? Or had he spent too many years alone, too many years relying on no one, too many years hiding from the truth?

And the truth was?

He ran his tongue over his teeth. The truth was he didn't think he had it in him to compromise and that was how he viewed marriage. A compromise. A series of 'I'll do this if you do that' kind of moments.

He loved his parents; they'd done everything in their power to give their children a stable home. But was it a happy home?

No.

It had been a childhood of knowing that his parents had made huge sacrifices for them. Knowing that he should be grateful they had made those sacrifices, but wishing that they had simply been there on the odd occasions when he needed them, instead of working every hour to provide the life they thought he wanted.

They'd compromised so much that eventually they realised they didn't know the people they'd become and had gone their separate ways.

His sister had always understood it better than he did. She played by the rules. She did what was required, followed her parents' wishes and became a police officer.

He drained the last dregs of coffee with an angry gulp.

But he'd joined the army and disappointed both his parents. There he'd found his niche in a tough world. Actions defined a soldier, not his words or ideology. Being part of the elite SAS may have hardened him, but it also gave him a family. The men in his squad were there for each other, they were there for themselves. If you didn't believe in yourself then you'd be letting your mates down.

And the way he saw it, the night the Blackhawk was shot down defined him. He'd survived, against all odds. Out of thirteen men on that flight, only one managed to crawl free. It didn't matter that he crawled right back into hell to try to save his mates – he hadn't even got one out alive.

He would live with that forever. Would live with the tearing grief of their funerals as he watched from the shadows, shielded from the public gaze. Would see the semicircle of rifles pushed bayonet first into the soil, topped with the sandy berets, surrounded by weeping family. Would lie awake tossing at times when sleep escaped him and the night pressed down on him.

And that led back to Morgan. If he had disappointed the people who'd raised him, and then failed to save the men who'd loved him as a brother, what was to say he wouldn't do the same to Morgan?

The sassy waitress floated past again, making eye contact this time and giving him a toothy smile. His own reflex smile brought an appreciative gleam to her eyes and he looked away.

Enough. Find the pattern in these emails and get some work done. Stop trying to analyse the impossible.

He sat forwards and focused on the screen again just as his mobile phone vibrated against his leg. Fishing it out of his pocket, he identified the number.

'Well, hello.' The warmth in his voice was echoed in his slow spreading smile. He couldn't help but register that his pulse had quickened, regardless of all his rationalising.

'Hello to you too.' Morgan's voice sounded breathless and he wondered if she'd been running.

There was a slight pause before they spoke over the top of each other and both stopped.

'You first, Morgan.'

'Is it all right to talk?' she asked, and something in her voice made him sit up a little straighter.

'Yeah, sure.'

'I just got back from a paddle on the surf ski around Double Island and Scout Hat,' Morgan told him. He pictured her in her kitchen, hip against the kitchen bench, hair wet from the water.

'Scout Hat?' His voice sounded rough in his ears.

'That little island south of Double. You can see it from out the front of my place. Haycock it's called on the maps, but it looks like a scout hat, so everyone calls it that.'

'I'll take your word for it.' He took note of her earnest tone. 'So . . . ?'

'So . . .' She hesitated. 'So there are some odd-looking crab pots moored off the south-eastern side of the island. I don't know what's in them, but they were too heavy for me to lift right out of the water.'

'Yeah?' He sat up, his spine straight.

'Yep, I've never found one I couldn't pull up before and these have little red strobes attached. Looked like they were filled with something wrapped up in black plastic. Hard to imagine a crab finding its way through that lot.' She stopped talking and he guessed she was chewing her lip.

'So . . . ?'

'So, I figured Thommo has been telling me for months that there were weird lights in the night out there. He even insisted there were answering flashes from up the hillside. Right now there are way too many strange things happening round here. Maybe he wasn't making it up and maybe they are all connected.'

'How so?' He was struggling to follow her logic.

'This guy who washed up on the beach, if he was part of a smuggling team, he could have been dumped in the water off Scout Hat. Plenty of boats moor up in the lee of Double Island, so no one's going to notice any unusual activity —'

'Except Thommo,' he cut in.

'Exactly. Only someone with nothing much to do at night would be sitting there watching both places.' She paused. 'So what if he saw something that night? Maybe the killer? Maybe someone doing a drop-off? What if they're storing the stuff up at the half built house on the hill? Thommo used to hide out there and that might explain why he's missing.'

'Is he missing or AWOL? Different scenarios.'

'He's missing.' Her voice was flat this time. 'Someone burnt his humpy down last night. I'm pretty sure he wasn't in it, but now he's disappeared. I spent a couple of hours trying to find him this morning. Only place left to look is up the hill.'

'Did you report the fire to the police?' Rafe asked.

BORDER WATCH

'Larry, the guy who cleans the barbeques, reported it. But if you're not interested I'll ring the police myself. I thought being Customs and . . .' The hesitation was tiny but he didn't miss it.

'What's else happened that you're not telling me, Morgan?' He hardened his voice.

'Nothing big,' she said dismissively. 'Just a dead possum in my pool's skimmer box. So, who should I tell about these pots? Customs or the cops?'

'Leave it with me. You okay?'

'Fine, just worried about Thommo. And hey, any excuse to hear your voice, you know how it is.'

'I do and you never need an excuse to ring me.' He wanted to press her further, but was fully aware she would only tell him what she wanted to. Stubborn woman. 'I'll be seeing you soon.'

'Okay. You take care.'

'Always do. Bye, Morgan.'

'See you, Rafe.'

He put his phone away and pulled his laptop across the table again. His fingers roamed over the keys. 'Scout Hat,' he said.

The name jarred in his memory and he returned to the list of emails. This time he reordered by date, expanding the subject line so the whole title was visible.

What he saw was like a quick punch to his gut. Within the last few words in a dozen of the emails were references to Scouts. It was the pattern they'd been looking for. Blindingly obvious now he knew where to look.

His fingers moved with restless speed over the keys as he pulled up earlier emails they'd intercepted. No matter how innocuous the title he scanned down them. It soon became obvious the content was of no importance. The information was contained in the subject line. References started to coalesce.

217

Arranged by date, the emails mapped out the timetable for several scheduled drop-offs at Scout Hat. The most recent one had taken place last night.

'Shit,' he swore to himself. 'Shit, shit, shit. It was right in front of us all the time.' How many hours had they wasted trawling the websites these emails alluded to, wading through jihadihst nonsense and Allah-be-praised rhetoric.

He tapped his phone, scrolled through his numbers. 'Yeah, it's me. I've found the pattern.' He continued talking for another five minutes, even as he transferred files over the internet back to his office.

'By my calculations, there's another party somewhere close to Cairns. Must be a local to know the alternative name of the island. It might be Wiseman. His file says he resigned from ASIS. What if he really got pushed? He'd have all the contacts, having been stationed in South-East Asia.'

He grunted at his boss's response, checking the time on his watch. 'Seems too convenient. He may well have been stalking Morgan before they began dating. Perfect view of the island from her house.

'I'd rather not use the local cops for backup on this one. Too many loose lips, too many leaks. Send one of our teams. We need to investigate this tonight. Inside six days and counting.'

He dropped a ten-dollar bill on the table as he left. For good or bad he was going back to Morgan again. Back to a woman who'd snuck under his defences and probably didn't even realise she had.

Morgan heard the knock through a sleepy haze. Sam scrambled to his feet and padded to the door, no alarm in him, so she sat for a moment with her feet on the floor, trying to clear her brain.

BORDER WATCH

The knock sounded louder this time, Sam's wagging tail reassuring her. Friend it must be, not foe.

'Rafe? What . . . ?' She was bewildered by the sudden appearance of the man standing on her doorstep. In her dreams one minute, doing things with hands and mouth that would drive a woman insane with wanting, and at her front door a second later, seeming far too controlled and normal.

His grin was boyish, embarrassed. Maybe even uncertain?

'Did I wake you up?' He reached out to straighten her hair. 'Looks like you just crawled out of bed. Early evening naps are for old people.'

'And you'd know, I suppose,' she flashed back, tugging at her sarong. She backed away from him, feeling breathless. One part of her wanted simply to fold against his chest and feel two strong arms hold her close. The sensible, predictable part – which was, thankfully, the stronger part – recognised that his expression was more confused than lusting.

'Coffee?' She swung on her heel leaving him to follow.

'Thought you'd never ask.'

Rafe closed the door, bending to ruffle Sam's thick fur. 'Hey, big fella, taking care of her?'

The dog's wise brown eyes seemed to mock him and he straightened, feeling wary, unsettled. That he'd driven straight here didn't sit comfortably with him. Ostensibly he was here to meet up with the team from Customs Special Ops. In reality, he should have driven out from Cairns with them, but then?

Then there would have been no chance of seeing Morgan.

And that need to see her made him a little angry even as he recognised it was futile blaming her for his actions.

'So did you find the crab pots?' Morgan's back was to him as she fiddled with the coffee grinder.

219

'About to go looking.'

'Right.' The coffee grinder drowned out any possibility of further conversation.

He leant on the counter, knowing he needed to keep some distance between them. Something in her dishevelled sleepiness crept past his defences. His body reacted to her slim strength, only partly shielded by the filmy sarong. The slope of her shoulders as she bent to take a mug from the cupboard were begging to be touched, to be kissed, to be soothed.

He turned away from the temptation, and his eyes lit on the dusted fingerprints on her windows.

'Morgan.'

No doubt surprised by his tone, she swung around as she pushed the button on the coffee machine to see where he was looking.

'Ah.' Her lips pursed before she lifted her chin, the coffee maker behind her kicking into action.

'And?'

'And.' She cleared her throat. 'And it seems I had a visitor while I was out this morning.'

'So the cops know about it?' His tone left no room for evasion.

Morgan nodded. 'Yeah.'

'And that's what Sam's doing here? Guard dog? Morgan, you can't stay here by yourself.' The anger burnt in his words.

Morgan visibly bristled at his tone.

'My house, Commander. I live here.' She turned back to the coffee and added a sugar to his cup in silence before sliding it across the counter. She didn't meet his eyes as she sipped from her own cup.

'Why didn't you tell me?' He recognised she was being deliberately obtuse.

'Why?' She kept her gaze level.

This time he gave in to a quick laugh. 'It'll take years of practice to beat me at that game, Captain Pentland, so don't bother trying.'

'What?' She lifted her mug again.

He walked around the counter and stood in front of her, crowding into her personal space. 'Answering a question with a question is lesson 102 in interrogation school.' He emphasised the two. 'You need to have passed 101 first, the non-verbal communication module.'

'Really?' She may have sounded uninterested, but he saw the pulse in her neck skitter and beat faster.

'Really. And these?' He ran one lean hand down her shoulder. 'And these tell me, you're wound up tighter than a generator coil, Morgan. If you stay strong forever, one day you might just snap. Unbend a little. Trust a little.'

She shrugged away his hand, irritation in her eyes.

'Thanks for the advice.' Her cup banged down on the counter top, the sound a sharp slap.

'Morgan . . .' Rafe raked a hand through his hair, trying to still the compulsion. 'Damn it,' he whispered as he lost the battle. Her skin was hot under his hands as he pulled her close. 'I know I shouldn't . . .'

The moment seemed to telescope into infinity, leaving Morgan helpless in the face of her overpowering want. His lips touched hers in a feather-light brush that melted her anger and sapped the strength from her legs. She swayed into him, hands raised against his chest, feeling the solid muscle through the crisp shirt. The kiss was everything and more than she'd imagined it could be. A gentle touch that deepened into a raging ache, that tripped across her cheekbones and wove around her neck then back across her brow before taking deeply from her lips again. She had no rational thought until his hands inched her away.

He sighed against her lips, rested his forehead on hers. Even with his dark eyes veiled from her, she felt the inner battle that raged through him, felt the push and pull of warring emotions and felt the moment when desire won. She offered her mouth up again as he crushed down on it with a desperation she returned.

The sunflower clock ticked silent minutes by as they shifted and searched for even greater intimacy.

Morgan knew her sarong was a hair's breadth from slipping down her body. Her fingers, shaky with desire, fumbled with his buttons but he captured them before she could bare his chest.

'No.' His voice was unsteady. 'No. God, Morgan. I'm sorry.' He held her hard up against him, as he looked down at her. 'You are driving me certifiably nuts, do you know that?' His smile spread across his face, the passion in his voice reassuring her. 'I'm here on work and you make me forget it in an instant. I'm sorry. I shouldn't have touched you.'

He let her go and breathed deeply, before he reached for his coffee. She could see the effort he was making to regroup. Returning them both to reality and all its ugliness.

'I'm meeting a team at the old boat ramp at Taylors Point so we can go take a look-see at your crab pots. Customs is very interested. It might just be the missing link. None of us knew Haycock was called Scout Hat. You've no idea how many doors that name unlocked for me this morning.'

'Really?' She retied the knot on her sarong, a corner of her heart relieved that, even as he controlled it, the desire in him was just as great as her own. 'Thommo told me lots of times he'd seen lights at night out past Scout Hat. I figured they were fishermen, but he always maintained there were flashing lights being directed to them from up on the ridge behind Range View.'

BORDER WATCH

'Where's that?' Rafe turned his dark eyes on her.

'Other side of the highway. There's an old bridle trail that scoots along the top of the hill and past the bunker.'

'Bunker? As in old war structure? Ruins?'

'No, nothing like that. Local gossip says it belonged to some chap with too much vision and not enough money. Started building his dream home on top of the hill. A delivery truck rolled on the steep drive and that was the end of his dream. The truth is probably a bit more mundane. It's a half-built ruin with a bad case of cement cancer. Squatters move in from time to time. You can see it from my back deck. It's just a bit too dark now.'

'Really? How do you get to it?'

'Its driveway comes off Range View Street, but the gates are chained and padlocked.' Morgan shrugged. 'Thommo's been known to hide out up there occasionally, but you have to hike the long way round from the university.'

'Yeah?' Rafe said, then pulled his mobile from his pocket as it rang. 'Yep. There already? Okay. I'll be there shortly . . . I'm just up the street.'

He met Morgan's raised eyebrows with an admonishing finger as he pocketed the phone. 'Uh-uh. You are not invited. Not even maybe. I'll drop by before I head into town.' He forestalled any more arguments by placing his finger over her lips. 'No, and that's final. This is work and my work almost got you killed once before.'

Morgan's mouth tightened with annoyance even though she knew he was right. 'Fine, so I give you the intel and you leave me out of it.'

'Intel? Where'd you learn that sort of language?' His smile rode over her again and she cursed under her breath. 'I'm acting on information received from a concerned member of the public.' He laughed at her, no doubt understanding the

223

mutiny in her face. She knew he was reading her like an open book.

'Module 101 in non-verbal communications was it? Where do I sign up?'

'You did already. Keep practising, Captain. You'll get there.' He ran a gentle hand along her jaw that left her skin tightening in its wake, before he headed out the door. Sam followed him, tail wagging, and watched him leave before he padded back to sit by a fuming Morgan.

'Bloody men,' she said, sinking her hands into the dog's fur. 'Haven't we already proved we can stand on our own two feet, Sam?' She stalked back into the kitchen and rummaged around in her fridge. She would cook and that would soothe her soul.

Then she would sulk.

A lot.

Well, maybe a little but . . .

But maybe not . . .

Morgan smiled. Commander Rafe's self-control was obviously slipping. Perhaps it needed a nudge. The thought tugged her mouth into a wide smile.

Oh yes.

That would be much more fun than sulking because she wanted this man. While it frightened her, it enlivened her. While it left her on edge, she craved more. While it sent rivers of desire coursing through her, it comforted her, warmed her. She didn't understand how, or why, or why now this had happened, but she would live in the moment and figure it out later.

27

The black inflatable manoeuvred through the small swell around the jagged, partly submerged reef off Scout Hat. No one spoke as the four big men rode the boat's erratic motion. The red eyes winking in the water marked a winding trail of bobbing floats.

As they came alongside the first one, the driver eased back on the throttle and swung the nose of the boat, bumping into the float. Rafe reached over with the boat hook and snagged the line. He could feel the weight of it and braced hard against the pull, his knees pressed into the taut rubber of the boat.

'Any chance this could blow up in our faces?' he grunted, straining with exertion as he heaved on it. None of the others answered him. 'Can I take that as a confirmed no?'

The man next to him, coiling the rope as Rafe hauled it in, grinned in the dark. 'You reckon we'd be sitting this close to you if there was a chance in hell this was going to explode? Best guess is still drugs.'

'Could be arms or explosives.' Rafe could feel the motion changing and knew that, whatever the contents, it was close to the surface now.

The radio crackled into life and they all pressed earpieces closer.

'Fast boat coming around from the north. Possibly off a trawler. Get out. Move.'

Rafe swore and heaved on the line as the driver swung the wheel. 'Knife, cut it.' The man beside him slashed down with the blade, cleanly slicing the line and Rafe swung the package into the boat as the throttle opened and they sped back to the west and into the darkness.

'It's not ticking,' Rafe said. 'Guess that's a bonus.'

The others were concentrating on scanning the horizon.

'Intruder's at the lines now. Cameras are rolling.' The scratchy voice on the radio belonged to the mission head in Cairns, who was perched among the trees on Taylors Point with the support team. 'Bring it home, lads.'

They made a quick entry onto the boat ramp and within five minutes the four-wheel drive and trailer bumped back down the rutted road headed towards town.

It took another hour before the surveillance team was satisfied the operation at Scout Hat was over. Rafe ambled back down Moore Street towards Morgan's house, his mood borderline euphoric. A good night's haul all in all. Excellent footage of the retrieval and the two men on the speedboat. One parcel was on its way to the techs for analysis. The parcel hadn't felt dense enough to be explosives and was too heavy for drugs.

The challenge was going to be tracking the other parcels the offenders had retrieved tonight. Fine line between tipping them off and keeping them under surveillance. They had another piece of the jigsaw puzzle and that put them a whole lot closer to closing down the operation before 9 November. It was lucky that Morgan had found the crab pots when she did or they would never have known about the drop-offs.

Her lights were still on and he could hear the soft tones of Norah Jones crooning a request to come away with her. The subtle smell of spices tickled his nose as he knocked on the door. Sam answered with a wag of his tail, peering through the glass with welcome in his bark.

'It's open,' Morgan called from somewhere inside. Rafe was disconcerted that even after a break-in she still didn't lock her front door. He had to admit the protective skills of the big mutt next to him might just deter anyone who wasn't a friend.

She was on the back deck, slick from the pool. Her tiny bikini didn't cover anything. The heat shot up to the base of his skull and Rafe clenched his jaw. God, but she was beautiful. A water nymph with hazy eyes and a smile that slyly tugged at him.

'Nice in the pool?'

'Come try for yourself.' She patted her shoulders with the towel before wrapping it around her, hiding her body.

'Thought I'd better report in before you mount your own investigation.' He ignored her invitation and kept his eyes on her face. 'Said I'd catch the boss later.'

'Dinner, then, before you go? Aged beef straight off the barbeque, mushroom sauce, hand-cut chips?'

His mouth watered at the thought of it, sex a temporary second best. 'Really? How aged?' His smile twitched.

'Old enough for you, Grandpa.'

'Hey, I wasn't the one having a pensioner nap.'

'Point to you, then. So?'

'So.' It was a statement that vibrated between them. Morgan brushed past him as he fiddled with his phone. 'So I guess I don't need much persuasion. Sounds great.'

'I'll light the burners, but the price is a swim in my pool.'

'Price?'

'Price. You're familiar with that system. You want some-thing, you pay the asking price. Price for feeding you is sharing my pool.'

'Weirdest transaction I've ever heard of.'

'Bartering. It's centuries old. Roman, I've heard.' She waggled the ignition wand at him as she sauntered back out to the deck. 'Smart man like you should study up on history a bit more. Might learn something useful.'

He followed her out, bemused by the playful siren luring him onto an island he wasn't sure he had the strength to resist tonight. Wanting her was one thing, acting on that want was another. Admitting that his self-control had become a little ragged just highlighted his weakened defences when it came to Morgan Pentland.

And this was not part of his game plan.

He watched her fire the barbeque into life with economical movements. Maybe tonight was right, maybe they could create a magic that would stop her running, stop him running. The soft fabric of a long, loose shirt drifted around her body and teased him with glimpses of curves and shadowy skin. He forced his mind back to work again.

'We picked up one of your packages and it's on its way back to base for analysis. Got some good video footage as well.'

'Really?' Her demeanour subtly altered as her interest refocused. 'Any ideas?'

'My gut feeling is guns, ammunition.'

'Good to see I wasn't just being precious then. No cray or muddie I've ever seen weighed that much.' She turned from the grill. 'I counted twelve little floats.'

'Yeah. We're pretty sure the boat that turned up as we were leaving harvested the remaining ones. Video images should confirm that. The one we took was at the end of the row so, hopefully, they'll think it snapped its float and sank. The rope should have unravelled quickly in the water after we cut it.'

She held out a glass filled with red wine. 'So Thommo was right. What else did he notice that no one else did?'

'You haven't found him yet?'

She shook her head, regret a shadow across her face. 'After whoever burnt his humpy down and chased him away . . .' She looked concerned. 'I just hope he's all right. I'll try and track him down tomorrow.'

Rafe's phone chirped and he pulled a face as he recognised the familiar voice. 'Boss.'

He nodded several times, turning away from Morgan. 'Yep, thought so . . . No, it can wait . . . First up in the morning then . . . Okay. I'll be back at the hotel later. Yeah, you too . . . Yep.' Internally he gave a triumphant high-five. No meeting with the boss tonight. So . . .

'Looks like I don't need to rush back to Cairns. My boss is tied up with someone else's problem.'

'That's a shame. You can pick the music then. Norah's almost finished.' She pointed at her sound system. 'Plenty there. I'll get the steaks.'

For an hour they talked of anything but work. Music, food, art. Almost a dinner date, thought Rafe.

Almost.

'So did anything get stolen in the break-in?' He savoured the last mouthful of beef, knowing he risked breaking the mood.

Morgan paused with her fork poised. 'And that would be lesson 103? Sneak in pertinent questions when the victim least expects it?'

'It would be a mistake to class you as a victim. Not finishing your chips? They're very good.' He reached over with his fork and speared one from her plate.

'And flattery doesn't wash either.'

He grinned, unrepentant. 'Doesn't hurt anyone. So?'

'No. Nothing stolen, just some damage.'

'To?'

'My clothes. Whoever it was slashed the clothes in my wardrobe, probably with the same knife they used to slit the throat of the baby possum they then left in my pool skimmer for me.' She got to her feet, gathering their plates. 'Harry's investigating. Doubt they'll catch anyone.'

'Why's that?'

'Didn't get any clear fingerprints. No witnesses, no motive.'

'No motive? Wiseman? Or your brother? He's got a rap sheet as long as my arm.'

'My brother?' The anger in Morgan's eyes surprised Rafe. It had been a throwaway line.

He shrugged. 'Just a suggestion. But you must have some idea. Nothing stolen, damage to your clothes and a senseless killing? Doesn't sound like a burglar to me.'

'Just because Ricky phoned me the other night. You don't understand.' She stalked into the kitchen and he let her go, cursing his slip. Why the sudden anger? Because he'd just admitted to doing some research on her family? Or because she didn't want to admit it might be her brother? The phone tap he'd listened to hadn't shed much light on anything. She'd told him to shove off. No collusion there.

His mind moved back to the problem of the drop-off they'd lifted. Lights on the hill needed investigating. Too dark now. He'd get on to that tomorrow. Time for the police to try to hunt down the elusive Thommo.

If he were still alive.

'Patrick is a deluded drug addict with mental health issues.' Morgan spoke with controlled anger as she picked up the

BORDER WATCH

pepper grinder. 'He's in Sydney with his two children doing god knows what. He may have been guilty of not fighting very hard for me when Mum died and he may be looking for a free handout, but he's not capable of killing baby possums.'

Rafe tilted his head as he turned to her. 'I was just running suggestions. Gavin mentioned you'd had family troubles. He wasn't very complimentary about your brother. You were pretty upset when he rang the other night.'

'There are not too many good things to be said about Patrick but . . .' She took a deep breath and perched on the chair beside him, still rigid. 'But I know why he is that way. I don't blame him for it, I don't accuse him of anything, but neither do I know how to forgive him.'

'Is it necessary to?'

'You're the one into meditation. You tell me. Wouldn't it be better for my soul if I could forgive him and move on completely?'

Rafe looked away from the pain in her eyes. 'Moving on is just another phrase for compartmentalising. People who move on simply lock away their fears. Better to deal with it, acknowledge it and embrace it.' He watched as her shoulders slumped.

'I told him I'd pay for rehab, but otherwise no money. He spat at me. I haven't seen him for twenty years and all he could do was spit at me.' She took a deep breath. 'He had a wife. He didn't say where she is now, but she's not with him. Maybe she had the courage to leave. He says it's not his fault but damn it . . .' Her uncharacteristic anger boiled over again. 'It is his fault. I made my choice. So did he.'

'Sounds like he regrets his choices where you don't.'

'They teach you amateur psychology in the SAS?'

'Of course. They have to or we'd all be certified when we left.'

231

'And you left because your whole team was killed in a chopper crash.' There was anger in her voice still, but also a note of enquiry. 'Because you felt guilty about being the only one to survive. The leader should go down with the ship, but by a freakish accident you were thrown clear and everyone else burnt to death.'

'Something like that.' He knew his face had closed down. She'd hit a very raw nerve, his own personal demons, and he discussed them with no one.

'And now we both have to deal with Gavin's death.' Her words bit into him.

'We do.' He watched her face, waiting. Finally she met his steady gaze and he continued. 'But neither one of us is going to let that define us now. The stakes are higher than one man's death. National security is at risk. This might all be tied in together and we need answers not recriminations.' They, he knew from bitter experience, would come later.

'You're right. If we can't stop whatever they're planning, then he would have died for nothing.' The glint of unshed tears glimmered in her eyes as she spoke, but she lifted her chin, defiant anger transforming into something else.

Recognition, he thought, or acceptance maybe? They were two flawed people who lived by their choices. That didn't make them better than anyone else, just stronger than most, more resilient than most.

'If we hadn't been shot down you wouldn't be sitting here. Fate.' Her last word was flat, final.

'Exactly,' Rafe agreed. 'Fate. Life. We get what we're given and get on with it or it would hurt too much in retrospect. Live in the moment because we can, because we have to, because we have the will to survive. We'll make it.' He didn't mean it as a metaphor or an invitation but, as the words fell into the silence, he heard the soft intake of her breath and saw her chin rise in challenge.

'Yes.' Morgan turned to him and he rose from his seat to meet her.

'Swim?'

She nodded but her eyes, luminous and soft in the low light, were the only answer he needed.

'Forgot my swimmers.' He tingled with unfamiliar nerves.

'That's a shame.' Morgan's laugh was breathless. In an instant the sexual tension they'd edged around all night was back.

The sound of his zipper, then the thud of first one shoe then the other hitting the deck, followed by the slither of fabric over skin, seemed loud in the quiet night.

He kept his eyes on her face and reached out to touch her shoulders, ran his hands down her arms and linked his fingers with hers. Her eyes were hooded, her pupils almost filling the misted grey. They never wavered, calmly held his gaze, as he drew her to him until they stood with chest, hips and thighs touching, only a whisper of fabric between them.

'Morgan . . .'

'Ssh,' she said, with a slight shake of her head, fine hair drifting around her cheeks. She lifted her head towards him and he leant in to meet her, feeling his pulse leap with erratic rhythms, then settle into a thudding, drumming roar. It was insanity. An overwhelming sense of falling, tumbling, but instead of an abyss it was the gentle landing of a kiss.

He tasted wine, spices and woman in the briefest of touches that anchored him, made it impossible for him to draw back, draw away, even if he had wanted to. Against his chest he felt her breasts, soft, pliant yet firm. Against his thighs he could feel the vibration of taut muscles held in check against a storm of desire that swirled between them.

Her fingers gripped his as her hips pressed against him, against the arousal that was consuming him, and he couldn't stop the groan of need, of want, that was ripped from him.

It was an aching, raging want that had everything and nothing to do with sex. An aching raging desire that swept away all the reasons this wouldn't work. An aching raging torrent that buried him in a deluge of emotions, and he heard it echoed in her deep sigh.

He freed his hands to tangle them in her hair, shifted his hips to draw her closer, felt her touch his chest, open his buttons and slide the shirt from his shoulders.

With her back ramrod straight, he felt the tension in every muscle and breathed in her scent, feeling the warmth of her skin against his.

She let his lips go with a tiny gasp and he lowered his head to nuzzle her neck, feeling the tremors that shook her and hearing desire, as great as his own, in each sharp intake of breath.

His hands roamed over her, stroking her shoulders, down her back, releasing the straps of her top inch by tantalising inch, sliding it down her body. As he captured her mouth, one hand slid around to cup her breast, pushing aside the flimsy bikini top. Having felt their softness pressed against him still hadn't prepared him for the sensuous roll of them across his palm.

Her skin was satiny under his fingers, her nipples puckered tighter, pressing hard against him. At his first touch, her mouth had opened and he drank deeply, sliding his tongue over hers, his fingers tracing the same path over the peak of her breast.

Drawing him still closer, skin to skin, her hands crept around his neck and she deepened the kisses. He shifted, spreading his legs so she fitted snugly between his thighs, moulding her body to his. When he left her breast and slid his hand lower,

BORDER WATCH

gliding around to her bottom, he felt the tight muscles of an athlete quiver under his touch.

Drawing her higher against him, his fingers caressed her curves more intimately, his hunger growing into a raging need. A need not just to touch her, to love her, to be with her, but a need to show her the woman she could be, if she could learn to trust again.

She shuddered as he slid inside the elastic of her bikini pants and touched her.

'Come into the water,' she whispered against his lips. 'I can't bear this.' She pulled away from him, but held his hand and tugged him into the pool.

Stopping on the wide platform of the bottom step that ran the length of the pool, she looked up at him with lips that were red, swollen from his kisses, and eyes heavy-lidded.

'Hmm?' She smiled up at him from under dark lashes and his surge of desire engulfed them both.

Feet planted on the bottom of the pool, effortlessly he held her in his arms as they fought to touch each other, every stroke, every kiss a little more intimate, a little closer to completion.

Captivated, he couldn't take his eyes from her face. All the tension had gone, the colours of sexual arousal bloomed across it and her hair floated like a dark cloud around her. Water clung to her lashes, her cheeks and he wanted to drink them from her skin and taste her.

Just when he thought he couldn't contain himself any longer, her eyes sprang open and she looked directly into his face with wonderment as she climaxed, a shuddering release that he captured with his kisses as he followed her over the edge.

'Where have you been all my life?' he whispered against her hair.

235

'Right here waiting,' she replied. 'I don't think I can stand.'

'Me neither.' He sat on the top step, cradling her close, over-whelmed by the rush of emotions that still cascaded through him.

The smell of coffee forced her eyes open, one at a time. Morgan struggled to sit up. 'What time is it?'

'Early, but I have to go.'

'Oh.' She took the cup from him, his fingers brushing hers.

'Yes, oh. Work.'

'Of course.' She tried to hide the rush of disappointment but obviously didn't succeed, as he sighed and sat on the edge of the bed, his shirt still hanging out of his jeans.

'I'm sorry, Morgan.'

'You have to go.'

'I'll be back.'

She giggled this time, a tiny sound of joy. 'Yes, Arnie.'

And he had to smile with her. 'Terminator I am not.' The kiss he brushed over her forehead was a whisper of the passion of the night. 'But I will be back.'

'When?' As soon as she said it, she regretted it. She sounded so needy, so desperate.

'Soon, but not soon enough.' Abruptly, he stood up, putting distance between them, she thought.

'See you, Morgan.'

'Rafe.'

She heard the front door close and an engine start and drew the sheets around her, searching for his smell in them.

Rafe.

Did she have the strength for this? There was nothing else in her memory to compare it with but . . . But this was love, unlike anything she'd felt, anything she'd needed, anything she'd ever craved. It left her breathless and dizzy and grounded and centred. It left her certain and confused, delirious and awash with tears. No emotion had ever overrun her like this.

And she hugged it to her as she summoned her courage.

She would try, try to find the courage and the strength, because she sensed it confused him as much as it confused her. She would be strong for the both of them.

28

When she woke again it was with a sense of purpose. Sometime in the drowsy hour after Rafe left, a thought had wormed its way into Morgan's head as she snuggled close to the pillow that still bore traces of his scent.

Had Carl started going out with her only for the view of Scout Hat or for her view of the ruins high on Range View as well?

Time to find out, she decided. With quick fingers she adjusted the focus on the binoculars and scanned the crumbling cement structure perched on the top of the cliff. Nothing moving. A dense stand of giant eucalypts grew right to the edge of the shale face.

She moved down the heavily wooded hillside and something snagged in her peripheral vision. A movement on the lower slope. With only a light breeze the trees weren't moving and whatever was down in the scrub was. Morgan locked her arms to her side and steadied the binoculars.

Thommo.

Her brain was telling her it was the familiar face of the troubled vagrant peering up the slope from beside a towering trunk.

BORDER WATCH

She swung her focus up the slope again. Something had changed since the last time she'd run up the bridle trail and along the ridge. She studied the building. Someone had added some planking, half blocking the entrance on the upper level.

Back down the slope she found Thommo again. Furtive, she thought; he looks furtive. Not so much scared as cautious.

She lowered the binoculars. Was he stealing food from whoever was squatting up there? Didn't look to her like he was part of the action.

One more time, she swung the twin lenses up to her eyes and focused where she'd seen Thommo. Still there. Looked like he was eating something. She moved her gaze along the ridge from the house towards the south and spotted a car. Rangers? It was a white four-wheel drive, backed into the undergrowth. Too new to be abandoned and squatters didn't usually drive cars, let alone expensive cars.

This time when she lowered the glasses, she chewed on the inside of her lip. The view from her house was perfect for watching both the little island and the vantage point high on the hill. That made it feasible Carl was connected with whatever was going on up there. She needed to find Thommo for some answers.

'Morning, Morgan. New birds in the garden?' A cheery Reg hailed her from his yard and she started, nerves just a tad jumpy.

'Not sure. Don't think so. How's my best mate this morning?' She could see the red coat of Sam through the wooden fence.

'He's just grand. Don't suppose you're going for a walk with him?'

'Can he wait till this afternoon? I've got some stuff I need to do this morning.'

239

Helene Young

'Yeah, no worries. Come get him when you want. Ta ra.'
Reg ambled back inside and Morgan squirmed at her dishonesty. She was going investigating. When Sam barked he could
be heard several blocks away and she didn't want him blowing
her cover up the hill.

She tried Rafe's mobile, but it went straight to voicemail.
A very official-sounding recorded message asked her to leave
her details so he could ring her back. She declined.

A part of her was uneasy at just heading up the hill alone
but then, up until a few days ago, she'd thought nothing of
running along any of the deserted forestry trails in the area.
Why change now? She jangled the keys in her pocket. Damn
it, she was going to check on Thommo and that was that.

Once more at the start of the trail Morgan rang Rafe's phone.
Same message. She closed her phone with a little more care
this time. She should have told Reg exactly where she was
going. Just a small insurance policy, she convinced herself as
she dialled.

It went straight to Reg's voicemail. 'Hi, Reg, change of plan.
I'm just off up the hill for a run. I'll get Sam for a walk after
lunch. See you then.' Enough to keep him in the loop, but
not enough to worry him.

She got out of her car and looked up at the hill. Would she
find Thommo up there? If he really wanted to avoid her, she
knew he could. And even if she found him, would he answer
her questions? Only one way to find out and that was to start
running. They were down to five days until 9 November.

29

Rafe didn't bother to keep the censure from his voice. 'You mean ASIO fucking knew Wiseman was on the fed's payroll and didn't tell us? Didn't share their concerns?'

His boss only raised a hand at him, palm out. 'This is unprecedented in Australia.'

'Not fucking unexpected though. Didn't they bungle that doctor's case badly enough to know we all have to cooperate?' Rafe referred to a case where in the aftermath of a bombing in Scotland the Australian agencies had ended up with egg on their faces and bad press for wrongful interrogation. Poor communication between the various branches had been identified as the root cause.

'We're not here to apportion blame. Leave that to the politicians and their witch-hunt. We need to find Nadal and Wiseman. In whatever order we can manage that.'

'This isn't our turf,' Rafe argued back. 'I provided all the information I could get from Morgan. They won't find out anything more if they haul her in and put thumbscrews on her. She was duped, used by a man ASIS trained to be the best little gigolo in Indonesia. Jesus Christ.' He strode across to the grimy window overlooking the mangroves behind the airport.

241

'And you're in danger of being biased.' His boss's words were a rebuke and he should have known well enough to back off, but this was different.

'Biased because I defend someone? Defend someone who has endured more than most ASIS or ASIO agents will ever face in their lives?'

'So let them bring her in and find that out for themselves. Besides . . .' The older man slid the filing cabinet drawer closed. 'It's out of our hands. I was only telling you as a courtesy. I know how much you've invested in this.'

'Do you?' Rafe asked bitterly. 'You have no idea.'

'You're wrong, Rafe. I do, and I don't want it all to be in vain.'

'It won't be in vain, despite their bungling.'

He left the room, resisting the temptation to slam the door behind him. He'd already breached protocol, but the worry was eating at him. His mobile phone showed missed calls and messages. Listening to them only increased his anger.

30

She closed the car door and stowed her car key in the wheel arch. Her little phone fitted into the back pocket of her running shorts.

She checked her laces before she headed up the slope past the barrier erected to deter cars. The padlock on the gate was hanging open, though the chain was still across it. Maybe the four-wheel drive belonged to forestry workers? No one else had the keys as far as she knew.

The sun was well up now, its heat already drying the dew from the night. The sealed road gave way to red dirt and she glimpsed the last of the university buildings through the scrub. Higher up, the road conditions worsened.

Morgan pushed herself to keep going up the steep incline. The loose gravel shifted under her feet, dry eucalypt twigs crackled with each step. Too hot to be going at this pace, she knew, but somehow she had to work off the tension in her long limbs. She reached the plateau. The view over Trinity Beach drew her and she slowed to a walk.

Cane fields were still dotted among new housing estates. Each year development took over more and more agricultural land. The sea breeze was a welcome relief from the humidity and she sucked air into her lungs. The Coral Sea winked in the strong light. Today it was a calm flat blue. The twin islands floated in the azure haze, the white coral beaches defining the water's edge. Perfect marine stinger weather with a light north-easterly breeze blowing.

She glanced up the track ahead of her. Not far to go to the bunker now. Would Thommo be there or was he hiding out lower on the slope?

There were tyre prints etched into the red dirt on the track. The rain hadn't come this far south yet so the dust layer was fine and silty, a shifting trap for the unwary driver.

Hopefully just forestry guys, she thought, pushing down on the uneasy twinge in her stomach. Not Thommo's mates with the lights.

She opened her phone and dialled Rafe's number again. This time when she got his voicemail she relented.

'Hey, Rafe, bring your running shoes next time you come to town. I'll give you a race to the bunker. Last one buys dinner. The view is pretty spectacular this morning. Ciao for now.' Pocketing the phone again, she shook her head. That wasn't quite what she'd wanted to say.

The exhilaration of last night still beat through her. It was impossible not to be optimistic about life when a girl had been so thoroughly loved, she decided. Even if it never went any further, even if Commander Rafe headed south and out of her life, she had a new benchmark to measure men against. No more bullies, no more control freaks.

She retied her hair into a tighter ponytail and stretched her calves against the lactic acid that had built up in the drawn-out hill climb.

But first there was Thommo to locate. There'd be time to contemplate Rafe later.

BORDER WATCH

Should she stick to the track or go cross-country to the old structure? She weighed up the risks. It was going to be easier simply to pretend she was out for a run and not looking for anyone if she stuck to the trail – just another deranged jogger torturing their body.

She took one last long look at the magnificent view below her before she started to run down the next small incline. One more hill and she'd be there.

The deep beat of a diesel engine drifted up the hill, the revs changing as the wheels churned through the soft dust, spinning, looking for purchase. Morgan slowed her pace, trying to judge how close the vehicle was behind her. Was it forestry workers out on routine patrol? This was a little more nerve-wracking than she'd bargained for.

The sound of stones moving under the wheels was clear now. The vehicle was close. She scrambled up the bank, clear of the track to allow it to pass. Last thing she needed was to be hit by a four-wheel drive up here.

The white vehicle was going at speed when it rounded the bend behind her, the driver obviously familiar with the track and its corners. It was a nondescript white Toyota, late model with tinted windows and two occupants, as far as Morgan could tell.

She waved at it, her eyes hidden behind sunglasses. Just as it passed her, the angle of the sun allowed her to see into the vehicle and for an instant she was sure her heart stopped. 'Damn it,' she swore. In that moment her brain recognised a glimpse of a profile.

She knew the driver and he'd just jammed on the brakes, the big car shuddering to a halt as both doors were flung open. She caught a glimpse of the dark metal of a firearm and knew it was not being waved by a friend.

31

Rafe hit the key again and pressed the phone hard against his ear. It was Morgan's voice, but her words were broken. Something about running and dinner. The view? What view? He'd been trying to reach her for almost four hours. Her phone kept diverting to voicemail and if he heard one more cheery 'Hello, this is Morgan', he was going to kick something.

He prowled around the outside of her house again. No car, no answer and the hairs on the back of his neck had gone past standing on end hours ago.

'Can I help?' Reg hung over the front fence. 'Looking for Morgan?'

'Hi. You must be Reg. I'm Rafe Daniels, with Australian Customs. Have you seen her?'

'She left me a message earlier. Said she was going for a run and she'd be back to walk the dog this afternoon.'

'Any idea where?'

Reg shrugged, his T-shirt shifting across his rounded belly. 'She said she was going up the hill, probably through the forestry land. Saw her looking up there through her binos this morning.'

'Really?' Rafe stopped moving. 'What was she looking for?'

BORDER WATCH

'Thommo maybe? She's dragged him down from there before when he's gone on a bender.'

Rafe ran a restless hand through his hair, leaving it spiking off his head at odd angles. 'She parks the car up there somewhere, does she?'

'Dunno, mate. I think the track starts from the uni, but I'm not sure. You could ask Gus — he's the one who told her about it.'

'Gus?'

'The old bloke who does the cleaning at the coffee shop.' Reg rolled his eyes. 'Another one of us old Vietnam veterans that hang around here. Morgan talks to anyone. I'll ring 'im.'

'No, I'll drop round there. The one on the front, is it?'

'Yeah, on the corner. Di's Place.' Reg was looking sombre now. 'You're just being cautious, aren't you? You don't really think someone would harm her?'

Rafe forced a smile as he turned to go. 'I don't know what to think. I just want Morgan safe.'

32

'Shit,' Morgan swore again as she leapt off the bank back onto the track, and started to run.

Guilt, fear? She wasn't entirely sure, but the expression on Carl's face was not welcoming and no way was she sticking around to find out what he was doing up here.

He was fit so she would have a battle to outrun him. Surprise had given her a fifty-metre head start, but she'd also been running for half an hour already and her legs were heavy.

She could hear the footsteps behind, but refused to turn around. Better to keep pushing it, she reasoned, veering off onto a track that cut through to the water towers further down the hill. Something slammed into a tree beside her before she heard his voice, closer than she'd imagined.

'Stop, Morgan!'

She didn't acknowledge him, just ran on, knowing she was risking injury at this breakneck speed, but a bullet was not an attractive option. Adrenalin gave her a much needed boost.

A shower of splinters sprayed over her as another bullet ripped through timber next to her and she ducked defensively, wobbling off-balance.

BORDER WATCH

'The next shot's between your shoulders, Morgan. Stop.' Morgan recognised the determination in that voice. It was enough to make her feet falter and land awkwardly.

She crashed down in a heap, rolling into the undergrowth, throwing up her hands to protect her face.

Pulling at twigs caught in her hair, she struggled to sit up and glared at the big man standing over her. Being defensive wasn't going to help.

'Trying to shoot me? You complete fuck-up.' Anger forced her feet to work and she ignored the belligerent expression on her chaser's face. 'There are laws against that, you piece of crap.'

His hand lashed out, a sharp cuff across the side of the head that almost dropped her again. 'Shut up,' he screamed into her face. 'What the fuck are you doing here?'

'Running. What the hell does it look like?' Morgan figured attack was her best option. 'You're insane. You can't shoot at people for no reason. This is a public trail.'

Another man came sliding down the trail behind them. Like Carl he wore a dark green shirt and pants that could be mistaken for a forestry ranger's uniform. His dark glasses hid his eyes, but his demeanour told her he was in charge here. Morgan felt her scalp tighten as a rising wave of fear flooded her. It suddenly seemed harder to breathe.

'Your girlfriend, Woomera? I thought you'd fixed her.' His accent was foreign, and the inflection was educated. He made no effort to hide his annoyance. 'Get rid of her.'

'Sooner said than done, mate.' Carl didn't quite defer to him, but still the pecking order was clear.

The other man stood impassive, arms folded. He looked fit and wiry, his swarthy skin burnt dark by the hot North Queensland sun, his hair close-cropped, military style. Everything about him screamed authority. 'It's your problem, deal with it.'

249

He walked up the track without looking back.

Morgan finished dusting herself down and glared at Carl. 'I'm leaving of my own free will. You don't need to ask me twice, dickhead.'

'You're not going anywhere, I'm afraid. I can't have you running off to your new boyfriend telling tales.' He'd moved in on her as he was speaking and his hand flashed out to grip her arm. 'He'll expect me to kill you, but maybe we can have some fun before that.'

'Get real, Carl. This is the twenty-first century in Australia, soldiers don't go around raping and killing. Get a life. You're mad.' She tried to shake his hand off.

He laughed, and the sound scared Morgan more than anything else in the last ten minutes. 'That's why I enjoyed our little interlude so much – you've got balls. But I haven't finished with you yet.'

He dragged her along after him, the gun hanging loose in his free hand. Morgan slumped against him and, as he turned towards her, she lunged at the firearm. She didn't stand a chance.

With a swinging arc, he brought it down on the side of her head, and pain was the last thing she remembered as he hoisted her over his shoulder.

33

It took Rafe almost an hour to track down a sleepy Gus at the caravan park in Clifton Beach. It took five minutes to determine that Morgan had driven past the balding old cleaner at eight o'clock with a cheery wave and no one had seen her since.

Rafe parked the car at the uni in the spot Gus had described and walked through to the start of the bridle trail. Morgan's car was parked by the entrance. He stooped to peer in the window. No sign of trouble, no sign of Morgan. The bonnet was hot from the sun, the tyres were cold. Hadn't been driven for at least a couple of hours.

He looked up the trail, hands on his hips. Nothing annoyed him more than not being in control. At this point, he had no proof she was in trouble, no proof he wasn't jumping to needless conclusions. He was standing here in the heat because of two missed calls, one distorted phone message and the state of the hairs on the back of his neck. Those hairs had never let him down before. His survival instincts were strong and well honed.

Only one way to go and it led up that bloody hill. He talked into the phone as he walked.

'Yeah, I'm headed up that way now. How fast can you get me backup if I need it?' He looked at his watch. 'Sunset's going to get us before then . . . Yeah, I know it's only a hunch, but there are too many loose ends that all lead to this bloody hilltop ruin . . . I'd appreciate you putting the guys on standby . . . Thanks. I'll be in touch.'

Satisfied that his boss was taking him seriously, he set off up the track. His ankle holster didn't make jogging very easy, but he wasn't going into this situation without his own hardware. He had another small gun jammed down the back of his pants, under his shirt.

The sun was making a stately exit, sinking to the west, but still lighting parts of the trail. The sweat was soon running off him and he wiped his hand over his face, checking his bearings against the glimpses of coast through the trees. As the shadows lengthened, he pushed his pace up. He didn't want to be stumbling into hostile territory in the dark.

Recent tyre tracks told him several vehicles had used the road. He picked out footprints in the dust – small enough to be a woman, with enough pressure to be someone running.

He reviewed the morning's events as he ran. The contents of the package they'd hauled up at Scout Hat were all Chinese manufactured. A surveillance team had the other material under watch as it was ferried south in a seafood truck headed for Brisbane. No arrests had been made yet. They were waiting for the bait to get further south to see what else they could shake out. The trawler that had collected the packages from Scout Hat was Cairns-based. The next step involved waiting for more drop-offs to see who was ferrying guns down from Cape York.

Rafe had long since given up wondering how people could become involved in this sort of illegal operation. There would always be the idealists, the fundamentalists doing their bit for

BORDER WATCH

the cause, but then there were others — normal, everyday people who, for a vast array of reasons, could be paid to do anything. He'd also stopped judging them for it a long time ago. If he were going to lose his trawler because illegal fisherman were fishing the oceans bare and someone offered him an easy ten grand what would he do? Thankfully he wouldn't ever have to face that decision.

The view stopped him dead in his tracks. Hell, no wonder the guy with the ruined house wanted to keep that view for himself. It was unbelievable, beautiful. The sea breeze ruffled around him, bringing instant relief from the heat of the western sun.

As he stood with his sides heaving he cocked his head to the sound that came in on the breeze. Diesel, and coming his way. He dived into the scrub, flattening himself hard against the dirt. The vehicle sounded loaded up, with the engine note straining before the gears were changed. It was going down the hill towards the university, bumping and rattling on the rutted slope. He didn't risk raising his head until the engine started to accelerate.

Tinted windows, but it looked like five heads, all men. No sign of Morgan.

He scrambled to his feet and resettled the second gun in the small of his back, then started off again. His pace was slower now. This sort of situation was fraught. If he hadn't been convinced that Morgan was in trouble, he would have staked this site out for at least twenty-four hours before attempting to penetrate it.

'Psst, psst.' The bushes to the left of him rustled and Rafe hit the deck, diving into the bushes to his right, the gun out of its ankle holster before he'd finished rolling. A cackle of laughter prickled the back of his neck.

34

The ground was hard under her cheek, the smell of old decaying concrete filled her nostrils. Her head throbbed, but Morgan kept her eyes closed as she surfaced. Pretend you're still unconscious and they'll leave you alone, she consoled herself, as she started to do an inventory of her body.

Her feet were bare so they'd taken her shoes, but her legs weren't tied up. Her hands were, and the binding was too tight and cutting into her wrists. She was still wearing her clothes, so that was a good sign. Her head felt like it had split open where the gun had hit her, but she knew from buried memories that the head could take a lot of force before that happened.

Damn, but you've been stupid, she berated herself. If you hadn't bolted you might have got away with just being out for a run. Now you're tied up, probably in the bunker, with god knows who and an angry Carl. His boss wants a quick solution. No one knows you're here and no one's going to come looking for you.

Rafe?

A tiny glimmer of hope tried to rise. If he called her back today and couldn't track her down then maybe he'd work it out. She pressed her cheek into the rough concrete. And maybe she was kidding herself. The message she'd left on his phone had been ambiguous to say the least.

Her best hope was Reg. When she didn't turn up to walk Sam, he might check with Lauren. Then again he might not.

She heard footsteps and slowed her breathing, relaxing her body again.

'Get up.' A toe pushed her and she lay still. 'Get up.' The foot prodded harder this time and she groaned and opened her eyes. Carl was standing over her, his chest bare, the banding of tattoos bulging around his biceps. The gun was gone, but the belligerent expression wasn't.

'I didn't hit you that hard. It was just a tap.' His sunglasses hid his eyes, but she could tell from the set of his mouth he was enjoying himself. She'd seen that expression before. She knew bullies got their thrills if you fought back, so she stayed compliant, dumbly gazing up at him. Would have been good if you'd remembered that bit of wisdom earlier, she scolded herself.

He held out a water bottle and she couldn't stop the involuntary lick of her lips. 'Drink, baby?' He raised it to his own mouth and drank with great greedy gulps, water running out the sides of his mouth and down his neck.

Morgan went completely still. A symbol, embedded in the Celtic tattoo on the inside of Carl's arm, was menacingly familiar. It was identical to the one on the back of the man she'd found on the beach. Much smaller and precise, but the same.

The icy blast of fear covered her in goose bumps. That was why the police insisted she look at all those tattoos after she found the body of the beach. They knew the guy was JI and they must have suspected Carl's link right back then. That must be why Rafe was sure they needed to find Carl urgently. Carl was part of a terrorist organisation. How could she have missed something so obvious?

They must have thought she knew more than she'd admitted. She fought to keep the fear from her face, but her heart pounded in her chest. If she managed to survive this day, she'd never doubt anything Thommo said again. He'd tried to warn her and she hadn't listened.

When he'd almost emptied it, Carl lowered the bottle and shook it, tempting her. 'Say "Please, Carl".' His smile taunted her.

'Please, Carl,' she croaked through dry lips, her voice shaky despite her best efforts.

'Sorry? Did I hear you say something?' He held the bottle towards her invitingly, the liquid sloshing in the bottom.

'A drink, I'd love a drink.' Morgan cleared her throat to give her voice more volume.

'"Please, Carl",' he repeated as he crouched down next to her and pushed his sunglasses up onto his forehead. 'Say it again.'

'Please, Carl.' She kept the fire from her eyes and forced her body to stay relaxed, preparing for the blow she sensed was coming.

'Love it when you beg for more, baby.' He upended the bottle over her, pouring the water down her face and her chest. She let it run, refusing to shake her head, refusing to let her eyes stray to the mark on his arm.

Carl laughed at his own cleverness. His hand shot out and grabbed her breast, her nipples visible through the wet fabric. 'Miss me yet?' He rolled his thumb over her nipple and tweaked it hard, forcing it to pucker. 'Thought you would. Big bad Customs man's been screwing my woman.' He dropped the empty bottle and grabbed Morgan's ponytail, forcing her to meet his gaze as his other hand roamed over her body.

He twisted her face up to him. 'Did you tell him you loved him?' His mouth closed over hers, his tongue trying to force

BORDER WATCH

its way into her mouth. Morgan kept her jaw clenched as he nipped at her lips. His free hand was between her legs now, his fingers digging into her thighs as she pressed them together.

Her brain told her what she needed to do to survive. Surrender.

His brutal fingers were almost inside her pants. A fragment of an image of Rafe's tender hands stroking that same soft skin overrode her brain's logic and Morgan twisted against Carl, scissoring her legs around his and toppling him to the ground.

He backhanded her again before he regained his balance and she felt the pain across her cheek.

'You want to fight about it first?' His grin was malevolent. 'Happy to oblige, babe. Come on.' He half crouched, arms out wide. 'Come and get me, babe.'

Morgan struggled to sit up with her arms tied behind her. 'Go to hell, Carl. You can't do this to me.'

'Oh but I can, babe. I'm ready.' He leered at her and Morgan looked away.

She took stock of the surrounds. They had her on the ground floor of the bunker and she was facing the ocean. No other voices so far. Where was the other man? She twisted her head around to see if the vehicle was still there. Was it just her and Carl?

'What's the matter? You want someone else as well?' Carl crouched down in front of her again, but out of reach of her legs this time. 'You want black, babe? I can get you one of those too. I can share, I don't mind watching.'

Morgan wished she had enough saliva to spit at him but her mouth was too dry. She contented herself with glaring at him.

'The boys are going to have fun when they get back.' He idly scratched his chest, that tattoo moving with his muscle and catching her attention again. 'Oh yes, indeed. Then a nice little accident. Over the cliff. Poor little Morgan must have got lost in the dark and fallen off.' He waved a hand. 'By the time anyone finds you, there'll be no need for a rape kit.'

'Piss off, Carl.' Morgan hissed the words, putting every ounce of venom she could muster into them. How the hell had she ever been attracted to him? she wondered. How could she so misjudge a man?

'Not yet, babe. Still too much to do. We're outta here tonight.'

'I need a drink.' She kept her voice flat, her eyes locked on his.

'Too bad.'

'Just release my hands, Carl,' she grated out through gritted teeth.

'So you can take a swipe at me?' He laughed in her face, a fine spray of spittle settling on her skin.

'I won't take a swipe at you.'

'Sure, babe, sure.' He shook the empty bottle at her. 'And I won't be untying your hands. Maybe I'll get you a drink later, if you behave.'

Morgan didn't reply. Carl only won if she let him demoralise her. Eventually he'd get tired of taunting her and leave her alone.

The sound of an engine drifted in. Distracted, Carl turned his head to listen.

'They're back. Let's see what they want to do with you now. You might be sorry you didn't get to have one last orgasm with me, babe. We were good together.' He reached across and touched her cheek, an odd, gentle touch. Morgan recoiled from it. He laughed at her again. 'You just might be begging for me by the time they finish with you.'

He strode out of the ruins. Morgan pushed herself to her feet and walked over to the southern wall. No sign of her

BORDER WATCH

shoes. She crouched down, her back wedged defensively into the corner, wondering just what they'd do to her. Death might be a preferable option.

The finality of that outcome prodded her brain into gear again. Her phone. Where was her phone? Hope flared and she contorted her hands to feel her back pocket. She couldn't reach it. She wriggled against the wall. The disappointment when she realised her pocket was empty was a physical blow. Her phone must have fallen out when she tumbled while trying to outrun Carl.

She took a deep breath, steadying herself. Perhaps she could get her hands free. She wiggled her fingers, searching for any sign of looseness in the bindings. It felt like tape. Maybe if she kept moving enough the sweat would help to soften it. And then?

Try using your head, girl, she lectured herself. Get free first.

She listened to the voices and counted as four car doors slammed. Men speaking a language she didn't recognise – a guttural, harsh language. Carl's voice was identifiable among them. His tone was wheedling. She steeled herself as their footsteps rang on the cement floor.

The five newcomers stood ranged out in a line in front of her. They were all wearing the same style of clothes. Easy to mistake them for forestry boys, she guessed. She met each pair of eyes one at a time, gauging their reaction as they talked among themselves. The laughter was lewd and the hand gestures suggestive. Her breasts seemed to fascinate them.

Only the leader stayed aloof, off to one side and bored. He eventually barked an order and the others turned towards him.

Carl switched to English. Morgan was sure it was for her benefit. 'Better to wait until it's dark. The boys might like to try her out before we kill her. Should be time later.'

259

Helene Young

'Enough. We're here to work. She's no better than a prostitute. Enough.'

'I still say we need to wait until it's dark to move.' Carl sounded sulky. His fun had just been curtailed.

Morgan kept her eyes on the boss, willing him to agree. That would give her a few more hours to get away. That left room for hope.

They reverted to the other language, but she worked out from their gestures that one man was being left behind to guard her for now. Carl and the others were off somewhere. The boss left without a backward glance at her. She caught the last couple of words as he walked away, speaking in English to Carl. It sounded like, 'The list of targets stands.'

Before she could process that, Carl walked over to her, regret tinging his face. 'Maybe later.' He bent down and hauled her to her feet, pinning her against the wall with one hand around her throat. The other reached between her legs for a last grope and Morgan forced herself to stay very still as he fondled her. 'Sorry, Morgan.' He kissed her lips one more time before he pushed her back down on the ground. 'Wrong time, wrong place, babe.'

He didn't look back and she listened for four car doors to slam again. Her new captor pulled a cigarette packet from his pocket and lit up. He offered it to her, but she shook her head, wary of what his next move would be. His dark eyes roamed over her, but she guessed he was taking his orders more seriously than Carl.

She got as comfortable as she could on the hard floor, knees bent in front of her. Piece by piece she started to sift through what she knew.

The indisputable truth stared at her. Carl was part of Jemaah Islamiya and the man who seemed in charge here was most probably Abu Nadal the bomb maker. That made this camp a

BORDER WATCH

staging point for men and equipment so they could be transported south. Terrorists not drug smugglers then. Arms, and probably explosives, were dropped off at Scout Hat by trawlers that came down from the north. Someone local picked them up and carried them further south.

Had Carl organised the collections?

Maybe.

Probably.

Carl had been hanging around for the best part of a year. Plenty of times when she was away he'd had 'friends' to stay. If Thommo could be trusted, and it seemed he could, then the flashing lights had been going on for almost a year. She ignored the quick rise of anger at being so easy to dupe, but squashed it. No time for self-pity, she reprimanded herself. They were getting ready to move out and she needed to let someone know she'd found Carl, and possibly Nadal. It irked her that the one vital piece of information was still missing. She didn't know what they were planning to attack. Was there anything in North Queensland worth blowing up? Maybe the naval base in Cairns? The port facilities in Townsville? The LPG gas tanks were close to the city centre. Then there were defence installations, the airport or maybe infrastructure like railways and bridges.

Whatever the answer she had to escape, and if she couldn't do that she had to at least raise the alarm.

How? She sifted through her memory from previous visits for anything she could use.

The terrain to the west was perfect for a training regime to harden fighting men in hot conditions. Uninhabited and hostile, not even bushwalkers ventured out there. So even if she managed to light a fire, unless it spread quickly, no one would notice in time. The nearest houses down the hill were too far away to hear her yelling out or screaming even. And

261

if they saw a fire they'd assume the Forestry Department was doing a controlled burn, commonplace at this time of year.

The old building had water and power connected, though it was pretty crude. It wouldn't run to a telephone line. Nothing to help her there.

Morgan tried to visualise the layout. They'd left her on the bottom floor in the front of its three rooms. The storey above had never been completed. One huge open space, it had gaps for the yet-to-be-fitted windows and doors. Above that was a flat roof.

The old cellar off to her right wouldn't have taken much to finish off. It would make a soundproof private bunker. The forestry guys didn't bother the squatters, providing they weren't burning the place down.

Without warning the sunlight was blocked out over her and she looked up, alarmed. Her captor gestured at her with his gun, pointing outside. He spoke to her again, his tone unmistakable even though she couldn't understand the words.

Reluctant to cooperate, she got to her feet, wondering if he'd been waiting just long enough to be sure the others weren't coming back to interrupt him.

He prodded her in the back before grabbing her hands and lifting them up her back. The pain ripped into her shoulders. No way could she get away from him now. Once they were outside he forced her over towards the scrub to the rear of the block. He pushed her at a tree and motioned for her to turn around with her back to it.

Only then did she realise he had a coil of rope over his shoulder. He looped it over her wrists then threw it up and over a thick branch. It was just long enough to allow her to sit down, but that was all. He grinned at her and said something that made him laugh at his own joke as he grabbed his crotch suggestively. When Morgan didn't respond, he reached

BORDER WATCH

across and cupped one breast, then the other, weighing them in his palm and running his thumb over her nipples.

Her captor licked his lips and for a moment Morgan was sure he was going to rape her. Instead, he hawked and spat into the grass at her feet then turned abruptly and walked back into the building.

Unwittingly, he'd given her the perfect vantage spot to assess the lie of the land. Aerials she'd never noticed before sprouted over the tops of the trees above the old cellar. A solid planking door covered the opening. Comms room, Morgan guessed.

An old air-conditioner sitting on a metal trolley had a pipe leading from it that disappeared into the ground. If you just happened by, it looked like a piece of discarded rubbish that had been dumped there. She could hear it humming though, and there was an orange power cord leading away from it.

Her captor was up on the second floor and she could hear the scrape of boxes or furniture across the concrete. Packing up. She tried to make sense of Carl's words. He'd said they'd be out of here tonight.

Where to?

All the while her brain was ticking over the problem, her fingers were flexing and straining against her bonds. She knew her best hope of escape was now, with only one minder. If she could just get her hands loose. Her fingers were already losing some feeling as the blood supply diminished. The pain in her head from where Carl had clipped her with the gun remained a dull constant ache.

Movement on the top floor drew her attention. Her captor had spread out a prayer mat and was offering prayers to Allah.

Well . . .

Her smile was wan. Maybe the threat of the prophet's wrath would keep her from being raped by this guy anyway. Shame Carl didn't take his religion that seriously.

263

It gave her a lead on the time of day though. She must have been out cold for longer than she realised. She squinted up at the sun. Getting late in the afternoon. Sunset could only be a couple of hours away.

Was Rafe even now wondering where she was and trying to track her down? If she got out of here alive, she planned on making some changes in her life. One of those was Rafe.

But first she had to escape.

35

'It's all right. I'm not gonna hurt you. You're Morgan's friend.'

Rafe stayed low, his gun levelled on the ageing drifter who scrambled across the track.

'They've got her up at the big house. Wiseman.' Thommo spat into the dirt beside him. 'He's no good for her. I've seen you.'

'And I see you. You're Thommo?' Rafe got to his feet, keeping the gun down but at the ready, his body tense.

'Yep, I watched you come up the trail. You've come for Morgan.' It was a flat statement and the older man nodded his head in answer to himself. 'There's only one of 'em left. A foreign bloke. Big bastard. With an even bigger gun, semi-automatic. But Carl won't be far away. Never is. We'll have to be fast or they'll kill her.'

'How much further?' Rafe nodded up the track, ignoring the urge to pick the tramp up and shake him as his anger, his frustration, his rage almost overflowed.

'Not far. Ten minutes. But you can't go that way.'

'Really?' Rafe eyeballed him. 'Where then?' Experience had taught him that crises bred strange bedfellows and this was a definite crisis. Ordinarily he wouldn't have been comfortable taking someone like Thommo into battle, retired war veteran or not.

'Up the cliff. You can climb, can't you?' Thommo's sly smile told Rafe that a mountain goat was going to be hard-pressed to go up this particular cliff without carabiners and ascenders. He'd already searched the hillside below the building from down at the beach. Even the binoculars hadn't managed to soften the angle of the cliff face where the old house sat.

'You showing me the way?'

'You'll need me. You can't stop them killing Morgan, but we can. I owe that big bastard. He tried to burn me. I seen him.'

Rafe took a deep breath, hanging onto his temper. He couldn't risk losing him, but the old man's ramblings were frustrating the hell out of him. 'So show me.' His palms were face up and Thommo slapped his roughened hands down on Rafe's.

'You trust me. I'll help you. But only because you're Morgan's friend.' He gripped Rafe's hand. The strength in the wiry fingers surprised the Customs man.

Rafe gripped back, meeting Thommo's eyes, expecting to see the edge of madness. Instead, there was a glimmer of tears as Thommo continued to speak. 'Morgan's my friend too. They'll die if they hurt her. Might die anyway.' He dropped Rafe's hand and shuffled off at a surprising pace towards the edge of the ridge. Rafe tucked his gun back in his holster before he followed, pulling out his mobile phone as he ran.

Damn it, would he be too late? He didn't want to let his mind even consider that option. If he let her down as well . . .

No.

It wasn't an option. He would never find a way out of the darkness if he lost Morgan. He had to find her before . . . His muscles bunched as he kept pace with Thommo, anger giving him strength, fear giving him focus.

He would find her.

36

'So who do you want first, Morgan?' Carl stood in front of her, his legs spread wide, arms folded across his broad chest, all dominant male on the offensive. He'd driven the car back into the camp with dust spitting from its tyres and wasted no time in finding Morgan.

She remained impassive, glaring back at him, not deigning to answer. The other man came and stood beside Carl, grinning, with his gun hanging slack in his hand. He said something in his own language. Carl laughed before he answered him and then turned back to Morgan.

'He wants to know if you were a virgin when we first met. Don't know why being a virgin is such a commodity. It's overrated.' He shrugged. 'So, what's it to be then? One last time with me and you can die a happy woman, hey?'

'Go to hell, Carl. I have no intention of letting either of you touch me. I'll die before I do.' Her chin was high, her shoulders straight, even as the excruciating pain in her head from the earlier hits, and now dehydration, blinded her.

She wiggled her fingers in her ties. When her captor had moved her back inside he hadn't bothered to check them and she had gradually managed to loosen the tape enough that she could slip her hands free. She would wait until she saw an opportunity and then run. If she got a bullet between the shoulders then so be it. At least someone would take the time to investigate a shooting victim. Better than ending up at the bottom of the cliff looking like an accident or, worse, a suicide, she'd decided with grim resignation. A suicide would be so easy for the police to fit to her. Poor Morgan, a troubled teenager after her parents' tragedy. Then that dreadful aircraft accident with her friend dying like that. No wonder the stress got to her. Couldn't blame her really.

She looked up at the sky. Darkness would descend shortly. In the tropics, night falling had special significance. One minute, broad daylight blinded you with its brilliance, lengthening shadows the only sign of impending night. The next, you were flat out picking out the trees a metre or so in front as the dark velvet smothered you. The naked bulb swinging above her head in the light evening sea breeze cast distorted images up the grey cement walls. The time was right.

Carl picked at his teeth with a fingernail, regarding her. 'Can't speak for my friend here, but I don't do dead bodies, so that will have to wait. I think my friend should go first. Watching might just whet my appetite.' He spoke to the man next to him and fisted his own pants at the crotch in a crude gesture. With a guttural laugh, Carl's mate propped his weapon against the cement wall and unbuckled his belt, dropping his pants.

Morgan kept her eyes on Carl's face. She couldn't quite block out the view of the other man's engorged penis as he swaggered towards her. 'You animal,' she snarled at Carl. 'How can you watch another man rape a woman? How the hell did I misjudge you so bloody badly?'

Carl chuckled as he sauntered up behind the other man. 'You didn't, but I had to get the gun out of his hand somehow.' The side of his hand flashed down as the other man leant towards

BORDER WATCH

Morgan. The foreigner dropped like a stone. Not a sound.
Morgan stared in fascinated horror as his dark head twisted at
an unnatural angle and he collapsed in a heap.

'Oh my god.' She backed away from Carl. 'Shit.' He followed
her back towards the wall.

'No one is having you but me. Shame I'm still going to have
to kill you afterwards. I made some bad choices. Now I need
to disappear. Tonight. Sorry, Morgan.' His fingers traced down
the side of her face and she flinched from hands that killed so
lightly. A sob caught in her throat. 'Ssh, ssh,' he crooned. 'I
won't hurt you. It'll be quick.'

'Won't hurt me?' Her voice wobbled. 'Killing me won't hurt
me? You're insane.'

Carl gestured at the body behind him. 'Did you see Yousef
complain? He'd offended Nadal so he had to die anyway. At
least this way he went to heaven a happy man to be greeted by
many virgins. Last things he saw were your tits and he almost
died on the job. What more could a guy ask for, hey?'

He reached across to stroke her breast. 'If you hadn't thrown
me out none of this would have happened.'

Morgan could only shake her head at him.

'This should have been an easy job. My final one. Instead,
it's showing all the signs of becoming a complete fuck-up.
And that started with you, babe, so I'm sorry, but . . .' His
hand circled her neck, his blunt fingers probing the soft tissue
around her spine, and she realised she might be drawing the
sweet night air into her lungs for the last time. That thought
enraged her and she twisted free from him. If she had to die
then she'd go with a fight, not compliant and cowering, nor
mesmerised like a rabbit bewitched by a python.

'Don't you dare blame me for this, you jerk.' She put all
the hate she could muster into the words. 'You are allowing
a terrorist organisation to bring hell down on Australia and

269

all you want to do is shift the blame to someone else. I didn't pick you for a coward but I should have.'

'Now, babe, you don't understand —'

'Oh I do, you arsehole.' She cut him off, the volume of her voice rising with an edge of hysteria. 'You set me up to take the fall for you. You bugged my computer. You killed a man at Trinity and god knows who else, helped Jemaah Islamiya enter Australia and now it's my fault you're going to kill me as well?' Her voice had risen to a scream by the time she reached the end of her accusations. Carl's face had tightened, his jaw set solid.

'They didn't listen when I warned them. They said I was being paranoid. Better they find out this way. I've organised it so it won't be that big. And I'll tip off the authorities before it happens.' He sounded like a sulky teenager.

'And if the terrorists go early or the authorities don't believe you? What then? How could you?' Her skin crawled with distaste. 'They were right. You are insane, you must be.'

'I'm not insane.' The note of pleading unnerved Morgan. 'Circular Quay could do with a revamp anyway. They'll have time to get the people out.'

Morgan felt a wave of cold wash through her body. She had to get out alive. They had to stop them. A bomb in Circular Quay during a Monday rush hour would paralyse Sydney and kill many, many people. She had to take her chance. Now or never.

'Go away, Carl,' Morgan hissed at him, adrenalin swamping her. She gestured with her head, willing him to turn around. 'Go and pick the spot to throw me off the cliff. Get it over with.' He obliged and spun away from her, his head cocked to one side.

She slipped her hands free and kept the elation from her voice as she carried on talking, raising her volume again. 'Find

BORDER WATCH

a nice deep section with plenty of undergrowth because once they find my body, Rafe and his mates will come looking for you.' She inched towards the fallen man's gun up against the building. Carl didn't turn and she moved a little quicker.

'Stop right there, bitch.' He swung around just as she leapt for the gun. Before he could stop her, she grabbed it with both hands and pointed it at him, fumbling to find a trigger. She pressed hard on what she thought was the firing mechanism and nothing happened. Damn it, she swore under her breath. A safety catch and she had no idea how to get it off. The bloody movies never showed this side of it.

'Oh, babe. You do have balls.' Carl laughed at her. 'But unless you're going to bludgeon me to death with it, you don't know what to do with a gun.'

'No, but I do.' The quiet words came from the gloom behind Carl. The overhead light glinted on the barrel of the handgun. 'Hands behind your head. Get down on the floor. I will not hesitate to shoot you.' Rafe's words were measured. 'Just looking for an excuse.'

Carl turned, but stood his ground, his body tensed for action. Morgan guessed he was weighing up his chances of taking her hostage again. She scampered away from him over towards Rafe, but kept out of the line of fire. Rafe looked as unpredictable as Carl did.

'Down. On your knees.'

Carl raised placating hands as he got down. 'Take it easy. She's not hurt. I was only amusing myself, giving her a bit of a scare.'

'Really?' Rafe's voice left no doubt that he didn't believe the other man. 'Hands behind your head. Now.' He waved the little automatic at Carl. 'Outside, Morgan. This is my problem now.'

271

Morgan hesitated as she sidled behind Rafe. She wasn't sure she wanted to take her eyes off Carl until he was tied up. She kept a wary eye on him as he knelt on the ground and she saw the danger an instant before Rafe.

Carl had knelt next to a pile of rubble and he grabbed at a lump of cement. Rafe and Morgan both reacted fast, but Carl was quicker. He hurled the rock not at either of his captors, as they were expecting, but at the single light bulb above them.

'Down!' Rafe roared. The sound of the discharge was deafening in the bare space. Shards of cement showered over them in the dark and Morgan cowered on the ground, covering her head with her hands.

She heard the solid hit of man against man. Somewhere close by in the dark, metal struck cement and Rafe swore. Morgan had a semi-automatic she couldn't use and now it sounded like Rafe had lost his gun.

The men were strangely quiet and Morgan hesitated, her eyes adjusting to the dark. She'd never witnessed a fight between two men with the same singular aim — to kill. There were no words, nothing intelligible. Just grunts of exertion and explosions of breath as hits connected. She didn't doubt this was a battle to the death and it galvanised her.

She crawled over the floor, sharp chippings digging into her knees and palms as she felt around for Rafe's weapon. It eluded her. Plenty of rubble, but she wasn't going to get a clear hit on Carl with any of that.

A new sound scraped in the dark. 'Come on,' snarled Carl, panting with the effort. 'Let me cut you.' Always the bully he needed to boast and it gave Rafe a slight advantage. Morgan could make out the two of them circling each other. She also registered that Carl was backing towards her and realised the danger she was in.

BORDER WATCH

'Run, Morgan, run.' Rafe's voice remained calm, but the urgency pushed her. 'The backup should be here. Go.'

Her feet reacted and she fled outside before skidding to an unsteady halt. Behind, she heard the clatter of metal on cement and a curse from Carl. Rafe had at least evened the odds again, but she knew Carl too well to think that would be enough to stop him.

'Damn it. I can't. I can't run twice.' Her legs wobbled and she knew she was on the verge of collapsing, but she wouldn't, couldn't run again. She saw with frightening clarity her mother's bloodied face, eyes open to the sky, her mouth slack, never to smile again.

Not Rafe too.

Not after Gavin.

Not after her mother.

The moon wouldn't rise until much later and it took several long moments for her eyes to adjust to the darkness. Finally she made out a bundle of reinforcing rods tangled in long grass. She swore at it as she struggled to free a length, dragging clumps of grass out by its roots. Staggering backwards as it came free, she whirled back to the doorway.

'You bastard,' she screamed, as she flung herself into the room, figuring surprise was her best weapon. What she didn't count on was distracting Rafe, who dropped his guard just enough for Carl to land a solid fist on his jaw. The big Customs man went over backwards. Carl followed fast.

Morgan swung the heavy rod, surprised by how long the tip took to follow. The metal wasn't as rigid as she expected. The space where Carl had been as she started the swing was now empty. Frustration made her hiss and she shifted her grip, balancing the rod between her hands like a baton twirler.

'Come on, you bloody coward. Come and get me,' she taunted, adrenalin giving her courage beyond her pain.

273

His low throaty laugh as he landed another solid kick on Rafe enraged her and she charged at him, her scream shrill in the heavy air.

Carl sidestepped easily, but she swung at him anyway and connected a glancing blow on his shoulder. At least she'd got between him and Rafe.

'You really are impressive, babe,' Carl half laughed at her, gasping for air. 'You deserve better, better than him or me. But you're too late. You can't stop it now. It's too late for Australia. They need to learn the hard way.'

'No!' Morgan yelled, her voice shrill. 'You have to stop this. No one neds to die.'

'Sorry, Morgan.' He shook his head. 'It's got to run a little longer yet. And I'm not getting caught here.'

Before she could answer, he turned and fled out into the moonlight. A deep groan from Rafe had her spinning back to him, the rod still gripped tight in her hand. A flash of light dragged her gaze back outside.

With a thump and a bright flare, fire leapt into the sky. A spindly figure she recognised as Thommo danced clear of the line of fire that now trapped Carl between its fierce burn and the cliff top.

Transfixed, she couldn't even scream.

'Gotcha now. You're not goin' anywhere. Burn my house down. I seen you,' Thommo cackled, spraying more fuel around.

In the moonlight the smoke wreathed around a whirling Carl. Flames licked closer to him, dancing across the ground as the petrol ran in rivulets. It cast huge shadows over the crumbling building.

With an angry roar, Carl charged across the fire at the homeless man, snatching the can of fuel from him. As he spun to fling it over the scraggy tramp, a flame ignited a pool

BORDER WATCH

of unburnt fuel on the ground. In an instant it leapt into the air, travelling back down the vapour trail to the can in Carl's hand. With a thudding whoosh, it exploded.

Like a grotesque parody of Balinese shadow puppets, the writhing figure of Carl beating at his head and clothes backlit a demented Thommo. The flames engulfed him and his shrieks sickened Morgan.

She remembered seeing a hose attached to a tap on the outside wall and ran towards where she thought it was. Laughter came from her left and she turned towards the sound.

'Thommo?'

The old man grinned at her. 'I brought Rafe 'ere. I saw you. I knew Carl was no good.'

'But the fire?' Morgan found the hose and struggled to turn on the tap. A trickle of water dribbled and gurgled from the end. She ran, tugging it behind her, to where Carl still writhed on the ground, and doused the flames. The grass, tinder dry from the heat of early summer, had flared brightly and then dulled to embers that blistered the soles of her feet. Rivers of flame dripped towards the cliff edge, but as the supply of petrol burnt out so too did the fire.

Thommo followed her and stood looking down at the injured man. 'He tried to burn me. Bastard. I seen 'im, I seen 'im. How's it feel?' The last was directed at the now wheezing man at her feet. The sounds of distress broke through Morgan's fascinated horror. Burning a man alive was not on her agenda.

'Thommo, we have to do something.'

'Too late. He deserves to die. I seen him kill that man. Then he tried to kill me, then you.' He patted her shoulder with his gnarled fingers. 'I seen them bring you here. I wouldn't let him hurt you.'

'Thommo.' Morgan sprayed water over Carl. Part of her wanted to help, but the corner of her brain that knew first-hand the violence in Carl still didn't trust him enough to get that close.

Smoke, petrol fumes and the smell of burning flesh coated her throat.

'Ha, how's it feel? Hey?' Thommo prodded the downed man with his sneaker before Morgan could stop him.

'Don't, Thommo. Don't. That's horrible.'

Rafe staggered up beside them, talking into his phone, which had somehow survived the battering his body had barely withstood. 'Need a chopper now. Medivac for a burns victim . . . Glad you enjoyed the show. And get the boss on the phone. I've got a location for the attack.' He tapped the phone ending the call, anger in his words. 'He's past being a danger now.'

Rafe rolled the moaning man onto his back.

'Stay still. The paramedics are on their way.' He took the hose from Morgan and played the water over Carl's head. The injured man tried to toss his face away from the cooling stream, each breath of air an agonising whistle through his blistering lips. Rafe kept the water playing through his fingers reducing the pressure of the spray. 'It's the only thing that will help you.'

Morgan crouched down next to them. 'It's Circular Quay in Sydney. That's what they are planning to attack. He told me.' She gestured at Carl, her voice uneven and hoarse. 'The rest of them left here about an hour ago. We have to find them.'

'I know. I heard what he said.' Rafe's face was grim. 'I've put out an alert. Thommo gave me the registration number for their car. We're doing everything we can now.'

Morgan sagged back in relief, resting on her heels. 'And Carl?'

Rafe met her eyes with a shake of his head. A trickle of dark blood was running down his neck from a cut to the back of his head. He looked like he'd been through hell.

'Will he live?'

Rafe didn't answer and Morgan asked again, her eyes drawn back to the ravaged face. 'Will he?'

'I don't know. Burns are difficult. I hope he does. We need answers.' Rafe's voice was tight and Morgan remembered the news reports she'd read on his SAS chopper crash. Everyone but he had burnt to death, though not immediately. Several had lingered in hospital for weeks before infections overran their bodies. The rumour mill said he'd received a medal for bravery for his efforts to save his team, but he'd been too badly injured himself to do much. Fire had been the killer. The smells must be carved into his brain, she guessed. How hard must this be to confront?

At the sound of pounding feet behind them, she spun around. Thommo melted back into the undergrowth as heavily armed, black-clad men in night-vision goggles stormed onto the plateau.

'Everyone down.' The orders were shouted from the back of the pack and the team arrayed themselves in battle sequence.

'About bloody time.' Rafe didn't bother to disguise his anger as he got to his feet.

'We saw the fire flare up and thought we'd better pick up the pace. Casualties?'

Rafe gestured at the moaning Carl. 'Just the one alive. One dead inside. I've phoned in for the chopper.' On cue the heavy beat of the twin rotors thudded low down in the valley, the sound drifting in on the strengthening breeze. The fire flickered and flared as gusts shifted it back and forth.

Several of the special ops group produced Cyalume light sticks and on Rafe's directions set up a temporary landing area clear of the buildings and scrub. Others doused the flames until smouldering embers were all that remained.

The dust that blew up in the rotor's downdraft covered them as they huddled near the building for protection.

Rafe still hadn't really acknowledged Morgan in all the turmoil and she hung back as the men talked in low voices. She saw him take a couple of phone calls, his face grim in the uneven light.

She felt very alone. The cool breeze blowing in over the edge of the cliff made her shiver, and she wrapped her arms around her chest. A tiny corner of her brain relived the urge to run, to hide, even as it celebrated her decision to stay. Big win, Morgan, she sighed to herself, but at what price? Rafe had done nothing but snap orders at her since he'd got here, and now she felt as though she was in the way.

Tears she'd contained all day flooded her eyes and no amount of willpower or blinking could stop them. Self-pity accounted for most of them, but the feeling that no one deserved to be burnt, no matter how dangerous or corrupt or evil, couldn't be banished.

A pair of warm arms came around her and she automatically tried to twist away.

'God, Morgan. You've made me age twenty years today.'

Familiar lips pressed into her temple and she sagged with relief into the comfort, the security of Rafe's arms, burying her face in his chest. The tears fell unchecked, a dam that had burst its banks and might never be contained again.

'Come and let the medics check you out. Did they hurt you?' Mute, Morgan shook her head.

The bruises would fade. Her feet would heal. The sunburn from being tied outside would leave her skin peeling for a while. But the fear?

Rafe half carried her over to the medics and held her hand while they did their job under the searchlights from the rescue chopper. Shadowy figures roamed over the plateau as the

BORDER WATCH

special ops team catalogued what remained at the site. The
dead terrorist was placed in a black body bag and lay beside
the chopper waiting to be loaded into it.

'She needs to go to hospital. Dehydrated, sunburnt, concussed,
cuts, bruises. We'll take her in with us.' Morgan shrank away
from the paramedic as he spoke, leaning into Rafe, whose dark
eyes sought hers.

He shook his head, squeezing her hand. 'Not in the same
chopper as those two.'

'She can't walk out. Nasty cuts on her head and who knows
what else?' The para shrugged as Rafe shook his head again.

Rafe was torn between wanting to be part of the clean-up of
the site and wanting to stay with Morgan. The smell of Carl's
burns stuck in his nostrils and the fear he still had of choppers
after the crash made him feel physically sick. More importantly,
they still needed to find the rest of the terrorists.

He looked down into her face and knew he only had one
option, and it galled him. He might not have put her in this
place personally, but he sure as hell was responsible for it and
he still couldn't be the one to comfort her. 'Take her with
you. I'll get to the hospital as soon as I can.'

The paramedic nodded. 'If we leave the stiff behind, we'll
all fit.'

'Thanks, but I've still got work to do. Call me before you go.'

By the time Rafe had spoken to the others, Morgan had
been strapped into a stretcher with a saline drip in her arm.
Her eyes were closed and he stood looking down at her. A
helpless rage burnt deep inside.

Life shouldn't be so bloody cruel. He didn't doubt she'd
build another layer of defences around herself, another layer of
armour that would keep the world at bay. He'd believed he'd
managed to find chinks in that armour last night, even as he

recognised that great sex didn't translate into a commitment of any real depth.

Her eyes opened, drowsy now, their focus soft as she looked up at him. He saw the shutters close and reached out to clasp her hand. 'How're you doing?'

Her smile was forced and she ran her tongue over her lips before she answered. 'I'll be okay.' She whispered something and he bent low to hear her words.

'One of Carl's tattoos is the same as the guy on the beach. That's why it looked familiar. I should have recognised it earlier. Maybe this wouldn't have happened then.'

He nodded. 'Yeah. He's an undercover operative playing both sides. Money? Ideology? Whatever. He crossed the line.'

'You knew? You knew already?' she croaked at him, confusion clear in her eyes.

'I found out this morning. ASIO weren't sure about him, but they didn't tell the feds let alone Customs. They let us investigate you instead.'

'Me?' He heard the outrage, the disbelief in the scratchy word.

'"Fraid so.'

'And you?' Her voice rasped with anger and hurt. 'Did you think I was involved with this? Was I just part of the job?'

He ran a rough thumb over her hand, trying to reassure with his touch, but knowing the newly forged link had just been broken. If he were ever to reforge it then honesty had to start now. No more lies.

'At the beginning, I didn't know, no one did. I was sent to watch you. Information about some of your missions had been picked up. Someone had loose lips and we needed to find out who. It took the device Gavin found in your computer to open a gap large enough for me to get through and unearth more information. As soon as you pulled up the package at Scout

BORDER WATCH

Hat, and told me about Thommo's theories on Wiseman, the investigation widened. The feds then found the connection between Wiseman and the body you found on the beach and they leant on ASIO, demanding answers. Wiseman got spat out. I'm just glad I made it in time.'

The contempt blazed from her eyes and she tugged her hand free of his. 'Thanks, mate.'

'Whoa, Morgan.' He took back her hand, but couldn't stop her turning her head away. 'I never said I doubted you. I've worked with you, seen you under pressure. I saw the tracker Gavin found in your computer. I believe you. I know you.' He hesitated. 'I trust you.' And, he added silently, I damn well might love you.

Morgan's hand stayed rigid in his and her eyes closed. She didn't answer.

'We'll talk about it more tomorrow. I couldn't – I just couldn't explain everything. It didn't matter that I knew you weren't actively leaking information. It was my job. Just the way it is.' He waited for her to speak, but she remained resolutely silent.

Rafe rocked back on his heels, running his free hand over his face. He should have told her everything once the team had decided she was an innocent caught up in the operation. It had all seemed so improbable before.

The paramedic touched his shoulder forcing him back to the present. 'Ready to go, mate. You can still come with us if you want?'

'Thanks, I'll catch her later.'

'She'll be right, mate.' The other man misread the concern on Rafe's face. 'Superficial cuts most of them. Nasty bump on the head.' He secured the drip to Morgan's stretcher. 'She'll be back on her feet in no time. You sure there's nothing you need?'

281

Rafe shook his head, releasing Morgan's hand. 'No, I'm right. Thanks.'

He got to his feet, feeling the weary ache in his body. Damn it to hell, he cursed, hearing the sounds of his men sifting through the building behind him. He'd made more bad decisions on this operation than in his entire career.

And it may have cost him the woman he'd come to love.

37

Rafe struggled to open his eyes, the sunlight intent on piercing his brain. He rolled onto his back, his legs tangling in the sheets, and groaned. Every bone in his body ached, every muscle screamed for relief. The climb up the cliff had been hell yesterday afternoon. He'd struggled to keep pace with Thommo, resenting the effortless way the stringy drifter clambered up the sharp rock.

He'd been dripping with sweat, muscles trembling by the time they reached the ledge below the ruined house. Gasping and out of breath, he'd listened to Carl taunting Morgan, trying to track any other voices on the plateau. Refusing to acknowledge the fear that he might be too late, he'd motioned to Thommo to show him the way over the top. The rest was literally burnt into his brain.

He rolled back onto his stomach, feeling the tightness of stitches on the back of his head. Carl had hands the size of house bricks and most of his punches had connected. The numbers on the clock radio swam into focus.

'Shit.' He shot out of bed, his body screaming in complaint. 'Ten o'clock. Shit.' He'd fallen into bed long after midnight so he might be entitled to carry on sleeping, but he had urgent matters to attend to.

His hair was wet when he slammed his hotel room door closed. At least a shave had made him feel halfway human again. It took him two laps of the hospital to find a car park. His footsteps were impatient as he hurried into the ward.

The winning smile he shot at the stern nurse didn't deflect her clear disapproval of the mobile phone clamped to his ear. As he reached the door of the room where he'd found a sedated Morgan being interrogated the night before, he ordered his body to relax. He plastered his best, most reassuring smile on his face and turned the corner.

Her bed wasn't just empty, it was stripped of its linen. Annoyed, Rafe headed back to the nurses' station. 'Morgan Pentland's room, thanks.'

'Oh, I'm sorry, you just missed her. She's been moved.'

'Where to?' Rafe asked, trying to keep his voice level.

'I can't tell you that.'

'Can't, or won't? This is bullshit. I need to see her.'

'I'll call security up if you like, sir. I don't have to put up with this.'

'Right.' He breathed out through pinched nostrils. 'Thank you.' Turning on his heel he'd dialled his boss before he got to the lifts.

By the time he'd rattled down four floors, he knew that Morgan was in protective custody under the gaze of ASIO. They had no intention of losing the only person who could identify the terrorists from the hill. The message he received was loud and oh-so-clear. Back off. Not your operation anymore. More important things to do.

The flutter of paper on his front windscreen did nothing to ease his mood. He scowled as he screwed up the parking ticket and tossed it on the passenger seat, and fumed the whole way

BORDER WATCH

back down the curving road to the airport and the Customs building.

The sparse office was open plan, a place for work and nothing more. The only thing welcoming about it was the air-conditioning. He waved an impatient hand at a colleague. 'Who's got the intercept job in the chopper?'

'I think it's Rob's team. Why? You interested?'

'Doesn't look like there's much else I'm allowed to do around here.' Rafe couldn't hide his frustration.

'They're out back loading the gear. I'll cover for you. The boss is out.'

'Thanks. Owe you one.' Rafe pulled his locker key from his drawer and headed off to get his own equipment. The other man's sympathetic smile followed him out the door.

38

Morgan knew she should close the fridge door, knew that nothing in it was going to appeal to her, understood that she didn't need food, only the comfort of cooking it.

'What the hell am I doing?' The door closed with a gentle hiss of its seals as she let it go.

She'd found the interrogation from ASIO far easier to handle than the concerned smiles and sympathetic enquiries from the nursing staff at the hospital. Right now she had two minders in and around her house and they weren't letting anyone in, not even Sam. She could hear the big dog doing patrols up the side fence, banished just because he'd taken an instant, and visible, dislike to the shorter of the two women assigned to her.

For two hours she'd sifted through the photographs they'd produced. Of the five men she'd seen at the house on the hill, she'd been able to identify four. The one who'd died from the savage chop of Carl's hand didn't make it on to any list. Not surprisingly, her minders didn't seem too concerned about discovering his identity. 'A dead terrorist is a good terrorist' seemed to be their mantra.

They agreed that Circular Quay was probably the target. They, like Morgan, saw no reason why Carl would have lied

BORDER WATCH

to her. Her body should already have been decomposing in the scrub below the steep embankment, not talking, walking and identifying his mates.

Four days left.

Four days until what?

Hell.

With Carl unable to answer questions, they needed another way to find the answers. She'd searched her memory for anything else that might help but had come up empty.

Unlike the interrogation she endured earlier in the week, these officers had been considerate, conciliatory and cautious. Probing rather than demanding, cajoling rather than hectoring, supportive rather than accusatory.

If one more person asked how she felt, she was sure she'd scream. She didn't know how she felt, so how the hell was she supposed to answer that question? Physically she ached in muscles she'd forgotten existed. She hobbled when she walked on feet tender from burns. Sunburn made her skin hot and prickly and someone had installed a jackhammer inside her head.

Other than that she felt numb. Emotionless. She'd been there before. Two, three, four times in her life. Who was counting? She knew the drill. Face what happened, deal with it, lock it up tight out of sight and move on.

'No point crying over the proverbial,' she said out loud. 'Wishes are for fishes.' She sighed, then added, 'Wishes are for dreamers.' She pushed the feeling of a warm pair of secure arms away from her. No point relying on someone else. Just get on with it. Rafe wasn't rushing to check on her and she was wasting her time waiting for him. He'd been investigating her all along, as well as looking out for his precious little cell of terrorists.

She didn't need a reminder that not only had she chosen a bully for a boyfriend, she'd chosen a terrorist as well. And if she believed Carl's words, he was a soldier of fortune, not even politically or religiously motivated. Just available to the highest bidder.

And then there was Rafe. Using her for his investigation. No doubt laughing at how easy it was to get her into bed. More fool her, she thought, refusing to give in to the wave of self-pity.

She spied the remote for the sound system and hit the button for the radio. A crooning Robbie Williams filled the room. It didn't make her feel any brighter. The fridge beckoned again. This time she snagged a bottle of juice out of it, poured a glassful, and headed for her back deck.

She'd dialled Rafe's number a couple of times, but never managed to push send. Part of her wanted to hear his explanation, part of her wanted to forget him. A corner of her heart wanted to listen to the dark, velvety voice tell her he believed in her, but her rational side reminded her that she'd just been part of his operation. Collateral damage. And she was kidding herself.

Great sex didn't mean diddly-squat. He never made any promises and right now he was probably up to his eyeballs in high-level meetings and she would be the last thing on his mind.

39

Rafe propped his foot on the bumper of the truck as the back doors finally closed. They were in a lay-by on the side of the Pacific Highway. The helicopter that had ferried them to the rendezvous was just starting to wind up again.

'Do we drive it into Brisbane or do we stop at the Sunshine Coast and leave it in the police compound at Maroochydore?' The burly man finished securing tape over the locks and waited for Rafe to reply.

'All the way to Brisbane and into the Customs warehouse out at Pinkenba. We can't risk this going anywhere we can't keep an eye on it. I want to be there when the feds sign for it.'

The other man nodded, jiggling the keys in his hand. 'Okay. I'll be there in about twelve hours. I've got your number.'

They shook hands then Rafe watched the truck leave in a cloud of dust and a grind of the gears. The local police cars used to pull the truck over followed at a more sedate pace.

The driver of the vehicle was handcuffed and wedged into the rear seat of the helicopter next to one of Rafe's team. Claiming ignorance of what you were carrying held no water with Rafe. The man knew more than he was saying. They just needed time to dig it out of him and time was a luxury they didn't have.

Rafe climbed in beside the pilot and pulled headsets on. 'Good to go, mate.' He signalled with his hand and the helicopter's rpm increased to a shuddering whirl. Third time in a week, he grimaced to himself. At least it had cured his chopper phobia. The gut-wrenching swoop as they accelerated forwards and up didn't help his nerves though.

He pulled his phone out of his pocket and sent a text to his boss. They'd made the right decision to intercept the smuggled goods. The package they'd pulled from the water may have been guns, but hidden under cases of prawns in the back of the refrigerated truck were boxes of detonators and plastic explosives. The whole shooting match would have left a crater as big as a house if it had gone off.

He felt a tinge of regret that intercepting it tipped off the receivers, but they couldn't risk letting that hardware hit the streets. Not with 9 November only four days away.

A tap on the shoulder made him turn and he accepted the water bottle his colleague handed him. He popped two painkillers into his hand and swallowed. He'd been conditioned to do without sleep in the SAS, but that was a few years ago now. He wasn't a young man anymore. The stitches still pulled in the back of his head and twelve hours' sleep in three days wasn't close to being enough. The edges of his brain were getting fuzzy. He leant back in the seat and closed his eyes, the familiar throb of the helicopter soothing him for the first time since the crash.

Micro sleeps always brought vivid dreams. A guileless, naked Morgan beckoned him from the cool water of her pool, enticing him with erect nipples and smooth shoulders.

Fire flared bright as the writhing figure of Carl teetered on the edge of the cliff.

BORDER WATCH

A young man crawling through the wreckage of a chopper, clawing his way back to his team, the rain pelting down on him, tracer fire flickering through the inky blackness.

Rafe woke with a groan and shook his head at the question in the pilot's eyes.

'Sorry, must have nodded off.'

'Yeah.' The pilot turned back to his controls as they navigated their way through the airspace.

Rafe stared out the window. Would it be too late when he got back to Morgan? Would the moment have passed? He'd give it his best shot, but Morgan built strong armour around her heart. Who could blame her?

His reflection stared back at him, wavering in the helicopter window. Grim faced, fatigue etched in every line, his dark eyebrows drawn together in a solid frown, he looked forbidding. It might have been too late for him to start with. Too long hiding emotions, too long needing no one and too long living alone. This sudden craving for softness, for comfort, was a weakness. Must be getting old, but he couldn't shake the desire, the need to have Morgan in his life, whatever the price.

He was used to planning strategies, campaigns, battles. Maybe he needed to do the same with Morgan.

But that would have to wait. He had a job to do first. Abu Nadal and his team were still out there.

40

'Are you sure that's the man you saw with Carl Wiseman? Abu Nadal?' Her minder's voice was gentle but insistent.

'Yes,' Morgan said. 'One hundred percent certain.' The grainy CCTV footage showed two men leaving the Circular Quay train station.

'Just keep watching. The face recognition software isn't infallible. We can't afford a mistake.'

'Right.' Morgan refrained from stating the obvious: that they'd already made many mistakes. The two men appeared on another camera as they emerged into the central entrance and the light. Nadal pulled sunglasses from his pocket and slid them onto his face. There was no doubt in her mind.

'It's him. And one of the other men I saw up there.' She watched as they walked outside and climbed into a taxi. The date and time stamp along the bottom told her the footage was less than an hour old.

'Okay.' Her minder was already keying a number into her mobile, relief clear on her face.

Morgan kept watching as the taxi left the kerb. Even she could see its licence plate. Maybe this would be the end of the trail finally. She'd watched hours of CCTV film, wading through lookalikes that the computer had identified as possible targets. With an ever-present minder leaning over her shoulder, the palpable stress in the room had got to her.

'Here, Morgan. They found your phone off the side of the trail.' Her other minder – the short one – handed over the compact mobile. It felt like she'd just been rewarded for giving them the right answer.

'Oh.' Morgan turned it over in her hand and peered at the screen. 'It's fully charged.'

'Yeah. I guess the techs had to plug it in to check it.'

'Of course.' Everything had to be vetted first. Nobody could be trusted. Morgan thumbed through the missed calls and messages.

Four calls from Rafe – all on the same day. All on that day, that day two days ago when death had crooked its finger at her and she'd survived. She skipped over them. She didn't want to hear his voice.

One call from Lauren followed by half a dozen text messages from her. That made Morgan smile. When Morgan hadn't replied to her messages, Lauren had called the house, then turned up on the doorstep and demanded to see her. Even her two minders couldn't stop Lauren.

Then there were two messages from Patrick. He sounded tentative, confused and something else she couldn't quite pick. After the second replay Morgan's finger hovered over the delete key. She hesitated.

She suspected Rafe was correct and she needed to find some way of forgiving Patrick. It shouldn't have worked that way, but Morgan couldn't dismiss the feeling that she had reached a point in her life where she was strong enough to face him, face her parents' death, and then turn her face to the future.

She sat in a chair on the deck, rolling the phone in her hands. The sunbirds were back, flitting in and out of the plants gathering fresh lining for their next offspring's bed. The male bird paused on the railing of the pool fence and turned its delicate head to watch her.

Something in that tiny movement, the optimism of its jaunty yellow breast, the bravado in its iridescent blue throat, touched Morgan.

She raised her phone to her ear and listened to Rafe's messages, heard the concern in his voice and knew it was real. Listened as each message grew more urgent. Listened until the final one, words distorted and crackly, finished in silence. The last message brought hope. 'Hang on, Morgan. Hang on, wherever you are. I'll find you. Hang on. I love you, Morgan.'

And he had. He'd found her. And maybe . . .

The insistent cheep of the little bird brought her back to her surroundings. Brought her back to the tears that wet her cheeks as she heard the truth in his voice. Brought her back to the thunder of her heart.

Maybe they could still make it.

But first she needed to finish off what had started twenty years ago.

She dialled.

And waited, her hand shaking until the call was answered.

'Hi, Ricky here.'

'It's me. Morgan.'

41

Rafe slumped on his couch, the sweat from his run still clinging to him, darkening his clothes. What the hell was he doing here? His austere one-room apartment was soulless. Except for the pile of books with titles that spoke of military campaigns and strategies, it could have been a hotel room. He got up and slid open the glass door which led onto a tiny balcony. Even the view of the Brisbane River and the sheer cliffs of Kangaroo Point did nothing for him this morning.

It was over. Nadal and his group had been picked up in an apartment hotel in Bridge Street, close to Circular Quay. In a quiet operation they'd been arrested and removed before anyone really became aware there'd been a problem. The AFP closed the hotel on the pretext a gas leak had been detected and the clean-up squad moved in. The bomb disposal team calculated the amount of explosives would have demolished Circular Quay's railway station and everything beneath it as it fell. Plans they found suggested the Sydney Opera House would have been hit as well. Now the blame game between security departments had reached feverish heights. And that would only get worse once the politicians sank their pearly teeth into the debacle. Sometimes a win could still be a loss.

And he'd been put out to pasture, which was driving him insane. He knew it was only temporary. He also knew his boss would sign the transfer papers releasing him to the Cairns office. But all that might still lead to a brick wall with haunting grey eyes.

Morgan Pentland had become an obsession that sent him running along the riverside walkway at five in the morning in an attempt to drive her out of his thoughts.

His eyes unfocused, he replayed in his head seeing her sitting in a hospital bed, still in her filthy running clothes. Propped against the sterile wall, he'd listened to her emotionless voice catalogue her day from hell to the two federal police officers. She'd answered their questions with resigned stoicism, no sign of the earlier storm of tears, just the bare, hard facts. She'd stared death in the face again and all because of him.

The railing of the balcony was cool and wet with dew. He leant on it anyway, reliving the last week and a half. Working from Morgan's descriptions and identifications they'd rounded up everyone from the ruins.

Rafe knew the federal police and ASIO had interviewed Morgan for several days. Debriefed as a hostage, analysed for possible Stockholm Syndrome since she had been living with Carl for almost a year, and eventually cleared of anything other than being used by a professional. He'd thought the intensity of that type of questioning might nudge her back towards him, but it seemed to have the opposite effect. It didn't matter what angle he tried, she kept pushing him away.

Gavin's funeral had been a very public affair on the same day the terrorists had planned to attack Sydney. Across the crush of mourners he'd seen Morgan and Lauren comforting Gavin's family. He'd paid his own respect privately to the grieving parents and he didn't feel he had the right to intrude at the funeral.

Morgan had acknowledged him with a brief nod before she turned away, her arm around Lauren. Her quiet dignity and composure must have taken some effort. That was the last time he'd seen her.

He walked back into the unit, flicking on the electric jug and digging instant coffee out of the cupboard. 'Admit it, mate,' he said out loud, 'you need help. You can't win this campaign on your own.'

He wasn't going to let her walk away without a face-to-face meeting, but even seeing her was proving impossible. When she finally answered his calls, she wouldn't even tell him where she was. If he could see her guarded eyes, he'd know whether she was being honest when she told him it was over.

Was it just his ego that was refusing to accept her assertion that they'd had a night of great sex and that was that? He really didn't believe so. The connection between them was stronger, more enduring than a fumble in the dark. It was a connection grounded in mutual respect, tested in extraordinary circumstances and, if he were honest, born in the instant she'd forced him to back down at their very first encounter. It was a fierce pull, deep enough to last a lifetime.

And she'd felt it just as deeply.

He knew it, would stake his life on it. Absently, he stirred sugar into his coffee. 'You need help.' The words were hollow in the morning silence. 'You need Lauren. She must know where Morgan is.'

The two hours to eight o'clock, and what he deemed a civilised hour, were interminable. He'd finished off all his paperwork by the time his watch ticked over the hour and he reached for his phone.

'Lovely Lauren. How're you doing?'

'Hey, gorgeous. Where are you?' Rafe could hear the delight in the young woman's voice and it lifted his spirits as she continued. 'Coming to rescue me from boredom or tell me you've proposed?'

'I'm in Brisbane and I need a little help, actually.' He felt his throat tighten with the admission. 'I seem to be having some difficulties contacting Morgan.'

'Her battery'll be flat. I spoke to her last night and she's doing okay. Not easy dealing with her brother and his disaster.'

Rafe pressed the phone to his ear, not quite understanding her words. 'No, it can't be I guess.'

'The kids are doing okay, but Patrick?' Lauren sighed. 'I think she's bitten off more than she can chew.'

'The kids?' Rafe resorted to his old techniques.

'Yeah, well, it's not like she's ever been a parent and two would be a bit of a handful.'

'Right.' Rafe kept his voice neutral and there was a pregnant pause.

'I think we'd better meet for coffee. You don't have a clue what I'm talking about, do you?' Lauren was half laughing at him now. 'Morgan's in Sydney. With her brother and his two kids. She hasn't told you anything, has she?'

'Seems not.' He kept the hurt from his voice. Maybe Morgan was being honest. Maybe she had moved on, away from him. 'Where are you?'

'Brisbane. I leave for Sydney tonight. I can be in the city in an hour. Somewhere by the river might be nice.'

'The Coffee Club near riverside? Nine-ish?'

'Don't be late, big guy. We can go shopping afterwards if you're interested . . .' The sly note in her voice made him laugh.

'Thanks, but coffee might be my limit.'

'Coward. See you in an hour.' Lauren's laughter stayed with him.

By nine o'clock the sun was high over Brisbane and the river still managed to sparkle despite its muddy flow. Rafe stopped by the ferry terminal to watch the City Cat manoeuvre onto the pontoon. It was packed with passengers even at the end of morning peak hour. Men in suits that were uniformly dark and sober, bustled off the ferry like a line of busy mynah birds. The women, on the other hand, were birds of paradise, flicking their hair, swiping a last coat of shine over their lips, tugging at clothes that hugged hips and breasts enticingly. There was something about the city that always brought a reluctant smile to Rafe's face.

'Perving like a middle-aged sleaze, Rafe?' Lauren tapped him on the shoulder before depositing a smacking kiss on his cheek.

He grinned down at her. 'Window shopping is fine apparently. I'm sure you were spouting that wisdom a couple of weeks ago.'

'Just don't touch it then. Coffee?' She nodded up the sloping walkway. 'I need my caffeine fix.'

It took Lauren all of five minutes to settle comfortably in her seat, twirl the order number between her fingers and cut to the chase.

'So all is not well in Camelot then?' She raised a wicked eyebrow at him. 'Cinderella escaped without the glass slipper, Sleeping Beauty didn't wait for the handsome prince to kiss her? Tsk, tsk. Very careless of you.'

Rafe leant back in the metal chair and raised his eyes to the ceiling. 'See, here's the problem. I need some information about a woman who's gone missing. Two ways I can go. Put out an all-stations alert with the police or . . .' He glanced over at Lauren. 'Or I can throw myself on the mercy of a smart-mouthed airhead with attitude. Why did I think the second plan was a better option?'

Lauren clapped her hands delightedly. 'Because you don't just need help, you need *my* help. And I'd do anything to see Morgan happy. So, let me start with what you do know.'

He ripped the top off a sugar sachet before he answered. 'The last conversation I had with Morgan face-to-face was in the hospital in Cairns after she'd escaped from the terrorist camp.' He hesitated. 'And I saw you both at Gavin's funeral. It didn't feel appropriate to intrude. You were with his parents. Morgan saw me, but she didn't look like anything would prise her away from your side.'

Lauren stared down at her coffee. 'I wouldn't have got through that day without her. I'm sorry I didn't see you.' She raised her head, tears shining in her eyes. 'She could have done with someone to lean on herself.' Her voice thickened and she waved her hand at him, before he could offer any comfort. 'Continue.'

The distress she was so carefully hiding was just below the surface and Rafe wished he had some words that would ease it. All he could do was keep talking. 'Since then I've had two short phone calls when she assures me she's fine, but she doesn't want to see me. So here I am, hoping you can help me.'

'You're not kidding, are you?' Lauren leant across the table, shock darkening her eyes, tears still clinging to her lashes. 'I had no idea. She said she'd spoken to you and you were too busy to get away. What is she doing?'

'Pushing me away with both hands.'

'Why?'

Rafe let his breath out in a rush. 'She figured out she was initially a suspect in the investigation. I was keeping an eye on her. She wasn't happy about that.'

BORDER WATCH

Lauren's harsh bark of laughter said she wasn't impressed either. 'Dear god. And you're surprised? A smart man like you?'

'No.' He shook his head. 'But I'd like a chance to explain. It was more complicated than connecting the dots, or in this case tattoos. I knew very early on she wasn't involved.'

'So you weren't sticking to her like glue because you fancied her. You played us all for suckers.' Lauren pushed her coffee cup away as she talked. 'You didn't trust any of us.'

'It's my job, Lauren. I don't have to like what I'm doing. At this particular moment I'd rather be driving a garbage truck than creating any more pain for Morgan.'

'Yeah, right.' Hostility was radiating from Lauren and Rafe met her eyes without flinching.

'I love her.' The words sounded flat even to him.

'So prove it.'

Rafe raised an eyebrow at her. 'If she'd just bloody well talk to me I would.'

'No, prove it to me and I'll help you. Don't, and I'll finish my coffee and walk away.'

'So I should have put out an all-stations alert then.'

'I didn't pick you for being a coward.' Lauren's chin jutted out.

'Lauren, what the hell do you want me to say?' He ran an impatient hand through his hair. 'I love her. That in itself was a revelation for me. I understand that she's built walls around her that will take a lifetime to dismantle. I know how hard she's worked to get where she is. I know she thinks she's a bad judge of men and all we do is screw her over, but that's not me. It's not what I ever intended to do.'

'But you did.' Lauren had her arms crossed now.

'Not through any choice of mine and certainly not after the aircraft was shot down. She'd been scratched off the list by then.'

301

He waved two fingers to the waitress. 'Same again, thanks.' Lauren didn't protest, which he took to be a good sign.

'You were right the night I found you in my bed.' He waited for her to bite. Instead she just widened her eyes at him. 'When you said you thought I was sweet on your boss. I was.' He nodded for emphasis. 'If it had been her in my bed, who knows where we'd all be today? Sliding doors, six degrees of separation or whatever you want to call fate.'

'So you had the hots for someone you were investigating? Isn't that improper?' Lauren was mellowing. He could see some of the anger leaving her.

'By then, I'd already sent in a report clearing her of anything except being used by a smart operator. It turns out Wiseman had a fat bank account in the Cayman Islands and a double life that would make James Bond proud. Unfortunately, no one bothered to tell Customs about it.'

'Never did like the jerk. Wish you'd decked him in the pub that night.' She leant forwards. 'So?'

'So I need to talk to her, need to convince her.'

'I can organise that, but . . .' She stopped and smiled at the waitress as she slid two coffees onto their table. 'But logistically, she's got a lot on her plate right now. You've obviously not heard any of it.'

'That's why I'm here.' He caught and held her gaze, trying to convey how serious he was.

'It seems her sister-in-law died of cancer earlier this year. That left her drug addicted, dysfunctional brother the sole carer for two children. The boy is the same age Morgan was when her mum died. That's the real reason Partrick tracked Morgan down. Family Services wants to take the kids away from him.' Lauren's words came out in a rush. 'Morgan will walk away from everything rather than let the system put them in foster care. She's been there, done that.'

BORDER WATCH

'Fuck.' Rafe's expletive fell into the silence. 'No wonder she's pushing me away.' He couldn't stop the quick catch in his voice.

'So now's your chance to run, and I won't tell her we've had this conversation.'

'Run?' He looked at her blankly. 'Why the hell would I run when she's going to need all the help she can get?'

Lauren shrugged. 'If you thought she had walls around her before, can you imagine what she's building right now? You'll need siege ladders to get over them. Are you up for it?' Her tone taunted him, making him bite down on his hot retort.

'Nothing a well-planned campaign can't overcome, Lauren.' His mild words were a rebuke, but she grinned at him.

'So let's get planning then.'

Half an hour later he found himself standing among the crowd at the Cenotaph in Anzac Square as the clock chimed eleven. The eleventh hour of the eleventh day of the eleventh month. Remembrance Day. The day that marked the end of the First World War.

Like those around him, he bowed his head and remembered. Remembered those who gave their lives in so many wars. Remembered his team in the SAS, his brothers in arms, who died for their country. Remembered Gavin, killed in a covert war that officially hadn't happened.

Two minutes later, as the noise of the city and the smell of car exhausts intruded into the moment, he'd made his decision.

He'd had enough of living with regrets. He needed to move on and only look back to learn. Looking forwards meant finding Morgan and winning his own private war.

42

'Hey, sister, give me five,' Lauren chortled, pumping her fist into the air as they walked out of the simulator centre on the Qantas Jet Base. 'We were on fire.'

Morgan obliged and slapped Lauren's hand, well pleased herself with their effort in the sim check. All they had to face now was a line check in the aircraft doing their job and they'd be back at work. 'So much modesty in one so talented,' Morgan drawled back at her.

'No point in pretending and hey, we've seen first-hand that all those procedures actually have a place and a purpose. That makes the lurching bat cave less daunting and more manageable.'

Morgan snorted this time. 'It will always be a lurching bat cave to me, no matter how many emergencies I might still face. You're just full of adrenalin.'

'Probably.' Lauren grinned at her. 'And I've organised a treat for us. Lunch at beautiful Bondi in one of those swanky restaurants overlooking the beach. Drink champagne, eat good food.'

Frowning, Morgan looked at her watch. 'Lauren, I'd love to, but I need to pick the kids up from school at three.'

BORDER WATCH

'So? It's only twelve o'clock now. And where's Patrick?'

'Methadone day at the courthouse. He has to get a blood test to prove he's taking his medication and not heroin. There's no guarantee he'll be home in time so I said I'd do the kids.'

'So we hurry then. The table's booked for one.'

'Can't we make it tonight? I can do dinner,' Morgan said. 'I really need to stop and buy some food on the way home.'

Lauren sighed. 'God, you're making this difficult for me. I'll try.' She pulled her phone out of her handbag and walked away from Morgan as she dialled, her finger pressed into her ears to shut out the roar of jets departing over their heads.

Morgan retreated back to her own thoughts. Dinner would be lovely. Meeting Ricky and his children had been confronting. Emma, wraithlike, had clung tight to his hand. Nathan had stood rock solid beside his father. Morgan could remember too vividly being the same age when her mother, his grandmother, had died. Twenty years had not diminished that pain, but had only changed it into a different hurt. An aching chasm that never filled, but still gaped deep inside her.

She didn't consider herself maternal, never had, but no way could she allow these children to face the world alone. Patrick might be making an effort now, but how long would that last? The first hurdle he came to might just shove him over the edge again. The genetic predisposition was ingrained. Their father hadn't had the courage to face what he'd done in a drunken rage. Hanging himself had been the coward's way out. Patrick was his father's son.

No, her life was about to change forever, maybe for the better, or maybe becoming more complicated. She hadn't worked out the logistics yet.

At least Rafe had stopped phoning her. It had got increasingly difficult to keep the pain from her voice. The feeling of his arms around her was a comfort she would treasure for

305

the rest of her life, no matter how empty she might feel, no matter how alone.

'All done then.' Lauren would have put the Cheshire cat to shame so wide was her smile. 'Seven tonight. I'll swing by and pick you up. Put on your party shoes and we'll celebrate.'

'I didn't exactly come packed for partying,' Morgan retorted, but the irony was lost on Lauren.

'Ha, so . . .' The younger woman looked at her watch. 'We have time to visit the QVB shopping palace for some retail therapy. Bet you've never managed to replace the clothes Carl trashed when he broke in to your place. Come on.' She grabbed Morgan's hand as they headed for the security gate. 'You'll be finished in time for the kids.'

Morgan didn't resist too hard. Lauren was a powerful tonic when she got going. The last few weeks had carved their mark into both women. It might be healthy to forget all those troubles for a while. What the hell. A new dress might be good for her. And Lauren was right. She did need to replace the stuff she'd thrown out after the break-in. At least the insurance company would pick up the tab for some of that.

'I still don't see how you can justify seven pairs of shoes, Lauren,' Morgan laughed as they loaded the car's boot.

'No justification required. I would be a thief to my own wallet to ignore such fabulous bargains. You should have bought more yourself.'

Morgan was still smiling as she slammed the boot shut. 'Three dresses are two more than I planned on buying, not to mention matching handbag and shoes.'

'So wear the red one tonight. It looks fantastic.'

'Lauren, Lauren, I'm not your Barbie doll.' Morgan tried to be stern, snapping the seat belt into the buckle.

BORDER WATCH

'No, but you'll make all the women in the restaurant jealous as hell. We're the perfect foil for each other. Young, beautiful and blonde with mature, dark and smoulderingly sexy.'

'You do talk crap, don't you?' It felt good to laugh at nothing more than Lauren's silliness, Morgan had to admit.

'Language.' Lauren wagged a finger at her. 'Did you ring Rafe back?'

The raised eyebrow should have been enough to make her back off, but Lauren wasn't afraid of much. 'That means no. Why?'

'Because.'

'That's not an answer.' With a toss of her hair, Lauren switched lanes, missing a truck by what must have been a coat of paint as she fought her way onto the overpass she'd almost sailed past. 'That's a cop-out. He's smitten.'

'Smitten.' Morgan put all the sarcasm she could muster into the word.

'Absolutely.' Lauren changed lanes again. 'He's even phoned me to check on you since you're not returning his calls.'

'Hmph.' Morgan stared out the window.

'So, as he's tried to call you, why not call him back?'

'I did. I left a message saying I needed space. That I had to go to Sydney.'

'But you never told him why?'

'Lauren.' Morgan's tone was a warning, but Lauren persisted.

'Well I told him. You can't keep stuff as big as this to yourself.'

'And why not?' Morgan was suddenly furious. 'It's my life, my decisions and I'm living it on my terms.' She glared at Lauren. 'You want the truth? Then try this on. I probably fell in love with Commander Rafe, but I'm about to become a mum to my niece and nephew. That's going to involve moving from my home. It means spending time with my big brother who I can't like, let alone love. It might even mean giving up a job I've fought bloody hard to have. So I can't . . .' She turned away so Lauren couldn't see the hot flood of tears that spilled over her lashes. But Morgan's voice betrayed her and shocked Lauren into silence as she continued. 'I just can't let him near me. I'm not that strong.'

'Morgan, I'm sorry. I had no idea.'

Morgan waved her hand at her friend, clamping down on the overwhelming tide of self-pity. There was no room for it.

'You still need to tell Rafe. He deserves that much from you.'

'I can't even tell you without falling apart.'

'He's got the right to know. Not go on thinking he's done something else wrong, apart from his job.' Lauren bounced back on to the offensive. 'Doesn't he deserve the right to decide whether he wants you along with a truckload of baggage? He's never struck me as a coward. He might surprise you with his answer.'

Lauren reached into the pocket on the side of the door and pulled out her phone, one hand on the wheel as she scrolled through her messages. 'He sent me one this morning. Here.'

She thrust the phone out to Morgan who turned it over a couple of times before she gave in with a sigh. Squinting at the screen, his words surprised her.

Take care of the boss. More fragile than she looks. Fly safe.

Morgan was silent as she digested it.

'You reckon a guy like Rafe bothers to send text messages unless he means them? He's in love.' Lauren dragged the last word out with a roll of her eyes. 'And he deserves to know why you're shoving him away with both hands. I know why he thinks you're doing it and he's wide of the mark by a country mile, but I'm not explaining everything to him.'

BORDER WATCH

Her vehemence surprised Morgan, forcing an apology from her. 'Sorry I bit your head off before. It just —'

'Hurts like hell that you found someone you care for and maybe can't have him. Got plenty of experience with that one, love.' Lauren pulled up in front of Patrick's house. 'My head tells me that I will eventually forget Gavin, but my heart tells me that when you meet someone who is so in tune, so intrinsically right for you, grab them with both hands. It might never happen again. A bit like the planets aligning once a century. If you let that opportunity go, it might not present itself again. Ever.'

Morgan didn't miss the quick well of tears in Lauren's blue eyes and bit back her acerbic retort.

'So, enough. Better go and convince Mum to let me have the car again tonight. I'll be here at six-thirty.' Lauren gave Morgan a hug before she loaded the bags into her arms. 'And wear the glamour-goddess dress. We'll sort something out.'

It was another half an hour before Morgan put her feet up and sipped a cup of coffee. Maybe Lauren had a point. To close this chapter once and for all, she needed to tell Rafe herself.

She selected his number then hesitated before she finally pressed send. It went to voicemail and the cowardly corner of her brain hit the end button before she could leave a message.

What the hell was she going to say?

Sorry, but the reason I can't see you anymore is because I've got an instant family which needs me.

And you don't.

And I need to be needed.

Sorry for falling in love with you and now putting two children ahead of you.

309

She retreated to her old comforter. By the time she headed out the door to walk to the school she had made enough food to feed them all for a week.

Nathan was still withdrawn, kicked stones all the way home.

Emma clung to her hand, brushing familiar fine dark hair back from her face as she chatted about her day. She perched on the corner of the kitchen bench as Morgan made banana smoothies and sliced carrot cake.

Her innocence was beguiling, a girl teetering on the brink of teenage-hood. There was no way Morgan would let her get caught in that storm and sucked up into the whirling, swirling turmoil. She knew how far and hard a young girl could fall.

Patrick came in and dropped onto the couch, morose and monosyllabic.

'How'd it go?' Morgan handed him the same snack she'd fed the kids.

'I'm clean. I didn't need their bloody tests to tell me that.' He didn't meet her eyes. She wondered how demoralising it must feel to be so untrustworthy you had to front up for a blood test every week to prove you hadn't fallen off the rails.

His other option was to do time in jail. That wouldn't help him or the kids, so she gave him grudging respect for at least trying. She just didn't think he'd make it.

'Lauren and I are going out for dinner tonight. There's a casserole in the oven and steamed vegies to heat up in the microwave.'

Patrick, didn't answer her, but Emma did.

'I'll do it, Aunty Morgan. I always did when Mum had to work.' Her lip trembled as she mentioned her mother, but in a gesture Morgan applauded the young girl took a deep breath and tried to smile.

BORDER WATCH

Morgan put her arm around the girl and gave her shoulders a quick squeeze. 'Thanks, Emma. Get your dad to lift the dish out of the oven though. I made enough to freeze the leftovers for another dinner so it's in the biggest dish I could find.' She smiled down into her niece's grey eyes. 'I'm twice your size and had trouble getting it out and these —' she gave Emma's biceps a gentle squeeze, 'have a long way to go yet.'

Emma giggled and snuggled closer. The warmth, the puppy-like wriggle of the young body, tugged at Morgan's heart. Some day, somewhere she wanted to give to this girl the things she'd missed out on herself. Then Rafe's quick teasing smile slipped into her head and she blinked at the sudden feeling of loss. No point wishing for second chances, girl. They only happened in books and movies.

Commander Rafe, with his warm hands and persuasive lips, was a memory she would keep safe in her heart, proof that someone had cared about her enough to hold her when she needed it most. Even if he'd had ulterior motives, she reminded herself, tarnishing the warming memory.

Protectively, she hugged Emma close again. The only thing she could do was protect Emma and watch over Nathan. 'So, homework, Em?'

The young girl screwed up her nose. 'Yeah, I guess.'

'Come on then. Bring it into the kitchen and let's see how much I can remember.'

Morgan couldn't miss the scowl on her brother's face. Bad luck, mate, she fumed to herself. You're allowed to miss your wife, but these kids need someone and, if it's not going to be you, then I'll make damn sure it's me.

311

43

With one last check in the bathroom mirror, Morgan squared her shoulders. At least she'd be able to tell Lauren with complete honesty that she'd tried to phone Rafe and his phone was diverting to voicemail. She heard a car pull up outside and hurried to say goodnight to the others.

Emma's eyes were huge as she gazed up at Morgan.

'Aunty Morgan, you look beautiful. You could be in a magazine.' She fingered the soft fabric of the floaty dress with wistful fingers. 'And you smell so cool.'

Morgan smiled, tucking Emma's hair behind her ear as she bent to kiss her. 'Thanks, Em.'

Patrick sat silent on the couch, his expression unfathomable.

'Where's Nathan?' Morgan asked.

Her brother nodded in the direction of his bedroom. 'Xbox.'

'Has he done his homework?'

Patrick scowled before he answered. 'Dunno.'

'Be good to find out.' Morgan struggled to keep the censure from her voice.

'Yeah.' Patrick stood up. 'Enjoy yourself.' He didn't look back or acknowledge her. His shoulders said it all.

BORDER WATCH

'And don't you look hot tonight?' Lauren grinned at her in the half dark of the car. 'We'll turn heads everywhere we go.'

'Just dinner, girlfriend. I need to get some sleep tonight. Tomorrow I'm dragging Patrick, no doubt kicking and screaming, to the lawyers to finalise Carol's will and make a new one for him.'

'That'll be fun.' Lauren pulled a face. 'So I was thinking, why couldn't they move to Cairns? They only rent. Patrick's not working. Nathan's going to high school next year. Emma's got a couple of years at primary school to go still. End of term's coming up. Good time to do it.'

Morgan almost laughed at Lauren's simplistic dissection of the problem. She'd examined all the options herself and not quite discarded that one. 'It's not that easy.'

'As easy as you want it. Their life has to change because their mum is gone. Move 'em to Cairns and at least you have stability. And good friends and great neighbours. You'd still have a job, a way of paying the bills.'

'Maybe I'm due for a change.' Morgan bit the inside of her lip.

'Maybe I can smell burning martyr from here,' Lauren retorted. 'So what did Rafe say?'

'Ah, yes. I tried. I really did. Three times. Went to voicemail.'

'And?'

'And I left a message saying sorry if I was rude, but I'm a bit busy and will be in touch when I get home.'

'Ha, what a load of.' Lauren sounded outraged. 'You fobbed him off.'

'No, I left him a message. It can wait.'

'Hmm.' Lauren focused on the road ahead and fiddled with the air-conditioning. Surprised by her sudden acquiescence,

313

Morgan examined her profile. Like the proverbial cat with stolen cream, she thought, narrowing her eyes.

'So you fly back tomorrow and our check flight's early next week. What are you going to do to keep out of mischief till then?'

'Got some things lined up. Figured you'd love me even more if I went and watered your garden. Sam will look at me with adoration if I take him for a run, and there's always shopping to be done.'

She tried to look sanctimonious, but ended up looking cheeky. Morgan returned her smile before closing in on her friend. 'So why did Brendan from the soup kitchen ring me to check out if you were reliable then?' She didn't miss Lauren's quick frown.

'I decided I needed to do something useful instead of spending money like the world was about to be collected by a meteorite. You do.' Her tone challenged Morgan, who ignored it.

'You'll have fun. They're a very eclectic bunch of people from very diverse backgrounds.'

Both women fell silent.

Maybe Lauren was right about North Queensland. Great place to bring up kids, thought Morgan. Wide open spaces still existed. Neighbours still chatted over fences. The air was cleaner, the sun brighter and the complications of the world were a little further away. What would Patrick think?

By the time they had found a park and walked to the restaurant it was well after seven and Lauren was fretting.

'Surely they won't give away the table just because we're fifteen minutes late?' Morgan protested, as she hurried in unfamiliar heels to keep up.

'You have no idea how much grovelling I had to do to change this booking,' Lauren shot back, pushing at her soft fall of hair as she hit the maitre d' with her high wattage smile.

BORDER WATCH

'Sorry, we're late. The parking is horrendous around here.' The beauty of the two women soothed ruffled feathers. Gratefully, they sank into plush chairs nestled at a table against the massive bay windows. The beach reflected white against the dark of the ocean. The restaurant lighting was subdued, their reflections in the glass softly muted.

'Cheers, my dear.' Lauren raised her glass of champagne and Morgan touched it with the soft ring of crystal.

'Cheers. To good friends.'

They lingered over the menu, discussing the choices. 'Almost as good as your cooking,' Lauren whispered as she turned to the desserts. 'Do I save room or just stuff it all in anyway?'

Morgan laughed at her indecision. 'You always eat double helpings at my place. Don't be put off by the price, my credit card's taken such a battering a little more won't hurt it.'

'It's not that. Hmm.' Lauren pursed her lips. 'Oysters to start? Share a dozen with me?'

'If you like,' Morgan shrugged.

'Mmm, then I think steak for me.'

Lauren pored over the wine list before charming the sommelier. 'What would you recommend with my steak? Something big and bold and seductive?'

She settled back once they'd ordered everything to her satisfaction and looked around.

'See? The place is full of jealous wives, peeved because their husbands are perving at us. Gotta love it.' She peered out through the glass. 'It's the perfect place for a romantic dinner for two, isn't it? A long walk on the beach after, kiss and cuddle on the sand. Bliss. Shame it's just us girls.'

'Your precious peeved wives probably figure we're a couple anyway,' Morgan teased, taking a sip of champagne.

'No, do you think so?' Lauren looked horrified. That was clearly not the image she had meant to project. 'God, I think

315

I need to check my make-up and flirt with a man somewhere then. Back soon.' She waved her fingers at Morgan and slid from the table, arching an eyebrow at the waiter who nodded towards the rear.

Morgan smiled into her glass then leant forwards to admire the view. The white of the surf break cut a line through the dark water. The Bondi Icebergs clubhouse, perched on the rocks at the opposite end of the beach, looked like an ice sculpture glistening in the night. Halfway along the beach the Bondi Pavilion, an iconic reminder of Australia's love affair with the ocean, shimmered pink in the moonlight. Maybe she could make a home here in Sydney. It wasn't her beloved Trinity Beach, but perhaps . . .

Lauren's chair moved and Morgan turned to speak, but the words never made it to her mouth. Her hand did, stifling a gasp before it could escape.

'Morgan.' The crisp white shirt looked good on him, the tailored trousers a change from the green uniform or casual shirts. She took it all in before she found her voice again.

'Rafe.'

'You look stunning. Do you mind?' He gestured at Lauren's chair. 'May I join you?'

'Ah.' Morgan looked around, feeling stupidly off-balance. 'Lauren's here somewhere. I'm sure they can fit in another chair. What are you doing here?' Her eyes were frantically scanning the restaurant, trying to catch the eye of the maitre d'.

'Looking for you.'

'What?' She focused back on him. 'Me? Why?'

'I would have thought a smart lady like you would have figured that out by now.' He reached over the table and picked up her restless fingers, which were creasing the tablecloth. 'You can stop looking for Lauren; she's on her way home already.'

'What? You sent her home?'

Rafe laughed, his teeth white and even against his sun-darkened skin. 'You think I'd get Lauren to do anything against her will? Thanks for the vote of confidence, but no. She organised this for us.'

'Oh.' Morgan looked down at her hand, still caught in his, feeling the heady rush of desire nibble away the edges of anger, the uncertainty of the last week. 'For us,' she repeated.

'She worked very hard to make this happen, especially when someone didn't want to do lunch.' He laughed at the look on Morgan's face. 'In fact, I had to find another restaurant because the one she'd booked was full for dinner. It took me all afternoon to find this place.'

Morgan felt nervous suddenly. She may have slept with Rafe, may have shared dinners with him before, may have dreamt about this moment, but she had never dared hope for it.

And now it was happening and it felt too rushed and she wasn't prepared.

She couldn't meet his gaze and instead looked out the window. The soft reflection threw his face back at her and he caught her eye, raising a quizzical eyebrow at her. The same calm belief she'd seen in his face the night they'd spent together was still there. The warmth, the approval that had made her want to run both to him and away from him, was still there.

'Did she order oysters for herself or you then?' Morgan asked his reflection, her mouth curved into a tiny smile.

'For us, I'm guessing.' He leant towards the shimmer in the glass, his voice seductive. 'Don't know why she thinks we need help in that area.'

Morgan had to laugh this time and turned to face him. 'Incorrigible. So what are you doing in Sydney?'

'I told you — looking for you.'

'Rafe, be serious.'

'Okay, finding you. And I have. So here we are.' The waiter took the change of guest in his stride as he delivered the platter of oysters and checked how Rafe wanted his steak cooked.

Rafe shook his head admiringly. 'She thought of everything, didn't she?'

'Hmm,' Morgan said. 'I should have been suspicious about her choice of food. Very un-Lauren to want half a side of beef on her plate.' She looked down at her plate, feeling lightheaded. Rafe had gone to a lot of trouble to be here and so had Lauren. It sent a flush through her whole body that people, friends could be this kind.

'So how did the sim ride go?' Rafe asked, picking up the champagne flute.

'Good.' Then she corrected herself. 'No, great. It felt great to be back in an aircraft and somehow . . .' She shook her head, searching for the words to explain it. 'Somehow, having survived being shot down by a missile made all those checklists and drills just routine. Another day in the office. Does that make sense?' She looked up at him with a slight frown.

'It does. The first time I survived a fire-fight in the desert, all the training was suddenly relevant. You'll never wonder again if you're good enough to fly that aircraft. You know you are, and you know the system works.'

'That's it, isn't it? Belief in yourself and in your training.'

He nodded in agreement, his eyes dark and compelling. 'So what else is happening in Morgan Pentland's life?'

She looked away, afraid he'd see the pain on her face. 'I think Lauren might have filled you in.'

'She's given me a thumbnail sketch. I'd like to hear it from you.'

BORDER WATCH

She emptied her glass of champagne in a quick gulp and smiled at the waiter as he poured red wine into elegant crystal. With her voice pitched low she told her story. Rafe listened in silence. When she finished she reached for the glass in front of her.

The warmth of his hand as it closed around hers on the stem of the glass shocked her with its intensity. His touch burnt into her and she felt its echo rippling into her heart.

'I don't have any answers for you, Morgan, just profound admiration for your determination to survive.' His approval meant more to her than she wanted to admit and it glowed in his eyes, came from the pressure of his hard hands.

She tried to maintain her composure. She didn't want to let her defences down, but he seemed to have already forded the moat and was even now banging on the citadel's doors. Abruptly, she changed the direction of the conversation.

'So, they caught them all.'

'Yes, before they could do any damage.'

'But there'll be a next time, won't there?'

'That's why people like you and I do the job we do. To prevent it.'

'And the politicians and all their secretive little departments?'

He shrugged. 'At least they acknowledged the herculean task of securing our northern borders. There'll be more funding, more boats, more aircraft, more resources. Wiseman achieved that at least.'

'What happens to Carl?' The question had niggled at her.

Rafe didn't let her hand go. 'He didn't make it. Probably better that way. He'd inhaled the fire. His lungs would never have functioned properly again and his face . . .' Rafe tilted his head. 'You saw how bad his face was. Third degree over sixty percent of his body. No doctor could work a miracle on injuries that severe.'

'Oh.' Morgan didn't know what to say, but couldn't stop her hand from trembling. The Carl she'd shared a bed with had been erased by the killing thug who would have carelessly brutalised her, but still he was another human being. 'And Thommo?'

Rafe eased back in his chair and picked up his glass with his free hand. He met her eyes over the rim. 'He's found a new home in a complex for retired Vietnam vets. He'd like to see you. He asked about you.'

His eyes didn't leave her face, but she couldn't read the expression in them. 'I'm glad he's okay. I never thanked him or you properly.'

'We both got a little busy.'

'Yeah, but still. Thank you. I thought I'd die that night and all I wanted to do was at least choose the way it happened.'

'If I promise to show you how to take the safety catch off a semi-automatic will you promise never to point one at me?' He laughed gently. 'Thommo said he saw you that morning and he wanted to warn you, but he couldn't catch up with you. You run too fast. He'd fretted all day, waiting for dark. Found a way up the cliff so no one would see him and then showed me the way.'

'I didn't mean to get you hurt.' Morgan looked down at the plate of food the waiter placed in front of her and smiled her thanks. 'I just needed . . . I needed to go back.'

'Because you weren't running away again.' His jaw was tight. 'Lauren told me you'd helped her understand that hiding and running weren't sins.'

'I couldn't run away again,' Morgan told him. 'I've always wondered if my mother would have lived if I'd stayed.'

BORDER WATCH

'And you are the wonderful woman you are today because of everything that's gone before. You can't change that, nor should you.'

She was silent, overwhelmed by what she saw in his face and felt in the soothing touch of his fingers.

Watching the sadness on her beautiful face, Rafe let the silence settle. He wondered how to steer the conversation onto less traumatic ground. He'd known, even as he'd colluded with Lauren, there was a chance their plan would backfire and he'd be no closer to Morgan than before. It wasn't quite panning out the way he'd intended.

'So your niece and nephew, how are they doing?' He kept his eyes on his plate as he waited for her answer, which was a long time coming.

'I see so much of me in Emma, it's scary. She even looks like me, or Patrick, I suppose. She's little, she's sweet and she's only ten. I don't think it's real for her yet.' She played with her food. 'Nathan is twelve. Already he's internalising it. And Patrick?' She sighed. 'Patrick has to want to get through this. It's early days still. I'll just have to give him time.'

'Are you planning on staying here?'

Morgan shrugged. 'I haven't decided. I have to be back at work next week. One day at a time.'

Rafe dug a little more. 'Can you transfer with Border Watch?' He was looking for clues in her face, but she was doing a good job of keeping her expression neutral.

'Possibly. I haven't asked yet. My little home at Trinity has been my refuge. I don't know if I'll find that again.' The hurt in her stung him.

'You will make a home anywhere you find a kitchen. People are more important to you than places.' He was satisfied with

321

the startled gratitude in her face. Unravelling the delectable Morgan might take him a lifetime, but at least he was headed in the right direction. 'You have to do what you believe to be right, honourable. Let me know when you've worked out where you want to live. My transfer papers to Cairns are just waiting for a new destination.'

She frowned, lining her knife and fork up and pushing her plate away. 'Rafe . . . It's not just me anymore.'

'I know.' He signalled to the waiter for the bill. 'I know. It's you and me.'

'That's not what I meant.' She flushed under his steady gaze and he was enchanted again by the delicate pink that bloomed across her face and made her seem less certain. 'Emma, Nathan.'

Rafe dashed a signature over the account. 'And Patrick. So you come with a family. Let's walk.'

He pulled her chair out for her and brushed the dark hair back from her face, feeling her tremble under his touch. The chemistry, the magic still shimmered below the surface and he knew this was one battle where defeat or surrender was not an option.

They crossed the sweep of grass and stopped on the edge of the beach. A cool sea breeze plucked at Morgan's filmy skirt. She bent and slipped her shoes off, dangling them from her fingers by their thin straps.

Rafe draped an arm around her shoulder. 'Do you remember me saying you were driving me certifiably nuts? You still are.' He felt the tiny tremor of a laugh shake her.

'You can push and shove at me all you like, but I'm not going anywhere.' He tightened his grip. 'I'm good at my job because I don't give up. About time I applied that to the rest of my life.'

BORDER WATCH

They'd reached the edge of the water and Morgan stood looking out to sea. Backlit from the streetlights, her face was in the shadows, but Rafe saw her take a deep breath before she answered him. 'I may actually love you. I know that. I also know, because Lauren keeps pointing it out, that we don't know what tomorrow brings, but I'm not planning just for me now.'

Rafe cut her off. 'But Emma and Nathan are different.' He saw her nod and turned her to face him as he continued. 'I understand that and I'm not asking you to make decisions right away. I think I realised I'd met a woman I could love the first time you sat me on my arse, what, six months ago now? Just wasn't ready to admit that right then. Shh.' He placed a finger over her lips as she started to speak. 'Shh. Men aren't good at this stuff. Don't interrupt.'

He cupped his hand under her chin, keeping her eyes locked on his face. 'I've never met a woman I wanted to wake up next to, never gazed into eyes that looked clear into my soul. I understand why you have a backbone of steel, why these children mean so much to you. It's just one of the things I admire about you, love about you.'

He stopped speaking and lowered his head to brush her lips with his. 'And I know this scares you, but I'm not asking you to give up control of your life. Just let me share it with you. Let me love you the way you deserve to be loved. Marry me, Morgan.'

She felt the breath catch in her throat. Marry him? Was he insane?

He didn't wait for her answer, just pulled her up against him and cut off her words with his mouth. His hands were warm as they slid down her arms and over her back. The ripple of desire started low in her belly and spread right out to her fingertips and toes.

Marry him.

Someone to love, someone to laugh with, someone to lean on.

She knew he didn't offer marriage lightly. He was a man who believed in commitment. Hadn't he already told her that in Weipa?

With a soft little sigh she melted against him and her hands reached up to frame his face. 'Do you really want to be on first-name terms with all the baggage I drag around with me?'

'You're not scaring me off, Morgan. Don't push me away again.' He held her, angling her so the streetlights shone on her face. It put his in the shadow and she couldn't read his expression. 'No is not an option here.'

'Why?' she asked.

'Grow old with me, Morgan. Learn the lessons you've taught me. Learn to trust again, learn to live again.'

'Together?'

'Always together.' His hands ran down her arms, their familiar warmth sending fire through her veins.

'Then Rafe Daniels, yes, but . . .' She didn't get to finish her sentence as he gathered her even closer and claimed her lips in a kiss that took the breath from her.

'But?' he whispered against her lips, not quite breaking the connection.

'But I hope you remember the difference between an adjective and an adverb.'

'For the vows?' He sounded bemused and she stifled a giggle.

'Year six homework is a bit more advanced than I remember.'

He laughed and she felt the rumble of it in his chest as his arms folded her close. 'New challenges for all of us then. New beginnings.'

Yes, Morgan acknowledged. Challenges she could only guess at now. New beginnings with the chance to draw a different set of patterns. A journey that would take them both beyond the borders she had so carefully guarded.

Acknowledgements

Any book is surely a 'village project' and mine is no exception. Thanks to publisher Bernadette Foley, editor Ali Lavau and the rest of the Hachette team for believing in *Border Watch*, rolling up their sleeves and polishing it to a high gloss. I'm privileged to have their support.

To Bronwyn, my sister, unofficial critique partner, editor and cheerleader, a huge long-distance hug to you. Your belief in me matters. Thanks to my parents who instilled a great love of books in the three of us. I assumed *everyone* read or wrote any spare minute of the day!

Thanks to Brett, Penny and Glen for technical advice. Discrepancies or errors in surveillance and security procedures are mine. I'll claim poetic licence as my defence . . .

Romance Writers of Australia and Romance Writers of America have provided many opportunities, resources and agony aunts, online and in person.

Peter Bishop, Creative Director of Varuna, asked insightful questions that made me dig deeper and write harder.

Thanks in alphabetical order to Albertina, Anita, Dana, Janice, Liz, Sala, Sandy and Simone — the girls are always there.

Finally, my husband, Graham, has been the steady beat in my somewhat erratic life that gives waking up in the morning more meaning and more joy.

Helene Young lives in Trinity Beach, on the edge of the Great Barrier Reef in North Queensland. Her work as a senior captain with a major regional airline takes her all over the east coast of Australia.

Helene is as passionate about aviation as she is about writing. 'I've been flying for twenty years, which gives me an "office" with the most spectacular views in Australia and I never get tired of looking down at the wonderful landscape.'

The idea for *Border Watch* started early one morning when Helene discovered a body washed up on the beach. While there was nothing sinister in that discovery it planted the seed of an idea.

This is Helene's first published novel, but she has written all her life. *Border Watch* is the first of a loosely linked three-book series.